The Hunt for Blackfoot Lion

The Hunt for Blackfoot Lion

A Novel

T. W. Hard

McCaa Books • Santa Rosa, CA

McCaa Books
1604 Deer Run
Santa Rosa, CA 95405-7535

First published in 2021 by McCaa Books,
an imprint of McCaa Publications.

Library of Congress Control Number: 2020922992 Paperback
ISBN 978-1-7358074-6-1 Paperback
Library of Congress Control Number: 2020924438 Hardback
ISBN 978-1-7358074-9-2 Hardback

Printed in the United States of America
Set in Minion Pro
Book design by Waights Taylor Jr.
Cover Design by Jane E. Baron

www.mccaabooks.com

Dedication

To Ellie: With much appreciation for your grace,
your beauty, your touch, and your love.

TWH

"Your religion was written on a tablet of stone
By the iron finger of an angry God.
Our religion is the tradition of our ancestors.
It is the dreams of our old men
Given to them by the Great Spirit."

(Chief Seattle, Duwamishi)

Contents

Part I

Reynolds Run

"What is life? It is the flash of the firefly in the night.
It is the breath of a buffalo in the winter,
It is the little shadow which runs across the grass
And loses itself in the sunset . . ."

(Crowfoot, Blackfoot Brave)

1

IN PLACES WHERE THE TREES ROSE more than a hundred feet, the spreading canopy almost obliterated the sky. A beam of sun penetrated this gloom, descending through the shadows until it fell upon a patch of earth. On this warm August afternoon, no birds chirped, no small animals scurried through the brush.

Moments before, a swirl of breeze had picked up a fragment of scent. The molecule was followed by a second and then a third, like the tiniest seeds of a dandelion, carried by puffs of wind. The odor that it brought was recognized by all wild creatures as the scent of death. There was danger here, and those beings that could fly, creep, or run slunk off to their secret spots of safety.

A paw stepped upon the illuminated patch of ground. It was light tan in color, perfectly camouflaged with the alternating shadows of beige and browns. When the foot lifted off the soft, moist earth, the depression left was more than seven inches across. There were no marks of claws. The claws, three inches long and razor sharp, were retracted in their protective sheaths. To the untrained observer, it might have been the paw print of a large dog. Yet there were no dogs here. Dogs move with yips and friendly exuberance. This animal moved with the stealth of an assassin.

Even in silhouette, he was huge. There have been bigger beasts that stalked the Montana forests, but mostly they existed in the Pleistocene, ten thousand years ago. During the spring, he had drifted down from the Canadian border, passing through vast uninhabited lands, unseen and unrecognized by man. And now he was hunting, his movements honed by the wondrous lathe of natural selection.

In power and speed, few animals in the forest surpassed him. A week ago, he had killed a four-hundred-pound grizzly. A month before, he had attacked a pack of wolves and slain them all.

For a moment he paused, this great beast, and the outline of his body so blended with the underbrush that he was hard to see. A faint scent caught his nostrils. His pupils dilated. A shiver passed through the massive sinews of his body. Elk. A doe and two fawns had traveled through the clearing.

He turned his head to catch the odor better. Instinctively, he calculated how long ago they had passed, and in which direction they had gone. And then he simply vanished, his form melting into the liquid shadows of the forest. There was no sound, no swaying of boughs. Except for the paw print that betrayed his passage, it was as if he was never there.

2

TRACY REYNOLDS STEPPED OUT of her white rental Ford that warm August afternoon and walked across the Elkhorn town square. She was the type of statuesque woman few people would forget. She was an unknown tourist in a small Montana town, yet everyone who came in contact with her remembered her presence. A man at a gas station told her the Aspen Café was just down the street. She said she was looking for a place to sit down, to make a few calls, to take a break from her drive.

As she strode across the square, past the large statue of Jeremiah Bates, sword raised, his mount frozen in bronze, she wondered what role in Montana history the figure had played.

Along the sidewalk, she passed the Bank of Montana building, a real estate office and art gallery. Later, two old-timers sitting on a bench would recall her passage. "Yeah, I remember her," one told the deputy. "She was a real looker."

Moving steadily, she detoured around a group of tourists standing in front of a white-water rafting store. In the window were displayed a series of photographs showing kayakers running the Arcata River. A disheveled, bearded man emerged from a grocery store and began loading his bike with supplies.

"Hey Cecil, you forgot your bread!" a storekeeper shouted. The man mumbled something, glanced at Tracy, and walked back into the store.

Jonathan Barnett was wiping tables at the Aspen Café when she entered. The restaurant was half full. In a back booth sat a family of Native Americans: a woman, two young children, an old man. A pair of tourists occupied a table next to the window. Across the room, along the opposite side of the café, perched a group of ranchers. The men were dressed in jeans and cowboy shirts. One wore a wide-brimmed straw-colored Stetson. Immediately, their conversation ceased. As the waiter led Tracy to a side booth, one whispered, "Where in heaven did she come from?"

Tracy Reynolds was five-foot-seven, twenty-eight years old. This afternoon, she was dressed in a pair of tight designer jeans. Her rose-colored blouse had a V-necked top, worn tight enough to reveal her well-contoured breasts. Her neck was slender and her face strikingly beautiful, her hair falling in waves around her shoulders.

She took a seat and then pulled out a polished leather satchel and proceeded to spread some papers across the table. She wanted a glass of water and a sandwich. Barnett tried to make idle talk, but she seemed preoccupied. When he asked where she was from, she simply replied, "California," and went back to her work.

Finally, when he was sure his other customers were attended to, the waiter wandered over to an empty booth next to her and cleaned the table. She held a cell phone to her ear. Without seeming obtrusive, he tried to listen to the conversation. Her voice seemed upbeat and excited. When she hung up, he moved to her table.

"I get you anything else? "

"Just a bill, please."

Once, maybe a month ago, a magazine crew had passed through town, working on a photo-shoot for a calendar. They'd stopped at the café for lunch. Barnett had waited on two college-age models, but neither were as attractive as this woman. Tracy glanced up and caught him staring.

"Your check . . ." he blushed.

"Thanks."

"You traveling far?"

"Whitefish."

"It's about an hour and a half from here," Barnett said.

"I was wondering about a good place to run."

"There's a high school track at the end of town," he suggested. "And sometimes guys like to jog the dirt roads by Johnson's Ranch."

"I was thinking about something more scenic," she replied. "Somewhere near the mountains."

"You got a map?"

She reached into her briefcase. Flipping through some papers, she found a roadmap of northwestern Montana. She unfolded the chart and spread the map across the table.

Barnett took a moment to identify the location and then leaned forward and pointed to a highway, following the route with his finger. "I know of a place you might like," he said. "You hit the main intestate about twenty miles from Elkhorn. The road runs parallel to the Arcata River. Follow the road until you find a sign for Henderson State Park. There's a campground and parking lot. An old logging road runs next to the river for a couple miles. Next to the parking lot is a sign marking the trail. I've seen joggers there. It's right on the way to Whitefish."

"Sounds perfect."

She placed the map and papers back in the satchel. Standing up, she paid her bill and moved for the door. Barnett glanced at the movement of her long legs, her tight buttocks, and was drawn after her like a magnet. He stopped at the window and watched her cross the street. When he turned back, he was greeted by a series of catcalls from the ranchers.

"Oh, how I love you." one taunted. "You get her number?"

"Ah, kiss my ass," he countered.

BY FOUR THAT WARM AUGUST AFTERNOON, Tracy Reynolds was speeding northward on Highway 29. Great swaths of forest lined the road. An occasional stream tumbled by. At a curve in the highway, she caught a glimpse of distant snowcapped mountains. Wonderful, beautiful country, she thought. She was happy and relaxed. She dialed the radio until she found a country western station. Willie Nelson was singing "Always on My Mind." She began humming along with the melody, her thoughts drifting.

Her meeting in Jackson, Wyoming had taken three days. Everyone was jamming about where the communications industry was headed. She'd given a short presentation, networked with a number of associates, thanked her boss for the great meeting, and headed north. Her fiancé had been hiking with friends in Glacier National Park. They planned to meet that evening for dinner. They would spend five nights together and then fly back to California.

She thought about her stop in Elkhorn with amusement. The waiter had fallen all over himself trying to gain her attention. She had noted the ranchers sitting at a side table and tried to ignore them. In this one-stop Montana town, she wondered what anyone ever did for amusement. Probably, she reflected, she should have worn a bra.

Tracy slowed at the sign marking Henderson Park. She turned, following a smoothly graded road. A half mile inside the park, she found a site labeled "Scenic View." Here stood a grove of trees. In the shade of a group of Douglas firs rested a picnic table. She saw no other cars.

Parking the vehicle, she stepped out of the Ford and walked to the overlook. The sun had begun to slip toward the horizon, giving a warm glow to the water. Steep, forested ridges rose from the opposite bank. A magpie darted through the trees.

As she stood, enjoying the view, an elk emerged along the river. The animal stopped, tested the wind, and then stepped cautiously into the shallow water. As if on cue, two fawns emerged from the forest. The mother elk was up to her belly by the time the twins caught up. The current was steady, and for a moment Tracy feared they might be swept downstream. Sensing the water was too deep, the mother turned back. The twins churned after her, trying to keep up. A moment later, they disappeared into the trees.

Tracy took a deep breath of cool mountain air and reveled in its freshness. The sun played in shimmering reflections off the water. She checked her watch. If she started now, she could get in a good two-mile run. The evening was perfect.

She returned to her car and opened the trunk. Inside was a neatly packed suitcase. When she was sure no one was watching, she took off her blouse and jeans and slid into a running bra, red jogging shorts and a white sweat shirt. She replaced her sandals with a pair of Adidas jogging shoes and tied her hair in a ponytail.

She locked the car and walked across the clearing. She had gone only a short distance when she came to a chain hung between two posts. A sign read "State Logging Road 5982." This was where the waiter had told her to run.

The logging road was little more than two ruts, but it was well cropped, and the trail looked easy to follow. Starting out, she began jogging slowly, trying to warm up. Gradually, she lengthened her pace, feeling her muscles pump easily with the longer strides. She had started running in college and kept it up for the past six years. She enjoyed the exercise immensely. It kept her trim and her muscles toned. She didn't think she would feel well without it.

She ran for thirty minutes. In a clearing, she sat on a rock and studied the mountains and the water and could feel the warmth of the sun. It was a glorious evening, and she marveled at the strength in her body and how well she felt.

When she checked her watch, she decided she'd gone far enough. She didn't know the area well, and she didn't want to get too far from the car. She stepped behind a large boulder to urinate and then started back.

It was then she heard the sound. The noise was a high-pitched cry, more of a mew than a call, and it sounded like the type of noise a child might make if someone was in trouble. The cry came only once. She paused and cautiously looked around. The logging trail stretched behind her toward the forest. A tingling worked up the back of her spine. This is silly, she tried to reassure herself. What out here could she be afraid of? She turned and began jogging again. Yet, try as she might, she couldn't dispel a growing unease that there was something back there, following. Hidden within the trees had been a shift of shadows. She couldn't tell if it was big or small, only there was a subtle movement along the edges of the forest.

She thought about the safety of her car. The vehicle was less than a mile away. She could almost sprint to it. Whatever was back there was moving silently, and it was traveling parallel with her, just out of sight.

A loud crashing erupted from the forest. Leaves swayed. Her heart jumped into her throat. Something big charged toward her. With a gasp, she jumped sideways as the brush exploded in front of her. Abruptly, three animals stampeded across the roadway. It was the mother elk and two fawns. In an instant, they were gone.

Tracy felt a sheepish sense of relief. Good grief, she thought. So that's what had scared her. Smiling, she turned and began the last limb of her run. She heard no further sound besides the pacing of her feet and the steady exhaling of her breath. In her mind, she was already with her fiancé, having dinner, enjoying a glass of wine.

As DARKNESS FELL, frogs and crickets chirped. A flock of ducks circled overhead, then sped downriver, wings whistling. A fox emerged from the shadows, trotting across the parking lot. Come midnight, Tracy Reynolds' car was still there.

Locked. Empty. Resting silently beneath the trees.

3

Dusk faded across the plains that August evening as the last rays of sun retreated beyond the mountains. To the West, great peaks stood like fingers of a giant's hand. A layer of clouds pushed heavily from the east.

Stepping out from a small two-bedroom house at Weasel Creek, staggered an old man. His body was bent. His hair, once long and black, was silvery white, his face tanned, like the leather of elk. He was dressed in a pair of frayed pants, his shirt stained and wrinkled. He wore no shoes.

George Two Feathers was in his late seventies. He was considered by some to be one of the last surviving elders of the Blackfoot tribe. He stood for a long time in the fading light, scanning the horizon. At first he stared in disbelief. A faint image emerged from the clouds. The figure appeared along the leading edge of gray cumulus. He could make out the ears, the outline of a head, the curve of a tail draped across Medicine Mountain.

"*Omahkatayo* . . . Could it be . . ?" He rubbed his eyes. When he looked back, the shape had vanished. Now there were only the swirling clouds, pushed silently by the wind. Nightfall was coming. He turned back toward the house.

Crossing the sparsely decorated living room, he entered the kitchen. His granddaughter, Sarah, stood by the stove cooking dinner. She was an attractive woman, twenty-two, with dark, slender features. She wore her hair in braids. She watched him carefully as he entered.

"Grandfather, you look as if you've seen a ghost. You sick?"

"No," he said slowly, trying to translate some meaning from the clouds. He muttered something in Blackfoot.

"Grandfather, why are you talking crazy again?"

He shrugged. What could he tell her? She wouldn't understand.

"Come on," she urged. "I think maybe you've been drinking again."

A baby cried in the back of the house and she excused herself to go and change it. Lord, how was she ever going to get out of this place? she wondered. She had two children and a husband who'd walked out on her, and now she was stuck on the reservation with a drunken grandfather who was still living in the past.

Too many times he'd gotten liquored up and ranted about some spirit he'd imagined or some omen that he was sure had special significance for their lives. If you believed everything he said, you might wake up one morning with a buffalo herd stampeding through your living room.

Still, out of respect, she tried to treat him with dignity and reverence. It was the Blackfoot way. The younger generation had always been taught to listen to their elders, even if they were occasionally drunk or crazy, or rambled about things that made no sense.

She changed the baby. Cradling the child in her arms, she moved over to a second bed where her three-year-old daughter was playing.

"Come on, Lindsey. It's time for dinner," she said. "Please go wash up."

When Sarah came back to the kitchen, George Two Feathers was holding a cup of coffee. His fingers trembled. He looked more unsteady than usual.

"Grandfather, do you need to see a doctor?"

He shook his head.

"How much drinking have you been doing?"

"Just a bottle."

"Just a bottle!" she cried. "You're going to kill yourself with just a bottle. How many times has the doctor told you to quit? Look at your fingers. You're so shaky you can hardly hold the cup."

"It's not the drinking," he muttered.

"We're going to see the doctor."

"No . . ." he waved his hand.

The three-year-old suddenly popped around the corner and darted into the kitchen. "Dranfather!" the child exclaimed.

The old man held out his arms. Lindsey ran up and gave him a hug.

"Dranfather, sick?" The little girl stared closely at his face.

"I'm all right." He pulled out a chair so Lindsey could sit with them at the table.

"Maybe it would be wise if you watched your children closely."

"What the hell is that supposed to mean?" Sarah answered with frustration. "I do watch my children closely. Maybe it would be wise if you watched your drinking."

Two Feathers did not answer. His mind drifted. He muttered something in Blackfoot.

"When's Bobby coming back?" he asked.

"Damn it," Sarah exclaimed with exasperation. "Grandfather, you know where Bobby is. He lives in Chicago. You know that."

"Maybe I should call him."

"You called him last week, remember?"

"I worry about Bobby."

"You worry about too many things," she answered. "Bobby is fine."

Sarah had thought of living close to her brother for a while, but living off the reservation was expensive, and without a high school degree, she couldn't find much work as anything other than a waitress. This would mean she would have to leave the children with a babysitter while she worked. She hated the idea.

23

At least on the reservation she could be with her children when they were growing up. Maybe if she had a husband who'd been willing to help, it would be different; but now, as a single parent, she felt it was more important than ever to raise them as she wanted. Native Americans had enough trouble making their way through an Anglo society as it was. In Chicago, people often ridiculed her and called her stupid names. Bobby was single and didn't have children to worry about. Her responsibilities to her family were different.

Sarah finished setting the table and turned toward George Two Feathers.

"I want to go to the market after dinner and get some supplies. You want to come?"

He shook his head.

"Maybe you'd better come and see the doctor," she persisted.

"No, there is something I must do."

She was suddenly suspicious. "Like what?"

Two Feathers shook his head. She knew it was useless to pry further.

They ate a quiet dinner that night, just as they always did. The television was turned on in the corner, and her grandfather watched for a while without speaking. Finally, Sarah gathered up the children and went into the back room to help them dress. She hesitated at the doorway. Turning back, she gave the old man a kiss on the forehead. "Please don't drink tonight."

It was almost dark when she loaded her two kids into the car. She switched on the beams and drove slowly out the driveway. When she looked back, George Two Feathers was sitting cross-legged next to the house. He had started a small fire, his face illuminated by the rising flames.

"Oh, my God!" she cried. "Grandfather. What are you doing?" She leaped out of the car and ran toward him. "You're going to set the house on fire!"

George Two Feathers did not reply. His arms were raised as he chanted toward the setting sun. "*Omahkatayo*, is coming," he whispered. He'd seen its image in the clouds.

4

THE ALARM SOUNDED SOFTLY. The room was dark except for a sliver of light that slid past a curtain along the eastern wall. Sam Hayden came out of a deep sleep, groping for the bedside table, then the alarm clock. Stopping the disruption, he eased back into the comfort of his bed, his body recoiling at the thought of getting up. Five minutes later, the alarm sounded again.

This time he raised the clock so he could see the luminescent dials. It was six in the morning. Except for an occasional creak, the house was quiet. Outside came the faint chorus of geese passing overhead. A quail called from across the field. Near the corral, one of the horses whinnied.

Suddenly, down the hallway, erupted the noise of scampering feet rapidly approaching his bedroom. Beneath the doorway came a snuffling sound. The door pushed open. With a rapid dash, a small gray-and-white dog sprinted across the room and leaped onto his bed.

Hayden buried his face beneath the covers. There was nothing worse than a dog's tongue slurping up your nose. The terrier rooted after him, pawing at his head.

"All right, Tobey," he muttered. "You're right. The alarm went off." He reached over and gave the dog a hug. "Everything's okay. I'll get up. Go easy, now."

Stretching, Hayden walked over to the window and opened the curtains. Faint wisps of clouds layered along the eastern horizon.

At the fenced edge of his seven-acre property, one of the horses bucked and danced, feeling the excitement of the coming day. A second horse galloped behind it. The two horses charged back and forth, chasing each other across the field.

Got to get some fresh shoes for those boys, Hayden reflected. His glance followed the corners of the fence, moving down to the barn and the corral, then the old tool shed. Probably should put a new coat of paint on that guy, too, he thought. A good storm this winter could tear the whole thing apart. Maybe he would get to it in the fall.

He moved into the bathroom and began to shave. He was forty-seven years old, five-foot-eleven, with dark hair and brown eyes. A trim mustache covered his lip. He was not quite as muscular as he had once been, but he was still in good physical condition. There was a slight gray to his sideburns and the beginnings of a bald spot on his head. Both changes—the graying and the baldness—had come rapidly after Maggie's death.

It was to be expected, the doctors told him. Loss plays hard on a man's life. In one year, he'd gone through two of the greatest changes a person could endure. He'd lost his wife and quit his job in Seattle and moved to Montana. On a scale of stress profiles for law enforcement officers, he had been close to one hundred. When you score over eighty-five, they told him, some men contemplate suicide.

Four years had passed. If Hayden hadn't moved out of Seattle, he wasn't sure he could have survived. Once Maggie was gone, there was no reason to stay. For his daughter's sake, he had to leave. Sooner or later, he would have ended up in the morgue, shot in a drug bust or nailed by a stray bullet with the SWAT team. So, he'd traded suburban Seattle for rural Elkhorn, Montana. And gradually, his sanity had returned.

He finished shaving and put on his uniform. He prided himself on the sharp crease of his shirt. Across his arm was the three-striped chevron of a sergeant. Over the left breast was the tri-county sheriff's emblem. Satisfied his uniform was immaculate, Hayden strapped on his revolver. He carried a .45 magnum. It was a handgun large enough to stop a charging bear or a threatening human. To his relief, he hadn't used it since coming to Montana.

"What do you think, Tobey?" he grunted at the dog. "I pass inspection?"

The terrier sat up, cocked his head, and watched. When Hayden walked to his daughter's bedroom, Tobey followed. As Hayden opened the curtains, a flood of sunlight illuminated the room.

"Got to be getting up soon, sweetheart." He reached over and kissed Ashley softly on the cheek. "How's my girl?"

"Good, Dad."

Her head was half-buried beneath the covers. All he could see was a corner of a large blue eye staring at him. It was always amazing how she could be sound asleep one instant and then be totally awake the next. Tobey leaped onto the foot of the bed and curled against her legs.

"Have a good day in school. I should be at the station all day." He started out the door, then paused. "Have Dolores fix you a good lunch. No junk food, please."

"Yes, sir." She gave a faint smile. Hayden knew damn well his housekeeper would probably throw a candy bar into her lunch, and more times than not, she shared a coke or bottle of soda with her friends.

"Oh, Dad," she said. "Do me one favor?"

"Yeah, what?"

"Hugs, please."

He came back into the room. Bending over, he gave Ashley a gentle squeeze.

"I'll be okay," she said.

"I know." He frowned. "I just don't want your gums to turn black or your teeth growing through your cheeks."

"Sounds pretty cool," she grinned.

HAYDEN REACHED THE STATION at ten minutes of eight. He parked the sheriff's Bronco and then went through the courtyard at the back of the building. He passed a bowl with fresh cat food next to the door. Pausing, he searched for the two stray cats the station had adopted. He found neither.

Inside, Mabel Browning, the station's fifty-five-year-old secretary, was already behind her desk. Officially, she started at eight. Over the past twenty years, no one had ever seen her arrive after 7:30.

"Morning, Mabel," Hayden nodded. "The cats all right today?"

Mabel fussed over the station's two cats as if they were children.

"I saw Bartholomew this morning," she answered. "And Max is probably sleeping in the bushes."

"How was your weekend?"

"Good," she answered. "Deputies waiting for you in the conference room."

Sometimes, Hayden thought, Mabel sounded like she was in charge.

"Lots of dispatches over the weekend. Lots of chatter," she remarked. "Pretty quiet this morning."

By now, Hayden was sure his secretary had canvassed all incoming teletypes and memorized most of the weekend reports. There was little information that escaped her.

Hayden walked back to the conference room. The four deputies were drinking coffee. Mabel had brought a half a dozen doughnuts. The men were trading jokes and talking about one of the ball games.

"Attention on deck!" a deputy shouted. Someone whistled two high-pitched notes, imitating a boatswain's pipe.

"At ease, ladies," Hayden grunted. He sat back in a chair and listened to the weekend reports. There had been a head-on collision on Merton's Road at two in the morning. Highway patrol had called the sheriff's department for help. Two of the occupants were helicoptered to Great Falls. Saturday morning, a kid with a skateboard had knocked over somebody outside one of the grocery stores. That night, two tourists had gotten into a fight at Bremerton's bar. Mostly, the reports were pretty routine.

The two oncoming deputies were assigned to the day's duties. One would go to the Blackfoot Reservation and investigate a report of a stolen vehicle; the other needed to be in court on a felony arrest. They chatted for a few minutes and finished coffee.

Hayden walked back to his office. By department standards, he'd been given a good place to work. The office was large enough to house a mahogany desk, a conference table, and several comfortable chairs. On the wall behind his desk was a photograph of the governor, several pictures of Ashley's Little League baseball team, and an "Officer of the Year" award he'd been given in Seattle.

Mabel had placed a morning newspaper on Hayden's desk. He glanced at the front page. "California Woman Missing," the headlines read. The article contained a photograph of an attractive woman named Tracy Reynolds.

He scanned the article with mild interest and then placed the newspaper to the side. Monday mornings rarely gave him time to read the news. Turning his attention to a stack of correspondence, he began to focus on administrative matters.

Mabel's voice came over the intercom: "There's a call for you, sir." He pushed down the button for the speakerphone.

"Sergeant Hayden?"

"Yes."

"This is Jonathan Barnett. I think we've met before. I work at the Aspen Café."

"Go ahead."

"In the paper this morning. The *Montana Times*. There's a picture of a missing woman. I think she was here at the café on Friday."

Hayden reached over and pulled the newspaper across his desk, staring at the headlines.

"I'm listening."

"The woman sat at one of the side tables, used a cellular phone, and did a lot of paperwork. The picture of the girl, Tracy Reynolds. I'm sure it was her. The article says she's missing."

"You at the restaurant?"

"Yes, sir."

"Stay where you are. I'll come over."

Hayden switched off the speakerphone and beeped the receptionist's desk. "Mabel, look through the dispatches and see what you have on missing persons this weekend."

Without hesitating, his secretary retrieved a fax from the inbound basket. "There is an all-agency alert. Woman named Tracy Reynolds was a 'no show' at a scheduled meeting with her fiancé. She was last seen at a conference in Jackson, Wyoming. Described as twenty-eight years old, auburn hair, green eyes, five-foot-seven. Bulletin is from the Highway Patrol."

"When you get a chance, punch up the name Jonathan Barnett on the state computers. He works at the Aspen Café. See what you can find."

"Are you talking about Jonathan? He's a student at Montana State. Working here for the summer. I think you know his parents."

"Just run a check," Hayden grunted.

HAYDEN FOUND THE WAITER at the rear of the Aspen Café. The two sat in one of the back booths. Barnett held out the paper and showed Hayden the article. It was the same story Hayden had seen in the office. Hayden wasn't sure how much the photograph had been touched up, but he was impressed with her looks. Even in the computer-generated print, Tracy Reynolds was a woman of exceptional beauty.

Barnett seemed nervous. As he spoke, his fingers fidgeted at the edge of the table. Occasionally, he looked away. Maybe he's telling the truth, Hayden thought. Maybe not.

"She wanted to go for a run," Barnett said. "Somewhere near the mountains."

"Go on."

"She had a road map of Montana. I suggested a logging trail in Henderson Park. I thought it would be a good place to jog."

"What else do you remember?"

"She said she was going to Whitefish," Barnett replied. " Even driving slowly, she could have reached Henderson Park by six. She would certainly have time to run."

"Anything else?"

"I got a good look at her car," Barnett added. "It was one of those white rental Fords. Had a small Avis sign on the back. "

"You seem to remember a lot about this woman," Hayden remarked.

Barnett blushed. "She was very, very good looking."

"Yeah, I'll put that in my report," Hayden said, scowling.

He stood up slowly. "Just do me one favor, would you, son?"

"Sure, anything."

"Until we get this solved, I don't want you leaving town."

As he left the restaurant, Hayden wondered about mobilizing the helicopter and then decided against it. The crew had been flying most of the night with the medical evacuation. If he drove to Henderson Park, he could see if her car was there. In truth, he didn't have more to go on than Barnett's story. Hell, she could be anywhere. He had followed too many false leads in his years of investigative work in Seattle to be convinced this would turn into a positive find. Still, if Barnett was right, he was obligated to check it out.

HE THOUGHT ABOUT ASKING one of the deputies to take the assignment but knew both were occupied for the morning. Truth was, he hated the routine paperwork of the sergeant's job. He'd been trained to patrol the streets, follow up leads, try to maintain law and order, not sit behind a desk all day generating memos. A good investigation was always hard for him to pass up.

Two trailers and a camper parked along the south entrance of Henderson Park. Hayden drove slowly, following the circular lookout next to the river. It wasn't until he circled back toward the entrance that he found the car. The white Ford was parked in the shade next to one of the picnic tables. He pulled up behind the vehicle. An Avis rental sign marked the border of the license. Hayden called in the plate. Moments later, he received a confirmatory reply. The car had been checked out to Tracy Reynolds on the 16th of August in Jackson, Wyoming.

Hayden stepped out of his patrol car and moved in a wide circle around the Ford, carefully searching for prints or any signs of a struggle. He found none. The ground was covered with pine needles and offered little chance for tracking. Moving to the car, he peered through the driver's window. On the passenger side, along the floor, he could see an expensive-looking leather valise. The back seat appeared empty.

He took out a pair of rubber gloves and tried the front door. Locked. He worked his way around the car, trying each of the doors. He carried a thin strip of metal he could slip down a car window and trip the locking mechanism but decided against using it. He would wait until he had more assistance.

He returned to the sheriff's car and radioed dispatch for a tow truck. He would haul the vehicle back to the station so a team of experts could go through every inch of the interior. Evidence could be anywhere. Then he caught himself. Where did he think he was, in Seattle? He frowned at the thought. The "experts" would be himself and one of the deputies.

Still, he was familiar enough with investigative techniques to undertake most of the work himself. You didn't need to be an expert in forensics to find blood. The identifying chemicals could light up anywhere. They would dust for prints. Blood and prints were the main things he would be looking for. And then possibly surprises. It made no sense this woman was running drugs, but you never knew. Cocaine and crack showed up in a lot of unexpected places.

And what about Jonathan Barnett? Hayden wondered if the waiter was holding back. They would check the car for prints and then run Barnett's for comparisons. Barnett had known where she was going. Maybe he'd come out and followed her.

Hayden left the car and walked along the roadway, surveying the terrain. On the western side, he found a logging road. He inspected the chain blocking the entrance. If Barnett was right, this was where she would have run.

Probably should get some dogs, he reflected. The dogs could follow a scent up to a week old and cover a lot more ground than he could. The nearest hounds were a tracking team in Shelby two hours away. Best take a quick look first, he told himself.

Moving slowly along the trail, Hayden searched carefully for prints. In certain places, the ground was covered with small gravel-like debris. Occasionally, he thought he found the heel mark of a boot. He had no idea what type of shoes she might be wearing, although he assumed they would be used for running.

He walked for a quarter mile before he stopped. He'd seen nothing unusual. He decided he didn't want to waste further time with this part of the investigation. He could mobilize a dozen men by early afternoon. The highway patrol and park service would have to be called in. He would bring out the helicopter as well. In the evening, they could fly over the area with an infrared scanner looking for a body. Sometimes the scanner could pick up heat emitted from a dead person for several days. But what if she was still alive? What if she had broken a leg, or somehow got lost, or maybe was assaulted and left for dead?

He was on his way back when he noticed a dark area in the middle of the pathway. There was a smudge along the short grasses between the two ruts of the road. There, in the dust, was a faint stain as if someone had spilled a bottle of wine. He wondered if it might be blood.

Hayden worked his way carefully around the spot, gradually widening his path in ever-increasing circles. Moving toward the river, he found several other stains, fainter and smaller. One splotch was several inches in diameter; the other seemed to be a set of drops.

So what is this? he wondered. If it was blood, was it blood from an animal? Maybe a bear or fox had killed something and dragged it toward the river. Or maybe somebody had been drinking and retched up some pizza and wine.

He turned toward the river. Picking up a stick, he pushed his way through the brush. He would explore the area for a few minutes and then return to the car. He followed a narrow animal trail. Walking slowly, he moved beneath a spacious canopy of trees.

As he reached the water, the river spread out before him. The surface was smooth and uninterrupted. Downstream ran a long section of rapids. Directly across the river stood a thick section of trees. Beyond that rose a massive set of ridges, leading toward the mountains.

When he studied the soft mud along the edges of the river, he found some hoofed depressions that he thought were deer or elk and a couple of prints of a large animal that he thought might be a dog. He poked his stick at a trail of boot tracks. Probably fishermen, he thought. Little else looked out of place.

He walked carefully up the embankment and started back towards his car. He'd seen enough. Enough to get a team of searchers, the helicopter, and some good tracking hounds. Now time was of the essence. Every hour that passed meant the trail grew colder, the chances of success more limited.

A pair of magpies flew from a clump of brush. The birds lit in a branch and chattered noisily. Something on the ground where they had been feeding caught his eye. Along one of the myriad of paths that crisscrossed the foliage was a small white object, partially hidden in the grass. He took his stick and walked over to it.

As he poked at the object, a dozen flies buzzed upwards. Swallowing hard, he pushed his way through the brush so he could see better. Half hidden in the grass was a jogging shoe. On top of the shoe was a stain of darkish fluid similar to what he'd found on the trail. He gasped once, then recoiled, suppressing a rush of bile. There, inside the shoe, were the unmistakable remains of a human foot.

5

THE HIGH SCHOOL LOOKED LIKE a brick fortress standing resolutely against the encroaching slums. The walls were marked with graffiti, the windows covered with bars. Inside, on the second floor, was a classroom filled with students. Most were Hispanics and Blacks.

These were ghetto kids from Chicago's South Side, kids who were the products of broken homes or members of teenage gangs, kids who didn't know their parents, or if they did, kids who were beaten by their father or put up with their mother's prostitution. Some were youths who at the age of thirteen had already witnessed family members murdered. Others had been on drugs or spent nights in jail. Some, Robert Wolfson reflected, had probably pulled the trigger themselves.

Wolfson stood well over six feet. His body, from a distance, looked slim. It was only when you came close that you could tell he was a man of immense strength. His black, shoulder-length hair was pulled tightly into a ponytail. On this day, he wore a white shirt and conservative tie with a paisley design. To all appearances, he could have been a college professor.

It was the third session of summer school. Here were some of the most difficult students in all the Chicago high schools. You didn't go to summer school unless you were in trouble, and not the third final August session unless you were on the verge of getting expelled. These were not students with C-minuses and D's. These were students with F's and G's. The G stood for "God Awful," one of his colleagues said.

Wolfson left his desk and began prowling down the rows of students looking at their notes, searching for those who needed help or were having difficulty keeping up. He moved catlike around the classroom. When he returned to the front, he wrote the number 1803 in large chalk letters on the board.

"So, what happened here? Why was 1803 an important date?"

"Napoleon," somebody answered.

"Go on," he replied. "What about Napoleon?"

There was silence in the class.

"Anybody read the assignment?"

No hands rose. It was a stupid question. He shouldn't have asked. How could you read an assignment when somebody had shot out half the lights in your building?

"So, Napoleon was the ruler of France, right? And France owned a huge five-million-acre plot of land in the middle of America that was giving him a headache. He had the port of New Orleans to the south, but he couldn't defend the land. He was already given fits by a gentleman named Toussant L'Overture in Haiti, and he didn't have enough troops to support all this land.

"France's territory stretched all the way from Louisiana to Montana," he continued. "Nobody had been in it, nobody had explored it, and as far as Napoleon knew, it didn't have much use. It was a wild land filled with dangerous animals and ferocious savages. No cities, no industry, no trade. Who in the world wanted it? Not Napoleon. He was living in France, half a world away."

Wolfson worked his way through the second line of desks as he spoke. "So, why was this important?"

"We wanted it," a girl answered.

"Good! And who is 'we'?"

"The United States."

"Why?"

"Because we wanted the land."

"But, we didn't know what was out there either, did we?" he replied. " Yet, we were concerned about growth, and we had a very shrewd president named Thomas Jefferson, who just thought he might be able to strike a deal.

"Go on," he encouraged, coaxing the kids to answer. "What else do you remember?"

"Lewis," a student said.

"Lewis and who?"

"Lewis and Clark," another answered.

"Who's Clark?"

"First baseman," a tall Black teenager snickered from the back. A murmur of laughter rose from the class.

"All right. Let's talk about Will Clark," Wolfson shot back. "Who did he play for?"

"The San Francisco Giants," the boy answered.

"What was his contract worth?"

"Fifteen million."

"And who else was on the team?"

"Barry Bonds."

"And what did Bonds make when he joined the team?"

"Forty million!" the youth exclaimed.

"You know a lot about baseball," Wolfson replied. "I hope you'll do as well in our class."

A snicker rose from the front row.

"So, we got Will Clark and Barry Bonds and a couple of base-ball players thrown in at sixty million."

Wolfson kept walking down the aisle, pressing his points, keeping eye contact with his students.

"Add a few outfielders, a catcher, five pitchers, and a shortstop, and you're up to one hundred million in a blink of an eye. What will that buy you today? Maybe, if you're lucky, a team of professional baseball players."

He moved to the front of the room and pulled down a large wall map. Sweeping his hand across the upper western half of the

United States, he started with Louisiana and went all the way to the Canadian border.

"Look what fifteen million bought Jefferson in 1803," he exclaimed. "Remember what this was called?"

"Louisiana Purchase," a Hispanic youth interjected.

"Oscar, that's great." Wolfson smiled. "I thought you were asleep."

The class laughed.

Wolfson traced the expedition route across the map. "They started here in St. Louis in May of 1804. In 1805, they were here . . ." He paused at the beginnings of the Continental Divide. "They had reached uncharted territory. There is a huge mountain range here, and they needed someone to help them through the passes. So, they searched for an Indian guide. And who did they find, do you remember?"

"Sacagawea," a girl said.

Wolfson cocked his head. "Stand up, Miss Paulson. Take a bow."

The young girl blushed, stood up to applause and laughter, and quickly sat back down.

"Anybody know how old Sacagawea was?"

"Twenty-four," came an answer.

"Eighteen," another said.

"Sixteen," Wolfson replied. "She was the same age as you. To make matters interesting, she was also pregnant. Despite this, she leads Lewis and Clark all the way to the Pacific. During this time, she delivers her baby then carries it on a papoose. She's one of the most important Native Americans in the history of the United States.

"Trivia question." He paused. "Who knows what tribe Sacagawea belonged to?"

"Crow?"

"Nope."

"Cherokee?"

"Absolutely not!" he scolded. "Cherokee were a thousand miles to the east. Sacagawea was Shoshone. And if any of you forget that on the test, you'll get an F."

"How come you know so much about Indians?" a girl in the front row asked.

"Yeah," another added. "Somebody said you is an Indian."

"The term is Native American," Wolfson replied. "I was brought up on the Blackfoot reservation."

"Somebody said you changed your name, too, teacher-man," a Hispanic boy said.

"Yeah, bro', I used to be Black, till I changed my name," the dark youth at the back of the room chimed in.

The classroom erupted with laughter. Before Wolfson could answer, the bell rang. There came a loud shuffling of students.

"Next assignment, we'll talk more about the Louisiana Purchase," Wolfson shouted above the noise. "And think about what happened to Lewis and Clark. They were young men at the beginning of the expedition. What happened to them?"

Even as he finished, the students were moving out the door. He wondered if they had heard anything he said.

As WOLFSON DROVE OUT OF THE high school parking lot that afternoon, he casually glanced at the graffiti covering the walls. Next to the scrawled "Fuck You" and "Eat Shit" drawings were the insignias of a dozen gangs. Across the street, a car had been lifted up on wooden blocks. The vehicle had been there for the three weeks he'd been teaching the August section of summer school. The engine had been gutted, the windows smashed, the tires stolen. He was surprised nobody had given it the torch.

At the corner loitered several teenage kids. One was a girl who looked all of sixteen. She was wearing a high hip-hugger skirt, a low-cut blouse, and had the suspicious look of prostitution. He wondered if the two guys with her were pimps or waiting at the corner to sell crack or speed. It was hard to teach kids inside the

41

classroom, he reflected, when their cousins were outside the front door peddling sex and drugs.

Wolfson tried to fix their faces in his mind. He'd get the police down here again. And he'd keep calling them every day until they got it cleaned up. These types could do their dealings downtown where the school had no control. But not next to school property, he raged. For him, it was a matter of principle.

It took him an hour to drive across town. He was slowed by the usual mid-afternoon congestion, complicated by an auto accident. He didn't reach his condominium until four.

Wolfson parked his car, took his mail from a small box, and then rode up the elevator to the fifth floor. Inside his one-bedroom residence, he poured a Pepsi, turned on some soft jazz, and sat down to open his mail. There were the usual bills, a postcard from a friend in Hawaii, an ad for a sports camp in the fall.

Tossing his mail onto the table, he went over to check his answering machine. The first two messages were from friends. These were followed by a request for some history references from an associate teacher. And then he heard his grandfather's voice.

He wasn't sure when the message had come in. Maybe sometime in the morning. His grandfather was speaking gibberish. Some of the words were in Blackfoot. None of it made sense. Two Feathers's voice seemed agitated and confused. Wolfson thought about calling back, but what could he say? How do you address an old man who seems to have lost all sense of reality?

At five, he grabbed a pair of jogging shorts, a t-shirt, and basketball shoes. He planned to drive out to the shoreline and take his usual run and then join some friends in a pick-up basketball game at one of the outdoor courts. He'd just started out the door when the telephone rang. He paused, listening. Two Feathers was calling again. The words were unclear, the voice garbled.

A frown crossed Wolfson's brow. What his grandfather needed was a nursing facility, some place with twenty-four-hour attendants where people could take care of the old man. Maybe later, when he had a chance, Wolfson would give his sister a call. His grandfather was still speaking when he closed the door.

As WOLFSON STARTED DOWN THE HALL, a poster rustled on his kitchen wall. The illustration depicted a captain standing at the helm of a sailing vessel, gazing across the ocean, with a telescope to his eye. The words "Santa Maria" were painted across the bow. Below, printed in bold letters, was the inscription:

WANTED:

CHRISTOPHER COLUMBUS

The Father of Our County

For murder, syphilis, infanticide, and rape.

6

A T FIVE THAT AFTERNOON, Peter Shoemaker and Jeremy Stone sped along Highway 29, trying to make Henderson Park before dusk. The two had left their families back at East Glacier and were ecstatic at having an afternoon to fish. Stone was an engineer who worked in Denver. Shoemaker lived in Kansas. The men had gone to college in Colorado and remained fishing buddies over the years. This summer, their families had decided to vacation in Montana together.

The map was easy to follow, and Stone pushed the rental car toward eighty as they hurried to Henderson Park. At the entrance, they found the road blocked by yellow police tape.

"What's this shit?" Stone muttered.

A deputy strode out from a parked Montana sheriff's vehicle. Stone rolled down the window.

"Evening officer, we came to do some fishing."

"Sorry, gentlemen, the park is closed."

"You're kidding. We drove all the way from East Glacier."

"There's an investigation in progress. No one is allowed inside."

"What's going on?"

"There's been a homicide. I can only tell you there's a search in progress. You'll have to turn around."

Stone glanced at Shoemaker. "What are we going to do?"

"Let's keep going," Shoemaker said. "There's a lot of river here. I bet we can find another access downstream."

Stone backed the car around. Driving rapidly, they headed west, following the Arcata River. Occasionally, Shoemaker caught glimpses of water through gaps in the trees. If they were lucky, they could still get in a couple hours of fishing. The Arcata looked like a perfect trout stream.

FIVE MILES FROM HENDERSON PARK, Stone slammed on the brakes. A dirt road came out of the woods and intersected the highway. The road led toward the river.

"What do you think?

"I think we'd better start fishing or we'll be catching bats."

"My thoughts exactly," Stone grinned. He swung the car around and turned onto the dirt road. They drove for a quarter mile until the road came to an end. Shoemaker rolled down the window. "Water, I can smell it!"

"You couldn't smell a turd in a punch bowl," Stone laughed.

The two men stepped out of the car and walked quickly down a narrow path. Within a hundred yards, they found the water. Here the river moved slowly in a series of S-turns. A column of fir lined the banks. A well-traveled trail led through the trees.

"Well, we've got a good path, and down there looks like a ripple section, which should be good fishing."

"Ten bucks says I catch the first fish!" Stone shouted.

"Ten bucks says you catch jack shit!" Shoemaker retorted.

By the time the two men had loaded up their fishing gear, slipped into their waders, and assembled their fly rods, the sun had dropped a few degrees toward the horizon. Steadily, the brightness of the day began to fade into the gentle violets of the approaching night. The surface of the river floated by in a kaleidoscope of colors. As Stone began to fish, he watched the endless images on the surface, mesmerized by a reflection of trees and clouds and mountains floating past.

The fish took on his eighth cast. He saw the roll, the dark shape of a dorsal fin breaking the surface, right where his fly had been.

The line swung tight as he raised the rod. Stone felt the deep, heavy vibration of a large fish. Steadily, he began to back toward the bank where he could maneuver the fish into shallow water. At first, he couldn't budge it. Then the trout leaped out of the water, taking Stone's breath away. Never had he hooked such a big fish. He yelled to Shoemaker, but his friend was at the edge of the rapids, too far upstream to hear.

When Stone finally brought the fish into shallow water, he took his rod and shoved it between his teeth and then grabbed the thrashing tail and pulled it out onto the grass. The fish lay there gasping, its big flanks heaving. He took a moment to gauge the size of the trout. Twenty-eight inches, seven pounds, he thought. He wondered if Shoemaker had brought a camera. Placing the fish on a safe spot in the grass, Stone hurried down the path to get Shoemaker. His friend would never believe him.

When he reached Shoemaker, Stone waded out into the shallow water. "How you doing?" he called, waving.

"Caught a couple of small ones, how about you?" Shoemaker yelled back.

Stone held his hands a yard apart.

"You shitting me?"

"Come see what I caught."

Shoemaker reeled in his line and waded toward shore. The two men started along the trail. When they reached the grassy area where Stone had left the fish, the trout was gone.

"It was here!" Stone exclaimed. He searched around trying to get his bearings. "It was here, right here," he kept muttering in disbelief.

A branch cracked in the underbrush. Both men paused.

"You know what I'm thinking," Shoemaker said. "I'm thinking leaving a fish here was not such a good idea. Maybe a bear got it, or maybe it flopped back into the water. Let's go. It's getting dark. I don't want to get caught on the trail when we can't see."

"Jesus, I don't want to leave that fish. It's the biggest fish I ever caught."

"I'll take a picture of a trophy in a fly shop for you." Shoemaker reached into his fishing vest and pulled out a small pen light. "Come on, let's get back to the car."

Stone lingered by the grassy spot, still searching for his fish. When he glanced up, he could see the small pencil beam of Shoemaker's light dancing through the trees. Cursing quietly, Stone made one last search through the grass, but the trout was nowhere to be found. Without a photograph, no one would believe him, he fretted. Stone hurried after his friend. He was surprised how dark it had become.

HE FOUND SHOEMAKER FROZEN in the middle of the trail. His friend backed up slowly. One hand held the flashlight, the other pointed the rod forward like a spear.

"Don't run," Shoemaker whispered. A tense hoarseness sounded in his voice.

"What is it?"

"Look on the trail. There."

Stone craned his neck to see what Shoemaker was staring at. There came a subtle movement, a shifting of shadows, and then Stone saw a pair of eyes reflecting in the night. A shiver shot up his spine. Shoemaker shoved in beside him.

"Back up slowly."

"What the hell is it?" Stone whispered.

"Looks like some kind of cat."

"A lynx?"

"Too big, this thing's a monster."

The two men continued backing cautiously toward the river. In another five steps, they reached the edge of a twenty-foot bluff overlooking the water. They were trapped. There was nowhere else to go.

Peter Shoemaker observed the animal steadily approach in the limited sphere of his pen light. For every step backward he took, the beast came closer. Then came a deep-throated growl as the glowing eyes grew to enormous saucers.

"Jump! Thomas, jump!" Shoemaker screamed.

7

S ERGEANT SAM HAYDEN WAS STANDING next to the big rock a mile down the logging trail when the dogs went crazy, barking and sniffing and pulling at their leashes. They paused next to a large boulder just to the side of the trail. A helicopter passed over and began a series of S-turns, swinging down river. A cadre of volunteers worked through the underbrush, shoulder to shoulder. An hour's search around the boulder brought no new evidence. A couple of used shotgun shells, a faded washcloth, a dozen crumpled cans—the detritus of ten years of weather and intermittent human use.

The dog handler went back to the rock and started the three dogs over again. They were big rust-colored hounds, and they homed in on the smell. There was a patch there, just behind the rock where Tracy Reynolds's scent seemed strongest. As they moved away, the trail faded, and the dogs began milling around aimlessly.

"Nothing?" Hayden asked.

The handler shook his head. "She was here. That's all I can say."

"Why would she come off the trail?"

"Maybe she stopped to take a pee," a deputy suggested.

Hayden scowled and kept following the dogs. It made as much sense as any other theory. Why else would a jogger step off a trail and go behind a rock? Or maybe she had been knocked out and lay on the ground, Hayden thought. Yet, there were no grass stains. If she had gotten into trouble, the evidence suggested it was where they had found the smudge of blood, back along the logging trail.

Hayden searched the area for another hour, but the trail seemed to be turning cold. Finally, they left and followed the logging road back to the chained entrance. In the picnic area where the car was parked, they ran the dogs for one more pass. By now, Hayden had a fair idea how she might have run.

The scent trail left the car and followed the logging road for more than a mile. At the big rock where the smell was strongest, she must have stopped and turned back. A quick field test of the reddish material along the road checked positive for blood. It would take the state forensic office, however, to verify it was human.

When they returned to the picnic tables, Deputy Campbell helped Hayden open up the car. On the passenger floor, they found a briefcase and a cellular phone. An open map rested on the front seat. Nothing was touched without gloves.

Hayden punched up the phone number on the cellular and then asked dispatch to run all telephone numbers of calls made during the past week. Perhaps there was a clue hidden in the transmissions.

Inside the trunk, they found a pair of jeans neatly draped across a small suitcase. Hayden pried open the suitcase. On top were several pairs of women's underwear, lace see-through panties, a delicate brassiere. The clothes were stylish and elegant.

Hayden's eyes caught those of his assistant. A flash of understanding passed between them. The underwear told a lot. She was the type of woman a lot of men might try to follow.

Hayden walked over to a picnic table and sat down. They'd been at it since dawn. He was hungry, fatigued, and discouraged with what little they'd found. Except for the car and the shoe, there was little evidence to help. Tracy Reynolds was still missing. Soon he was going to have to call Tracy's family and tell them the news. He pressed his hands to his forehead, dreading the thought.

Somewhere out there were going to be some terribly distraught people. Relatives, lovers, friends, clinging to the slimmest hopes that their loved one was still alive; that maybe she had had a flat tire or changed her plans or maybe she had wandered into the woods and become lost. Or maybe she just hadn't had a chance to phone. And a voice they'd never heard was going to say that her car had been found at an isolated park near a remote river in Montana. "And, by the way, there was a foot in a tennis shoe . . . We think it might be hers . . . If you wouldn't mind coming down to the station . . . Maybe you could identify the toes . . ."

You're getting pretty cynical, Hayden reflected. Certainly, he'd seen worse. Even after twenty years of work in Seattle and hundreds of investigations, body parts were something he'd never gotten used to. They represented fragments of a whole, parts of the truth, and until he got everything back together again, Tracy Reynolds was nothing more than another missing person. Got to be some clue, somewhere out there, he thought, maybe something they had overlooked.

Hayden left the search site at noon and returned to the station. He would remain here for an hour making a few calls and then join the deputies and continue the search until dark.

His secretary looked up with surprise as he entered the doorway. Hayden appeared haggard and exhausted. Heavy circles shadowed his eyes. There was a defeated look to his expression.

"You're back early," she said.

"I'm thinking of calling it quits. I don't think we've left a stone unturned."

"Nothing?"

"Twenty searchers, shoulder to shoulder. Five hours with the helicopter. Three bloodhounds. Gone without a trace." Hayden tried to smile. "What's happening here?"

"Oh, we're surviving," she answered. "I placed all the reports on your desk. The office of pathology called and said they should have a preliminary report for you early this afternoon about the foot. Dr. Perkins, is working on the case. The family of Tracy Reynolds called. Her fiancé heard you may have some news. He said the family would be arriving tomorrow.

"The governor also wants an update on the search," she continued. "Seems the Reynolds family is a pretty big deal back in California."

"So I'm beginning to understand, " Hayden said. "How you holding up?"

"I can't say as I enjoy you men being gone, but it does keep things interesting. Your daughter called. She wanted me to be sure to tell you she was hoping you would pick her up this afternoon."

Hayden frowned. "I don't think I've had time to say much more than 'good night' to her the past couple of days."

"She's a pretty spunky lady," Mabel added. "Told me if you didn't come and get her she was going to call 9-1-1."

"Sounds like her," Hayden nodded. "What did you tell her?"

"I wasn't sure what time you'd get back. I just said you were awfully busy on the missing person search. I think she understands. She wanted me to tell you that she loved you and not to forget. "

"Already learning how to turn a man's heart." Hayden smiled faintly and started for his office.

"If pathology calls, interrupt me. And see if you can get hold of Jonathan Barnett. He should be working at the Aspen Café. I need to talk with him for a couple of minutes."

Back in his office, Hayden turned to a stack of reports on his desk and began thumbing through the documentation of various calls that had occurred over the past twenty-four hours. Unfortunately, the march of crime went on irrespective of higher priorities. There were several incidents, some investigations half complete, others new filings. He rapidly scanned the reports. There had been an attempted robbery in the town of Alder Ridge. Three kids had been caught vandalizing one of the elementary schools in Elkhorn, and Ray Peterson had gotten drunk and assaulted a customer at the Silver Saddle Saloon.

As he flipped through the remaining papers, one item caught his eye. The incident had occurred on the Arcata River several miles from the search site. Two tourists had been wading along the river, fishing. At dusk, they reported that a huge cat-like animal blocked their path. The two jumped into the river to escape. The memo indicated one of the men had almost drowned. The reporting deputy had sent a referral to Fish and Game.

Hayden spent a moment thinking about the incident but could make no connection. It seemed another mishap of idiot tourists—a pair of vacationing fishermen wading in unfamiliar waters. Probably a bear, he thought.

He could remember no other confrontations with grizzlies, coyotes, or any other type of dangerous game. The only animal encounter report to cross his desk the entire summer was from an enthusiastic tourist who had been gored by an angry buffalo.

As he tried to finish the reports, he found it hard to concentrate. His mind wandered back to Henderson Park. So, what happened back there? There were a lot of questions about Tracy Reynolds's disappearance that needed answers.

Mabel's voice came over the intercom. "Sergeant, I have the pathologist."

Hayden's pulse quickened. Perkins was an expert in forensic pathology and was well known throughout the state. Hayden flipped on the speakerphone. "I thought you guys had forgotten me."

"Sorry about the delay," Perkins answered. "There's a lot going on back here. The specimen you sent—" he continued, "I wanted to give you a follow-up. In case it would help."

"At this point, anything would help."

"The foot is certainly that of a woman. There is evidence of toenail polish, and the size and contour of the foot is typically female. In addition, there are callus marks on the heel and lateral sides of the foot, which indicate the person has worn high heels. We have been in contact with the Reynolds family. Tracy Reynolds wears a size nine, the same size as the Adidas running shoe."

"Yeah, that's what I figured," Hayden said.

"There's more. The brownish stain on the grass and bits of dirt you sent. The blood matched the A-positive blood typing of Tracy Reynolds. Again, we'll tie all this up with DNA testing, but I have to conclude it's all from the same source."

"Anything else?"

"We need a body."

"I was hoping to find one."

"Nothing yet?"

Hayden clicked his tongue. "Nothing. Not a clue. We're starting to go back over the same ground."

"Couple of other things," the pathologist added. "There were no drugs in the blood samples. No cocaine, no heroin, no alcohol, no marijuana. The lady was leading a pretty clean life."

"Yeah, so how did she die?"

"I can say the foot was apparently separated from the body after death. If you're worried this was done by some type of ax murderer, a dismemberment-type of killing, I'm not seeing it here."

"How do you know?"

"A microscopic look at the bone fragments revealed it was not cut evenly. The bone was severed with short, crushing lesions. A knife leaves a straight-edged cut. This looks like the work of an animal."

"You talking about a grizzly or a wolf?"

"Could be. Even a fox or coyote might find a body and gnaw through a bone like this, postmortem. Whoever, or whatever, worked on this leg had a pretty strong jaw."

"You don't think it's human?"

"Until we get a look at the body, all bets are off. I'm just telling you about the foot. We found several animal hairs."

"Go on."

"All the same species, *Peromyscus maniculatus.*"

"Come on, speak English."

"The common name is a wood mouse."

"Oh, that's just great!" Hayden snorted. "I'm supposed to tell the governor our lead suspect is a mouse? "

Perkins laughed. "Just telling you what we found."

8

Lake Michigan ruffled in the breeze. A freighter chugged along the horizon. To the north tacked a fleet of racing boats, sails arched sharply against the wind. A long, green park ran the course of the waterfront where a myriad of people moved, some jogging, others rollerblading, all following a path next to the water's edge. Two families were flying kites. A dozen dogs scampered across the grass. At the southern tip of the park was an elevated freeway jammed with afternoon traffic. Behind the highway rose the skyline of Chicago, a mass of glass and steel reflecting the afternoon sun.

At the western edge of the park was an outdoor basketball court, and this evening, it was jammed with players. Here was a favorite place for good athletes to come. Some were executives, others factory workers, a few still in college, working their way through school.

By six that evening, Robert Wolfson had played for more than an hour. In the game, he was point guard. He dribbled the ball well, passing to his big men, setting up the shots. He had a good eye and natural gift of hand–eye coordination. On occasion, he took several three-point shots and made them all—the best, a fade-away jumper that arched above the court and swished through the basket. On that one, even his opponents cheered.

After the game, he drove back to his apartment. He took a shower and then hooked up with a couple of friends at a pizza parlor for dinner. It was nearly midnight by the time he returned. Remembering he had to get up early for a conference, he went into the bathroom and got ready for bed.

He'd just turned out the lights when the phone rang. He had a premonition it was something bad. No one called this time of night unless it meant trouble. He picked up the receiver.

"Bobby?"

Sarah was calling from the Blackfoot Indian Reservation. As he listened to her speak, his expression turned to a frown. Her voice was high-pitched. Her words came in a rush. It was something about their grandfather, something about him acting crazy. And now he was in the reservation hospital.

The words came so fast, Wolfson tried to slow her down. "How did this happen?"

"He's gotten confused, Bobby. He's been hearing voices and having dreams, and he's been asking for you constantly. He started having chest pains this morning. When I took him to the hospital, they said he was having a heart attack."

"How can I help?"

"You need to come back. The doctors don't think he's going to last."

"Lord, Sarah. I'm in the middle of teaching," he said." It's not that easy to drop everything and leave."

"God, what kind of reality are you in?" Sarah cried. "Don't you understand anything I've said? I'm calling from the reservation hospital, and they think he's going to die. Do you hear me, Bobby? If you want to see him before he passes, you'd better come back."

"Sarah, I've got a full week of classes to teach."

"It figures. I didn't think you'd give a shit."

"It's not that . . ."

"Oh, fuck you, Bobby! What the hell do you care? Your grandfather spent half his life trying to raise you, and you could give a rat's ass. Piss off. I'm sorry I even called."

The line went dead.

Wolfson stared at the receiver. His hands were trembling.

Memories of his days on the reservation began to tumble back. Memories of his mother and father when he was a child. They were disjointed, uncomfortable images in which he felt helpless and out of control. There was a terrible hurt there, buried beneath his conscious mind, a hurt so horrible that he'd spent most of his adult life trying to get away. His mother was gone when he was eight; his father, six months later. His grandfather became his custodial parent. And now, George Two Feathers was about to die.

He spent a few moments pacing the room, trying to clear his head, trying to think of what to do. Finally, he picked up the telephone and dialed one of his teaching colleagues. There was an unexpected family emergency, he explained. They would have to cover his classes for a day or two.

By three in the morning, he was still awake, heart pounding, trying to catch his breath.

9

IT WAS NEARLY MIDNIGHT BY THE TIME Sam Hayden returned home. He'd spent another six hours at the search site. No new evidence had been found. Pulling into the driveway, he locked the sheriff's car and staggered through the front door. He found his housekeeper sleeping on the couch. Dolores was half Mexican, half Blackfoot Indian. She was a heavyset woman with a long braid and pleasant smile. Not long after he arrived in Montana, she had appeared at his doorstep and asked if he needed help. Truth was, he didn't think he could get along without her.

"If you want to spend the night, it's all right," he said.

"No, that's OK," she answered. "I got Ashley home from school. She did her homework and had dinner. She went to bed early."

"I may be gone tomorrow, too," he replied. "We've got another day's search ahead."

"What time do you want me here?"

"I'll need to leave by six."

"I'll be here, Mr. Hayden," Dolores nodded.

He walked her to the door, thanked her for staying late, and went upstairs to his daughter's bedroom. Tobey was sleeping at the foot of the covers. The dog perked up and wagged his tail. Hayden sat down at the side of the bed. Reaching down, he gently kissed Ashley's cheek. Light from the hallway spilled into the room. The whiteness of her skin shocked him in its vulnerability. She had the same curl to her lips, the same curve of the nose, as Maggie. God, he missed his wife. There were times when he wasn't sure he could go on.

Ashley stirred once but did not awake. Thin locks of hair fell across her cheek. Hayden gently pulled the strands away from her face. Rolling at his touch, she murmured something and then tucked back into the pillow.

On the bedside table was a picture of the four of them in Seattle. Ashley was only six then and Tobey was two. Hayden sat next to Maggie with Ashley, the dog crouched in between. It was a life that seemed an eternity ago.

He went quietly into his bedroom and undressed. On his pillow was a plate with four cookies. They were his favorite—chocolate chip. Tucked beneath the plate was a handwritten note:

Dad, I thought you might be hungry.

I made these for you.

Love, Ashley

He ate one of the cookies and then fell into bed exhausted. The next thing he knew, the alarm was ringing and Tobey was licking his face.

THE HUNT FOR BLACKFOOT LION

10

KIMBERLY BENSON STOOD IN FRONT of a bank of monitors at station KPXL in San Francisco. Her segment on a toxic spill came next to last, buried somewhere between the sports and weather. The lighting was bad, and her choice of background poor, marred by a hundred cars passing along the freeway. Worse, her hair seemed unkempt and windblown. She'd wanted to get that image of a roving television reporter working against the elements, but now she realized it was a bit overdone. God, she looked Neanderthal, she thought with chagrin.

She felt a twinge of envy to see her colleague Stephanie Peterson's segment on the mayor inserted as the first segue after the national news. Stephanie looked neat and trim. The brunette's makeup was seamless, and her hair didn't have a strand out of place. In front of the camera, Stephanie's delivery came off smoothly and to the point.

Glancing at a clipboard, Kimberly searched for the next day's assignments. Except where there was a fast-breaking story, she could usually predict the working location from a printed list of options. Given no unexpected disasters, tomorrow's shoot involved a trial in San Mateo over a convicted felon who was scheduled for a life sentence under California's "Three Strikes" law. Of interest was the third strike—stealing a pack of cigarettes from a convenience store.

The tug on her shoulder came a second time. "Boss wants to see you."

Jeremy Wong wore an earphone and mic. He'd come across from the main console to get her attention.

"What's up?" Kimberly asked.

"He just said if you were out here, he asked to see you in the office."

"I just wanted to catch the end of the news."

The engineer frowned. "I got the impression he wanted to see you now."

She nodded and left the main editing room. Holding on to the clipboard, she walked down a long corridor to Alvin Kessler's office. In general, she felt she had a good working relationship with her boss. Kessler had always treated her fairly, even though sometimes he was a tyrant.

The station manager was sitting at his desk, elbows out, hands clasped behind his head. He swung around, watching, as she entered.

"I've got a job for you."

Usually, assignments coming from the boss were a positive sign. They often meant the top brass had assessed a story and were specifically picking a reporter who might represent the station's best interests.

"Do you mind doing a little traveling?"

"Never," she answered quickly. Her mind spun. Where were they sending her? To Sacramento, to speak with the governor? Maybe to Washington, to interview the Secretary of State?

"There is a prominent San Francisco family in the publishing business who has a daughter missing. The Reynolds girl. I'm sure you're familiar with the story. So far, they've not had a lot of breaks in the case. She disappeared near a small town in Montana. I'm sure there are the usual incompetent law enforcement agencies. We thought it might make an intriguing segment for the news."

"Montana?" Kimberly frowned. This was not a top-of-the-news item. Yes, she was familiar with the story, but from what she'd heard, the woman had probably been kidnapped and killed. Besides, the story was already several days old. This was "I read it yesterday" stuff.

"When are you talking about?" she asked cautiously.

"Tomorrow."

"What about the Three Strikes story?" she protested. "I'd planned to shoot the trial in the morning."

"I'll assign it to somebody else. Maybe Stephanie can pick it up. She's got some time."

"Who are you sending as my camera man?" she asked cautiously.

"Eric Stafford."

She turned away so that Kessler could not see her disappointment. Stafford was heavyset. He wore a beard and smoked constantly. He had just started working at the station during the past month.

Kessler noted her dismay. "Stafford came highly recommended. I thought it would be a good opportunity to see what he can do."

She studied Kessler, trying to see behind his facial expression. There was no obvious hidden agenda she could detect. Yet, the facts were there. She was being taken off a lead story and reassigned out of state with a rookie cameraman. Stephanie would be picking up her assignment, along with one of the top photographers.

She tried to regain her composure.

"How long you looking at?"

"Couple of days. I thought it might be an interesting piece. Maybe there's something else out there you can uncover. The area got its share of "whackos." You got the Freemans. It's not far from Ruby Ridge. Dig around. See what you can find."

"Alvin, I wasn't born yesterday," Kimberly said. "Why are you taking me off a lead story?"

Kessler looked down at his pipe and tamped it lightly on an ashtray.

"I just thought you needed a break for a couple of days. Some of the staff have noticed you're a bit difficult to work with recently. Your reports seem to have lost a little edge." Kessler turned away, avoiding her glare. "It's from the top, Kimberly. From management. They like Stephanie a lot. They want to look at her for an anchor."

The words cut into Kimberly like a knife. Anchor positions didn't become available for women often, and when they did, there was always fierce competition. If the station was going to pass her over, she would have to look for another job. There were a lot of stations around, but KPXL was one of the best.

"So, where does that leave me?" she glared at her boss.

Kessler walked to the window. Gazing across the street, he turned back. "You know there are some things in this business that are out of my control." He pulled slowly at his pipe. "If I were you, I would go to Montana and file your usual outstanding reports. Try to make a good trip of it and come back and continue working, like you have. This is a short temporary assignment, as a personal favor for the Reynolds family."

"Yeah, thanks," she answered sarcastically.

"There are tickets for you at the reception desk. I think there's a flight at seven."

11

THE THREE KAYAKS SLID SINGLE FILE into the Arcata River. The temperature rose to a comfortable warmth; the Montana sky was deep blue. Paddling steadily, they eased into the main current, then, one after another, peeled off. Immediately, they were swept downstream.

The best and most experienced of the kayakers was a college kid named Jack Clayton. He'd been kayaking over seven years and was a skilled paddler. Larry Tarantino was a good intermediate. The least experienced was Jonathan Barnett. Today was the waiter's afternoon off, and Barnett had joined his two friends on the river.

At the end of the first rapids, the three pulled together, hanging in the slack water of an eddy. The river had changed since Clayton had run it two weeks before. The water seemed up, the current out of the biggest chutes, more violent than he remembered.

"You all right here, Jonathan?" Clayton asked. "Some of this looks a little bigger than I thought."

"I think so," Barnett answered. He glanced at the rapids ahead. "Which way you recommend I take these?"

"Avoid standing," Tarantino joked.

"Give him a break," Clayton said. "If you keep to the left, you should do fine."

This would be a good beginning challenge, Barnett thought. The rapids were short and not too rough. Yet, in places, the Arcata was much rougher than he expected.

65

"I'll try to go down backward on the right," Tarantino announced, pointing to the chute ahead.

Clayton smiled. "Don't try to get too bold too quick, or Jonathan and I will have to pull you out. Let's shoot these first ones straight. We can try some of the tricky stuff after Henderson Park."

Tarantino raised his paddle. "Adiós, amigos."

Tarantino entered the main stream, classic kayak style, paddling out from the eddy going upriver. The nose of the kayak edged into the swifter water and then pulled around as if caught by a sudden hand. Tarantino took a couple of paddles, slid across a small rapid in front of a boulder, and then bounced over the chute. Clayton followed. Then came Jonathan Barnett.

The youth could feel his heart jump. Before he knew it, he was paddling frantically, darting in and out of the boulders, following the crest of the river. The run lasted for nearly a minute as he worked his way a hundred yards downstream. At the end of the rapids, both Clayton and Tarantino had paused in the slack water, waiting.

"What do you think?" Clayton cheered.

"Fantastic!" Barnett exclaimed. "What a thrill!"

"Better than sex." Tarantino laughed.

"A little scary at first." Barnett nodded. "Not so bad when I remembered to paddle."

"We've got some deep water here at Henderson," Clayton said. "Then things will speed up."

They paddled slowly following the current past a bend in the river. A pair of uniformed deputies walked along the bank searching through the brush. A sheriff's Bronco stood on a low bluff. Next to the vehicle was a picnic table covered with gear. A number of law enforcement officers gathered around the table. They stopped and eyed the kayakers as they passed.

"This where the tourist lady disappeared?" Tarantino asked.

"Over there." Barnett pointed to a grove of conifers next to the picnic area.

"Any news?"

"Nothing. A blank."

"They find out how she died?"

"All they found was a foot."

"They think it was murder?"

"Come on, Larry," Clayton interrupted. "Jonathan's probably pretty exhausted from the whole thing. He was one of the last people to see her, you know."

"You're kidding?"

"Yeah, I'm still one of the suspects," Barnett nodded. "The sergeant thinks I might have followed her out here."

"You?" Tarantino snorted. "You couldn't poke your way through a paper bag."

Jonathan shot him an angry glance.

"Well, let's get on with it, gentlemen," Clayton said impatiently. "We've got some rapids to ride."

The river narrowed and picked up speed. At the beginning of a steep canyon, Clayton pulled them into shallow water. Here the three rested, splitting a candy bar. Ahead was a deep trough where the water pressed together, rushing tightly between two huge boulders. At the end of the chute rose a seven-foot standing wave.

"Gentlemen, may I introduce you to Widow Maker."

"Wow!" Barnett exclaimed, his eyes widening.

"You feel up to it?"

"Sure," Barnett said with a nod. "Give me some pointers, I'm game."

"Try to keep on the left. Keep your boat upright and paddle fast. Larry and I will probably try some acrobatics here. For you, Jonathan, just try to get through. Follow the seam. You'll do fine. We'll meet you at the other end."

Barnett raised his fingers in an O.K. sign.

"If you dump, try your flip maneuvers. If that doesn't work, kick out. The water should be deep."

"See you after the dance," Tarantino waved.

Barnett entered the main section of the river upstream, moving steadily outward until the current pulled him sharply around. Taking a deep breath, he stroked into the faster water. Suddenly, things began happening too fast for him to control. Paddling rapidly, he tried to drive his boat to the left of the big wave, but he was moving too slowly. The surge of current caught his kayak and swept him up the face of the wave. He had time to yell, and then he was over the top. He could feel his stomach fall away. The kayak crashed heavily into the turbulence and then he was upside down.

His helmet took a tremendous bang. He saw stars. He could feel his consciousness ebb as if he had been pulled into a violent whirlpool. He tried to flip upright, tried to remember how to coordinate his hips and jam the paddle in a reverse thrust that would turn the kayak upright. Upside down, underwater, the massive current flung him like a doll. Got to get air, he thought. Got to get air, or I'm going to drown.

Five feet beneath the myriad of bubbles were little islands of clarity. Abruptly, he became trapped by something large and pink, underwater, waving in the current. He kicked violently off the bottom. Then the rapids dislodged the object and whipped it down stream.

Clayton grabbed Barnett by the back of his life vest and pulled him into shallow water. Barnett staggered over to the shore, coughing and spitting, trying to catch his breath.

"You all right?"

"God, I couldn't break free. Something trapped me down there. I thought I was going to die."

Tarantino paddled his kayak in next to them. "That it?" he pointed downstream.

There in the slack water of an eddy, floated a large, pinkish, white object. At first the kayakers thought it was a large towel, or sack. Then the figure rotated slightly. Breaking through the surface came the fingers of a hand.

12

"Ashley, your dad is here! It's the sergeant!"

Hayden could hear the words repeated by assorted children as the message carried across the school playground. A dozen kids played on swings or skipped rope; others were jumping hopscotch or hitting a tetherball. Hayden searched for his daughter but could not find her in the swirling motion of colors. Then, out of the mass came a cry: "Dad!"

Ashley ran out of a cluster of children playing by the swings. Her hair was braided into pigtails. She wore a pair of jeans and a brightly colored T-shirt imprinted with a cow jumping over the moon. She had fine, well-formed teeth and a cluster of freckles across each cheek.

Hayden grabbed her arms, hoisting her upwards. "Boy, are you growing!" he exclaimed. "I can hardly lift you anymore."

"You're just getting soft, Dad."

"You ready to go?"

"What am I going to do with my bike?"

"I'll put it in the back of the Bronco."

"Can we take the horses for a ride?"

"You bet."

Ashley helped saddle the horses, and the two rode off the property following a small dirt road that ran for nearly a mile next to the forest. Tobey scampered after them, barking and yipping to keep up. They passed over a small creek then cantered along a forested trail, emerging through a broad meadow.

The afternoon was warm and lazy, and Hayden could feel the tensions of the search ease away. Across the field, two larks whistled. A pair of butterflies floated past. He watched his daughter ride ahead as Tobey sniffed alongside the trail. Ashley jabbered about school and a girlfriend who had a sick horse, wondering if they were going to have to put it down. Hayden half-listened, leaning back in the saddle, feeling the gentle sway of the horse beneath him. They were halfway across the meadow when his cell phone rang.

He pulled the phone from his belt. Deputy Peter Campbell was on the line.

"Sergeant, sorry to bother you. I thought you'd want to know."

"I'm listening."

"Some kayakers found a body in the Arcata River."

"Tracy Reynolds?"

"Without an autopsy hard to tell. "

"You need help?"

"Station's pretty thin. We'll need to make out a report. They wanted us to send the remains to the state pathologist ASAP for review. Perkins told me they might be able to get to it tonight, if we can get the body there fast enough."

"I'll be right in," Hayden gave a deep sigh. Just when he had the afternoon off, he fretted. And now he had to go back again.

Ashley reigned her horse until Hayden caught up. "You have to go?"

"I should be home for dinner," he said. "You okay if I'm gone an hour?"

"One condition," she grinned.

"What's that?"

"You're it!"

Before he could answer, she wheeled her horse and kicked it into a run. With a shriek of delight, she galloped off, leaving

Hayden in the meadow. Little Tobey dashed after her, barking madly. Hayden swung his horse around with a yell. He might have caught her if he had pushed it, but Ashley was going fast, and he kept behind her just enough to make it close. By the time he closed the gap, she was out of the meadow and running along a tree-lined path. Ahead was a narrow ravine with a small creek. Her horse plunged into the water, raising a shower of spray.

Hayden hit the creek behind her, close enough to get drenched by Ashley's splash. She took great pleasure in seeing him soaked. Finally, just outside the main gate, she pulled up, out of breath, laughing so hard she almost fell off her horse.

"I'll get you, little lady!" he shouted in false protest. He made an awkward reach, but she was too quick. Ducking beneath his hand, she edged her horse away.

"Maybe you need a little more practice riding, Dad," she teased.

"You're meat, kid," he growled.

LATER, WHEN HE HAD TIME TO REFLECT, when he was driving back to the station to help tag and ship the remains of the body found in the Arcata River, he thought about his meeting with the Reynolds family.

Arthur Reynolds was a distinguished-looking man in his sixties with a thin mustache and silver hair. His wife was blonde, statuesque, in her middle fifties. Hayden could see where Tracy would have inherited her attractiveness. Her fiancé was tall, handsome, with short cropped hair. The three had been angry and frustrated and thought Hayden's office was not doing enough.

As he watched the rising anguish in their faces, Hayden tried to reassure them he would call immediately if there was any further news, but he knew words were little help. Tracy Reynolds was missing. And there was no way to relieve the pain of such a loss. Seeing their despair only brought painful memories for himself. He'd had a comfortable life and loving family in Seattle when he'd received an unexpected message from Maggie one day. The doctors had found a lump. It seemed the tumor had spread

Hayden went home that evening and took Maggie in his arms, and that night when she was feeling too weak to walk, he lifted her up and carried her into the bedroom. For the first time, he realized how much weight she'd lost. He promised he was going to take her to Hawaii over the Christmas holidays, and, by God, even if he had to carry her on the plane, they would go back to where they'd first fallen in love. They would lie on the beach and feel the warmth of each other's arms.

Maggie never made it. In two months she was dead, and in another six months, Hayden was on his way out of Seattle, following an old friend who'd taken leave and gone to work as a deputy in Montana. His daughter had never ridden a horse before they came to Elkhorn, and now he realized what a good rider she'd become.

When he thought about it, Ashley was more accomplished in a lot of things than he wanted to admit. Time was passing, and she was growing fast. Somewhere in the distant recesses of his mind came a pain that edged into his consciousness like a thorn. One day, she would be grown and have a family of her own. But right now, he reflected, he was all she had.

13

T HE ONE-ROOM CABIN WAS HIDDEN in a thick section of forest bordering the Arcata River. The nearest highway was three miles away, the town of Elkhorn twenty five. A small two-lane trail led to the cabin, although access was limited to vehicles with four-wheel drives.

A century ago, the cabin had played a role in the silver rush in Montana. Now, few people knew of its existence. During a rainstorm, the ceiling leaked, and there were sections where the wind whistled through the walls. Still, it supplied shelter, and for Cecil Reiss, it was home.

Gradually, over the years, he'd shored up the structure. New planks of wood were inserted to replace the old. Glass windows were added, and a second set of logs cut to stabilize the roof. Next to the clearing, Reiss had cultivated a small garden. There was no mortgage, no rent, no landlord to deal with. All in all, he couldn't have asked for a better place to live.

It was late in the afternoon by the time Reiss peddled his bicycle back toward the cabin. He was whistling loudly, pleased with his luck. Early in the morning, he'd ridden his bike out to the highway and then hitchhiked into Elkhorn. Now he was returning, loaded with supplies. Often he had to wait several hours for a ride. Today he was picked up almost as soon as he put out his thumb. There were some good folks in Montana, he thought. It was a place where people were always willing to help.

He was a short, wiry man. A dishwater-blond beard fell to the middle of his chest. Most days, he wore the same clothes, usually a pair of jeans with suspenders over a set of long johns. A century before, he would have fit in well with the miners who poked around these mountains. Now, he was thought of as reclusive and odd.

As he peddled around the corner and drove into the clearing, he noticed something wrong. The deer carcass he had hung along the front porch was missing. He parked his bike and searched around the cabin. The body had been dragged behind some brush.

"What's this? We got visitors?" he exclaimed.

Some animal had torn off a large section out of the deer's shoulder. He paused to survey the rope. The deer had been hung with a cord as thick as his finger. It looked as if an enormous force had snapped it in two. What kind of animal would do this? He searched around the ground, but there were no tracks. "Got to be bear," he muttered.

He unloaded his supplies, then came back and dragged the carcass out into an open spot, leaving it in a clearing some distance from the cabin. Back inside, he unzipped a high-powered rifle from its case and opened the window. Satisfied the carcass was clearly visible through the scope, he took a bottle of scotch and poured himself a drink.

"Well, let's just see who comes calling, shall we?"

Turning on his radio, he found a station to his liking and began to drink. Thirty minutes passed. Humming loudly, he poured his third glass of scotch. As the sun slipped steadily to the west, long shadows drifted across the clearing. Reiss's eyelids became heavy. His breath eased. Gradually, his humming faded to a snore.

Reiss awoke with a start. It was dusk and the light was fading rapidly. Staring across the clearing, he realized something there—something huge. A large dark shape crouched over the carcass.

He rose up, trying to see the figure clearly. What he saw was no bear. It looked to be an enormous lion.

"Holy bejesus!" he muttered.

He moved slowly, bringing the rifle up, poking the barrel through the open space in the window, looking through the telescopic sight. His fingers trembled. Holding his breath, he tried to steady the rifle. He slid the crosshairs onto the chest of the beast and pulled the trigger. The explosion almost knocked him off his chair.

He quickly reloaded and then looked back through the telescopic sight. There was only the carcass of the deer. The lion was gone.

"Be damned!" he cursed.

Rushing toward the door, Reiss grabbed a flashlight and hurried into the clearing. He spent a few moments searching back and forth around the carcass, but it was too dark to see. Even with the flashlight, he found no blood. Maybe he'd missed it altogether.

"Keep out, you son of a bitch!" Reiss shook his fist at the forest. "Wherever you are, there is more where this came from."

With a grunt, he dragged the deer back to his cabin. Cutting off a slab of meat, he tied the carcass to a rafter then went inside, locking the door. Soon he was drinking again. A venison steak sizzled upon the stove. When he thought about the lion, he chuckled. Maybe he was too drunk, or maybe the rifle had moved and the shot was off. Don't matter, he told himself. Probably scared the bastard all the way to the Pacific.

It was dark by the time he finished preparing dinner. He brought the steaming plate over to the table and sat down. The aroma of meat made him salivate. Pouring another glass of scotch, he stuffed a napkin under his chin and started to eat.

A shudder rocked the cabin. Reiss stared at the ceiling. A shower of dust drifted from the rafters. He pulled off his napkin and eased over to the rifle, his eyes fixed on the wooden beams. One of the rafters gave a groan. Something up there, he thought. Something big.

He checked the rifle to be sure there was a cartridge in place and then clicked off the safety. Moving quietly, he grabbed the flashlight and tiptoed to the door.

"You come back for a little visit?" he said quietly. "Come back to see old Cecil, did you? Well, I got something for you, big boy."

Clutching the rifle in his right hand, he stepped outside. He held the torch in his left hand and switched on the beam. The circle of light fell across the upper corner of the cabin. He took a step backwards, flashing the light across the roof.

Nothing. The roof was empty.

He breathed a sigh of relief and then edged around the cabin, searching the surrounding area with his light. He saw no glint of eyes. Whatever he'd heard was gone. He turned back inside and locked the door. Maybe he was getting edgy, he thought. Maybe it had been his imagination.

He rested his rifle in the corner and sat at the table, stuffing the napkin into his collar. Refilling his glass, he lifted the scotch, eyeing his reflection in the window. The room looked warm and inviting. The smell of venison brought saliva to his lips.

"Here's to you, Cecil," he toasted.

As he raised his drink, an enormous shape crashed into the room. The window exploded in a hundred shards of glass. Reiss was knocked off his chair. The table overturned. Plates and silverware clattered across the floor.

Reiss found himself on his back, groping desperately for his gun.

14

HAYDEN HELPED DEPUTY CAMPBELL finish writing his report on the body found in the Arcata River, arranged for a quick transport to the state coroner's office, and then returned home. He had a pleasant dinner with Ashley, went over her homework, and put her to bed. He was back at the station at 8:10 in the morning. He nodded to his secretary and proceeded to the conference room. Peter Campbell met him in the hallway. The deputy held a sheaf of papers.

"Autopsy's in."

"Already?" Hayden could feel his pulse quicken. "What did they find?"

"You're not going to believe it."

"Yeah, what?"

"I think you can take Jonathan Barnett off your 'most wanted' list."

"What are you telling me?"

"This is the preliminary report. They won't be releasing the final version for a couple days."

Campbell handed the fax to Hayden. "Maybe you'd better sit down when you read this, sir."

Hayden nodded without looking up. As the printed words rushed toward him, he shook his head. Grabbing the side of the table, he eased into one of the chairs. The report was a dozen pages.

He read quickly through the preliminary findings, stopping with the summary at the end.

OFFICE OF THE SHERIFF'S CORONER
Case number 7438—Preliminary Report
Forensic Division
Helena, Montana
Summary of Autopsy Findings

Despite significant water immersion, the body is identified by blood type, dental records, and DNA tracing as missing person Tracy Reynolds. Findings are consistent with the amputated lower foot found in Henderson Park.

The autopsy shows significant deformity and tissue removal from the left chest wall, anterior ribs, and portions of the internal organs, consistent with predation by a large carnivore. Unusually deep puncture wounds at the back of the neck caused extensive damage to the cervical vertebrae, severing the spinal cord and probable cause of death. Microscopic hair particles found along skin surfaces and adjacent to macerated areas are consistent with Felis concolor.

In summary, there is overwhelming forensic evidence that the deceased was killed by a mountain lion. The separation of fang marks at the back of the neck indicates this may be an animal of extraordinary size. It is to be noted the deceased was menstruating at the time of death.

Part II

Paw Prints of the Lion

"The antelope are gone.
The buffalo wallows are empty.
Only the wail of a coyote is heard . . ."

(Chief Plenty Coups, Crow)

15

IN THE BEGINNING, he was no bigger than the palm of your hand; a tiny ball of fur, blind, spotted, and completely helpless. His den was a hidden cave along a section of cliffs above Kintla Lake. The area was one hundred miles from Elkhorn in a section of Glacier Park along the Canadian border. Here the primordial forests encroached upon the great mountains of the Continental Divide. It was desolate and remote; there were few roads, no towns, and only an occasional telephone line. Other than rare visits by park rangers, it was a place where the chances of seeing another human were low.

Yet in the beginning he did not know of such things as man. He only knew of his mother's warmth and her nutritious milk, and the high-pitched, purring chirp, which called him back to safety. In terms of feline beauty, his mother was magnificent. Her face was round with black crescents on either cheek, her body sleek and graceful. For hours she would lie with her three cubs, cleaning their faces, licking their bodies, nursing them when they were hungry. These were her first cubs; had she lived a normal lion's life, she might have raised two litters more.

Two weeks would pass before his eyesight developed. When the world first took form before his eyes, it must have seemed a miracle. Perhaps, like the growing light at dawn, he gradually became aware of his surroundings. Yet even at night, he began to see well.

As time passed and the cubs grew, he became increasingly interested in the outside world. At one month, when venturing to the entrance of the cave, he could see the mountains and the green sweep of forest, and far below, the turquoise waters of Kintla Lake.

The cave was supremely situated for the family's needs. One hundred yards below, within easy access of the stair-step rocks, a path led downward from the ledge. During these first months, his mother would leave the cubs on occasion to hunt for food. Here, in the luxurious undergrowth of the forest, she caught deer and hare, badgers and marmots. Once she brought back a three-striped blue-backed lizard.

As the young lion's confidence and coordination grew, it was tempting to try to explore outside the lair. During these periods, his mother would often growl or cuff the cubs back, knowing well there would be a time when she could no longer keep them safely. And it was thus one morning, on a bright summer day, that he learned his first lesson about the unforgiving hostilities of nature.

The three cubs were basking in the sun at the edge of their den. The mother had left to hunt. Aware of their sudden freedom, the cubs set upon each other, leaping and stalking along the rocky ledge, hissing in mock combat.

An hour later, their mother emerged from the forest with the body of a hare. Between their small skirmishes, the cubs watched her approach. Suddenly, she dropped her prey and bounded upwards. She could not roar, lacking the flexible hyoid bone of the African lion. But the call she emitted was harsh and shrill and one of great danger. It was a cry the young male would never forget.

There came a rush of air, a cushion of wind, pushed forward by the rocketing shape that descended upon them. Suddenly, the eagle was there: a huge white-headed bird with talons like sabers. With scarcely a flare of its wings, the great bird snatched his hapless sister and was gone.

His mother reached the lair a second too late. Leaping at the eagle, trying desperately to stop it with a swipe of paws, she didn't touch a feather. She could only watch and listen as the cries of her offspring tore into her heart. For a long time she could hear the faint disappearing mews of the cub. Later, even in her sleep, the sounds came back in recurring nightmares.

The mother herded the two cubs back into the cave. For an hour she lay down and nursed them. She had no speech, no way to tell them what had happened. But intuitively, she knew she would have to move. That night, she took the two remaining cubs, and under the cover of darkness, she carried them one by one to a second lair. This cave was closer to the valley floor and more protected from the cliffs.

Like his mother, even when he was no more than a yard long from nose to tail, the young male was fearless. When the eagle had struck, he had not cowered, but leaped at it, claws out, baring his fangs in a needle-toothed growl. Despite such courage, his diminutive size compared to the eagle's was a joke. Still, he had stood his ground, and it was this uncompromising fierceness that would distinguish the rest of his life.

As he grew, fearlessness, agility, and sheer size would become his main characteristics. In all three, he was extraordinary. Where most lions might fear man or dogs or bears, he had inherited no fear. Already, at eight weeks, he was significantly larger than his littermate. At one year, he was over a hundred pounds; at two years, two hundred. Hunting records by Boone and Crockett list the largest recorded North American Mountain lion as weighing 265 pounds. Undoubtedly, there have been bigger lions in the history of the continent. He was one. When he was fully grown at four years, he weighed over 280 pounds. For the species *Felis concolor*, he was a giant, a genetic variant that occurred only once in a thousand years.

At four months, the mother began to take her two offspring into the forest. By now they were the size of dogs. They could run and escape most predators, and the mother worried less about them every day. During these periods, they would watch her hunt, occasionally sharing in the chase. Here, they began to smell and understand what the mother was after. As they joined her stalks, instincts fired like rockets in their brains.

The chase, at first an exciting opportunity to run, now became a deadly effort on which their lives depended. As he grew, the young male followed his mother and learned from her patient tutelage. Because he grew so quickly, by the end of the first year, the three lions, hunting together, were almost like a pride. Whereas the success of a single mountain lion hunting by itself is estimated at one kill in four chases, with the family together, the kill-to-chase ratio increased to seven in ten.

The territory that the lions covered was nearly five hundred square miles. Sometimes they were gone for weeks. Traveling up along the Canadian border or ranging westward along the flanks of Kintla Lake, they hunted and roamed through the days of spring and summer.

The young lion did not have the mental capabilities to reflect deeply upon such things. He only knew this period of his life, hunting with his mother and sister, were the most pleasant times he had experienced.

Then, during the fall of his second year, an event occurred that would forever change his life. The three lions had traveled north, following a series of tree-lined ridges, moving over a mountain pass that led onto the fringes of the Canadian border. It was late September, and the quaking aspens were aflame. Periodically, snow dusted the mountains. The game was plentiful.

They had been following the scent of a herd of elk one night, when they heard a crashing of animals coming through the brush. The noise sounded like a frightened stampede. The three lions bounded after the animals, curious about the chase. Moving silently, they traveled through a section of forest and then paused at an open meadow.

The herd of elk bolted through the clearing. There were seven in all, and they covered the ground in sprinting leaps. As he watched, the young lion saw a pack of gray animals emerge from the forest. The pack loped after the elk, gliding like shadows.

When they reached the far side of the meadow, the gray shapes stopped. By now, the elk were too far ahead and they abandoned the chase. One of the animals leaned back on his haunches and howled. The sound was an ascending cry that rose in a melancholy wail. The young lion had never heard such a call before. Even as he listened, an instinctual shiver passed through his body. When he glanced toward his mother, he was astounded to see she was trembling.

The wind changed. For a long moment, the wolves stared in the lions' direction. Abruptly, they came loping across the meadow toward them. What were these strange creatures? he wondered. What danger did he not understand?

As his mother turned and bounded into the forest, the two young lions followed. She led them for a mile, crossing a stream and then ascending a narrow ridge. When she paused to catch her breath, she tested the wind and carefully listened. The two cubs crowded next to her. Through the trees came the noise of pounding fleet. An instinctual look of terror crossed his mother's face. Suddenly, she took off. His sister followed.

Confused by this behavior, the young male found a large boulder next to a steep incline and pulled off the trail. In two leaps, he gained the top of a rock. He crouched there, surveying the forest below. And then he heard a sound that made his heart quicken. From far in the forest came the screech of a mountain lion. It was a short, rapid call, and it came only once. Even in its quickness, he recognized the cry of his mother. He rose from his perch, ears cocked, tail twitching.

A chorus of howls rose. There were three, then four, in rapid succession that hung over the valley like a shroud. Then everything became silent. What had happened? Where were his mother and sister? What were these strange gray shapes that pursued them so relentlessly? And then he heard a cry that carried across the forest and stabbed into his soul.

It was his mother's voice, and her cry was one of terrible urgency. It was a cry he had heard her make only once before, when the eagle had taken his sister. He had been a small cub then, helpless and defenseless. Now he was a giant, and her summons came as a cry for help.

A hundred feet he plunged, paws wide apart, tail trailing like a rudder. He landed on the forest floor, crashing through the trees, hitting the ground at a run. He followed no trail. The noise had come from the south, and he charged in this direction, his great hind legs propelling him in massive leaping bounds.

Soon he could hear the noises of the gray shapes and the occasional hiss of his sister. He ran faster, charging with all his might. He'd been moving so rapidly through the dense underbrush that he was suddenly in the open, surrounded by the pack.

His sister was up in the branches of a fir. She peered down from her perch, ears back, snarling. The wolves frothed and slavered beneath her, leaping at the trunk of the tree. He was not sure whether the gray shapes could climb. He only saw his sister stranded seventy feet above the ground. He sensed her vulnerability, and it made him insane. Charging forward, he lunged into the wolves.

He hit the first wolf so hard he knocked the animal off its feet. With a swipe of claws, he filleted the wolf's snout in four parallel gashes. He dispatched the second with a bite to the neck. He slammed the third with a stinging blow that knocked it head over heels. The fourth wolf backed against the tree, growling ferociously. The lion plowed into this wolf, grabbing its open jaw, his fangs splintering the bone.

The remaining wolves charged after him. One almost got a piece of his flank only to be hit by a blow that knocked its breath away. A second lunged for his neck. The lion turned in mid-air and grabbed its throat, shaking the senseless animal like a rat.

The remainder of the pack pulled back. Out of eleven, only four remained.

He watched the wolves slink off into the forest and then turned back to the remaining injured wolves. Here he went methodically from wolf to wolf, dispatching each with a bite to the neck. Grabbing one of the wolves in his jaws, he carried it up the tree and deposited it along a spreading limb, forty feet above the ground.

It was as if he was bringing an offering to his sister, to show her he had taken care of the problem. If she had desired, he'd even have brought her something to eat. He climbed higher until he reached his sister and gently licked her face. After a few minutes, she seemed to relax and began purring softly. It took another hour before she would descend the tree. Even then, she had periods of uncontrollable trembling. At dawn, the two lions started on the trail again.

He thought then, somewhere in his limited reasoning, that perhaps his mother had gone ahead and escaped the wolves. He would never see her again. Over the next month, the Great Lion and his sister turned south, hunting game, killing elk, working their way back to the eastern borders of Kintla Lake.

A WEEK LATER, AN ANIMAL EXPERT came upon the scene. He was tall, large, African American, and he wore a Department of Fish and Game shirt. Howard Lassiter was in the area performing a survey for the government on the health of predators in this section of the mountains. The numbers looked good. He had seen many tracks of grizzlies. He'd found signs of lynxes. There'd even been some wolves.

Lassiter was driving a government vehicle down a logging trail when he was alerted to the flapping of ravens and the raucous calls of jays. He thought at first he would find the carcass of a moose. It made sense that a grizzly had killed something and left the remains.

But the sight that he came upon was beyond his imagination. He carefully surveyed the area. There were six carcasses. All wolves.

Something had killed them. This was not the work of a disease or natural calamity. Some immense force had slain the pack.

Taking a stick, he poked at the partially decomposed bodies, going from one to the next, astonished at the mutilation. Sides were ripped open, jaws broken, skulls severed to the bone. And then the flap of wings from a tall fir drew his attention. He looked upward, squinting in the afternoon sun. A raven had been feeding on something in the boughs.

He walked around the base of the tree, trying to ascertain what was there. The object was gray. He could recognize a tail. He raised a hand to shield his eyes. What was this? The body of a wolf? Good God, he thought. What could have possibly done this?

A week later, the first winter storm came, blanketing the ridges in white. The land could be inhospitable and harsh. Howard Lassiter was glad to complete his survey and get the hell out. He was the last human to ride down the logging trail for a year. But what he had seen remained indelibly in his mind.

During October, the storms began to pile up, one after the other. The temperature dropped. Snow flurries came constantly. The afternoons were overcast and gray.

As the days shortened, moose grazing in the high country worked their way down to more protected marshes. Grizzlies fed on berries along the ridges, gorging until they could hardly walk. The strange, whistling staccato of elk announced the coming change. For the lions, too, came change. His sister became edgy and irritable, often growling at him. With the family split up, things were not the same. His sister left him one morning to hunt. He did not follow.

The storms continued through the winter. From time to time, the temperature fell to a wind chill of forty below. In places, the snow piled in thirty-foot drifts. Food was scarce, movement impossible. Practically all living things took shelter. The young lion moved down past Kintla Lake for the winter, finding refuge in the deep forest. He was by himself. Occasionally, he killed a deer or moose and managed to stay alive.

IN HIS FOURTH YEAR, HE DRIFTED SOUTH, down past Bowman Lake and the Beaver River, hunting near the boundaries of Lake McDonald. Here he saw humans for the first time. Usually, he remained hidden and tried to avoid them. Once, during the wee hours of the morning, he walked through a camp of six hikers. During this time, he entered a tent and silently sniffed the faces of the sleeping humans. The strange beings snored as loud as grizzlies he'd encountered.

He remained that winter near Fish Creek. Come spring, he was still wandering, still exploring, still traveling south. He stayed largely in the hidden forests, away from human inhabitants. Here he hunted deer and elk.

By now, he was a truly magnificent animal. His coat was two inches thick. From stem to stern, counting the front of his nose to the tip of his tail, he measured twelve feet. His weight was over 280 pounds. His great canine fangs were almost four inches long. One of the fangs, it is to be noted, had broken slightly at the tip during the take-down of a bighorn sheep.

Like the occasional Olympic athlete that grows far beyond the average, this lion was a unique specimen for his species. As a predator, he was a remarkable killing machine: hunting, eating, resting, and then moving, constantly changing his environment, steadily pushing the outer perimeters of his world.

As he ranged along the southern boundaries of Glacier Park, he entered lands that were heavily occupied by man. Here were highways and roads and the incessant flow of traffic. He acknowledged the bewildering bustle of humans with their strange machines and generally avoided them. Most of the time, they never knew he was there.

AND THEN ONE AUGUST, he crossed the Arcata River in the pursuit of a mother elk and two fawns. He was stalking silently along the tree-lined boundary of a trail inside Henderson Park when a young, statuesque woman crossed his path.

Hidden behind a row of trees, he watched her disappear behind a boulder. When she reappeared, the woman began jogging back in the direction she had come from. The bounce of her ponytail piqued his curiosity. He watched for a second, watched her long, graceful legs, and then he slid over to the rock where she had rested. There was a spot of dampness here and he touched it with his tongue, raising his lips to take the odor better. Mixed with the pungent smell of urine was the tantalizing scent of blood.

And this was all it took. A microscopic gate inside his brain, switched from "off" to "on."

16

As the commuter jet circled Elkhorn and then began to descend, Robert Wolfson gazed out the aircraft window. A ridge of mountains passed below, rising along the southern border of Glacier Park. The Blackfoot Reservation was out of sight to the east. The nearness of the plains and the familiar sights of mountain peaks he'd known as a child began to bring back a flood of memories.

He could try to escape his heritage and ignore his past, but the facts were this remote corner of Montana had been his home. This was where he had been brought up under the steady tutelage of George Two Feathers. He had to come back, if for no other reason than respect. Sarah was right. He owed it to his grandfather to return.

As the aircraft taxied toward the terminal, he reflected how ironic it was that this was the same airport he'd used to try to escape for most of his adult life. It was here he'd taken a flight with his championship high school basketball team to a tournament in Denver. He'd been a junior then, and it had opened his eyes to an entire universe out there waiting for him—an enticing, fascinating world in which there was nothing that could hold him back.

It was on the bus after the game, after the speeches and the trophies, that Wolfson had recalled a homeless drunk sprawled next to the stadium, yelling at the team for a handout. The man had long black hair with dark skin and coarse features. There was vomit on the side of his clothes.

Wolfson noted the man was Native American. And for the first time in his life, he became concerned about his heritage. He wanted to hide, to erase his past. It was an undercurrent of embarrassment to their victory, and it hung there like a scab.

It was at this airport, too, years before, he had waved goodbye to his father for the last time. Strange, but it was the strongest memory he had of his father. Maybe subconsciously, he had had a premonition something bad was going to happen. He was eight then, and he remembered his frustration of not being able to journey with him. His father was traveling to Washington, D.C. to try to raise dollars for education for the reservation. Wolfson's mother had died that spring, and when his father returned, he began drinking again. Six months later, his father was dead, killed in an auto accident, another sad statistic of the Montana highways.

Wolfson's final departure was when he'd flown to Fort Benning to join the Army. He'd known then he was leaving for good. If he ever was going to make a future for himself, he had to break out of the traditional Native American mold and leave the reservation. He was determined to chart a course of his own.

While in the army, he changed his name. For a fee of thirty-seven dollars and a copy of his birth certificate, he eliminated Bobby Running Wolf for good. The old name just didn't fit with what he wanted to do in life. After the change, all the wolf calls and kidding ceased. He seemed to become a more integral part of the groups he worked with. It was a subtle difference but a significant one. In the melting pot of the military, and even with the diverse class of teachers in Chicago, nobody was sure of the heritage of Robert Wolfson. Hispanic, Eurasian, Middle East? Mostly people didn't care.

WOLFSON WAS THE LAST PASSENGER OFF THE PLANE. As he came down the ramp, he spotted a young man standing off to the side of the concourse. The youth looked to be in his teens. Dark hair splayed across his shoulders. He was dressed in a T-shirt with jeans and cowboy boots. There was a familiarity about him that Wolfson could not quite place. When the youth waved, he suddenly recognized the face. It was Franklyn Yellow Pine. There was at least ten years of difference between the two. The last time Wolfson had seen him, Franklyn must have been eight.

"Hi, Bobby Running Wolf!" Franklyn shouted. "Your sister sent me to pick you up. I've been watching every flight since noon."

On the reservation Wolfson knew they would revert to his tribal name. But that was okay. He would not be home long. This weekend they could call him whatever they wanted.

"Plane out of Chicago was delayed," he answered. "And I missed the connecting flight in Denver." He shook the youth's hand vigorously. "God. The last time I saw you, you were this big." Wolfson pointed to his knee.

"Come on," Franklyn laughed. "I was never that small!"

The front of Franklyn's T-shirt displayed the design of a runner with mountains in the background. The caption advertised "Mountain Marathon."

"You running?" Wolfson asked.

"A little."

"Competing?"

"Yeah, some."

"The Mountain Marathon sounds pretty serious. How'd you do?"

"Third in the state."

"You're kidding!" Wolfson gave him a friendly slap on the shoulder. "Maybe we could do a little running while I'm here."

Franklyn nodded. "I'd like that a lot."

As the two walked into the airport, Franklyn spoke of his parents and what he was doing. Wolfson waited for his bags while Franklyn went outside to bring up his truck.

A dozen suitcases tumbled down a conveyor ramp. Passengers crowded forward to collect their gear. Wolfson waited patiently in the back. He noticed an attractive blonde woman at the edge of the crowd. A large Black man stood next to her with a camera over his shoulder. The insignia: "KPXL" was stenciled on the back of his jacket. The two made an unusual pair.

When Wolfson recognized his bags, he edged forward between passengers. On top of the ramp, a suitcase twisted sideways and then tipped over. The top sprang open and the contents spilled out. An assortment of underwear and cosmetics slid down the ramp.

"Oh, my God," a woman's voice exclaimed.

Leaning forward, Wolfson rescued a handful of clothes. The blond woman with the photographer pushed in beside him, grabbing at her garments.

"How, embarrassing," she muttered.

Wolfson helped her pick up the clothes. Reaching over, he collected a blouse and pair of panties.

"I'd wear these, but I don't think they'd fit," he chuckled.

"Thank you." Her face flushed. "God, I knew that suitcase was a problem."

"You with the news?"

"Kimberly Benson." She held out her hand and gripped Wolfson's firmly. "Station KPXL, San Francisco."

"How come you're here?"

"We're doing a story on a missing person. And you?"

"Just coming back to the reservation."

She finished pushing the remaining clothes into her suitcase and motioned for her cameraman to pick up a large metallic container coming off the ramp.

"You Native American?" she asked.

"Was . . ." he answered.

"Maybe we could talk sometime."

"I'm probably not the best person to speak," he answered. "I'm just back for a couple of days."

"Well, how could I get in touch?"

"Send up a smoke signal."

"In English or French?" she laughed.

"Blackfoot," he shot back.

He grabbed his suitcase. Kimberly Benson was still collecting her bags as he started toward the exit. When he looked back, she waved.

"Thank you," she mouthed

THERE WERE TWO DOGS IN THE BACK of the pick-up, both mongrels. Wolfson swung his bags into the open flatbed and climbed into the front. As they circled the airport toward the main highway, Wolfson noticed the blond reporter standing next to a rental van with her assistant. He could have given her his name, but the last thing he wanted was an interview about Native Americans. Mostly, he hoped to get in and out of the reservation anonymously. He would visit his grandfather and return to Chicago as soon as he could.

The drive to the reservation took nearly an hour. Along the way, Wolfson sat back and tried to relax. The two spoke about the Denver Broncos, the summer weather, and the influx of tourists coming into town. The road ran parallel to Glacier's southern boundary, following the Arcata River.

"What's going on with the tribe?" Wolfson asked.

"There's talk of a putting a road through the reservation."

"So what's the big deal?"

"One of the big mining companies wants to run a road up to Canada to help bring some of their drilling gear back and forth."

"Through tribal ground?" Wolfson asked.

Franklyn nodded.

"I think that would be a travesty."

"They're offering a lot of money to the reservation. I'm told there's enough for everyone to take home $10,000. I could do a lot with that kind of money."

"And you can bet there's some big corporate boss, skimming a million dollars into his pocket." A twinge of anger touched Wolfson's voice. "Better give the asshole ten thousand and keep the rest for the reservation."

"Maybe," Franklyn said. "But if it will bring some real money, we would be stupid to turn them down."

"And the elders want this road through tribal land?"

"Well, it would be a small road," Franklyn replied.

They both laughed.

"So who's behind all this?" Wolfson asked.

"Some business folks in Denver. They were up here last month talking with the elders. It all looked pretty good."

"I bet," Wolfson said. "Let us take your land, Red Man. Great White Father bring many presents. Beads, tobacco, looking glass . . ." He stared at the youth. "Is that what you really want?"

Franklyn pondered the question. His answer came back slowly. "It's hard, very hard for many of us to make a living on the reservation. The only people who've done well are people like yourself, who've left. I know it flies in the face of our ancestors. But maybe we've got to move on. The road idea is being pushed by some of the more militant members of the tribe. They're having a tough time here, Bobby. The schools aren't great. People want to get their money and leave."

"Sounds like another example of being fucked over by the Anglos."

"Yeah, maybe," Franklyn answered. "But, if you need the money, and you need work, and you see your life flushing down a drain, why not?"

"You enjoy getting screwed?"

"In all due respect, you're a fine person to talk," Franklyn glared. "You're not here. You're not living on the reservation. Word is, you changed your name and left. And there are a lot of people back here who are having a tough time existing in any kind of fashion.

Do you think I like working at the Dairy Queen for $7.50 an hour? And I'm doing a lot better than a lot of guys my age."

"What about college?"

"Good luck," Franklyn replied.

"Why not?"

"Because my grades suck. Because you need at least a three-point to get into the state universities. I don't think my average is above 2.5."

"Then what about running?"

"Nobody has scholarships for runners these days."

Franklyn fixed his eyes on the road. They drove for another ten minutes in silence.

As a teacher, Wolfson knew Franklyn could go on to school and get a college education if he really wanted. The trouble was the issues were confusing, and kids Franklyn's age often had no real direction. The move outside the reservation was scary; it required a lot of motivation, and even in the best of circumstances was not always successful. A number of Native Americans, his sister included, had tried to leave the reservation but came back.

"Any other news?" he asked.

"There was a missing tourist a couple of days ago. Her remains were found in the Arcata River. First, they thought it was murder."

"Sounds like Chicago," Wolfson grunted.

"The state pathologists ran an autopsy. Rumor is they found some fang marks and animal hairs. They're pretty sure it was a lion. It was front-page news this morning."

"Years ago, I remember someone being mauled by a lion. And grizzly attacks occur in Glacier all the time. So, why all the press?"

"I guess it's because the girl's from some kind of well-to-do publishing family in San Francisco."

"Anything else?"

"Well, Billy White Shoes went out to the river after they completed the investigation and looked around. He saw some lion's tracks. He thought he found an area where she was knocked down and dragged off. At first, the sheriff discovered a foot, but they needed to find the body to confirm the cause of death."

"So, who found it?"

"Three kayakers running the river. Nobody's real sure how the body got into the water."

"White Shoes say anything else?"

"He said the paw prints of the lion were this big." Franklyn lifted hand, spreading his fingers as wide as he could.

"I think he must be drinking," Wolfson replied.

"I'm just telling you what he said."

"And Grandfather?"

"Not good," Franklyn paused. "Sarah wanted me to bring you right to the hospital. The doctors aren't sure how much longer he's going to last."

As they drove, Franklyn began to talk about fishing and a new girlfriend, who was half-Irish, half-Blackfoot, and the "most beautiful girl" he'd ever met. Mostly, Wolfson listened and watched the scenery. Despite his reluctance to come back, the view of the mountains, the tall ridges, the fresh smell of pine were a feast to his senses.

He'd always loved the conifer forests. For the first twelve years of his life, when he wasn't in school, he'd spent almost every spare hour with his grandfather, wandering pristine valleys, tracking game, exploring areas where his ancestors had roamed.

He tried to imagine what would become of the reservation in another twenty years. In his most pessimistic version, the mining company would build a road through sacred land and contaminate the area for miles.

He was surprised the thought stirred such strong emotions. In reality, he was out of it. He no longer thought, lived, or existed as a Native American. Franklyn was right. He wasn't qualified to comment. Such things were no longer his concern.

17

THEY REACHED THE RESERVATION HOSPITAL at five. Franklyn pulled his truck into the parking lot. Wolfson's sister met them in the waiting room. When Wolfson stepped forward to hug his sister, Sarah drew back.

"It's nice to see you," she said flatly. "I'm glad you could get away."

They stood for a few moments exchanging cautious pleasantries. The meeting was awkward. Sarah seemed tight-lipped and angry.

Wolfson had always liked his sister. Once he'd flown her out to Chicago, but the jobs were scarce and she didn't make the adjustment well. After hugging Lindsey, Wolfson tried to pick up the baby. The infant promptly regurgitated a flood of milk on his shirt. A faint smirk crossed Sarah's face.

"She's got a way of showing affection," Wolfson said with amusement.

"It's her reaction to strangers," Sarah replied. "Maybe you should come more often."

"I'd better let you two talk." Franklyn politely excused himself and started for the parking lot. Wolfson thanked him for the ride and then turned toward his sister.

"Why didn't you take him to a hospital in Helena? Someplace like a university medical center where he could get proper help?"

"Oh, God," Sarah replied. "Because, this is where he belongs!" Her voice lowered. "Look, if you don't want to see him, I'll tell him you couldn't come . . ."

"Sorry," Wolfson said softly. "I didn't mean to be critical."

"Then just visit him," she burst out. "Tell him you love him. Make him feel that you care."

They sat together for a few moments in silence. A nurse stepped out from the hall and ushered Sarah down a side corridor. Wolfson followed. They paused outside intensive care, looking through a large plate-glass window. Inside was an old man lying on a gurney. Wolfson was shocked at the sight. George Two Feathers was hooked to a bank of monitors. An intravenous line ran into his arm. His grandfather's face looked gaunt, his skin pulled back like parchment.

"Are you Bobby?" the nurse asked.

Wolfson nodded.

"He'll be glad you came. He's been asking for you constantly."

The nurse motioned for them to follow. Inside, they moved quietly to Two Feathers's bed. The old man seemed to be sleeping soundly, his chest rising and falling rhythmically with the beeps of the monitors.

"Grandpa . . . Grandpa, wake up." Sarah reached forward and shook him gently. "Look who came to see you. Bobby's here."

Two Feathers gave a faint shudder. His eyes fluttered.

"Grandpa . . . wake up," Sarah repeated. "Look who's here!"

Two Feathers looked toward Wolfson. The faintest smile crossed his lips. He raised a gnarled hand to grip Wolfson's fingers.

"It's good to see you, Grandfather."

"I . . . I'm so glad you came." His voice fell to a whisper. "I don't have much time."

"No way! We'll have you out in a couple of days."

"Not this time, Bobby," he murmured.

There came a long pause. "I tried to call . . ."

"I know. I got your message, Grandfather. I came as quickly as I could."

"We need to talk . . ." The old man's words came with great effort. "Sarah, I need Bobby alone."

Sarah shrugged and turned to Lindsey. "Let's take a walk," she said.

George Two Feathers watched her take the children out of the room and then tried to raise on one arm, but he was too weak. He sank back in bed, staring at Wolfson. He motioned for him to lean closer.

"Bobby . . ." His voice rose. "*Omahkatayo* is here."

"These are visions, Grandfather."

"No, I saw its image in the clouds. This time there is no mistake."

"I think this is your imagination," Wolfson frowned.

The old man shook his head. "How does the goose know where to fly in the fall? How does the elk find grass below the snow?" His voice quavered. "The lion has killed someone. It was no vision that did this."

"A lion killed a tourist, Grandfather," Wolfson said. "I came to see you and help you get better. You are my concern, and I want to get you well."

The nurse entered the room. Reaching forward, she adjusted one of the intravenous lines. "Be careful of getting him too excited," she cautioned. "His pulse has gone up by twenty beats just since you came."

Hesitating at the bedside table, the nurse made a few notes on a chart and then started out the doorway. As she departed, she brought a finger to her lips with a sign of caution.

Wolfson felt a sudden pain at his wrist. The old man had grabbed his arm. The nails dug into his skin like claws.

"I have thought about it much." Two Feathers's voice faded into Blackfoot. "Whatabe malaka entebbe. Asanga . . . Asanga . . ."

Then, very faintly, whispered words came from deep within his throat: "You're the last blood of great chiefs," he said.

"Eyes-in-Shadows, Long Walker, Red Cloud. You will need strong medicine. Talk with Raven Crow. She knows the ways."

Two Feathers's voice trailed into mumbled Blackfoot. The old man's eyes closed. His lips formed words, but no sound came. Like an aspen stirred by the flutter of a passing breeze, George Two Feathers trembled once and then became still. Finally, there was only the ping of the monitors.

As they left the hospital and walked toward Sarah's car, a group of children caught Wolfson's eye. The kids were standing next to the side of the building, clustered around a woman wrapped in a brown blanket. She had coarse gray hair and a rough, weathered complexion. Below a beaded headband, two silver earrings flashed. The children stood in a semicircle, watching intently.

Wolfson paused to see what the kids were so fascinated with. The woman had her hands out, the tips of her fingers touching in a circle. Two thrushes moved up and down her arms.

One of the birds suddenly fluttered off her wrist and flew to a bush. Another circled overhead and landed on her shoulder. The birds appeared wild yet approached the woman without fear.

Wolfson turned to the car and helped Sarah strap her two children into car seats in the back. As he slid into the passenger side, he saw the strange woman rise up and glance in his direction. Backing from the parking lot, Sarah drove away from the hospital. When Wolfson looked in his side-mirror, the blanketed figure was staring after them.

"Sarah, who is that?"

"Her name is Raven Crow. Some call her Bird Woman."

"How does Grandfather know about her?"

"I don't know, why?"

Wolfson made a mental note to ask his grandfather more about this strange woman. He never had the chance. An hour later, George Two Feathers was dead.

18

LIKE MOST FARMERS IN THE ELKHORN AREA, Lute Olsson was having a tough year. During the past two seasons, the wheat crop had been poor. Too much rain in the spring and too little during the months of July and August had thrown the harvests off. Olsson found himself in debt to the bank again. There were times like this when he wished he was out of farming. He had inherited the land from his father, and he had worked the property for over twenty years.

The location was pristine. He had two hundred acres in a narrow valley with Swan Lake on one side of the property and a backdrop of the Bear Mountains on the other. One hundred seventy-five of his acres were flat and fertile; and he could grow, during good years, a crop of wheat that would bring in forty thousand dollars. His family didn't need half that to live. But this year was the third year of too much precipitation during the spring, followed by a summer drought. The whipsawing of moisture ruined the quality of the wheat.

If he didn't get a good crop soon, he was looking at the beginnings of financial trouble. He'd barely been able to pay off the bank last year. He had had to take out another loan. Now they were asking to take the mortgage on his farm as collateral.

He sat at the head of the dinner table that evening, surrounded by his wife and three children. As they did before every meal, he bowed his head and said the blessing. They were a good Mormon family. Lute thanked God for the health of his children and the food before them and asked for forgiveness of their sins.

Olsson's wife sat at the opposite end of the table. Kate was a modest woman, attractive though heavy set. They'd married during Olsson's senior year in high school and lived together for twenty years. His three children were ten, twelve, and eighteen. James, his only son, would be going to Brigham Young that fall. That, too, would be a financial strain. Even though the boy had a partial scholarship, there would be costs for room and board.

After the blessing, Olsson's wife and daughters served dinner, carrying healthy portions of vegetables, meat, and potatoes. A large black mastiff lay beneath the table, waiting patiently for scraps. It was eight in the evening. The sun slipped beneath thick clouds. There were no sunset colors that night.

"Looks like rain, Pop," James said.

"I hope so," Olsson replied. A frown of frustration crossed his brow. "Even a little drizzle would give this crop a boost."

"Why don't I stay home this fall and help with the harvest?"

Olsson shook his head. "You need to get on with your studies. We'll make it okay."

His wife placed a cup of gravy on the table and sat down.

"The real estate man called again," she said.

Olsson took a mouthful of potatoes and began chewing quietly. He nodded for her to continue.

"Says he has someone interested in buying the property."

"He knows I'm not selling," Olsson replied, angrily. "Why does he keep calling?"

A whinny came from outside the house. One of the horses sounded distressed. Everyone at the table paused. The mastiff rose to its feet and went to the door.

"Something spooking the horses," James said.

Lute held up his hand for silence. They had six horses in a small corral, two hundred yards from the house. In years past, a bear would occasionally wander through the property. Whenever they turned the dog loose, Abe would chase it away. No animal wanted to mess with a dog the size of Abe.

"Do you want me to go see?" his son asked, standing up.

"Let's wait," Lute said with a shake of his head. "Maybe it was just a scent on the wind."

The sharp whinny sounded again. Lute could hear the horses snorting, moving restlessly in the pasture. The dog whined, pawing at the door.

"All right, Abe, go see what it is," Olsson commanded.

He stood up from the table and let Abe out the door. With a growl, the dog dashed into the darkness. Olsson watched him disappear and then came back inside.

"Got to be a bear or coyote," he said. "Coyotes getting so bad, James Robertson told me he'd seen a pack of eight the other day."

Olsson turned back to the table. He'd just sat down when he heard the loud barking of his dog and the frantic high-pitched whinny of his horses. There was an element of desperation in the sounds.

"Got to be a bear," James said. "Sounds like a grizzly."

Olsson stood up from the table. "Jimmy, get my flashlight and gun."

The boy lunged out of the room. In a moment, he was back holding a large-beam torch and his father's twelve-gauge shotgun. Lute opened the breach and popped two shells of double 0 buckshot into the chambers. He took another six and shoved them into his pants pocket. Close up, the twelve gauge had enough firepower to rip open the chest of a bear and blow its heart to oblivion. Even from fifty yards, the large double 0 buckshot would hurry an intruder on its way.

The commotion continued outside. A sudden, loud-pitched barking rose from the dog.

"Abe's onto something," James exclaimed.

A frantic scream rose from the darkness, a sound Lute Olsson had never heard before. He thought at first it was a cry made by a wild animal. Suddenly, he had the sinking feeling it was his dog.

"What the hell's out there?"

He bolted through the door with his son right behind. The beam of torchlight stabbed into the darkness.

Olsson whistled for his dog. The horses started up again, whinnying and snorting. He cocked the shotgun and moved toward the sound of the rearing animals.

"Abe! Here, Abe!"

There was no answer from the dog.

When they arrived at the corral, Olsson handed the shotgun to his son. He grabbed one of the horses by the halter. The horse tried to buck and leap. Olsson took a rope and tied the horse to the fence. The other horses were still snorting, milling about. God Almighty, he thought. The only time he'd ever seen the horses act like this was in a fire. Something was scaring the hell out of them.

Olsson called for the dog again, but there was no answer. He shined the beam across the meadow, straining in the darkness to see if something was there. A movement caught his eye.

"James! Give me the gun!" He took the shotgun and started across the meadow at a jog. He held the torch in his free hand. They were three quarters of the way across the pasture when Lute stopped. He shined the light back and forth across the fencing, swinging the beam past the trees, trying to pick up movement.

"Dad!" James whispered. "There!"

The silhouette of a huge form stood in the outer edges of the light. A sudden flash of eyes reflected in the glare. It looked like a lion. It had to be a lion. Only it was the biggest lion Olsson had ever seen. The beast was standing next to the fence with the dog in its mouth. The cat dwarfed the dog, holding the mastiff like a house cat might carry a rat. With a giant leap, the lion lunged over the fence.

By the time Lute could get the gun to his shoulder, it was too late. He fired both barrels in the direction he'd seen the lion. Twin explosions echoed off the trees.

Lute threw two more shells into the chamber, and blindly fired again.

"He's took Abe," James choked. "He took our dog!"

Olsson stood stiffly, flashing the light back and forth across the trees. He heard a distant crashing in the brush—then all was silent. Slowly, the realization of what had happened began sinking into Olsson's mind. No animal could pick up a dog the size of Abe and leap over a fence, could it? Yet, it had happened. It had happened right before his eyes.

19

THE DOOR OPENED TO HAYDEN'S OFFICE as an attractive blond woman stepped inside. She had blue eyes and a pleasant smile. She met Hayden with a firm handshake and direct stare.

"Kimberly Benson. Station KPXL, San Francisco." She handed Hayden a business card. "I apologize for barging in like this. Thank you for fitting me in."

Hayden offered her a seat at the conference table. "How can I help you, Miss Benson?"

"The station sent me out to get a fix on Tracy Reynolds's death. The family is well known in publishing circles in San Francisco. I wanted to put the story to rest. I'll be here only a couple of days. I thought it might make sense to get some information from you, if I could."

"I can tell you what I know," Hayden nodded. "All the evidence indicates she was traveling through Elkhorn to meet her fiancé. She'd been at a conference in Jackson, rented a car, and stopped in Elkhorn for a break. A waiter gave her information on a place to run near the Arcata River. We think she was jogging. That's when the accident occurred."

"You have many lion attacks like this?"

"Rare," Hayden answered. "Park Rangers tell me there hasn't been a death like this in several years."

"How sure are you this was a lion?" Kimberly asked.

"I've got to go on the post-mortem exam. The findings are pretty convincing."

Kimberly took out a yellow pad and began making notes. "Do you mind if I bring in a cameraman and do a short interview?"

"Interview me? Ha!" Hayden shook his head. "Not a good idea, Miss Benson. I generally like to keep out of the news."

"Then, Sergeant, how do you go about hunting a lion like this?"

"Look for tracks, sometimes bring in dogs. Mostly, it's a job for Fish and Game."

"You are aware, sir, there were a couple of fishermen that almost drowned."

"Yeah, we got a report," Hayden nodded with annoyance. "We think the men had been drinking. They jumped into water over their heads and were swept downstream."

"I understood they were charged by a large animal."

"I'm not sure what they saw. We passed the report on to Fish and Game."

"Thomas Stone said there was no question in his mind. The animal was a lion."

"You talked with one of them?" Hayden asked with surprise.

"He wasn't hard to reach," Kimberly answered. "Works as an engineer in Denver. I got his number from Fish and Game. They were fishing a few miles from where Tracy Reynolds was killed. He told me they couldn't get through the police barrier at Henderson Park. That's why they went downstream."

"Sounds like you've been doing your homework. "

"Elkhorn is a small town, Sergeant. I've been here two days. Time to get out to the Arcata River and look around, time to talk with store owners, people at the bars, the kayakers who found the body. This kind of death is pretty big news. Everybody seems to have an opinion."

"Who else did you speak with?" Hayden asked with interest. The reporter was much more prepared than Hayden expected.

"Jonathan Barnett. The Reynolds family."

"Maybe I should be asking you the questions, Miss Benson."

"What makes you think this lion's gone?"

"I have to go on advice from people who know this type of thing better than I," Hayden answered. "Game wardens tell me the animal's most likely drifted back into the mountains. I think Tracy Reynolds was in the wrong place at the wrong time."

"You seem pretty casual about this, Sergeant."

Hayden could feel his anger rise. "This is a very big wilderness up here, Miss Benson, and there are a lot of large predators. Trying to figure out who did what, to which person, is sometimes a tall order."

"And what if somebody else gets killed?"

"We can cross that bridge when we get there," Hayden answered.

"There must be some way to trace a lion like this?"

"Yeah," Hayden replied. "You give him a lie detector test. Ask him where he was on the evening of August nineteenth, and if he doesn't come up with a good answer, you cut open his belly and look for human remains. That's kind of the way law enforcement works in this country, isn't it?"

"Don't mess with me, Sergeant," Kimberly retorted.

"You got any answers?" Hayden asked her. "I'm all ears."

"Just keep me posted, would you?" The reporter stood up. "I'm staying in town. I would like my station to know you're doing everything you can to bring Tracy Reynolds's death to a satisfactory conclusion. The family would like closure."

Hayden nodded. "I think we owe them that."

Hayden escorted the reporter out to the front door and then turned back into the station. His secretary stopped him at the reception desk.

"A woman named Kate Olsson called." Mabel said. "Her husband left at dawn tracking a large animal that made off with the family dog. The horse returned a few minutes ago with an empty saddle. She thinks it was a lion."

20

Seventeen miles north of Elkhorn, Hayden turned the sheriff's Bronco off Highway 29 onto a dirt road leading toward Olsson's ranch. Deputy Peter Campbell sat next to him. Campbell knew the locals well, and a second officer on a search of this nature was always an asset, Hayden figured.

A mile in, they crossed a cattle guard and entered Olsson's property. Two large pastures were separated by a triangular split-rail fence. Within a quarter mile, Hayden pulled up to a ranch-style house next to a barn. Along the back of the property glistened a lake. Toward the horizon rose an ascending line of distant mountains.

Eighteen-year-old James Olsson greeted them at the doorway. Kate was in the kitchen, her daughters by her side. Her face looked drawn. Her daughters' eyes were red.

"Thank you for coming so quickly."

"Kate, I don't want to take too much time," Hayden answered in a rush. "I've got the helicopter on alert, in case your husband's been injured or needs medical attention. Deputy Campbell is a good tracker. Tell us what happened."

Kate Olsson carefully reviewed the events of the night before. After she finished, Hayden held out his arms.

"I wouldn't be too concerned, yet," he told her with a reassuring hug. "Maybe the horse bolted and Lute fell off and injured himself. Or maybe he's out there on foot, trying to make his way back."

The family huddled together, clinging to his words.

"Let's see if we can follow his prints. If we can't find him quickly, I'll call for help," Hayden said.

James Olsson led them to the fenced pasture where his father had confronted the lion. In the soft grass, next to the fencing, Hayden found footprints where Olsson and his son had stopped. They spent several minutes searching the area, walking back and forth next to the fence. Campbell crouched down, spreading the tall pasture grass. After a short search, he found several spent shotgun shells.

"That's where he fired," James said. "My dad was pretty excited."

Hayden walked carefully around the area but could find nothing more. Campbell climbed over the fence and began searching the ground along the opposite side.

"Blood here." Campbell pointed to several smudges. Dark stains colored the leaves.

"Blood from the lion?" James asked.

"Maybe," Campbell answered. "It's high and fresh. Could be the dog, or maybe your dad got a piece of the lion."

Hayden climbed over the fence and searched the area alongside Campbell. The two spent a few moments wandering in circles around the site. Abruptly, Campbell gave a whistle.

"Olsson rode his horse here. There are fresh hoof prints coming from the trees."

The deputy studied the tracks and then gestured toward the forest.

"It looks like Lute came here this morning. He got off his horse and walked around looking for signs. I see his boot prints here. Then he mounted. The horse's hooves go there . . ." Campbell pointed in the direction of the forest.

Hayden glanced at him. "Shall we go in?"

"Do you want me to bring some horses?" James asked eagerly.

"I want you to stay here with your mom," Hayden said. "She needs you, son."

The boy looked disappointed but obeyed Hayden's suggestion and remained at the fence. Hayden followed Campbell into the forest. The horse prints were easy to track, and the two officers moved with relative ease across a small clearing and through an open section of lodge pole pines.

"Let's search for a short distance, then turn back," Hayden said. "I don't want to go too far without help."

"There's a track mark back there I think you should see . . ." Campbell said.

There in the soft earth was a tri-lobed heel-print with four pads. There were no claw marks. It looked to Hayden like the footprint of a very large dog.

"I'm not an animal expert," Campbell said. "But if this is the lion, we are dealing with a very big animal."

"I'm wondering if we ought to go back and bring help," Hayden said, frowning.

"The trail's pretty clear. Even if we call now, it will take a half hour to get the helicopter. Let's follow a short distance. See where it goes."

"Lead on," Hayden said.

Abruptly, the hoof prints led into a dense portion of forest. Gradually, the trail narrowed. Large trees obliterated the sun. There was a certain gloom about the place that made Hayden uneasy. He unfastened his pistol and gripped it in his right hand. The feel of the gun gave him comfort.

In some areas, the undergrowth was so thick the two men had to turn sideways and force their way through. In other places, they could see only a few yards ahead. At first, Hayden was not sure how Olsson could have tracked the lion so well. When Campbell began to point out small drops of blood here and there, Hayden realized Olsson must have been following the blood. Observed from saddle height, the trail would not be that difficult to follow.

Campbell stopped. "Look . . ." he said, pointing. Here was a second set of hoof prints, traveling in the opposite direction. "Olsson's horse coming back."

The tracks branched off the trail and continued at an angle to the side, disappearing in the direction of Olson's stables. These second hoof prints were wide-spaced, with deep impressions along the backsides of the hoof. Even Hayden could tell the prints were made by a horse that was running.

Hayden checked the cylinder to his handgun and loosened several bullets along the side of his cartridge belt. The gun was loaded and ready. All six bullets were in place, and he had access to another twenty at his belt. But the quarters were tight, the visibility poor. If the lion came at them, he wasn't sure how much time he would have to shoot. He fingered the safety to his revolver.

The two moved quietly, sliding softly through the brush. The shadowy light became a somber blend of tans and browns. Occasionally, small birds flitted through the upper boughs. They saw little other movement.

They traveled another fifty feet when Campbell paused. "Olsson's track . . ." he whispered. A boot print pointed toward a cluster of trees. "And there, the lion."

The four-pug track was almost as big as Olsson's boot. Hayden felt a tightening in his gut. The man and the lion were going in the same direction. Had Olsson been following the lion . . . or *had the lion been following Olsson?*

At the base of a large fir, Campbell stopped. A look of confusion crossed his face. Squatting, he pulled Hayden down. Hayden started to speak when Campbell put a finger to his lips. "There . . ." he whispered, pointing.

Hayden followed the direction of his hand. Off to the side of the trail was a small clearing. In the middle of this space was a clump of brush composed of dead limbs and broken branches. Beneath this loosely assembled mound was a barely visible shape.

As Hayden stared at the figure, there came a shock of realization. Buried beneath the brush was the body of a man. The legs were twisted grotesquely, one foot bent backward. A boot emerged from a corner of the pile.

"God, Jesus," Hayden murmured.

"*Hs-s-st*," Campbell cautioned.

Hayden froze. The saliva dried in the back of his throat. They'd found Lute Olsson's body. But where was the lion?

Hayden squinted into the dense tangle of brush. A moment passed. There was no sound. The faint twittering of wrens and occasional jays ceased. It was as if time had stopped.

Hayden kept waiting for something to happen, some explosion of movement. Nothing moved; everything was deathly still. The pugmarks disappeared near the base of the tree. A curtain of brush blocked their path.

A drop of liquid landed on Hayden's shoulder. He was vaguely aware of it, out of the corner of his eye, but was concentrating so hard on the brush he was afraid to turn his head. A second drop fell on his right forearm, staining his shirt in an expanding ring. The liquid looked like something from inside a rusted engine.

He thought at first it might be sap or the unusual droppings of a bird. But bird droppings were white and sap was yellow. A third drop hit the side of his elbow. It was not the color of blood. If it had been red, he might have reacted more quickly. This was brownish-black, more like something from inside the remnants of decaying bowels.

Hayden looked upward. His gaze followed the rising trunk, searching for the source of the liquid.

Fifty feet up, the tree spread a series of perpendicular limbs. Higher up, four to five feet above the first branches, rested an irregular mass, lodged in a crook of the tree. It took Hayden a moment to recognize the shape.

Abruptly came a massive movement in the boughs. Branches shook. Pine needles showered downwards. A limb swung sideways as the body fell, bouncing heavily from one branch to the next.

Hayden took all this in. At the same time he was aware of the body falling, he saw the distinct image of a huge shadow soar above his head. The form passed in an arching leap that landed beyond the impenetrable veil of forest.

Firing wildly, Hayden emptied his revolver after the disappearing beast. These were desperate attempts aimed from the hip as he was falling backwards. Deputy Peter Campbell never had a chance to shoot. By the time he brought up his gun, Lute Olsson's dog came crashing through the trees.

21

THE HILL ROSE TO A GRASSY PLATEAU that fell into a deep valley. From the summit came an unobstructed view of the great mountains. On this clear afternoon, the glaciered peaks looked close enough to touch. The spot formed a fitting location for the final passage of George Two Feathers, esteemed elder and patriarch of the Blackfoot tribe.

A dirt road led toward the base of the plateau, and along this path flowed a stream of cars. It seemed the entire reservation had come to honor George Two Feathers's passing. Many parked their vehicles at the base of the knoll and ascended the last quarter mile on foot.

The plateau was devoid of trees except for a gnarled spruce at the very tip of its western edge. Scaffolding, composed of stout, freshly cut pine, had been erected in the center of the knoll. The ceremonial platform stood six feet off the ground. On top of this structure rested a crude bed of limbs that were fastened to wooden pillars. On this final bed rested the body of George Two Feathers.

The old man's head faced west, arms folded across his chest. Red and yellow swirls were painted on his face. He was dressed in the ceremonial clothing of a chief. A feathered headdress crowned his head. Around his neck was a grizzly claw necklace, worn over an elk-skin vest. A pair of deer-skin moccasins covered his feet.

The crowd gathered in a circle around the platform to pay their respects. A medicine man adorned in a buffalo-horn headdress began to chant in a soft, wavering voice. Two men dressed in Indian robes pounded on a pair of drums.

The Running Wolf family stood at the front of the inner circle of mourners. Sarah wore a light tan deerskin dress with a repeating bead design. Her hair was pulled back in a braid. Two horizontal streaks marked her cheeks. To honor the ancient customs, she had cut her forearm with a knife. The parallel lines across her cheeks were drawn with two fingers dipped in her blood.

Wolfson stood next to her, dressed in a sports coat, white shirt, and tie. Except for hair pulled back in a ponytail, no other markings suggested his Indian heritage. As he watched the ceremony, he swallowed hard, and tried to suppress his grief. He was surprised at the depth of his emotions. A deep sense of loss tore at the back of his mind. He knew he could not cry, yet found the tears difficult to hold.

The drums increased in intensity. The medicine man's voice rose, chanting in waves, his words drifting out to the plains. Far in the distance, a hawk shrieked.

As if on cue, Wolfson stepped toward the platform and placed Two Feathers's bow and quiver upon a small table next to the scaffold. His sister followed. Here she laid a folded suit and pair of pants. Then came her daughter, Lindsey, with a knife and scabbard, placing them next to the clothes.

A hawk called, circled over the plateau, and then swooped down, as if to inspect the ceremony. With a final cry, it flew out across the plains. A good omen, tribal elders said. George Two Feathers's spirit would soar in peace.

Sarah Running Wolf lowered her head and cried. Covering her face, she pulled the baby closer to her. Lindsey stood next to her, clutching her mother's dress. Scattered women began to wail. Finally, when Wolfson could no longer hold his grief, a tear rolled down his cheek.

After the funeral, Wolfson stood at the edge of the crowd, shaking hands, speaking with various people in the audience. Some he remembered from the past. Many he did not know. A group of tribal women introduced themselves, and then several men. They thanked Wolfson for coming back, for honoring his grandfather so. For thirty minutes, he mingled with the crowd as they lingered after the funeral.

At the end, Sarah Running Wolf stood across the knoll with her two children, talking with a group of friends. Wolfson walked over to the edge of the cliffs. He paused by the lone, gnarled tree, gazing off onto the plains. Memories of his childhood flashed through his mind, previously suppressed but now resurfacing fresh and vivid.

Wolfson remembered his grandfather as a kind and gentle man, and, in his early years, as an endless source of information. His father was gone a lot, and even before he had died, Two Feathers had taken over much of the parental role. When he was hardly six, his grandfather taught him how to follow animals. By the time he was ten, he was one of the best trackers on the reservation. As a youth, he spent hours exploring the region with his grandfather, sometimes on horseback, sometimes on foot, learning about the wildlife and the land. Yet, it was his grandfather who cautioned him about the limitations of the reservation.

"You must understand, the days of our tribe as a great confederation are gone," Two Feathers emphasized. "For me, I'm an old man. My ways are fixed. But for you, you must prepare for the future. Look to the outside, Bobby," he urged. "If you want to compete in an Anglo world, go to college, get an education. Make something of yourself. Leave a trail others may follow . . ."

A swoosh of wings startled Wolfson's thoughts. A crow landed on a branch near his head. He looked up with surprise. The crow gave a caw.

A muffled whisper sounded in his ear: "It is good you came back."

He spun to find a woman with dark hair and a scarred face staring at him. She was covered in a blanket, the corner pulled over her head. "Your grandfather asked that I speak with you."

Wolfson glanced at her cautiously. "Who are you?"

"I am Raven Crow."

"When did you talk with him?"

"Last night."

"Last night he was dead," Wolfson said, emphatically.

"The spirit never dies," she replied.

The crow flew out of the tree, soaring over the cliffs, and circled back. Wolfson watched it land upon a rock next to the edge of the precipice. Here it stretched its wings and cocked its head, listening.

"Your grandfather was having visions before he died."

"I heard that," Wolfson said.

"There was a woman killed by a lion at the Arcata River."

"Yes, I am aware of that."

"There was another man killed yesterday. An Anglo farmer."

"Lions kill people. They are predators," Wolfson replied with a shrug.

"This is not an ordinary lion." Her voice rose.

"My grandfather was sick," Wolfson said. "In his last days, he thought a bear was sleeping in his bed. My sister told me he dreamed he was running with a pack of wolves. He was seeing a lot of things. I'm not sure what was real and what was in his imagination. But the lion, wherever it is, is not my concern.

"The tribe needs you, Bobby Running Wolf. You're part of the legacy of our people. The tribe needs someone with your training, your education, your experience."

"I have a good job in Chicago," he said flatly. "There are no jobs here, no income. There is nothing for me to do."

"You are turning your back on your people."

Wolfson's gaze turned to the open plains, following the rolling hills toward the mountains. The crow hopped off the ledge, took wing, and landed on the tree above his head. It cawed twice, peering downward at him.

"And what about the lion?" she insisted.

"The lion?" Wolfson questioned. "I came back for my grandfather's funeral." He said the words with finality. "As soon as we settle his affairs, my business is finished. I'm sorry. I cannot help. The lion is not my concern . . ."

Wolfson rose from his crouched position and started to rejoin his sister. After the ceremony, he had removed his sports coat and carried it under one arm. Before he could take another step, Raven Crow reached forward and grabbed his shirt. Fabric ripped. Buttons popped. Wolfson was astonished at the woman's strength. His shirt was torn open, exposing his chest.

Raven Crow pointed a gnarled finger at the faint outline of a tattoo beneath his breast. It was the size of a postage stamp, dark purple in color. The discoloration looked like a birthmark.

"You are marked with the sign of great chiefs, Bobby Running Wolf," she hissed. "*It is you the lion hunts . . .*"

22

EVENING. THE SUN, ORANGE AND BLOATED, sank slowly below the western horizon. Gradually, the forest became engulfed in a rising tide of darkness. Flowers, brilliant in their reds and yellows, folded their petals and withdrew. Boughs darkened. Trails disappeared. Trees seemed to coalesce into an impenetrable wall.

With nightfall rose a chorus of noises. Frogs and crickets chirped. Wings fluttered as small birds sought their resting spots. A raven croaked and darted through the pines. Mice, dormant through the day, scurried at a frenzied pace, their tiny, high-pitched squeaks adding to the symphony of sounds. Off in the distance, a coyote howled.

Stars blinked like distant candles. In places, the trees were so big and the canopy so vast, even the Milky Way remained hidden. Steadily, the forest became an abyss of blackness—unfathomable, somber, and mysterious.

To the human eye, used to city lights and electric bulbs, these darkened corridors presented an impermeable barrier. A man standing here would have little sensory interpretation. He would hardly be able to see or smell, and those noises he could hear would be largely indecipherable.

Yet, others in the forest were much more adept at navigating the night. Some had optic cells that amplified the faintest light, light so dim it was practically invisible to the human eye. Their retinas worked like parabolic receptors, collecting faint shards of illumination, focusing on mirror-like membranes, magnifying the light a hundredfold.

To these animals, night was almost like day. Although they did not see color in the darkest recesses of the forest, they saw well enough to navigate, to feed, to run. To the forest inhabitants, the emerging scents, now heavy and pungent, left trails as clear as footprints. The odor of fur told a rabbit had crossed nearby. Fainter still lingered the smell of a fox, an hour old and a hundred yards away.

A pair of radar-like ears turned and focused on every sound. The tiny scrapings of a chipmunk were picked up, identified, and located in a bush. A faint crackling of bark was the gnawing of a porcupine. Such sensory clues provided a continuous stream of information. They told of peril, of allies, of where food was located, and of what kind of animals were there. And sometimes they warned of dangers, of indescribable horrors that roamed the shadows of the night.

It was thus in the blackest recesses of the forest that a doe emerged. She paused next to the trunk of a spruce. Scanning the pathway ahead, she constantly tested the wind. The deer lingered here, watching, her ears tuned toward the faintest sounds.

A gurgle of water came faintly to her ears. She could smell the sweet odor of evening grasses, and she remembered how hungry she was. When she could resist the gnawing in her stomach no longer, she gave a snort.

From out of the brush, a tiny fawn emerged. The baby was barely a month old, no taller than a man's knee. It stepped into the clearing in the same gingerly fashion as its mother. It was already beginning to learn its mother's caution, and the fawn paused here, testing the air, trying to learn what new smells were about.

Unable to hold back its hunger longer, the fawn gave a snort and nudged against its mother, gently butting her belly. The doe turned to the side and extended her rear leg so the fawn could nurse.

The mother waited until the fawn had finished and then started down a trail that led to the stream. The pair moved silently. Every few yards, the mother paused and tested the wind.

She did not relax. Complacency was fraught with risk. Often when she felt most safe were the times she knew she must be most on guard. Always have an escape route, she learned. And always be ready to flee at the slightest warning.

The fawn knew nothing. The youngster knew how to nurse and how to sleep and how to run for brief spurts. Everything else was dependent on its mother. The fawn had not yet learned who to trust and what to fear. Had there been a wolf on the trail, the fawn might have given it a curious sniff. The fawn by itself could not survive.

The mother moved hastily toward the stream. She had made this trip dozens of times before, and she knew the turns and twists of the path intimately. She paused at the scent of a raccoon. Then she proceeded through an open meadow toward the water. Her safest strategy was to drink quickly, spend a few minutes feeding, and then retreat.

A mink slid into the river. She watched it disappear, bobbing with the current. Glancing around, the doe waited until all seemed safe and then cautiously bent down to drink. The fawn remained in the clearing. It had fed well and was feeling good. Soon, it began to play. Once it jumped straight up to test its legs. As it landed, it skittered twenty yards in one direction and then turned and sprinted back.

The mother had taken her third head-down gulp of water when she sensed danger. She wasn't sure if it was a sound, perhaps a movement, or maybe a smell, but some instinct brought her head up. She turned to face the meadow and gave a warning snort.

The call told the fawn to come immediately. The fawn ignored her. Turning on its heels, the baby sprang in the opposite direction.

The doe pawed the ground impatiently. She was watching her offspring stilt across the meadow in a series of light-hoofed jumps, when her heart froze. There in the darkness, at the edge of the clearing, crouched an enormous beast.

The doe gave a deep-throated cough and raced into the meadow. A darkened shadow flowed outward from the trees. The fawn looked up in time to see a huge form descend upon it.

By a miracle, the fawn's reflexes took over. Abruptly, it leaped like a rocket, shooting ten feet in the air. The jump was enough to elude the springing lion. Skittering sideways, the fawn lost its balance, tumbled over, and then caught its legs and surged back toward its mother.

The mother had one desperate gamble. Her choice was made without hesitation, without thinking. She would use her body as a decoy. She would risk her life to save her fawn. If she turned and fled, the fawn would be taken. The infant would not know how to escape or which way to run.

Hoping for a moment of confusion, the mother ran directly at the lion. As the fawn jumped to escape, she darted in front, giving the lion an unexpected target. The beast saw the mother flash across its path, and the size and the closeness of the deer were too tempting to resist.

A paw lashed out, raking the mother across her flank. A fraction more, a quarter inch, separated life from death. Had its claws struck deeper, it could have pulled her down. Then its great fangs would be at her neck. Instead, the talons slipped across her hide, slicing shallow furrows through the skin.

The mother's momentum carried her briefly out of danger's grasp. The lion had to stop and change directions. It lost a second in the transition, and in this desperate chase, a second was like eternity. It was that second that gave the fawn time to take a different path and move away from the lion—a second for the mother to gain her legs and flee in a bounding sprint.

The doe realized there was little hope of escape. She might be able to outrun the lion, dodging erratically through the brush, but the fawn was doomed. What else could she do? If she hesitated, the lion would kill them both.

With a rush, she charged out of the forest, moving away from the river. She ran toward unknown territory. Leaping blindly, she dodged between trees and dashed across a narrow ravine. Miraculously, the fawn stuck with her.

Ahead was a flat patch of black, slippery rock. The sight raised new fears in her mind. It was something she'd learned never to cross. But she couldn't stop. Behind came certain death. She waited long enough for her fawn to catch up and then plunged out onto the highway. Her hooves slipped on the hardened pavement. A pair of blinding lights rushed around a curve. And then the eighteen-wheeler was upon them.

PAUL MISHKIN LET OUT A GASP and reflexively jammed on the brakes. Even then he knew it was a mistake. It would be stupid to risk jackknifing the rig for nothing more than a deer and fawn. Mishkin let off the brakes, but the load of lumber was too great to stop. There came a shower of sparks and the scream of twisting steel. Cursing the animals, he pulled on the air horn, splitting the night with a blasting shriek.

The mother and fawn passed directly in front of the cab and disappeared beneath the right bumper. He waited for a sickening crunch, but there came no bump, no thud, no hesitation of the wheels. His partner was asleep, dozing in the right seat of the cab. He awakened instantly. Out of the passenger window, in the glare of moving headlights, glowed the reflection of two eyes.

"What the hell?" he cried.

"Hold on, Steve!" Mishkin yelled.

"I thought I saw a lion!"

Groping madly, Mishkin desperately tried to regain control, to slow the truck, to keep from slipping off the road. There was another screech of brakes and then the agonizing groan of shifting lumber as the trailer slid across the highway, turning sideways, spinning down a ravine.

LONG AFTER THE HIGHWAY PATROL lit their flares and the flashing lights of emergency vehicles passed, the Great Lion moved silently through the darkness. As he traveled back along the river, a growing hunger gnawed at his stomach. The doe and fawn had escaped. He'd been so close that he almost ran into the truck. Leaping away, he had disappeared back into the forest.

Now he prowled the edge of the river, moving along a canyon and then toward a series of low-lying hills. There were horses and cattle here. A week before, he had taken a buck who was grazing in the fields.

Once he thought he heard the distant cry of a female lion. When he reached a clearing in the trees, he rose up and scraped his claws along the biggest pine, tearing at the bark. Here he left a calling card no animal could miss.

Moving steadily, he covered two miles, traversing a series of ridges and then descending into a valley. He gazed now at the twinkling lights of a settlement. A highway ran through the valley a mile to his left.

He crossed this road sometime after midnight. No headlights illuminated his presence. No one saw him pass.

Before him glowed a painted sign:

Welcome to Elkhorn

Gateway to Glacier National Park

Population 7,635

23

KIMBERLY BENSON CHECKED INTO a $135 suite at the Pinecrest Motel. Here she set up camp with her photographer, Eric Stafford. Initially, they had taken adjoining rooms; however, Stafford snored so loudly she could hear him through the walls. After spending a sleepless night, she quietly moved to a spot at the opposite end of the building.

The room she now occupied had an adjoining space where she could work. She plugged in her laptop and searched the television channels for updates on the news. Because of the remoteness of Elkhorn, she was frequently knocked off-line by surges in electricity, and her attempts to access the internet for various news groups were often aborted in the middle of her search. She thought about better accommodations, but the nearest AAA motels were in Whitefish or Great Falls, several hours away.

She left San Francisco on a Wednesday, scouted the area at Henderson Park on Thursday, and completed her interviews with Hayden on Friday. The sergeant had not wanted to be interviewed on video, and she respected that. He was not essential for her report anyway, especially now Tracy Reynolds's body had been found, and a mountain lion had been implicated in her death. On Friday evening, she air-expressed a canister of uncut video back to San Francisco, thinking her assignment in Montana was complete. It was time to get back to San Francisco and report on more pressing news.

She sat impatiently in the motel that morning waiting for a telephone call from her boss. At least, Kessler could have left some word on her answering service. It was as if she and her cameraman had dropped off the face of the earth.

Out of curiosity, she punched up "Blackfoot Indians" on the Internet. The reservation occupied a prominent portion of land near Elkhorn, and she was curious about the history of the people. The Blackfoot, she learned, were a nomadic tribe that had inhabited the plains of Northern Montana and lived off the buffalo. Some historians felt the tribe could be traced back five hundred years. Before that, their history became murky. They were a proud, fierce people, part of a large confederation of Native Americans who had inhabited the plains just east of the Continental Divide. Sometime before the Lewis and Clark, they had divided into three groups: the Bloods to the north, the Piegans along the Canadian border, and the Blackfoot to the south. All three groups were connected by a common Algonquin language.

The *Pied-Noir*, as the French trappers called them, probably derived their name from a peculiar black stain that colored their moccasins. Some claimed the name originated when the tribe traveled on foot and crossed burned, charred prairie. At these times, their moccasins took on a blackened stain from ash and soot. The name Blackfoot was used interchangeably with Blackfeet, she learned, depending upon the author.

With the coming of the horse, everything changed. The Blackfoot became expert riders and terrorized their enemies with frequent raids. For a hundred years, their society flourished. And then, the white men arrived. With them came whiskey and smallpox and forced internment on government-assigned reservations.

By 1890, the last buffalo herds were gone and the Blackfoot nation was left to survive on government rations. A million acres was set aside in northwestern Montana for the Blackfoot reservation. Each family was allotted 120 acres, and for a time, ranching seemed to offer hope. Their history was one of continued frustration. During the droughts of 1920, most of the cattle died, and soon they were back on government handouts. To Kimberly, it seemed a sad fate for a proud and noble people.

The telephone rang. She sprang for the phone. Soon they would be heading home.

"Hi, Kimberly. Alvin Kessler calling." She listened patiently to her boss. "I understood you called. Don't forget there's an hour's time difference here in San Francisco. I just got into the station."

"I think we're finished up with the Reynolds story," she said. "I'd like to get a flight out later today. Did you have a look at my interviews?"

"Yeah, they were fine."

There was a lack of enthusiasm in Kessler's voice. Troubling, she thought. Something about his tone sounded as if he was holding back.

"So, I would like to head back, Alvin. The food is shit and the town is knee-deep in rednecks, and nobody is eager for an on-camera interview. Other than that, we're having a great time. Anything breaking at the station?"

"No, everything's fine," Kessler answered matter-of-factly.

"There's a flight this evening that will get us into SFO around eight. I can be at the station first thing in the morning."

"I was thinking," Kessler said. "You know the California Mountain Lion Initiative comes up for the voters this fall. Based on the autopsy report that came over the wire service, if it's true that Tracy Reynolds was killed by a lion, maybe you could stay for another couple of days. See what you can dig up on this lion story."

There was too much to do back at the station to get stuck in Elkhorn, she worried. The president was coming to San Francisco, the mayor was having a crisis with the Muni bus, and there was talk of a misappropriation of funds from the City's housing commission. This was front-page news, the type of report she liked to work on. Not some "lion story" in the backwoods of Montana.

"I was thinking, while you're out there, take a look at how the state is handling their predator problem," Kessler continued. "Send back some interviews on what the ranchers think, how people feel about things like the lion. It would be nice to know what states have what laws and who else is having problems with these animals."

Kimberly tried to read between the lines. It didn't make sense they would keep her in Montana for another week. Unless . . .

"Alvin, it sounds like you are hanging me out to dry." She leaned back in her chair. Her lip trembled. She tried to clear her voice. "I thought I came out here as a favor. For a couple of days, remember? Now you're changing my assignment and telling me a couple more days. Are you telling me to start looking for another job?"

"I'm telling you, we've had some problems with your ratings, Kimberly," Kessler answered bluntly. "And, I think there is a story in Montana for you. You asked, I answered. I'm trying to look out for your best interests."

WHEN SHE HUNG UP, moisture clouded her eyes. God, she'd given her life's blood for the station. She couldn't remember how many times she'd canceled a date or told a friend she was unavailable because of a breaking story. For the past three years, she devoted almost all her free time to KPXL. A frustrated boyfriend told her once: "Dating you like is like dating the six o'clock news." But she didn't care. Her singular goal in life was to become the best possible reporter she could. And to do this, she realized, she would have to work incredibly hard, be accurate, and try to keep at top of the breaking news.

And now Kessler was saying her ratings weren't great? Well, fuck him, she muttered. But the thought of change and uncertainty and maybe having to work at another station brought a surge of anxiety to her mind.

A loud knock sounded at her door.

"Coming."

Eric Stafford waited outside. "I tried to reach you all morning," the photographer said. "Any news on when we're pulling out?"

Stafford stood there, smiling politely. He had dark curly hair and the beginning bristle of a goatee. This morning, he was dressed in a faded T-shirt with suspenders. He looked like an oversized kid, waiting patiently for permission to play.

"Kessler wants us to stay a couple extra days."

"You're kidding!"

"He wants us to do something more on the lions."

"God, I think he wants us killed," Stafford groaned. "This is crazy."

He pulled out a cigarette and lit it. The smoke drifted past Kimberly's face.

"Eric, do you mind?"

"Sorry." He raised his hands in a shrug.

"If we're going to work together, we're going to have to have some understanding between us." Before she knew it, she was venting with an unbridled rush of frustration. "You know how I hate smoking. So, why do you do it?"

"Bad habit," he answered. "I'll try to keep it away from you."

"And dammit, while you're at it, you've got to wear some fresh clothes. Look at you, Eric. You've got food stains all over your shirt. And when did you take your last shower? When you get sweating, quite frankly, you don't smell so good. And the other night when you ate all that garlic with your pizza, you kept burping. You've got a gross streak, Eric, and you're not always the most pleasant to be around."

The photographer stared downward, taking her criticisms like blows to the chin. He knew there was a germ of truth in what she was saying. It reminded him of the uncomfortable moments when he was an awkward, oversized kid, and the children were teasing him that he was fat and looked like a pig. He was not a fighter, and his body size was something he'd never been able to control.

He raised his eyes. "If you want, I can go back to San Francisco. I don't want to be here if I'm offending you."

"No! Christ, Eric. I'm just pissed that we didn't get out of here. Every minute we spend here, I feel like I'm losing my job to Stephanie Peterson."

"Stephanie?" A surprised expression crossed the photographer's face. "She doesn't hold a candle to you, Kimberly. You've got the reputation of being the best-prepared, the most professional reporter at the station. I asked to take this assignment. I haven't had a chance to work with you. I thought it would be a privilege. All Stephanie has is big boobs."

"Well, unfortunately, in ratings, sometimes that's all that counts."

"Aw, that's bullshit," Stafford answered.

"I apologize, Eric." She shook her head. "It was wrong for me to come after you like that."

"No, what you say is right. I'll try to be better." His voice raised. "Hell, if Kessler wants a report on lions, let's put something together that'll knock his fucking socks off!"

"Deal!" Kimberly reached out and squeezed his hand.

As she watched the photographer stroll across the parking lot with his awkward, rolling gait, she had to admit Eric Stafford was a pretty reasonable guy. At least he was willing to improve.

Her beeper sounded. She went back into the motel and dialed up her answering service. The message was from Sergeant Hayden.

"There's a special town meeting about the lion tonight," Hayden said. "If you're still around, I thought you might be interested in stopping by."

24

SEVEN BLOCKS NORTH OF THE TOWN SQUARE stood the Elkhorn High School campus. The building was an old T-shaped brick structure, the front decorated with Corinthian columns. Along the street hung a large sign: "Home of the Champion Raiders." At the rear of the property rose the gymnasium, a tall, two-story building, reminiscent of a hangar. During the high school playoffs, the gym held a thousand fans.

To prepare for the town's emergency meeting, bleachers had been lowered. Workers added a hundred folding chairs. At one end of the court stood a speakers' table. By eight that evening, the room was packed. Sergeant Hayden waited along the side, next to one of the exit signs. A few last stragglers rushed into the meeting. A hush came over the audience.

Townspeople were scared. Two people had been killed by a mountain lion, and they wanted somebody to do something now. Word about deaths from the lion spread like wildfire, not only in Elkhorn but across the state. The sheriff's office received numerous calls from citizens wondering what the authorities were planning. Three news agencies requested information, indicating they were sending reporters.

Things were getting pretty crazy, Hayden thought. Rumors were rampant. Someone asked if there were tigers and leopards on the loose. Time to correct the citizens, he reflected. Time to be calm and establish law and order.

Mayor Eliju Miller was a short, heavy man with a bald spot at the crown of his head. This evening, he was dressed in a polyester jacket and white shirt. Next to him, seated along the speakers' table, were a dozen members of the city council. Miller nodded to Hayden as a last couple scurried into the gymnasium. Hayden stepped forward and closed the doors.

The mayor stood behind a podium. He rapped once on his microphone. "Ladies and gentlemen. It's after eight. Why don't we begin?"

A chorus of "*sh-h-hs*" flowed through the auditorium.

"As all of you are aware, the body of Lute Olsson was found Monday morning by Sergeant Hayden. There will be a funeral for Lute Friday afternoon, and our heartfelt sympathies go to his family."

A murmur of agreement passed through the gathering.

"Based on the footprints we found, there is evidence, fairly strong, I think, that this is the same lion that killed the young lady, Tracy Reynolds, along the Arcata River."

"Yeah, yeah," came an anxious murmur. The audience rustled in their seats.

"I want to remind you there is no reason to panic. People have encountered lions in this region before. Like grizzlies, these animals are a species we deal with from time to time. Wildlife is one of the things that we share in this great state, and it is part of our heritage. For many of us, that is why we live here."

"Come on, Mayor," a rancher yelled. "Get on with it. What's your office doing about it?"

"Yeah! Get to the point!" another cried.

Miller held up his hand. "I want to caution you, this is a very dangerous animal. Please don't try to take it on by yourself unless you are an experienced hunter. Sergeant Hayden called the state this afternoon. They will be sending a professional hunter in the next several days."

"That's good! That's something!" a voice cried from the back.

"Thank you, Mr. Bertolli. I'm glad we're finally doing something that meets with your approval."

A chuckle rose from the audience.

"I wanted you to know that I, as your mayor, and Sergeant Hayden, in charge of law enforcement, are doing everything possible to make the citizens of Elkhorn safe."

Hayden glanced across the room. He recognized the faces of many of those present. A few he knew intimately; others were familiar by association and casual conversation. Kimberly Benson was seated at the back of the auditorium with her cameraman. If he had video equipment, however, it was not visible. The mayor had told her he wanted no live footage of the meeting. Afterward, if people were willing to give interviews, that was not his concern. What he didn't want was his image, or those of the council, flashed on the evening news. This was a small town, and these were private affairs, Miller explained; and right now, as they began to consider the issues at stake, the less media coverage, the better.

"We wanted to call this meeting to let you know we have set a course of action," Miller continued. "What we absolutely want to avoid is people taking up arms and shooting up the countryside."

"Easy for you to say, Mayor. You ain't got no children!" a man shouted.

"This ain't no small lion either!" another yelled. "Bret Hawkins went out to Olsson's farm. He said they were the biggest cat prints he ever seen!"

"I'm going to carry a gun," an old man yelled. "I don't give a damn what you say!"

A chorus of angry shouts rose.

"Hold on!" the mayor cried. "This is the reason we called this meeting. I want you to know, we are going to do everything we can to catch this animal. I asked Sergeant Hayden to speak with you to cover some of the points we agreed upon earlier today. Please hear him out."

Hayden moved up to the podium. Before the meeting, he had stationed two uniformed deputies inside the building at the front and back entrances. There was a sense of formality to their presence, which he felt important to show. His men stood for law and order, and he wanted that image to prevail. The last thing he needed was a bunch of panicked citizens taking up arms.

"I know you're worried, and I know these happenings cause everyone a lot of concern," Hayden began. "Remember, I have a daughter, too." He nodded respectfully at the man who had yelled at the mayor.

"And I wanted to emphasize what the mayor said, that we're doing everything we can to bring this to an end. The state department tells me there have been no more than a handful of deaths by lions in the past century. This means you have a greater chance of getting killed by lightning than you do by a lion."

"Well, there's two deaths now!" a man yelled.

"Yeah, you tell that to Lute Olsson's family!" a woman cried.

"Let him continue," someone countered.

"I know," Hayden answered. "I was there, and my heart goes out to the Olsson family."

A restless murmur passed through the assemblage.

"We don't know exactly why this lion is in the area. This is a dry summer. Fish and Game tells me a number of deer and elk have come out of the mountains and are feeding on the plains. You may have seen an increase in these animals at your ranches. Lions normally prey on these species. It makes sense this particular lion came out of the mountains to pursue its natural prey."

Hayden spoke slowly, hoping his words would help appease the crowd.

"I can't tell you not to carry guns," he said carefully. "I know we live here on the frontier, and guns are part of our lives. But, I caution you . . . guns can also hurt people. They go off by accident, and a significant number of deaths happen each year because of this. So, if you're not familiar with guns, please don't start carrying them. I want to let Fish and Game handle this lion, and let's go about our business as everyday citizens."

"Sheriff, with all due respect." A tall man stood up. "I'm out on a ranch most of the day, and I normally carry a gun. If I see a lion—any lion—I am going to kill it. You can have all the Fish and Game people here in the world, but until you assure me this lion is taken care of, I'm going to shoot any lion I see."

"Me, I'm carrying a gun, too," a young man added. "I've got a long walk to my house at night, and I am not about to be bushwhacked by any damned lion."

"Yeah, me, too!" a middle-aged woman cried. "I work in real estate, and I drive the neighborhoods all day. You can say what you want, Sergeant, but I want to defend myself."

She drew from her purse a large .357 magnum and waved the pistol in front of the crowd. Hayden cringed. He didn't know if the gun was loaded, and the barrel was pointing back and forth across the audience.

"Madam, please!" Hayden shouted. "This is the very thing we want to avoid. This is exactly how somebody gets hurt."

Some of the audience slid down in their seats, afraid the pistol might go off. Others yelled and nodded. They were determined to carry guns, too, and nobody was going to tell them different. For an instant, the room broke into angry shouts.

Hayden tried to whistle for silence. When he saw he was getting nowhere, he waved to Deputy Peter Campbell. Campbell worked his way through the seats until he could reach the woman and disarm her. The mayor moved back to the podium and raised his hands for silence.

Gradually, the room quieted.

"We'll get this lion," Miller said firmly. "Sergeant Hayden has a helicopter at his disposal. A professional hunter is coming. Give us a couple of days. That's all we ask. Until this is resolved, I don't want any of you to panic."

"You know where to reach my office," Hayden added. "We'll add a couple of deputies. With a little luck, I'm sure this will come to an end very quickly."

"What about this rumor that the Indians are talking about?" a man in front interrupted. "Some of the Blackfoot are saying this is a 'spirit cat,' an animal from the past. They're saying the only one who can kill it is an Indian."

The mayor looked at him and scoffed. "I can only tell you, sir, in the history of the world, I have never heard of an animal that can live through a sixteen-ounce bullet with a muzzle velocity of two thousand feet per second."

Laughter rippled through the crowd.

"So, go home," the mayor concluded. "Rest assured the town is safe. Elkhorn has nothing to worry about. Sergeant Hayden and I have everything under control."

A loud bang erupted from the rear of the auditorium as a door burst open and a young rancher stumbled into the room. His face was covered with perspiration, his hands trembling. He carried a heavy object wrapped in a blanket over his shoulder.

With a grunt, he heaved the bundle onto the floor. The mass landed with a thud, like a large tuna flopped upon a deck. An arm slipped out from underneath the covering. The skin was half gone, the meat exposed.

"There's been another kill!" he cried.

A shocked hush fell over the gathering. Then a woman fainted, and everyone began to scream.

25

Clouds scuttled past a crescent moon. Stars blinked and shimmered and then disappeared. From the air, the town looked as if it was lit up in a Fourth of July celebration. Streetlights marked roads like a crosshatching of yellow flares. Every porch light was on. People were scared. The body of recluse Cecil Reiss had been discovered inside an old miner's cabin near the Arcata River. The death toll had risen to three. A huge cat was prowling the vicinity, and it was killing human beings.

Sometime after eleven, Vincent Bertolli's dog began to bark. Bertolli had gone to his art gallery after the town meeting. He was hoping a tourist might come back and buy an oil painting he exhibited, and he was wondering if he should call the man to encourage him to return. And then he was thinking of getting out of town. He'd never really considered leaving Elkhorn before, but things were getting a little out of hand. Everyone was jumpy as hell. A home was supposed to be a safe refuge, he thought. And now, bodies were popping up all over the place.

Bertolli began working at his desk, checking from time to time, to see if anyone was using the parking spot out front. There was a small saloon down the street, and sometimes the young men littered the sidewalk with beer cans. As he returned to his accounts, he recognized the booming voice of his dog. He'd raised Randy as a pup and often tied the dog on his porch at night. But it was unusual for his dog to bark like this. He wondered why the animal was so excited.

Alice Chapman lived in a small house three doors away. She couldn't sleep because of the racket the dog was making. She worked with Jonathan Barnett at the Aspen Café. This evening, she'd gotten off at nine and was exhausted. As she listened to the incessant barking, she felt like calling Bertolli and telling him to shut the dog up. The noise was disturbing the tranquility of her rest.

Along the main square, Deputy Peter Campbell checked the door at the front of the Montana State Bank. Everything seemed locked and tidy. He strolled across the green toward his squad car. In the distance, he could hear the echoing boom of a dog. Something sure bothering that animal, he thought. The noise was coming from beyond the square, in the vicinity of E Street. He knew Vincent Bertolli had a big dog, and the barking sounded as if it was coming from the vicinity of Bertolli's house.

Martin Riggs stood in his kitchen watching television. He was sipping a cup of coffee when he heard the dog. It sounded as if the dog had stuck its head in his front door and was barking at the top of its lungs. Riggs was forty-seven. He resided in Elkhorn on a modest disability pension after injuring his back. He lived across the street from Bertolli's house.

He listened to the dog for another minute and then went to the telephone and called Bertolli's home. When there was no answer, he rang Bertolli's Art Gallery. Riggs didn't especially like dogs, and he very much disliked dogs that disturbed the neighborhood. He figured he would get an answering machine and give Bertolli a piece of his mind. He was surprised Bertolli answered.

"Your dog is making one helluva racket, Bertolli. Can you please come and shut him up?"

"I'm busy working, Mr. Riggs. Maybe you could walk over and offer him some water."

"And maybe you could kiss my ass. You got any insurance?"

"That dog's never bitten anything bigger than a flea," Bertolli retorted. "Go see what's bothering him. I just can't leave now."

Riggs sighed and hung up. Muttering to himself, he walked over to the front of his house and opened the window. He could see Bertolli's dog in the illumination of a porch light. The animal was standing stiff-legged, facing down the street.

"Hey! What's going on there! You lie down and shut up!"

He watched the dog, waiting for a reaction, but the animal didn't stop. It just kept barking. The dog was staring toward something moving up the street. Puzzled, Riggs arched his head and peered out the window. It was then he saw the lion.

It was just a glimpse, a flash of motion that passed through the outer fringes of a streetlight and moved toward his house. At first, he thought it was another dog, but the size of the beast was too large. He had to blink to be sure what he was seeing, and by then, the animal was gone. He wondered if he was hallucinating, if maybe the town meeting had made him jumpy and prone to visual disturbances.

An unconscious shiver rippled through his mind. "Jesus H. Christ," he muttered.

He shut the window, making sure the latch was locked. The lion must have covered the entire length of the street during the time the dog was barking. And now it was coming directly for his house.

By now, Bertolli's dog was going crazy, lunging and churning on his chain. Staring through the window, Riggs saw another flash of movement, and then a massive shape drifted across his front yard, disappearing over his fence. This time, he knew it was no mirage.

Riggs dashed across the front hallway and around the stairs and into the back of his house, trying to follow the animal's course through the windows. But now, he could no longer find it. He only knew that the lion had jumped his fence and disappeared. He ran back toward the kitchen, locking windows as fast as he could. When he reached the telephone, he dialed 9-1-1.

His voice came in breathless gasps. There was a lion in the center of town. This was no mistake. He had seen it. When the operator tried to get further details, he came unglued. "Just get the fucking sheriff's department before someone gets killed!" he yelled.

The second call came thirty-two seconds later from Riggs's neighbor, Alma Singleton. She was in her early sixties and had just come out of a bath on the second floor. She walked into her bedroom with a towel wrapped around her midriff, noting that her pet cat, Samantha, was crouched at her bedroom window.

Suddenly the cat arched its back and began screeching at something outside. Another one of the neighbor's cats, she fumed. They'd been trying to mate with her precious Samantha for weeks. Grabbing a shoe, she started for the window. Without thinking, she angrily opened the pane and raised her arm. What she saw made her scream.

On top of the garage roof, looking directly through the open window, stood an enormous lion. The beast stared at her for an instant and then leaped off the garage, disappearing around the side of her house.

Trembling, she moved to the telephone and dialed 9-1-1. Her voice quivered. She was told to stop and take a deep breath before she continued. At this point, dispatch realized this was no hoax. Immediately, the station sent out a bulletin for all hands.

By now, a cluster of residents had come out of their homes next to Bertolli's house. They stood in a group, speaking in hushed, excited tones. Many carried guns. Flashlight beams darted in every direction. Several pointed toward the fence where Riggs had seen the lion. The animal had cleared a five-foot chain-link barrier as if it were a shrub.

At 11:17, Anthony Renfree and his nineteen-year-old cousin, Duncan, drove their pickup down M Street. They'd just come out of the Cattleman Saloon. Renfree was twenty-seven and worked on his uncle's ranch. He was a tall man with a handlebar mustache. His cousin was shorter with thick sideburns and a protruding abdomen.

A gun rack stood behind the driver's seat. Renfree carried a 30/06 rifle and a 12-gauge shotgun. For as long as he could remember, he had owned a gun. He was a Montana rancher and he knew how to shoot, and he was damned proud of it.

As he drove, he spoke animatedly about a horse he'd considered purchasing, going over the pros and cons of buying the mare. He wanted one that he could use for roping. The owners were asking more than he had saved. There was a rumor, too, the mare had once been lame.

He was driving twenty-five miles an hour, leisurely watching the road, when a tawny form leaped across his headlights. The movement was so unexpected, he blared the horn, jamming on his brakes.

"Lion!" Duncan cried.

They watched as the beast raced across the street onto a neighboring lawn. The lion hesitated at a large hedge and then turned back toward the street. In its mouth was a small brownish object that looked to be a dog.

"Get a gun!" Renfree cried. Duncan grabbed the first gun he could lay his hands on. It was the 12-gauge shotgun. As he pulled two shells from the glove compartment, he clamored out of the vehicle. His cousin jumped from the passenger side. When they looked around, the lion was gone.

"We'd better call for help," Duncan said.

"Not yet," Renfree grunted. He lunged back to the truck and pulled out a flashlight from the glove compartment. Flashing the beam across the lawn, he spent a minute searching for the lion. Next to the house was a large garage. An open window stood along the side.

"There!" Renfree pointed.

"Go ring the doorbell," he told his cousin. "Tell them there may be a lion in their garage. Have them call the sheriff's department."

"What about you?"

"I'm going to stand by the window. If the bastard's in there and he comes out, he's going to be greeted by two barrels of double 0 buckshot. Now! Quickly!" he cried. "There's no telling how long he'll stay."

Renfree ran up to the side of the garage. He checked the safety on the shotgun and crouched next to the open window, listening. He wasn't sure what he might hear. Maybe the noise of crunching bones or maybe heavy breathing or maybe growling. He could feel his heart pound wildly in his chest.

The garage looked empty—no cars inside. He could see a faint reflection of light from a grease stain on the concrete floor. Across the space was a cabinet with neatly stacked shelves. A bicycle stood against the wall, and there was a corrugated pegboard with tennis rackets and a couple of shovels. Nothing moved. The garage looked empty.

Rapid footsteps approached. "You see him?" Duncan yelled. "Nobody answered the door."

"Sh-h-h," Renfree hissed.

He searched through the window, following the light beam, peering into the darkness. Still nothing. Was it possible the lion had gone somewhere else? But what if it was still there? He'd heard of animals choosing dark holes as if they might be caves. Maybe they had startled the lion and it had jumped inside to escape.

"Don't you think we should call the sheriff?" Duncan asked.

"Quiet. Let me think."

His mind worked rapidly. What if they had the mountain lion trapped inside the garage? He'd never killed a mountain lion before, but he had shot a lot of deer and elk, and he had hunted all his life. With a shotgun, he knew a couple of blasts at close range would drop any animal. Most likely, it would blow a hole through the lion's chest, big enough to stick your fist in.

145

Movement. At the bottom of the garage door a sliver of light shifted slightly to the left. A shadow slipped across the door.

Renfree leaned in through the widow, pointing the light to his left, trying to illuminate the garage wall. He brought the shotgun up and slowly pushed his head and shoulders through the window.

"Careful!" Duncan cautioned.

"Quiet . . ."

Renfree flashed the beam across the garage floor. Abruptly, he froze. Directly below was the shape of a small dog. The dog lay in a pool of blood. Renfree's heart leaped into his throat. The lion was in the garage!

Renfree had the sudden realization that the beast must be much closer than he thought. He tried to ram the barrel of the shotgun through the window and aim downward, but he was too slow.

A flash of claws raked his face. Blinded by a gush of blood, he fell sideways against the window. He grabbed his head with both hands, dropping everything. The shotgun clattered onto the floor. His torch spun wildly away.

A massive paw caught Renfree by the neck. The claws dug into his skin. He fought desperately, trying to keep his balance, gripping the window, bracing his legs against the wall. He could feel his body slipping, his head pulled inward through the window.

"Help me, Duncan!" he screamed. "It's killing me. It's pulling me inside!"

For an instant, Duncan watched in disbelief. Then he turned and sprinted for the truck. There was no time. No time to grab a gun or run back or try to get help. He lurched into the driver's seat. He had a moment to realize the fetid odor was his own bowels. Then he turned on the ignition and floored the gas. The truck surged over the curb and headed for the house. He did not slow down. He was still accelerating as he crashed into the garage.

26

KIMBERLY BENSON STOOD IN FRONT of the statue of Jeremiah Bates at one end of the Elkhorn town square. It was eight in the morning. She wore a blue blouse with a pearl necklace. Her hair was carefully combed, her makeup immaculate. Despite the early hour, a crowd gathered around the statue, watching her work.

Eric Stafford gave a thumbs-up sign. The video camera blinked. Kimberly spoke directly into the lens, using no notes. She seemed very professional. Her sentences were concise, her cadence unruffled.

"As the sun rises this morning," she began, "this small mountain hamlet in western Montana is living in dread that a mountain lion may return: a lion so bold that it stalked the city streets for more than an hour last night, killing a small dog and mauling a young man with its claws.

"Today, at noon, the mayor is calling for an emergency meeting to consider such things as curfew at dusk, posting armed guards, bringing in the National Guard.

"Last week, a northern California tourist named Tracy Reynolds was killed by a mountain lion while she jogged along the Arcata River. Three days ago, the body of Lute Olsson, a local rancher, was found after he chased a lion that killed his dog. Yesterday, the body of a third victim was discovered inside an old miner's cabin near Henderson Park. People are understandably scared. No one feels safe.

"Then last night, shortly before midnight, a rancher named Anthony Renfree was driving with his cousin through town. They witnessed a lion cross the road in a residential neighborhood. When the lion jumped into a garage, Renfree went after it with his gun. He was terribly mauled. After four hours of surgery this morning, doctors are hopeful they have saved his life.

"Law enforcement officers are quick to warn, this lion is extremely dangerous," she continued. "If seen, the sheriff's department advises immediately calling 9-1-1.

"Unless something is done soon, the citizens of Elkhorn are rightfully concerned this lion might strike again. In short, it is a town under siege, a community terrorized by a big cat, who so far has eluded all attempts to find it by authorities."

Earlier in the morning, Kimberly had completed the background for her report. She had taped short interviews with the first two citizens who called 9-1-1 and then interviewed Renfree's cousin, Duncan, standing in front of the wrecked garage. The structure looked like it had been struck by a bomb. Broken glass and fractured boards were everywhere. Three-quarters of the truck was still buried in the wall.

Although the descriptions of the lion varied slightly, in one respect they were all the same—the animal was huge.

"Until then," she concluded, "This is Kimberly Benson reporting from lion country in western Montana. Stay tuned and I will keep you posted . . ."

Part III

Death in the Tall Pines

"When your time comes to die,
Be not like those whose hearts are filled with the fear of death,
Sing your death song and die like a hero going home . . ."

(Tecumseh, Shawnee)

27

IN GEOLOGICAL TERMS, it passed in the blink of an eye, a period twelve thousand years ago called the Pleistocene. It was a time marked by the last retreats of glaciers from the Ice Age, a time when early man crossed the Aleutian land bridge following woolly mammoths south. Fossil remains in tar pits at La Brea indicate that extinct horses, camels, and long-horned bison roamed the American West. Along with these herbivores came a variety of predators. Dire wolves, foxes, even coyotes thrived, many not too different from species we recognize today.

The most spectacular of these early predators were the big cats. A huge American lion (*Panthera atrox*) stalked the plains, as well as packs of saber-toothed tigers (*Smilodon californicus*). Likewise, there were several species of cougars, one *Felis dagretti*, sizably larger than the current North American mountain lion, *Felis concolor.*

What happened to these great feline predators? Why some species lived and others became extinct is one of the great mysteries of the past. Yet, the basic structure of cats has changed little over the ages. The exceptional build, the superb coordination of musculature, the rapier teeth and gripping claws—all give these animals an extraordinary edge for survival. Except for minor variances, the body type of the house cat is modeled on the same genetic template as the Bengal tiger. It is a design supremely suited for hunting prey.

Kimberly thought of these things as she sat in the back of the Bank of Montana building that morning, waiting for the arrival of the state animal-control expert. A couple of references and a quick search about mountain lions on the internet had given her the basic information. During her research, she reflected upon her cat at home. She loved animals, and she especially liked cats. But even common house cats had the same cruel, killer instinct as many of their larger relatives. Kimberly had seen her cat cripple a mouse and play with it before she angrily took it away.

Her small cat posed no threat to human beings. But what if the sizes were reversed? What if her house cat were larger than a man? Would it purr and treat you with affection? Probably not, Kimberly reflected. Most likely, it would eat you for its lunch.

When she checked her watch, it was nine o'clock. By now, all members of the city council were present. The conference table had seats for twelve. Hayden's secretary made sure there were enough coffee and refreshments for everyone invited. Mayor Miller lounged at the head of the table, discussing issues with other members. Two of Hayden's deputies were seated at opposite ends of the room.

The town seemed to be placing great stock in the government hunter, Kimberly thought. She wondered with increasing anticipation what he would look like and how he would act. She was curious how someone would go about hunting the lion, and she was pleased Hayden had invited her to join the meeting. As a reporter, she especially liked the fact that she had been there from the beginning.

The door burst open as Sergeant Hayden entered the room. An audible gasp rose from the city council. Following Hayden was a giant of a man. He was so big that his frame almost filled the doorway. His skin was dark, and he had a short gray beard. He was dressed in a western shirt, jeans, and a pair of dusty boots. A bandanna draped around his neck.

In addition to his size, one of the striking things everyone noticed was what he carried on his belt. Strapped at his right hip was the scabbard of a ten-inch broad-blade knife. On his left hip, jutting from a leather holster, rested a large western revolver.

His presence was so unexpected it took the mayor a moment to realize he was followed by a tan spotted dog with long tail and floppy ears. As he stopped in the middle of the room, he turned to the dog and pointed toward an empty corner.

"Go, Ringo. Stay," he commanded.

The dog obediently walked over to the side of the room and sat down.

"Ladies and gentlemen, this is Howard Lassiter," Hayden announced.

Lassiter moved around the table shaking hands. Mayor Miller was impressed that his own fingers seemed no larger than a child's in the man's grasp. Mrs. Kellogg, secretary for the town council, was even more amazed at the dog. The animal came into a room with a bunch of strangers. It had no leash, and it sat down next to the wall at a whispered command.

James Benson, Elkhorn town treasurer, liked the sound of Lassiter's voice. It was deep and rich, and when the big man took a place at the end of the table, there was a certain air of confidence that Lassiter was the best in the business. The hunter had a quick smile and gentle, easy laugh. Any fears the town council had about the competence of a hunter the state might send were quickly dispelled.

"I'm sorry I could not be here earlier," Lassiter apologized. "I was in eastern Montana. You didn't give me much time."

"We thank you, sir, for coming," Miller answered quickly. "Everybody's a little freaked over this lion thing. We felt that a man of your experience was needed."

"Understood," Lassiter said with a nod. "Early this morning, I stopped at the Arcata River. I followed the logging trail, then went out to the cabin where they found the body of Cecil Reiss. After the meeting, I want to look around town, then have Sergeant Hayden take me out to Olsson's ranch. I need to have a good look at the tracks and be sure this is the same lion. Then, I can put together a plan."

"How much time are you asking for?" James Benson asked.

"To kill the lion? If it's in the area, we should be able to get it in a couple days. If it's a transient, then it becomes more difficult. Big male lions like this, if they are moving through an area, can travel thirty miles a day. So, we may have to wait until it shows again before we can pin it down."

"Well, obviously, the sooner the better," the mayor said. "After last night, people are getting a little jumpy."

"Does it make sense that this lion is injured or wounded?" Mrs. Kellogg asked.

Lassiter broke into a deep laugh. "Are you asking why it attacked these people? Is it a crippled lion? That theory is hogwash, ma'am. They used to think animals that killed humans were either injured or somehow too old to feed on their usual prey. Lions are opportunistic feeders. Granted, they have predictable hunting patterns; but, if someone comes jogging down a path who looks, smells, and acts like prey, they might try to take them down."

"Then why don't we have more attacks like this?"

"These big cats are very intelligent, ma'am. Most times, a human standing on two legs doesn't look like prey. Usually, lions hunt after dark, and most times, they live in the high mountains where there aren't many people. If you begin to crowd their habitat, however, you're going to get some problems.

"There have been more lion attacks in the past ten years than in the rest of entire century put together. So, part of the problem is the gradual encroachment on the lion's habitat by civilization. People are camping, hiking, and farming more and more in the lion's territory. Then, too, it's been a dry year. Many deer and elk have come down from the high country for water, and lions are likely to follow."

"What's the chance this lion is going to learn that people are a good thing to eat and become a man-eater?" the mayor asked.

Lassiter lifted his hands in a shrug. "Ah, well, that's the big question, isn't it? The lion has killed three people. It knows now it can kill human beings. I understand the rancher who was killed had no dogs—he tracked it with a horse, and may have been pushing the lion off its prey. Sometimes they get a little fussy when you do that. The autopsy report on the Reynolds girl stated she was menstruating. She was jogging down an isolated lumber trail. The lion may have been hunting in the area when she accidentally came along.

"The old recluse out by the Arcata River, I can't figure. I found the body of a deer carcass near his cabin. But the lion did not feed on much of it."

He paused while Mabel offered him a cup of coffee.

"Will this lion kill again?" Lassiter wrinkled his brow. "That's why you asked me to come, isn't it? I don't want to give this lion a chance to get into more trouble than it already has. We'll find it and take care of it, and you can go on with your business."

"Maybe you could outline how you will approach this for the council," Hayden said.

"Well, we've got a couple of choices," Lassiter said, nodding. "One of the ways we use is to set out baits and poisons. If a lion is in the area and feeding actively, and you set out six or eight baits, it will usually feed on one of the baits in a couple of days. Cyanide was what the old 'wolfers' used, and they killed a hell of a lot of predators. The problem with this method is that you kill other game indiscriminately, and most of the conservation groups have a problem if you end up taking innocent animals."

Councilman Benson choked on his coffee. "You got to be kidding! Go have the conservation groups speak with the Olsson family and see how they answer that question."

"I know," Lassiter answered patiently. "Remember, I work for the state, and we get our funding through the governor. And I, personally, got to be a little careful about upsetting too many of the animal rights people. We end up accidentally poisoning a couple of bears, and it will not look good. You got to trust me on this." He shook his head. "These are the political realities of the times."

"So, what are your other options?"

"The best choice, of course, is to make a clean kill. We identify the cat and hunt it down, and we kill the offending lion. We demonstrate this is the lion that has been doing the damage. And we leave the environment intact and go on our way."

"And how, sir, do you intend to do this?"

"I would suggest that we search for this lion in two ways. We'll need to drive the dirt roads and look along the shoulders as well as local streams for fresh tracks. Your local ranchers can help. A lot of us looking together will be much better than one or two. If we don't find much, we wait for a lion sighting or look for evidence where it has made a fresh kill. Then, old Ringo and I will take up the pursuit."

The dog had been watching Lassiter intently. When his master spoke his name, Ringo lifted his ears and gave an eager whine.

"I've got three dogs, and they know lions probably better than any dogs in the state. We get to within a day of that lion, and they'll find him. Then, it's just a matter of catching up to the dogs and killing the lion. That's the easy part. The hard part is locating where he's feeding and finding scent fresh enough that the dogs can follow."

"And what if you can't find him?" Mrs. Kellogg asked.

Lassiter snorted, pulling at his beard. "I've hunted a lot of lions, ma'am. And, I haven't found the lion yet that will get away from me for long."

"We have a limited city budget," the mayor said. "How much are you going to charge for this?"

Lassiter laughed, and the deep, booming richness of his voice carried through the room. "Sir, you've been paying me through your taxes for as long as I have been working for the state. The governor asked especially that I come help. I don't expect our budget is going to run out very soon."

The hunter glanced around at the hopeful faces at the table. "Give us a couple of days," he said reassuringly. "If the lion is here, we'll find him."

After the meeting, after Lassiter had gone to search out areas through which the lion had passed, and after the mayor and the city council had dispersed to continue their day, rumor drifted through Elkhorn that a very large man had come to this small Montana hamlet to kill a very big lion. It was somehow strange, they thought, that an "Afro-American" should be the person to come into this redneck region and provide safety for their population of mostly Whites.

Anyone who raised this question admitted that no, they personally had not met Howard Lassiter. Later in the afternoon when he came back and began to look around town and then ate dinner in the Aspen café, people drifted into the restaurant just to have a look.

"Must have played football," someone said. Then a rumor started that he'd been an all-pro athlete back east. Another story circulated that he'd killed a lion with his bare hands. People scoffed at this, too—until they saw him.

Getting rid of the lion problem, they concluded, was just a matter of time.

28

THE SMALL TWO-BEDROOM HOME rested on a side street at the back of Weasel Creek. The roof was old, and the exterior cracked and chipping. Wolfson stood in the back of his sister's house going through his grandfather's closet. The sum of the old man's wardrobe was a pair of pants, two tattered coats, several shirts, and a sweater. Wolfson took the last coat from a hanger, folded the garment, and placed it in a cardboard box. He could still feel the sadness of his grandfather's death. The loss was greater than he had expected.

On the floor of the closet, Wolfson found a pair of shoes with holes in the bottoms. He placed these on top of the folded garments and turned toward a bureau where Two Feathers had stored his belongings. Wolfson started at the bottom drawer. There wasn't much. A couple of undershirts, some patched long johns, several pairs of socks. The total of his grandfather's possessions filled one-half of a cardboard box.

He glanced up as Sarah came into the room. "Grandfather didn't have much, did he?"

"He didn't have much money, if that's what you mean," she answered sharply. "A man's riches aren't always measured by his possessions."

Wolfson turned back toward the bureau. As he continued searching through the drawer, he found a portion of a folded blanket, wrapped around some irregular material, tied with a cord. He laid the blanket on top of the bed.

"What's this?"

"That was his medicine bundle," Sarah answered.

Wolfson knew that "medicine bundles" were objects of magical significance to the older generation of Blackfoot. Most of the early braves were superstitious. Medicine bundles contained things of religious or spiritual importance to their owners. Often the items were considered good luck totems that gave the possessor special powers.

Untying the leather thong, he opened the folded blanket. His eyes widened as he took inventory of the items. First came a broad knife, seven inches long, with a bone handle. Next to it, wrapped in a piece of cloth, were the clenched talons of an eagle's foot. Then came the mummified body of a small owl, tightly wrapped with crossing strips of leather.

In a hidden fold of the blanket, Wolfson found several small pieces of rock. One was black. Scattered through the surface were tiny crystals of glittering metal. Wolfson wondered if it was gold.

He continued opening the articles, unfolding them one by one. Wrapped in a separate piece of cloth was a large foot from some type of animal. He held it up and turned it over in his fingers. It looked to be a lion's paw. The foot had been preserved so well he could press on the pad and the claws would extend.

At the bottom of the blanket, Wolfson found a small folded piece of skin, wrapped in a circular scroll. On one side were the remnants of buffalo hair. The other side contained a series of primitive drawings. The figures reminded him of pictographs he had seen as a youth on the cliffs at Buffalo Ridge.

"What's all this supposed to mean?" he asked.

"The skin was given to Grandfather by his great-grandmother. It tells the story of Washaka and how he was saved by a lion. Before he became the great chief, Eyes-In-Shadows.

Wolfson nodded. The story was familiar. It was a legend Two Feathers had told him as a child, the Legend about a "spirit cat, *Omahkatayo*"

Reaching down, he picked up the knife, closely inspecting the handle. The bone seemed solid. He ran his finger across the point. The edge was impressively sharp.

"So, where did this come from?"

"Grandfather told me the knife belonged to one of his ancestors called Red Cloud. It was considered a magical knife. The handle was made of bear bone. He said that it gave great powers, that Red Cloud saved it for his most important battles."

Twisting the blade, Wolfson could see a dark smudge along one side. He wondered if it was blood. The Blackfoot were superstitious about such things. Warriors were known to keep the dried blood of enemies on spears and blades they had used. Was this from someone Red Elk had killed? Maybe somebody he had scalped? Wolfson shuddered at the thought.

"And this?" Wolfson held up the mummified owl.

"From Crooked Beak."

"You know this stuff pretty well."

"Well, it's part of our heritage," Sarah replied.

"Pretty pathetic, isn't it?" Wolfson said.

"Oh, fuck you." Tears welled up in Sarah's eyes.

"What are you talking about?"

"Just go fuck yourself. Why are you even here?"

Wolfson frowned, surprised at her sudden anger. He started to say something when she cut him off.

"Why didn't you call?"

"I did call," he replied angrily.

"Bullshit!" she snapped. "Grandfather called you every day toward the end. You could have called back. One call might have made a difference. But you were too busy, or you didn't know what to say, or he was talking Blackfoot and you couldn't be bothered.

You don't know how he cared for you, Bobby. You were his light, his life, and you didn't give a shit."

"Come on! What are you saying?" Wolfson cried.

"You're gone. You're not here anymore," her voice rose. "What the fuck do you care?"

"That's not true," Wolfson shouted back.

"Then why didn't you call?" Tears flooded down her cheeks. A shudder rose within her body. "You could have called. Just a word or two that you cared. That's all he needed. God knows what was going through his mind."

She broke into a sob, her shoulders slumping. "And now, what am I going to do? What are we going to do?"

Wolfson reached forward and took his sister in his arms.

"I love you, sis," he said softly, "and I loved him. I didn't mean it to come out like this."

"After you left, he was all I had," she murmured.

"I'm so sorry," he blurted out. "I didn't mean to do this to you. To him. You're right. I should have called. But, there's no way to undo that now. I never meant to hurt you."

"He always talked about you, Bobby. You were always on his mind."

Wolfson stood for a moment, trying to control his grief, trying to hold back his tears. He rubbed Sarah affectionately on the shoulder. "Why don't you come back with me," he said gently. "To Chicago. I can help take care of you there."

"I can't, Bobby." She shook her head. "Right now, my life is predictable and stable, and I need that for the kids. Maybe when they get older . . ."

Sarah looked up, staring at Wolfson. "Why don't you think of coming back to the reservation?"

"God, sis, what would I do? How could I make a living?"

"Then, I guess we're both stuck, aren't we?"

Sarah's three-year-old daughter came into the room. She looked at them strangely. She'd been awakened from her nap by raised voices, and she was not sure who was arguing or why. "Mommy, I'm hungry," Lindsey said.

"We'll eat in a minute." Sarah wiped her eyes and tried to regain her composure. Pulling away, she stepped over to her daughter and picked her up.

"Everything's okay, sweetheart," she murmured. "Everything's going to be all right."

Wolfson turned back to the bureau and began folding the items back into the blanket. He thought about placing the medicine bundle in the box with the rest of George Two Feathers's clothes but decided against it. Carefully, he returned the blanket to the top drawer of his grandfather's bureau. As he opened the drawer, he found a pair of false teeth.

"And what do you think we should do with these?"

"Try them. Maybe they fit," Sarah answered.

He dropped his head for a moment, long enough to push the teeth into his mouth, and then turned back and made a Halloween face at Lindsey. The teeth stuck out the side of his mouth.

The young girl shrieked with delight.

A faint smile touched Sarah's lips. "I'd better feed the kids."

WOLFSON LISTENED TO HER FOOTSTEPS fade down the hall and then turned back to the bureau. A deep hurt welled up within his mind, a pain he could not easily shake. His grandfather was gone. All that was left was a couple of mummified objects, an old knife, and some stick drawings on a cloth. The old man had had no investment stocks, no retirement savings, no cash.

In a way, his sister was right, he thought. A man shouldn't be measured in terms of physical possessions. It reminded him how out of place Blackfoot tradition was. In past days, a great chief was rich by virtue of his power and respect from the tribe. A "rich" man in the 1800s might have a large teepee, a dozen horses, and a couple of wives. Everything else was shared for the common good of the tribe. If a man was brave and demonstrated remarkable courage in battle, he would be considered a "wealthy" man. These were not attributes that could be bought and sold. Richness to the Blackfoot was measured in character, fierceness, and courage.

As he closed the drawer, Wolfson realized he had forgotten to include the skin scroll with the blanket. He tied the holding cord and placed the bundle inside the drawer. As he did this, a large coin fell out of the blanket, striking the bureau with a clang. The object spun on the wooden surface and clattered to a stop.

The coin was the size of a silver dollar, faded brown with age. On one side was an imprint of two arms shaking hands. On the other, the picture of a man. Wolfson scraped at the metal with his thumb. The number 1803 emerged from the tarnished surface.

My God, he wondered. Was this one of the original Jefferson Peace Medals, made in 1803, minted especially for the Lewis and Clark expedition? He'd read about such medallions in his history studies. Had this coin been given to one of his Blackfoot ancestors by Lewis and Clark? He felt the metal, marveling at the thought, turning the coin in his fingers.

An approaching car sounded outside

The vehicle stopped in front of Sarah's house. There came a second and then the sound of the brakes of a third. There was a sharp rap at the door. Wolfson could hear his sister move across the living room.

As the front door opened, the vibration of trampling feet entered the house. Men's voices. Wolfson placed the box with his grandfather's belongings in the closet and started for the door.

In the living room stood six men. Wolfson recognized one of the individuals as a council leader named James Black Kettle. He was stocky, in his late fifties. He wore his hair in braids.

"Bobby, I am glad we found you," Black Kettle said. "The council wondered if you would be willing to do a sweat lodge? We could smoke pipe. It would be an honor."

The men crowded toward him, nodding with approval.

Wolfson hesitated. "It's been a long time . . ." He looked over at his sister. She caught his glance and nodded.

"I'm sure he would be delighted," she said.

29

WOLFSON TOOK A FEW SWIMMING STROKES then walked into the shallows. The lake water seemed like ice. Shivering from the cold, he emerged with the others and toweled off. Near the shoreline was a sunken enclosure that looked like a circular hut covered in tarps. The men led him to a small flap-like opening.

Entering the doorway, Wolfson followed the elders into the darkened interior. At first, he couldn't see. Everything was pitch black. As his eyes became accustomed to the dark, he could see red-hot coals glowing in the center of the structure.

He sat cross-legged on a blanket next to the wall. Here he rested in silence, staring at the heated rocks. Someone said something in Blackfoot. A gourd of water poured over the coals. The sharp hiss of steam rose. A voice began to chant.

As clouds of vapor spread through the enclosed chamber, Wolfson felt as if he was in a blast furnace. Sweat oozed along his forehead and collected across his chest. Soon the heat became so oppressive, it was difficult to breathe. A drum pounded slowly in the background. The chanting continued almost at a whisper.

He felt someone nudge his side. Reaching blindly in the darkness, he found a long pipe thrust into his hands. He raised the pipe to his lips and took in the smoke with a slow, deep inhalation. As the aroma drifted into his lungs, his mind began to haze, his vision cloud. He took several puffs and passed the pipe to an unseen man on his right.

Gradually, time began to blur. He thought first about returning to Chicago and teaching high school, completing the semester. He would have to leave the reservation soon. Substitute teachers could cover for him a couple of days. After that would be difficult. He had a lot to do back home, and the summer was quickly passing.

And then his mind turned to his grandfather and the funeral, and the strange contents of George Two Feathers's medicine bundle. Images came to him beyond his control. Steadily, the veneer of civilization began to peel away, stripped like layers of cloth, until there was only him, sitting naked in the darkness.

As Wolfson stared into the fire, the incandescent coals became a pair of glowing eyes. Gradually, Wolfson could feel muscles tremble beneath him, muscles that seemed to be of enormous strength. He recognized he was in the forest. It was evening, and in the growing darkness, he could see and hear everything. For a moment, his senses became extremely acute: no movement, no sound, escaped him.

As he glided silently, vast landscapes passed before his eyes. The feeling was one of omnipotence. The lion was looking for him. And even in the darkened confines of the sweat lodge, he could feel the presence of its gaze.

30

A MILE NORTH OF THE ELKHORN TOWN SQUARE stood a small municipal park named after William Tanner, an early trapper who had settled here. A baseball diamond marked one end of the space, an open green, the other. A grove of aspens lined the park's eastern boundary. Behind home plate rose a cluster of pines.

Howard Lassiter crouched next to a soft spot in the earth. Reaching down, he brushed several twigs from the indentation of an animal print. The hunter removed a glass plate from his satchel and placed it on top of the track. As he outlined the print with a grease pen, a shadow crossed his hand.

"The sheriff's office told me you might be here," Kimberly Benson said. "I was hoping we could talk . . ." She held out her business card.

Lassiter studied the card then turned back to his work.

"So why's a California reporter interested in a Montana lion?"

"For one, Tracy Reynolds comes from a very well-respected San Francisco family," she replied. "The station sent me out to investigate her disappearance. Secondly, there is a voter initiative coming up in California on hunting lions. The station wanted me to get a perspective on how Montana approaches the problem."

"Yeah, I know about California," Lassiter grunted. "You can't shoot anything that walks, squawks, or mews, and it's got to be caught in the act of killing something to get departmental approval. You got more tree huggers out there than you got trees. God help you if you make a mistake and take the wrong animal."

He took a piece of paper, outlined the print, and then smoothed it over with his hand.

"What are you collecting here?" she asked.

"Footprints," he answered matter-of-factly. "Footprints of a lion."

Lassiter took a ruler and measured the width of the foot. The toes were four elongated ovals with three lobes at the base. "Looks like a young male," he said.

"Are you telling me there are lions coming through this park?" Kimberly asked with astonishment. "Right in the middle of Elkhorn?"

Lassiter stood up. "Ma'am, there are lions all over the place. Last night, I found the tracks of a female and two juveniles on the high school football field. And over there, next to the swings, is the print of a big male. Maybe the one we're looking for."

"That's hard to believe," Kimberly said.

Lassiter shrugged. "Place like this turns into a crossroads at night for a lot of animals." He paused to write the name, location, and time of the lion print and then placed the outline in his satchel. He glanced casually toward the reporter.

"If you'll pardon me saying so, ma'am . . . you're standing on a piece of coyote shit."

Kimberly jerked her foot away. Her face flushed.

"Remember, I've been doing this a lot of years," Lassiter chuckled. "It always helps you to know where you're stepping."

"So I see," she murmured.

The hunter started back to his truck. Kimberly hurried after him. "Howard James Lassiter. Tight end. Denver Broncos, 1981–1985. Three years Pro Bowl. Before that, All-American, Syracuse University."

"You seem to know a lot about athletics, ma'am."

"You weren't hard to find," Kimberly said. "I punched your name into the internet. Everybody's got a past there somewhere."

Lassiter eyed her carefully. "Those were good years." He tossed the satchel into the front of the truck and walked over to the driver's side.

"I'm heading into town," he said. "If you want to talk, why don't we meet at the Aspen Café?"

THEY SAT AT A TABLE IN THE BACK of the restaurant. The hunter ordered a soda and cheeseburger. Kimberly asked for a bagel and tea.

"My treat," she said. "I'll write it off as business. Category: Interview. Topic: Lions. Question: Why did the lion cross the road?"

Lassiter looked up and smiled. "Three reasons, Miss Benson. Eat, mate, and defend home territory from other males that also want to eat and mate. Reduced to its simplest equation, that's all there is."

"And why are you out here hunting lions, Mr. Lassiter?"

"Fish and Game's got a half a dozen hunters on their payroll. Me? I started working for them after I blew out my knee. When I was recuperating, I got the idea of going back to school, so I went to the University of Montana and got my master's in environmental sciences. I worked for the Forestry Department for a couple of years. When they had a problem with a coyote population near Billings, I helped track a bunch of them down. I liked the work, and I liked being outdoors, and it seemed to fit. The rest is history, as they say."

"Do you hunt everything?"

"Anything that causes a problem," he answered. "Mostly, we try to dart the difficult animals and haul them off. Bears are the chief offenders, and they take up half my time. The other half is spent on coyotes and sometimes packs of livestock-killing dogs. Wolves aren't much of a problem anymore, but a couple of years ago, I had to go after a big black that was taking calves along the Canadian border. And then, there are the lions. I get called because of a problem lion two or three times a year."

"You think I could go with you on a hunt?" Kimberly asked.

"I'm not sure that would be a good idea," Lassiter said. "Once the dogs start running, there is a lot of riding; and I'm afraid you'd be pretty much in the way. This is a big, dangerous male, Miss Benson, and I wouldn't want you to get hurt."

"You seem to put a lot of faith in your dogs," she said.

"Ringo is the leader of my pack," the hunter replied. "He can smell a lion a mile away. I've never known him to be wrong. Blue and Sampson are the others. The three of them do all the work. They chase and tree the lion. I'm just the mop-up man."

"You ever had a dog killed?"

"Never." He shook his head. "Mostly, the lions are afraid. Once the dogs get on their trail, the lions usually climb the nearest tree. I'd say we've taken thirty lions, and I've had no serious problem. Once in a while, the dogs get scratched across the nose. Blue got a claw in the eye once. The lions are a lot different than grizzlies. Some of those old bears are mean as hell. They'll stand toe-to-toe and fight to the end. Not the cats. Lions generally don't want to fight. Mostly, they turn and run."

"And what about this lion, the lion that killed Tracy Reynolds?"

"It's crossed the boundaries," Lassiter replied. "One death might be accidental. Occasionally, if this happens in the parks, they let the animal go. But, the killing of a third person raises the suspicion this lion may be going after humans. This big boy needs to be taken down."

"You're seem pretty sure about this."

"Lions are habitual animals," the hunter said. "Often they cover the same areas, prowl the same boundaries. Sooner or later, this one is going to show, and we'll take him. My dogs are too good to let him get away."

"Well, I wish you luck," Kimberly said.

"Yeah, good luck with your story," Lassiter replied.

31

THE TWO RUNNERS CAME OVER THE RIDGE, jogging steadily. Wolfson was in the lead, Franklyn Yellow Pine, a step behind. Crossing a section of forest, they ran through the afternoon shadows, moving past a cluster of firs, and then along a trail leading through a strand of spruce. Water exploded off their heels as they plunged through a stream. A herd of deer scattered before them, prancing in stiff-legged leaps.

Still running, the pair crossed another ravine and then went up a rise leading behind the housing settlement of Weasel Creek. The trail turned again, rising through a boulder field and over a second ridge. Wolfson struggled to keep his pace. Gradually, he began to falter.

"Give up?" Franklyn shouted.

"Never!"

As the climb increased, Franklyn edged around him. When Wolfson reached the top of the incline, he had to stop. Bending over, he held his side, heaving for air. Franklyn increased his kick and moved rapidly ahead.

"Hey! Wait a minute!" Wolfson gasped. "I can't keep up!"

"Let me finish five miles," Franklyn yelled. "I'll circle back." His voice faded as he disappeared into the forest.

Wolfson shook his head, awed at the tireless speed at which Franklyn ran. He could keep up with the youth for two miles. After that, he wasn't even close. And Franklyn was only eighteen. He still had three to four years of training left before he would reach peak speeds.

From his vantage point on top of the ridge, Wolfson watched Franklyn moving in and out of the trees, his white shirt and blue shorts flashing here and there. A half a mile away, Wolfson saw Franklyn turn and descend through a meadow into the valley.

Wolfson caught his breath and began running down the steep incline, taking two yards at a bound. He reached the base of the valley and slid behind a cluster of trees to wait for Franklyn to come running along the trail. Leaping out, he grabbed Franklyn from behind and pulled him over in the grass.

"Caught you!" he yelled.

"You cheated!" Franklyn cried.

The two rolled on the ground, laughing.

"That's the only way I can beat you."

Franklyn glanced at his watch. "You're ruining my time."

"Tough shit!" Wolfson answered.

He pulled himself to a sitting position. Franklyn stood alongside him. A small stream meandered through the valley, lined by cottonwood trees.

"Look at you! You're not even winded," Wolfson said. "I don't think I could have gone another mile."

"A little out of shape, old man?"

"More than I'd like to admit."

"You know, if you came back, we could run every morning," Franklyn said.

Wolfson took a deep breath. "I like the view. Even the air smells good."

"So, when are you leaving?"

"Couple of days."

"No way I can persuade you to stay?"

"I'd like to. It's just that I got to cover the last part of summer school. And then, there's the beginning of the fall semester. It would put me behind for weeks."

"Why can't they get someone to sub?"

"They can. I just hate to dump the work on anyone else."

Franklyn grabbed Wolfson's hand and pulled him to a standing position. "Come on. We still have three miles to go."

"No, you have three miles to go," Wolfson answered. "I'm finished."

Franklyn adjusted his watch and waved goodbye.

"Stop by the Dairy Queen. I'll treat you to lunch," he yelled.

Wolfson watched him disappear down the trail. Smiling, he broke into a jog. He felt good. The cool morning, the mountains, and the fresh scent of grass and trees were invigorating. It was a far cry from running in repetitive circles on a paved track in Chicago.

In five minutes, he caught a second wind and jogged easily along a path toward Weasel Creek and his sister's house. He saw a pair of deer standing by the edge of the forest. Crouching down, he began to slip from tree to tree, gradually working his way toward them. He wondered if he could touch one. His grandfather had dared him to do that once.

Moving cautiously, he approached within twenty yards of the animals and then charged outward at a sprint. He ran after them, vaulting over a log, dodging through a section of aspen, but they were too fast. He finally stopped, watching the pair bound off into the shadows. Better leave the running to Franklyn, "*old man*," he smiled to himself.

32

Howard Lassiter drove out to Olsson's ranch that afternoon to see what had happened. A dog, 110 pounds, carried up and deposited in the boughs of a tree. It was something that was hard for Lassiter to believe. He'd been in the game control business for a lot of years, and he'd never seen anything like it.

Crouching next to a large pine, he studied a paw print in the soft earth, marveling at its size. Big lion, he thought. Damn big lion. He spread his fingers, measuring the size of the print. Paw prints could be deceiving. Sometimes, a big cat had only a medium-sized print, and sometimes a medium cat had a large print, but this print was enormous. This was no mistake. The owner of this print was huge.

Lassiter bent down and surveyed the clearing where Lute Olsson's body had been found and then shaded his eyes, squinting upwards, following the trunk to a broad intersection of boughs forty feet above the ground. It was here the dog had been deposited.

He marveled at the strength needed for carrying a heavy dog up the trunk of a tree. Cougars don't cache prey in the limbs of a tree, do they? Occasionally, he heard reports of big cats hauling deer and sometimes smaller game into trees where they could feed in safety from other animals and wolves. But these events were rare. And then a memory flashed across his mind.

He'd been on assignment for the Department of Forestry, riding a fire trail during the summer near Kintla Lake. There he'd had a strange encounter, something he'd never seen. Wolves—seven of them—massacred, decimated, laid at the base of a tree, and one dead wolf carried into the boughs.

He got down on one knee, studying the track. What had happened back there at Kintla Lake? he wondered. And then a stunning realization occurred to him: maybe this was the work of the same lion. What was he dealing with here . . . something out of the Pleistocene?

He stood up slowly, his mouth dry.

"We'll get him, Ringo," he grunted. "He'll show again, and he's ours."

The dog had been sitting a short distance away. When he heard Lassiter's voice, the animal stood up and trotted to his owner's side. Lassiter patted him on the head and mounted. With a cluck, the hunter started through the forest, the sound of hoof beats fading gradually through the trees.

33

BY MID-AFTERNOON, the sheriff's station was running at a frenzied pace. Mabel fielded a number of calls. Sergeant Hayden asked for the typed revision of a child-abuse investigation. Deputy Peter Campbell came through the office, reporting on an alleged assault at Alder Ridge. Best Campbell could tell, the offenders were a couple of drifters who'd been hitchhiking nearby.

Mabel was seated at her desk. She noticed a commotion in the courtyard. She happened to glance out the window, watching one of the station's cats, when a crow flashed across the yard and flared above the water. The cat leapt backward with a hiss. As the bird spread its wings, the cat ran. The crow hopped onto the edge of the cat's bowl and took a drink. The secretary left her chair and walked over to the window.

Standing at the back of the courtyard was a Native American woman wrapped in a gray blanket. Although her face was partially hidden beneath the cloth, she appeared middle-aged, her features dark and scarred. The woman remained in the courtyard, waiting.

Unable to control her curiosity, Mabel walked out the door.

"Can I help you?"

"I would like to speak with the sergeant."

"Do you have an appointment?"

The woman shook her head.

"Is there something I can do?"

"It's about the lion."

"I'll see if he can fit you in. Can you come inside?"

"No, I will stay here."

"Who shall I say you are?"

"Raven Crow," she answered.

Mabel shook her head and went back into the office. What does a Native American woman have to do with a lion? She wondered. She reluctantly rang Hayden on the intercom. "Sorry to bother you, sir . . ."

Hayden listened, frowned, then finished a report he was writing. Ten minutes later, he stepped out into the courtyard.

"Hi, I'm Sergeant Hayden." He held out his hand. Raven Crow ignored him. She remained next to the hedge, trying to coax a small thrush into her hand. Hayden watched with amazement. The bird seemed to have little fear. The woman made several soft whistling sounds as the thrush hopped tentatively onto her fingers. Reaching forward, she stroked the bird on the head. A second thrush came out of the bush and lit on her shoulder.

"Do you like birds?" she asked.

"You wanted to see me?"

"You can hold one if you want."

The bird jumped forward on her arm, moving out to the tip of her outstretched fingers. Abruptly, the thrush flew to Hayden's shoulder and perched next to his head. He had to fight a reflex to bat it away. Turning, he tried to watch the bird out of the corner of his eye. The thrush pecked at his ear and wiped its bill on his shirt. Suddenly, it flew off. In an instant, it was back, hovering about the strange woman, lighting on her arm.

"My daughter would love this," Hayden said. "How do you do this?"

"I have come to talk about the lion," she said.

"Yeah, I'm listening."

"There will need to be someone with special powers to take this lion, Mr. Sheriff. Neither you nor your deputies have this medicine. It will need to be a Native American. A Blackfoot. Someone with ties to the past."

"And who do you propose this is?"

"There is only one."

"With all due respect, this lion has killed several people," Hayden replied. "I can appreciate what you're saying, but this lion needs to be eliminated so that our streets are safe. I can't wait another week. And this office will do everything we can to support that position."

Raven Crow shook her head. "You don't understand. Your people will not be able to kill this lion. The lion is not your affair."

"We've called in a hunter from the state. I have the utmost faith in his abilities."

Raven Crow pulled the corner of the blanket away and stared at Hayden fiercely.

"The lion will kill this man."

"Look, I don't know what to tell you," Hayden answered. "It's a matter of public safety, and we've brought in a government hunter to take care of the problem."

Raven Crow shrugged. "Your daughter is not safe."

"Nobody is safe until this lion is killed," Hayden answered. He drew back in disbelief. Was this a threat? What the hell did she know about his daughter?

Raven Crow pulled the blanket over her head and turned away. As she walked out of the courtyard, the small birds fluttered after her. Just before she disappeared, a black form darted from the roof. Hayden heard a swish of feathers and ducked, just in time to avoid a crow swooping inches from his head. The crow flapped across the yard and lit momentarily in a tree. Cawing loudly, the bird disappeared after the figure of Raven Crow.

Hayden walked back into the building, shaking his head. It was one of the strangest encounters he'd ever had.

"Pretty odd woman," Mabel said. "What did she want?"

"Sounded like a lot of hocus pocus, Hayden replied. "Something about an ancient lion. Something about needing medicine from the past. Not a lot of it made sense."

Mabel broke into a broad-faced grin.

"What the hell's so funny?"

"It appears her friend left a little message on your shirt, sir," she chuckled.

Hayden reached up and discovered a small whitish glob of bird excrement on his shoulder. He tried to flick it off but caught the dropping on his finger. Glancing at Mabel, he gave a frown of annoyance, then headed for the sink.

34

ROBERT WOLFSON BROUGHT HIS LAST ITEMS to the cash register: a box of diapers, a dozen oranges, some paper towels. He waited at the counter. Across the green rose the bronze statue of Jeremiah Bates. Past that was the Bank of Montana Building, and then Bertolli's Art Gallery and the white-water rafting store.

"That'll be $38.50," the woman at the counter said.

Wolfson took two twenties and placed them on the counter.

"You from the reservation?"

"Visiting," he answered.

"You look familiar."

"I was raised here."

She stared at him for a moment in astonishment. Her eyes widened. "Oh, my goodness," she exclaimed. "You must be Bobby Running Wolf. Little Bobby Running Wolf. I never would have believed . . ."

She rushed around the counter and gave him a hug. "I remember . . . You used to come in here with your grandfather. You always liked those little candy treats. Now look how grown and handsome you are."

Wolfson reddened. "It's been a while."

"What a pleasure to see you, Bobby." She edged back around the counter. "I'll tell my husband. He'll be interested that you came . . ."

Wolfson thanked her and lifted the two bags of groceries, placing one under each arm. He started across the green. When he reached his sister's car, he placed the groceries in the passenger side and walked around the front.

A sheriff's Bronco pulled along the street next to him. Two officers sat inside. Sergeant Hayden rolled down the window.

"Robert Wolfson?"

"That's me."

"Can we talk?"

"Yeah, sure." Wolfson waited as Hayden drove the patrol car down to the corner and parked. Walking back, Hayden introduced himself. The two shook hands.

"Word is, you used to be one of the best trackers on the reservation."

"How do you know me?"

"Small town. A lot of gossip. I was going to try to catch up with you sooner or later."

"I'm not sure where you got that information," Wolfson said. "There's many people out here better than me. I've been gone for a lot of years."

Hayden paused to let a car pass. "There's a woman come to my office. A woman from the reservation."

Wolfson squinted at him.

"She was talking about this lion that's attacking people. She said there was only one person that could kill this animal. Someone from the reservation. I just wanted to get your take on this."

"That all sounds pretty crazy," Wolfson said.

"That was kind of my sense," Hayden replied. "But I was just wondering—if we needed assistance—if we have to go to Plan B, so to speak—if you'd be okay, me giving you a call."

"Thanks, I don't think I would be much help," Wolfson said. "I hear you've got a good hunter from the state. I wish you luck."

Hayden reached out and shook his hand. "Sorry about your grandfather. I got a housekeeper that lives on the reservation. She knows your sister. She said he was a good man."

Wolfson watched the sergeant walk back to the sheriff's vehicle. It was amazing how quickly word spread through a small town like Elkhorn, he thought. In Chicago, no one gave a rat's ass what you did. Here, you coughed once, and the sheriff was knocking at your door.

He placed the keys in the ignition and took a moment to sort through the groceries. He suddenly realized he'd forgotten the baby's formula. Jogging back across the green, he'd just reached the grocery when Kimberly Benson walked out of the Aspen Café. The two almost collided along the sidewalk.

"Hi. How's your reporting?"

She looked at him for a second in confusion. "You're . . . ?"

"At the airport."

"Oh, yeah, thank you," she said with embarrassment. "I don't think I ever got your name."

"You were going to send a smoke signal, remember?"

She laughed.

"Where's your cameraman?"

"I was just trying to set up some interviews. I gave him a break for the afternoon."

"How's the work?"

She shook her head. "A tough town to penetrate. A lot of people are reluctant to go on camera. I think they're afraid I might embarrass them. But I'm really just trying to get information, you know? Sometimes it's easier if I don't have a camera along. People are much more open if they don't think they're being filmed."

"Makes sense," he said.

She eyed him cautiously. "What I do know is that nobody from the reservation will speak with me. We went out yesterday. I've never had so many doors slammed in my face."

"An attractive blond reporter with a black cameraman digging around the reservation?" Wolfson snorted. "You're lucky you weren't stoned."

"So how do I get through to them?"

"I'm not sure you can."

"Well, it was just a thought."

"Sorry, I wish I could help."

He started for the store when Kimberly stopped him.

"The smoke signal?"

"Yeah?"

"I didn't get your name."

35

A SHLEY HAYDEN STOOD IN THE MIDDLE of center field, waiting for the last player to hit. It had been a warm afternoon, and Little League practice was winding down.

"Hey batter, batter!" she chanted, joining the playful taunts from the rest of the team. At bat was a young boy, wearing the number 14. On the first pitch, he swung and missed. Everyone jeered.

On the next pitch, he swung again. This time, there was a solid crack of wood. A flyball sailed toward center field. Ashley raced after it, her cap skewed sideways. She held out her glove and caught the ball on the run. Raising the ball, she waved back to the team triumphantly.

"Great catch!" the coach yelled. "That's it. Everybody in!"

Joe Lugatti had coached the team only a year, but he seemed to know baseball, and no one cared as long as they were winning. The kids ran toward first base and crowded around him.

"Good practice," he said. "Remember to tell your parents the game will be at nine Saturday morning. Tanner Field."

He reached over and patted Ashley on the shoulder. "Nice going, young lady. Good fielding."

The kids milled about, laughing and shouting at each other. Ashley jogged over to the fence behind home plate and let Tobey loose. The students were allowed to bring their dogs to the school as long as they leashed them on the playground. Tobey barked excitedly and then ran over to the edge of the fence and raised his leg. Finished, he bounded back to Ashley's side. Refreshments of orange juice and cookies were served. Several parents helped with the treats.

"Wait, I've got to finish my school project," Ashley said. She lined up several players and took five photographs with her portable camera. She caught one of the kids in the shadows of the dugout with an orange stuffed in his mouth. The flash momentarily blinded him.

"You look like Wilmer the pig!" she teased.

"Yeah, let me take yours, moose face."

The boy chased her in a circle, the two finally tumbling over, laughing.

"Who else needs a ride?" Lugatti shouted.

"We've got our bikes," one of the girls replied. "Ashley and Barbara and I can ride together."

"The three amigos, eh?" the coach chuckled. Both his ten-year-old son and eleven-year-old daughter played on the team. In the past, they'd often ridden their bikes. When he thought about it, he didn't like the idea. With the number of lion problems recently, he wasn't eager to have the girls ride by themselves.

"I think you'd better come with us," Lugatti said.

"We're just going into town," one of the girls answered. "It's not far."

"And what about our bikes?" Ashley asked. "If we leave them here, somebody might take them."

That could be a problem, Lugatti thought. His van was already packed with baseball gear, and he didn't have enough room for his kids, three girls, and their bikes. He would have to leave something behind.

"All right," he agreed. "But stick together. And go directly home."

The girls nodded obediently.

"Isn't your dad supposed to pick you up?" he asked Ashley.

"Yeah, but he's always late, and if he doesn't find me, he'll know I've gone with my friends."

Ashley asked the coach to take one last photograph of them together—the three Little League girls in their uniforms, posed with a bat, standing next to their bikes. Then they started off. Pedaling toward town, the three girls disappeared around a corner with Tobey in hot pursuit.

At 6:30 that afternoon, Sam Hayden pulled his squad car into the baseball field parking lot. Booking a drug suspect had taken longer than he thought, and he still needed to fill out more papers for the jail. He saw a few parents and several kids playing at the diamond. He searched quickly for his daughter but could not find her. One of the fathers was pitching to his son next to the batter's cage.

"Hey, John. You seen Ashley?" Hayden shouted.

"I think they went home. Practice ended thirty minutes ago."

"Did the coach take them?"

"The girls rode their bikes."

Hayden went back to his car. As he drove out of the parking lot, a growing discomfort edged into his mind. Maybe the girls had gone to the Dairy Queen for an ice cream cone. He was surprised he had not seen them on his way to the baseball field. Better catch up, he thought.

A block from the town green, he found two of the Little League girls riding their bikes. Ashley was not with them. A knot worked into his stomach.

"You girls seen Ashley?" he asked.

"She started with us, but she said she wanted to go home and feed the horses. She left a while ago."

"By herself?"

The girls nodded.

"Oh, man . . ." Hayden muttered. He thanked them and started up the street.

At Pine and 5th, Hayden slowed behind a large RV blocking traffic. The vehicle was stuck momentarily at an intersection with a red light. The driver was obviously a tourist.

He turned on his siren and carefully edged around the vehicle, moving through the intersection. Once free, he stepped on the gas.

How long to get home, and which way did Ashley go? he worried. If she took the farm route, he should catch up with her easily. His ranch was only two miles outside town. But if she rode through the forest that bounded his property, she would be traveling on her own.

He was late and he had missed Ashley again, and he cursed himself for being so careless. He should have called Dolores or Mabel or even one of the deputies to pick her up. Maybe she had enough sense to take the farm road, he tried to reassure himself. But his thoughts brought little relief.

ASHLEY WAS A MILE OUTSIDE ELKHORN when she pulled off the road. The sun slipped westward toward the mountains. Long shadows flowed across the trees. As she started up again, she pedaled leisurely, singing to herself. It was a great evening for a ride, she thought. She'd made the run a hundred times. The biggest danger was a truck or unsuspecting driver coming from the opposite direction that might be going too fast. This evening, she saw few cars. She turned along an access road until she reached a junction. Here she stopped to rest.

"You all right, Tobey?"

The little terrier panted heavily.

"Here, have some water." She took her bike bottle and squirted a stream of water into Toby's face. The dog lapped it eagerly. Her small disposable camera fell forward. Swinging the camera around her neck, she started up.

When she reached home, she heard the telephone ring. She dropped her bike, fumbled furiously for the door, and raced through the living room to the kitchen. When she picked up the receiver, the caller had already hung up. Maybe it was her dad.

As she hung up the telephone, she heard a scratching at the door. She went to the window and saw Tobey standing on the porch. She opened the screen door as the little dog raced inside.

"You need a bath," she scolded.

She considered changing clothes, but it was getting dark, and she knew the horses were her first concern. Get the horses fed and then back into the house and wait for Dad, she told herself.

When she went out the back door, Tobey tried to follow.

"No, you stay inside!" she ordered. She remained by the door, watching. Tobey tried to push the screen with his nose.

"I mean it!" she said sternly. She pointed her finger at the dog.

The terrier glowered at her and then reluctantly lay down. Moving quickly, she left the porch and hurried toward the corral. The forest looked dark and ominous, and she glanced in its direction with concern.

The horses seemed nervous. "All right. Easy, guys," she said. She poured feed into a metal trough and reached for the gate leading into the pasture. The horses almost trampled her, running past. Strange, she thought. Usually, they would come up and nuzzle for food.

She grabbed a hose to fill a bucket with water then turned back toward the barn. A loose halter had fallen from the fence, and she picked it up. Walking in the darkness, she went through the barn door and placed the halter on a post. A dim light illuminated the barn. And then she saw the lion.

There had been no noise. One moment there was nothing, and then the huge beast was there, blocking the doorway. It stood in the semi-darkness, its body an extension of the shadows.

Ashley froze. There was no time to think, no time to scream. Spinning sideways, she turned and ran. She glanced over her shoulder, terrified to see the enormous beast follow. Then, her legs tangled and she pitched forward, landing on her side. As she fell, the disposable camera slammed onto the ground. The bulb went off. There was a brilliant flash.

Struggling to her feet, she pushed the camera into the lion's face and pushed the shutter. A second flash. The lion stopped, dazed.

Rolling to the side, Ashley fired a third flash into its eyes at point-blank range; and then she was up, running from the barn, sprinting with all her might. As she ran across an open space, she tried to click the camera, but no flash came.

Ducking into the old shed, she leaped through the entrance and pulled the door shut. She lay on her back, pushing the door with her feet, trying to keep the door closed. She was breathing heavily, her temples pounding. Her heart raced like a flywheel.

From outside the door came a horrible, snuffling sound. Was it smelling for her? Was it playing with her like a cat with a mouse? She pushed her weight against the door, bracing herself.

There came a sickening crash. A side of the shed fragmented before her eyes. A paw reached through the jagged hole, claws out, working its way along the woodwork, trying to find her. The animal launched against the shed again. Another crash. This time, the structure shuddered.

There was nowhere to run, no place to hide. She shrank against the back of the shed, thinking frantically, trying to formulate a plan. She had run out of options. She was trapped. There was nowhere else to go.

Barking. The noise became steadily louder. Suddenly, she realized Tobey was outside the shed, charging after the lion. He must have escaped the house. He'd come to help.

She screwed up her courage to look through the jagged opening in the shed. The little dog danced and charged at the lion, spinning like a dervish. Ashley had never seen him move so fast. A swipe of claws almost caught Tobey in the head. If she didn't help, the lion would kill him.

No way, she thought. No animal was going to take her pet like that. Determinedly, she groped along the back of the shed. Her fingers found a broom. She charged out of the shed, swinging at the lion.

The broom caught the lion in the face. The beast spun toward her, snarling. Then Tobey lunged after it, nipping at its tail.

Ashley squared off, raising her broom like a bat. "Go on! Get out!" she cried. She swung the broom again, this time with all her might. The lion caught the handle in its mouth and snapped it in two.

"Oh, my God," she murmured. Staggering backwards, she reached desperately for something else to fight the lion. There was nothing. Only the crumbling wall of the shed.

The lion took a menacing step forward. Ashley shrank back and held her breath. She brought her arms defensively across her face, huddled against the wall, bracing for its charge.

The rising wail of a siren approached. Headlights flashed. A rotating red light blinked. It was her father, and he was roaring up the driveway toward her home.

As silently as it had appeared, the great beast was gone, drifting back into the shadows. Tobey raced after the lion, barking ferociously. A moment later he returned, jumping into Ashley's arms.

"Oh, you beautiful dog," she said.

36

LIKE ANCIENT DRAWINGS IN A CHAMBERED CAVE, florescent images flashed across the helicopter's infrared monitor. The figures were pale, ghostly—animals running, caught with the million-candle search beam like bleached figures on a blackened wall.

A pair of deer ricocheted across a field. A herd of elk stampeded through scattered timber. The animals were blinded, confused, sprinting in frightened desperation. Twice they saw bears, and if they'd not been hunting lions, Hayden might have killed them all.

Since eight that night, an hour after he'd come home and found his daughter huddled in the back of the half-torn shed, he'd been in the air, combing the countryside, searching for the lion. They flew the helicopter in grids, just as he'd do for a missing person. First to the north, five miles out, a horizontal run two miles east, then a quarter-of-a-mile turn, and a reversal back, constantly watching the monitor, looking for life, lighting up anything that moved.

He'd taken the right-hand door off the aircraft and belted himself into the passenger's side, leaning out the open space with the shotgun in his hands. A half a dozen magnum shells were stuffed into the zippered pocket of his flight suit. The infrared monitor was sensitive enough, on this cold evening, to light up everything from a newborn fawn to the steaming droppings of moose.

He hoped they would trap the lion within the grid, and when they saw it bounding across the terrain, he would direct the helicopter in low, running on top of it, blinding it with the Night Sun until he could empty both chambers into the beast at point-blank range.

When fuel was running low and they had canvassed a ten-mile radius, big enough to cover the distance a large cat could travel in an hour, they had found no traces of the beast. Maybe, he thought in some primitive way, even if he didn't find the lion, the noise of the helicopter would give it a message that violent machinery protected his property. He didn't know what else to do.

In the end, when they finally put the helicopter down next to his house, he realized he had wasted two hours of jet fuel and the pilot's time on a desperate hunt without success. Maybe Lassiter would have more luck in the morning. He thanked the crew, watched the helicopter lift off, and turned to go into his home.

His housekeeper had come over as soon as he called. He found Dolores with Ashley, watching television. Tobey was tucked into the foot of the sofa. Neither looked any the worse for wear. In fact, Ashley seemed to be holding up a lot better than he. Hayden escorted Dolores out to her car and came back through the front door. He was still carrying the gun.

Unloading the weapon, he placed the shells in a desk drawer and rested the shotgun along one wall. In the past, he hadn't kept guns visible around the house. Now, times were different. If the lion came back, there would be no scramble for arms. He would be prepared.

He led Ashley and Tobey upstairs. He felt terribly vulnerable. For the first time since he'd come to Montana, he wondered if he should go back to the city, pull up stakes, and settle somewhere in a community with nice safe parks, a good school system, and a police force that at least managed human beings a lot better than he was doing with the lion.

They slept together in Hayden's bedroom that night, Tobey on top of the blankets between his legs, and Ashley tucked under his arm. Before he drifted off to sleep, he thought of the woman named

Raven Crow. She had predicted no "Anglo" was going to kill this lion. She had said even his daughter was not safe. Well, sure as hell, she was right.

She said there was only one person who could hunt this lion. What the hell was she talking about? Was there something there? Or was this the strange ramblings of a half-crazed woman who spoke in riddles and befriended birds? So far, Hayden reflected, the sum of his efforts wasn't worth a damn.

37

THEY WERE TEN MILES OUTSIDE ELKHORN, walking across a vacant field. Ahead was a small church, surrounded by several piles of rubble. As they moved toward the building, Robert Wolfson studied the older man. Black Kettle was the elected chief of the tribe. He'd been raised on the reservation and then gone away to school. He was in his fifties, a handsome man with dark features. His voice was deep, and he moved with a certain dignity and grace. This morning, he was dressed in jeans and a leather vest. He insisted Wolfson come. Before Wolfson returned to Chicago, there were things he wanted to say.

"Your father and I were schoolmates together," Black Kettle said. "Your dad was full of life and mischief. He was one of my best friends. We were both altar boys here."

Black Kettle pushed at the front door of the old church. The wood gave away with a resounding squeak. Inside were a dozen pews and a small altar. Some of the side windows were boarded up. Behind the altar rose a set of stained-glass windows depicting the Crucifixion. Scattered cobwebs hung along the ceiling. A small steeple adorned the roof.

"The church is all that's left," Black Kettle said. "The school was torn down after you left the reservation."

They walked slowly toward the altar, their footsteps echoing off the walls. The building didn't look as if it had been used in years.

"One morning, I remember your father put a couple of frogs in the baptismal water." Black Kettle chuckled. "The priest was performing a baptism. When he dipped into the water, he almost fainted. The mother shrieked. Everyone was madder than hell. They never found out who did it. Martin and I laughed about it for years."

Wolfson smiled. They turned and started out of the church.

"I was always fond of your mother," Black Kettle said. "Half the men in the tribe were in love with her. She was the most beautiful girl on the reservation. When Martin took her as his wife, we were all secretly jealous."

Wolfson nodded. He couldn't remember much of those early years, but he appreciated Black Kettle's narrative.

"When your mother died, it broke Martin's heart. We were all so shocked. To this day, I'm not sure exactly what happened. I was back in New York, working on my thesis, when she passed away. Martin was in Washington. They said she bled to death, but it was totally unexpected. She was alive and healthy one day, and the next, she was gone. When she died, I could sense some spark of Martin's gone. He was never the same afterward."

"Most of the memories of my parents are lost in a lot of hurt and pain," Wolfson said. "I remember much more about my grandfather than I do my father."

"Your grandfather did a great job bringing you up. George Two Feathers was always one who loved nature, who knew the ways of the deer and the owl and the fox. Your father was more for making change. He wanted to help the future of the tribe through the political process. Those were things that were most important to him."

They left the old church and drove ten miles north, past pastures of rolling prairie, and then turned off the highway and followed a dirt road through a set of barbed wire fences. Wolfson stepped out to open each gate and waited for Black Kettle to drive through.

Ahead, the country spread out in a flat plateau. Black Kettle stopped his truck and stepped out. Wolfson followed. They walked over to a series of cliffs. The precipice fell to a river two hundred feet below. At the bottom of the cliffs were several plots of land marked by grids of string. A half a dozen workers excavated through the layers, searching for artifacts and bones.

"These cliffs were used as a buffalo jump," Black Kettle said. "They'd run the animals over the edge and then harvest the meat and skins. The university sent some men down last year, and now they've turned it into an archaeological dig. I'm told the finds go back a thousand years."

Black Kettle sat down on a rock. He motioned for Wolfson to join him. A flock of swallows darted along the cliffs.

"Our people have been here a long time, Bobby," Black Kettle continued. "Much longer than most historians have written."

A hawk drifted along the river. It shrieked once. Far in the distance rose an answering call.

"After four years at New York University and a graduate degree at Columbia, there are still a lot of things I don't understand about the old times. There were people, medicine men, old squaws, with special powers that we have no explanation for. People are saying this lion has come back for a reason, and that a Blackfoot is the only one who can kill it. Does that make sense?"

He shook his head. "Not everything in life makes sense. Your father tattooed you with a lion's paw in remembrance of times past. He had great aspirations for you, Bobby. I think if you were to follow his footsteps someday, take up the torch where he left off, that would be a good thing. I can't tell you what to do. I just thought these were things you should know . . ."

Black Kettle put his arm around Wolfson and squeezed him affectionately. It was a tender gesture, something a father would do to a son. The two started back for Black Kettle's truck.

As they reached the vehicle, Black Kettle pulled out an object wrapped in a blanket from the back seat. "I brought this for you," he said. Carefully unwrapping the blanket, Black Kettle uncovered a bow. The wood was a deep mahogany, the surface honed and smooth. The weapon measured six feet from tip to tip. He handed the bow to Wolfson.

"Look at the strength of it, Bobby."

Wolfson turned it over in his hands, feeling the solidity of the wood. The bows he remembered were more like his grandfather kept—shorter, more flexible bows used for hunting buffalo from horseback. This was a magnificent long bow.

Black Kettle pulled an arrow from the blanket. The arrow was a half inch in diameter and four feet long, the flint point solidly fixed with finely wrapped cord. The shaft looked as if it had been honed with a lathe.

Black Kettle took the bow and strung the arrow. "If you'll permit me," he said. With a lift of his massive shoulders, he pulled the bow and aimed at a tree fifty yards away. There was a sharp twang of string. The arrow streaked forward like a rocket, striking the midsection of the tree, burying its head with a dull thud. There was no vibration of feathers. The shaft stuck there as if it had been driven by an ax.

"Where did you learn to shoot like that?" Wolfson asked with amazement.

"The bow was found in a Blackfoot burial site," Black Kettle said. "It was given to your father. I thought you might like it before you leave."

Wolfson took the weapon, marveling at its power. There was much to think about, he reflected. His father had had great aspirations for him, Black Kettle said. Leaving the reservation was no longer as easy as he thought.

38

THE HELICOPTER ROSE IN A CLOUD OF DUST, lifting off the driveway, accelerating to the east. Below, parked along a loop of road next to the corral of Hayden's ranch, were a dozen vehicles. Howard Lassiter watched the aircraft disappear and then rode up to his trailer and dismounted. His three dogs were milling about, whining. Hayden approached as Lassiter leashed the dogs to his truck.

"Any luck?"

The hunter shook his head. "Tracks down there by the creek. Looks as if he was stalking something parallel to the road. If I had to guess, I suspect he might have been following your daughter."

"The big male?"

"Too big to be anything else."

"I sent the deputies out for one more search this morning. So far, they haven't found a thing."

"Didn't think they would. Helicopter's all right for polar bears. Not much good for cougars. The terrain is too rough, and they can hide too easily."

"Where do you suppose he went?"

"I thought for a while we were on a fresh scent, but we lost it in the forest. Probably scared him off. Too much activity. Too much noise."

"I got a little carried away," Hayden said.

"You did what you had to do. If it was my daughter, I would have done the same. Let me handle the tracking and searching from now on, OK? You guys may be great at finding missing persons, but it's not going to work with a big cat. They're too slippery to catch in the open."

"So, where do we go from here?"

"I think we keep searching the high roads and timber trails. He's got to be holing up around here, somewhere. I've got my scouts."

"Thanks for coming," Hayden said.

"Glad to help." Lassiter turned to lead his horse into the trailer. "Looks like your daughter's going to be famous."

He nodded toward the tool shed where Kimberly Benson and Eric Stafford were about to tape an interview. Ashley was speaking to the television reporter. Tobey was in her arms. Kimberly began fussing with Ashley's hair, combing it back, and then took a makeup brush and touched up Ashley's cheeks. Ashley was smiling and laughing, her eyes wide and excited.

Hayden watched his daughter with amusement. Ashley gabbed away about the lion as if she were describing a stroll in the park. When they started filming, she seemed to have no fear of the camera. Kimberly hugged her when she finished.

"Ashley, you're fantastic!" the reporter exclaimed.

Hayden turned to Lassiter. "You got time for lunch?"

"I can always use something to eat," Lassiter grunted. "Let me get the horse watered, and I'll join you."

Inside the house, Dolores stood at the kitchen counter, preparing sandwiches. Lassiter lounged in a corner, speaking with one of the deputies. Eric Stafford sat on a chair, adjusting the battery of his video camera. Two of the neighbors were across the room chatting. Hayden pushed in next to his daughter, watching the veterinarian listen to Tobey's lungs. The little dog stood on top of the butcher-block table, waiting patiently, while the vet finished his exam.

"I don't see any serious damage," he said. "Ribs are intact, the heart and lungs clear. The nose cuts look pretty superficial. I don't think they need sutures. Maybe a little Neosporin. Pretty close call, eh, Tobey?"

He patted the dog affectionately and lowered him to the floor. Putting his stethoscope in a black bag, he closed the lid.

"Send me a bill, John," Hayden said.

"There's no charge," the vet replied. "I'll get it back on your horses."

The telephone rang. Ashley ran and answered. She listened for a moment and then turned toward her father.

"It's the *Denver Times*. They want to do a story."

"Tell them we'll call back," Hayden replied.

"Sam, I would just like to do one more sequence, if I might," Kimberly said.

The telephone rang again. This time, Hayden answered. He listened for a moment and then placed his hand over the receiver. "It's the *Salt Lake City Tribune*."

He turned to Kimberly. "They want to do an exclusive story with the photographs. What should I tell them?"

"I think you should sell it," she said.

"I don't know what to even ask."

"Let me talk with them."

Kimberly took the telephone. "Hello, this is Kimberly Benson . . . Yes, we can do that for you. You want exclusive rights to the story? Well, understand the television rights are taken, but if you want to do something in print, I'm sure we can arrange it . . . Sure, I think $10,000 sounds right . . . Yes, a cashier's check would be fine . . . Of course, talk with your editors. You call us when you've made a decision. Please understand the price may go up. We're getting a lot of offers."

They only needed one more sequence. During an interlude between phone calls, Kimberly motioned for her photographer to come into the living room. Here, on the coffee table, stood a pile of five-by-seven prints taken with Ashley's disposable camera. Most showed Ashley's baseball team in various poses. There was a shot of the three girls with their bicycles taken by the coach, a shot of Ashley running down first base snapped by one of the parents, and a number of teammates Ashley had photographed after practice. Two pictures were of horses. The most striking images were of the lion.

The first photo was taken when Ashley tripped and fell. Everything looked askew. You could see the night sky, the top of the barn, and a thick tan-colored leg that looked the size of a tree. Little else was recognizable.

The second snapshot showed the lion up close, ears back, lips pulled in a snarl. The third image was a close-up of the lion's head, mouth open, teeth bared. One front tooth was slightly shorter than the other, as if it might have been chipped. You could see a set of whiskers and the black, cavernous yaw of the lion's mouth and the huge canine fangs, white and blurred in the action of biting.

"Let's try a close-up of this image," Kimberly told her photographer. "Move in tight on the photo. Then pull back and show Ashley and the dog. Can you get it?"

The telephone rang. Hayden took the call and then put his hand over the receiver. "It's the *Los Angeles Times*."

39

Kimberly Benson orchestrated the sale of Ashley's photographs for $18,000 to Robert C. Babcock Associates, the parent company for a syndication of newspapers in the western United States. In an exclusive arrangement, Kimberly agreed to delay her videotape so that her report could run simultaneously with the first editions of the press. In Elkhorn, the photograph appeared on the front page of the *Rocky Mountain Times*. A close-up of the lion's mouth introduced the story with a large caption: "GIRL ESCAPES KILLER LION!"

A two-column article followed, including photographs of Ashley and Tobey, with a detailed account of how Ashley escaped the beast. A smaller photograph of Ashley and her two Little League teammates was inserted toward the bottom. The numbers on the uniforms were reversed.

Hayden came into the Aspen Café early that morning. He had just taken a seat when Alice Chapman brought a newspaper for him to see.

"Your daughter is famous," the waitress gushed. "Front page news. We have a celebrity in town!"

Hayden smiled and took his coffee.

"You should be very proud."

"I'm just glad she wasn't hurt." A note of deep concern touched his voice.

"How's she taking it? I mean with the scare and all? If it happened to me, I don't think I could sleep for a week."

"Surprisingly well. Much better than me," he answered.

"Well, you tell her I send my love. And if she gets in here one of these days, I want her autograph."

Hayden finished reading the article and folded the paper under his arm. As he stood to pay the bill, a strong hand grasped his shoulder. He turned to find the owner of the Diamond Creek Ranch standing next to him. Austin Smith was in his early sixties, a tall man with gray hair and broad shoulders. He ran a large cattle operation west of town.

"Great story on Ashley," the rancher said. "Any news on the lion?"

Hayden shook his head.

"One of my wranglers said Lassiter found some tracks this morning."

"I hadn't heard that," Hayden replied.

"Yeah, a couple of big prints above the ranch on one of the high passes. I'm told he may go up this afternoon."

"Let's wish him luck."

"Good to see you, Sergeant. And give that daughter of yours a hug."

AT NOON, KIMBERLY BENSON FOUND Howard Lassiter outside the sheriff's substation office. The hunter stood next to his horse, brushing the animal's flank. His three dogs were tied to the side of the truck. The trailer was hitched and ready to go.

Lassiter finished straightening the horse's mane and led it by a halter into the trailer. As he walked back to the rear gate, Kimberly approached.

"I hear you found fresh tracks," she said.

"Word certainly gets around." He eyed her cautiously.

"I would like to come with you."

"It is no place for a woman," the hunter said, shaking his head. "The terrain is rough, the going vigorous. I may be out three or four days. You would just be in the way."

"Why don't you let my cameraman and me come?" she countered. "We can stay at the camp. If it looks like we're getting in the way, I'll leave."

"I've got no tents for you, ma'am. No food. No water. No blankets, no sleeping bags. I can travel much better alone."

"We can supply our own tents. And, I'll bring the food."

"You've got no horses. How are you going to keep up?"

"We've found some horses. We can trailer them behind you."

"Can you ride?"

She avoided the answer. "I wouldn't go if we were going to be in the way."

"I would have to clear it with my boss." He frowned. "Frankly, I'm not too keen on the idea."

"Your boss thought it would be a good idea."

Lassiter stared at her with surprise. "Who the hell you been talking to?"

"The governor." She said simply. She paused to let the words sink in. "Remember, the first fatality of this lion was the daughter of a prominent San Francisco family. When I spoke with Governor Erickson this morning, I reminded him how important it would be to get you on film, how good it would look for the state to show that the department was doing something for the community here. The governor strongly endorsed the idea."

"God damn," Lassiter cursed. "You're not here by two, I'm leaving without you."

SAM HAYDEN DROVE INTO THE STATION PARKING LOT. He nodded to Kimberly Benson as she stepped into her car, then noticed Lassiter standing next to his trailer, feeding the dogs.

"I've been looking for you, Sergeant," Lassiter said.

"I heard you found some tracks."

"Man, word gets around."

"I ran into Austin Smith from Diamond Creek this morning."

"Yeah, well, I wanted to tell you we're going to set up a campsite this evening."

"I thought you'd already gone."

"A little delayed," Lassiter said with frustration. "I got roped into taking Kimberly Benson and her cameraman."

"Interesting," Hayden replied.

"Don't ask me how, but I think she's gone somewhere and gotten some horses and a trailer. The goddamned stupid thing is she talked to the governor this morning. She got the whole thing cleared before I even knew."

"What are you going to do?"

"I don't even know if she can ride, dammit."

"Well, I hate to tell you where she got the horses."

"You're kidding!"

Hayden shook his head. "After she helped sell Ashley's photographs, I asked her what I could do in return. She wanted to use my horses. I didn't see how I could refuse."

Lassiter whistled softly. "You, of all people."

Hayden sighed. "She didn't actually indicate where she wanted to go. I just thought she just wanted to take Ashley for a ride."

"Yeah, well, maybe if I'm lucky, she won't show."

"Why don't I go up there with you?" Hayden said. "I know the country well. Let Miss Benson and her cameraman tag along. I'll help you set up camp. If they're totally useless, you're going to need some help putting up the tents and securing firewood, anyway. Maybe if I'm there, she won't be so much in the way."

"Well, I'm not running any dude ranch, I tell you. And so help me, God, if she or her cameraman gets in my way, I'm going to shoot them both."

"Understood," Hayden said.

"You find this pretty amusing, don't you?"

"Nah, just glad I'm not the only one in life who's got to answer to higher authority. It'll work out. I've got great faith in you."

"How the hell can I do my work when I got a camera shoved up my ass?" Lassiter fumed.

"I don't know," Hayden chuckled. "Maybe they'll like the view."

40

THE CAMPSITE STOOD NEXT to a logging road along the crest of a mountain pass. Looking west, you could see the tiny town of Elkhorn, nestled in a broad valley. To the east was Diamond Creek Ranch. At the end of the road rose a deserted fire lookout. Further still were the Great Bear Mountains, marked by a series of rugged peaks.

They came in three vehicles. Hayden helped Kimberly Benson rig his trailer and load the horses. To Lassiter's chagrin, they arrived promptly at two. The group left Elkhorn in a small convoy with Hayden's Bronco in the lead. The vehicles followed the highway north until they reached the entrance to Diamond Creek. Five miles later, the group drove up a winding loggers' road. At the crest of the ridge, they pitched camp.

The tracks Lassiter pursued came across this narrow pass. To the hunter, it looked like the lion might be using this corridor to descend on its nightly forays. If they were lucky, he thought, they might be able to catch the lion early in the morning, coming back into the mountains.

Lassiter wanted a campsite at least a mile from the site of the tracks. No sense parking right on top of the animal, he said. From his perspective, their location near the fire lookout was perfect.

Hayden helped pitch tents, while Stafford scurried around for firewood. Kimberly assisted with the dining table and helped prepare dinner. By seven o'clock, a large fire burned in the center of camp. Lassiter excused himself for a half hour and rode down the mountain by himself. He left the dogs chained to a tree.

The hunter returned at sunset. He tethered his horse to a large pine and strolled into camp. The tents were pitched, the fire warm and crackling. A small table was covered with a sheet. Kimberly Benson came over and offered Lassiter some food.

"Smells good. You cook?" The hunter pulled a fallen log next to the fire and sat down.

"I thought I'd do my share," she answered. "My mother ran a catering service for a while. I used to help her when I was in high school."

"Maybe you'll be some use after all," the hunter grunted.

Stafford sat down next to him. Hayden came over to the fire. Here he helped himself to dinner and then rested back on a canvas chair. They ate for a few moments in silence.

"Well, I've got good news," Lassiter said. "I found a lot of tracks. Very big cat. It's the one we're searching for."

The dogs stood up and began whimpering, pulling at their chains.

"Easy, boys," Lassiter called. "We'll go after him in the morning."

The hunter continued eating, speaking between bites. "Ringo would follow a lion all night if he had to. But I don't want him getting hurt. Sometimes, if you got a lot of dogs, on some of these paid trips, you know, where the guy pays ten thousand dollars to kill a lion, they'll send the dogs out at night, and they'll tree a lion and keep him up the tree for several days. The hunter calls his client in New York. Says he's got a lion. The client takes the first plane out, flies into Billings, drives out to the ranch, and shoots the lion in the tree."

"Sounds like great sport," Hayden said.

"Some call it that," the hunter scowled.

"And when do they become man-eaters?" Kimberly asked.

"The history on African lions and Indian tigers shows some very famous cats get a particular liking for human flesh and have a tendency to repeat. Humans are really pretty simple to take, and some of the well-known man-eaters have eaten hundreds. There was a cat called the Tiger Empress in India. Killed over four hundred people. Used to feed on a native a week."

"Delightful." Stafford shivered.

"Got so bad with the tigers in Indonesia that they discovered the best protection for workers in the rice fields was to put a mask on their head with eyes facing backwards. For some reason, many of the big cats need someone looking away or bending over. They use stealth and ambush techniques, and their natural tendency is to attack if they think their prey has not seen them. When a man bends down in a rice paddy, his back turned and head down, the tigers see him as prey. Once he puts on a mask with two large eyes painted on the back, the tigers don't attack. A cat will not stalk something it thinks is watching."

"You bring any masks?" Hayden laughed.

Lassiter chuckled. "The biggest purchasers of Donald Duck masks in India are the rice field workers. For a couple of bucks, you get a surefire tiger repellent."

"And where does this lion fit in?" Kimberly asked.

Lassiter poked at the fire. "Lot of things about this lion don't make sense. It's almost as if it's a throwback to the old days. Centuries back. Like it's come out of a time warp. Mountain lions rarely haul prey into a tree. Leopards do that.

"I think back, maybe a thousand years ago, when the lions were out on the plains, maybe they would carry their kills up into a tree to keep their food away from other predators. Cougars don't have to do that anymore 'cause there're not many wolves. And the size of this animal? It's like some freak of nature. Like some genetic variant that crops up every thousand years. But tomorrow, we get him treed, I'm not going to be asking any questions. After he's dead and skinned, I figure we can do all the measurements we want."

Down by the trucks, one of the horses snorted.

209

"Better see what that's all about." Lassiter stood up and tossed the remainder of his coffee into the fire. A column of steam rose with a sharp hiss.

"Yeah, I've got to head back," Hayden added. "I promised Ashley I'd be home before bedtime. Good luck tomorrow."

Hayden moved forward and shook Stafford's hand and clenched Kimberly's shoulder. "And good luck with your filming."

"Thank you for the help," Kimberly replied with a grateful glance.

She watched the two drift off into the darkness and turned toward Eric Stafford. "How you doing?" she asked.

"If you want the truth about the matter. I'm scared absolutely shitless." the photographer said.

FAR PAST MIDNIGHT, A PACK OF COYOTES started a high-pitched, strident yelp. The dogs in camp began to answer. One of the horses whinnied and shuffled on its feet. Eric Stafford lay on a small cot in his tent, wide awake, shivering in the cold. For more than an hour, he had been listening to Lassiter snoring softly. The fire had practically gone out, and the canvas walls of Stafford's tent were faintly illuminated by the coals. Kimberly slept along the opposite side of camp. Occasionally, she turned in her cot, but for the most part, she seemed quiet.

Stafford thought for a while about his wife and his two-year-old son and how much he missed them. Then the coyotes started yipping again, and Stafford thought about the lion. Ever since they had come to Montana, it seemed Kimberly had been pushing things to the brink of recklessness. He wasn't sure how much Kimberly knew about horses. What he did know was that he had absolutely no knowledge of riding, and he felt they had no business trying to chase the lion. Their presence had all the makings of a disaster.

So, they were going on a lion hunt in the morning. He had a growing suspicion this was going to be a far more difficult hunt than anyone expected. When Lassiter saw the photographer couldn't ride, maybe the hunter would make him stay in camp. And that would be just fine. A thousand yards and a 1600 mm telephoto lens were about as close as Stafford wanted to get to any lion. Especially one that seemed to have a fondness for killing people.

When the coyotes started their high-pitched chorus at five in the morning, he was still awake, tossing on his cot. Despite the cold, he worked up his courage and went outside to urinate. The coals in the fire were down. The faintest pink rose along the eastern horizon.

The dogs stood up and sniffed silently as he passed. He returned and rolled back into his blankets, shivering. When he finally fell asleep, he had a nightmare that a bear was chasing him and he couldn't get away.

Stafford woke with a start. A shadow played across the tent. He stared at the shape with a surge of panic. Something was shuffling at the flaps of his tent.

Lassiter's head poked through.

"Time to get up," the hunter boomed. "We've got to be going soon."

41

THEY BROKE CAMP AT DAWN. After breakfast, Lassiter saddled his horse and waited for Kimberly and Stafford to join him. Stafford stood back, fumbling with his camera gear. He didn't know the first thing about cinching a saddle. Kimberly made some motions with her horse but clearly was doing something wrong. She had ridden a few times as a young girl, but it had been a long time, and the western tack was unfamiliar.

"Damn, how in the hell did I ever agree to this?" Lassiter muttered. He walked over to Kimberly's horse and helped her with the bridle. "You got it all backwards." He finished helping Kimberly and turned toward Stafford.

"You need help, too?"

"Yes, sir, please," Stafford answered, respectfully.

There was no sense in false pretenses. Stafford tried to smile, but Lassiter just shook his head and cursed. The hunter led the horse over to a stump so Stafford could climb on.

"Mount on the left side," he commanded. "Use the stump as a foot lift."

The photographer struggled onto the horse and Lassiter handed him the camera.

"Look, if things get tight, I can't wait for you," he said. "I'll help you the best I can, but if the dogs get after the lion, I may have to leave you two behind. If you lose me, try to make your way to this access road. If we're down in the valley, just remember to go uphill until you find the road. If you follow the road, you'll be able to find camp."

He looked angrily at the two of them, studying their faces. "Whatever you do, don't panic," he said harshly. "And for Christ's sake, keep out of my way."

Lassiter took his three dogs by a long leash and mounted up and rode his horse across the logging road. Kimberly and Stafford followed. The start was easier than Kimberly was expecting. Hayden's horses seemed well trained, and they moved at a steady walk, single file.

Lassiter led them along a game trail, gradually working his way downward until he crossed a broad meadow. Kimberly and Stafford followed close behind. At a small river, the hunter got off his horse and walked slowly back and forth along a sand bar, searching for tracks. At a curve in the stream, he whistled for them to come.

"You won't find a bigger set of prints," he said.

Kimberly dismounted and asked Stafford to take a video of her hand spread out next to the lion's print. "How fresh are they?"

"Couple of hours," Lassiter replied.

The dogs began whining and straining at their leashes. Ringo lunged forward, barking excitedly. Lassiter crouched down and unleashed the dogs.

"All right, boys, go find him," he urged.

There was a flurry of activity as the dogs dashed here and there, running into the brush and then returning. Suddenly, Ringo gave a yip. The other two bolted after him.

"Let's go where we can watch," Lassiter said. "I usually prefer to be above the dogs when we're on horseback. Mostly, the lion will run upward if it's chased, and that will shorten our ride."

Lassiter helped Kimberly mount and then swung into his saddle. With a cluck, he urged his horse into trot. Stafford followed close behind. The trotting was especially difficult for the photographer, and he found that he was constantly holding onto the saddle horn. They passed through a thick forest of spruce and then moved upward toward a second meadow.

From the distance came an occasional yelp, but there was no excited bawling of dogs on fresh scent. Even going slowly, the riding became vigorous. On one occasion, Lassiter led them through a thick forest and up a steep embankment. By now, both Kimberly and Stafford showed signs of fatigue. The heavyset cameraman was sweating profusely, and Kimberly had difficulty catching her breath.

They waited in a small meadow, listening carefully.

Lassiter raised his hand. "I think they're beginning to circle toward us."

"Maybe if we wait here, they'll come back," Stafford said hopefully.

Below their position, the cameraman studied the valley floor. At the bottom of the depression ran a small creek, coursing through a cluster of trees. Here grew aspen and cottonwood. Along the opposite side of the valley spread thick tongues of fir. Although Stafford could not see the dogs, the sound of the animals carried well, and their occasional yelp and barks marked their positions as they ran. Stafford took the camera off his shoulder and shot some footage of Lassiter sitting on his horse. Abruptly, the voices of the hounds changed. The dogs began to chip and bawl in a high-pitched, excited fashion.

"There on!" Lassiter cried.

There came a rising chorus of howls as the sound of the chase advanced, steadily approaching. The noise of the dogs now changed to high-pitched, frenzied barking.

"He's making a stand," Lassiter yelled. He started in the direction of the hounds. "Either follow me or stay," he shouted after them. "I've got to get down there. If you stay, I'll come back for you later."

Spurring his horse, Lassiter crashed downhill, galloping through the brush.

"I say we wait," Stafford said, but his horse took off, following Lassiter's lead. The photographer jerked forward. He held onto the saddle with one hand, barely escaping a fall.

"Oh, man!" he cried. "Kimberly, are you there?"

He saw to his surprise she was right behind.

The horses flew at a gallop, following Lassiter through the forest. Sprinting down a narrow trail, they crossed a small stream. Stafford tried to slow his horse, but the mount ignored him.

At an open space, Kimberly's horse darted in front. Stafford hung onto his camera with one hand, ducking and bobbing to avoid low-hanging branches. The cameraman saw the jump too late. A fallen spruce blocked their path. The log crossed two feet above the trail, and Lassiter's horse jumped it with ease. Stafford had little time to prepare. He saw Kimberly's horse vault over the trunk; then his chest struck a low-hanging limb. Falling backwards, he tumbled off his horse. He landing in a heap on the trail. Here he lay, stunned, gasping for breath.

Kimberly kept up with Lassiter until they came to an open stream. Lassiter charged across the water and disappeared into the brush, still hot on the heels of his dogs. Kimberly's horse lost its footing and lurched sideways.

She used both hands, trying desperately to grab the saddle horn, but her forward momentum was too much. She flew over the neck of the horse, landing with a splash in the water.

Kimberly pulled herself out, feeling stupid and embarrassed. Gamely, she tried to wipe the mud off her face and then scrambled out of the water to dry ground. Her horse had not gone far. With a little effort she was able to grab the horses reins and lead it back along the trail.

She could hear the dogs braying in the distance. She yelled for Stafford but had no response. Had he fallen? She had lost sight of him after her horse jumped the log. She wondered if she waited, maybe the hunter would come back for her. Then she remembered Lassiter said he would not stop. If the dogs were after the lion, he would be going on. When it came to a choice between humans or dogs, Lassiter made it clear which side he would take.

She started back along the trail, leading her horse on foot, hoping to retrace the prints of the horses in the direction they had come. Every few yards she stopped and yelled for Stafford.

The photographer came limping out of the forest, holding his back.

They walked to a small clearing and sat down. "You don't look so good, Eric," she said.

"Took a little fall," he answered. "At least I can walk."

He paused. "You don't look so good yourself."

Kimberly's clothes were covered in mud. She raised a hand to her forehead and wiped away the debris.

Stafford began to smirk. "What if the station could see you, now?"

They both started to laugh.

"Worst, most stupid decision I've ever made. I could have gotten us killed."

"Always a pleasure to work with you." The photographer bowed.

She stood up. "Let's get your horse and see if we can make it back to camp."

The distant sound of a rifle rolled through the valley and echoed off the hills. The two stopped and stared at each other.

"He's got him!" Stafford cried. "Lassiter's got the lion!"

42

THE GYMNASIUM DOOR WAS JAMMED. Wolfson tried to open it and then yanked more forcefully. On the third try, he was able to wedge the door open enough to slip his body through. It didn't look like anyone had used the entrance in weeks.

Entering a broad, dark hallway, he groped along the interior until he found a light switch. A trophy case occupied the central wall. He stared through the glass at the assortment of trophies. Standing in a prominent position along the center of the case was a huge trophy from his senior year in high school. The plaque read: "Class AA State Championship, Blackfoot Indian Reservation, Elkhorn, Montana." Next to the trophy was a team photo. He squinted, trying to see the players better and then nodded as he recognized his picture. Man, did he look different then.

The case contained another half dozen trophies and several framed photographs of winning teams dating back to the 1940s. Some of the teams had players he remembered. Young men from the reservation had a talent for basketball, and one, Jon Winterstorm, had played professional ball for the Celtics. Missing, however, were trophies from current teams. The most recent championship was over ten years old.

As he moved along the display, studying the pictures, the noise of a basketball started inside the gym. He was surprised anyone was playing. Walking down the corridor, he entered the main gymnasium through a set of levered doors. Two youths were shooting baskets at the opposite end of the court.

The lighting in the gymnasium was poor. Two of the overhead floods were out, another blinked erratically. In places the wooden floor had become buckled and warped. Several windows were cracked.

Wolfson walked down the court and took a seat in one of the bleachers, watching the boys play. The two looked to be twelve or thirteen. One wore a pair of blue sweats, the other, a Chicago Bulls T-shirt. The boy in sweats had a good shot and was consistently making baskets. Wolfson waited for a few minutes and then walked onto the court.

"Hi guys. How'd you get in?"

"Back door," one answered. "It's easier than coming through the front."

"Do you play for a team?"

"Naw, we just like to hack around."

"What grade are you?"

"Seventh."

"You guys look like you're good players. Is there no league?"

The youth with the Bulls T-shirt shook his head. "There's a league, but there was no coach last year, and this year, only four of us wanted to play, so there weren't enough players for a team."

The boy introduced himself as Jimmy, the other as Paul.

"And who are you?" Jimmy asked.

Wolfson started to use his formal Anglo name and then changed his mind. "Bobby Running Wolf," he answered.

"I've heard of you," Paul said. "You played on one of the great teams here, didn't you?"

"Long time ago," Wolfson said with a nod.

"Well, nice to meet you." The boy came forward and shook Wolfson's hand and dribbled back to the basket and took a shot. The ball banged off the rim.

"Mind if I give you a pointer?"

"Sure," the boy answered.

"Try to use more leg in your shots. The spring of your knees will give the ball an extra lift. Don't shoot only with your arms. Especially as a game goes on and you begin to tire, you won't be able to carry your shots consistently with just your hands. Know what I mean?"

The boy tried bending his knees. His first shot was a little to the right.

"Not bad. Try again."

The second shot hit the backboard and rimmed out of the basket. The boy's third shot sailed through the net.

"You got it!" Wolfson exclaimed.

The other boy looked at him. "It would be nice if you could help us from time to time."

"Wish I could," Wolfson answered. "I live a long way off."

"Your father was George Two Feathers, right?"

"He was my grandfather," Wolfson answered with surprise. "Did you know him?"

He was really good to us," the youth said. "He spent a lot of time with me and Paul showing us how to track and teaching us about the wilderness."

"I'm sorry that he died," the second added. "We really miss him."

"He was a good man," Wolfson said.

"Want to play with us?" Paul asked.

"No, I was just passing through."

They thanked him and returned to shooting baskets. As Wolfson walked to the front of the gymnasium, he thought about his grandfather. The breadth of the old man's teachings was amazing. Even recently, George Two Feathers had been working with the kids, sharing his wealth of knowledge about nature and the wilderness. Young boys needed someone like him, he reflected.

As he stepped out of the building, he heard the sound of a helicopter. The noise grew steadily louder. Abruptly, the aircraft soared overhead, roaring like a rocket. The blades made such a clatter that the gymnasium shook. Banking, the helicopter made a sharp turn and then swung rapidly back and landed in the parking lot.

Wolfson turned away from a violent rush of dust kicked up by the blades. His first reaction was anger. He wasn't sure who the hell it was. The blades were throwing a spray of pebbles that ricocheted off his sister's car. It must be one hell of an emergency, he thought.

A large sheriff's insignia was painted along the side of the aircraft. A man in a white helmet and blue flight suit opened the passenger door and jumped out, ducking beneath the blades.

The deputy ran toward him. As he reached Wolfson, he pulled off his helmet. He was breathing heavily. "You Wolfson? Robert Wolfson?"

Wolfson nodded with surprise.

"There's been trouble with the lion," the deputy exclaimed. "Sergeant Hayden needs you right away!"

43

ERIC STAFFORD LOOKED as if he had survived a war. The photographer's pants were ripped, his shirt was torn, and he walked with a limp. Following Lassiter's instructions, they were able to find the fire road and follow it up to camp. Kimberly changed clothes and combed her hair. A large bruise discolored her arm. Her face was covered with scratches.

By now it was nearly dusk. At the edge of camp, along the top of the fire ridge, they watched a search party move methodically along the valley floor. Kimberly rested on a canvas chair. A wave of worry crossed her face. Stafford had spread his video camera on a towel and was working on the sprocket mechanism. In the clearing where they had parked the trailers were three sheriffs' vehicles. Hayden's two horses were tethered a short distance away. The noise of a helicopter rose and fell, working its way through the valley.

"Got it!" Stafford tightened a screw, closed the camera lid, and pushed the record button. He held the camera to his ear. A look of satisfaction crossed his face.

"We're running. I don't know how long, but we're running."

"Do you think you lost any of this morning?"

"Nope. I think we're good."

"I just hope Lassiter is O.K.," Kimberly fretted. "I can't imagine something happening to him."

"Me, either." Stafford shook his head. "They'll find him. We heard the shot. He must have killed the lion. Maybe his horse spooked and he injured his leg."

"I feel so stupid, Eric. What if he got really hurt, and it was our fault?"

"You can't blame yourself, Kimberly. I don't think we slowed him down. Maybe if we got close to the lion and caused a problem, that would be different. Even if something happened, nobody's going to hold you responsible. Hell, during the chase, I never saw more than the butt of his horse."

He held the camera up and began panning across the campsite. "What I would like most right now is to see Lassiter coming into camp with that damn lion over his shoulder. That would be a good shot. A good ending to this day."

The noise of the helicopter rose a pitch, as if the blades were straining, pulling something heavy. The deep whoop-whoop increased in intensity, echoing off the mountain. Kimberly searched into the valley and watched the aircraft rise above the trees. It looked as if it was carrying something.

"They're coming!" She rose from her seat. As the aircraft drew nearer, she could see it was hauling a litter by a long line. Fifty or sixty feet below the helicopter hung a body-sized stretcher. Inside was the shape of a man.

"Eric, they got him!" she cried. "Look! They're bringing some-one up! It's got to be Lassiter. Thank God! He must be all right. Can you get this on film?"

Stafford nodded. The red light on his camera blinked. Squinting through the viewfinder, he swung his lens past the trees to the aircraft. The helicopter approached slowly, moving so as not to disturb the litter it was hauling.

A sheriff's Bronco suddenly roared around the corner. Hayden drove directly into the clearing, jammed on the brakes, and jumped out. A second sheriff's vehicle followed. Robert Wolfson leaped out of the passenger's side and joined him.

The helicopter carefully lowered the litter to the ground. Hayden and a deputy ran forward, released the cable, and waved the pilot off. A shower of debris blew through the clearing. Moving steadily, the helicopter rose upward and headed for an open spot along the road.

Kimberly hurried toward the clearing. Why was everyone moving so slowly? It looked as if things were happening in slow motion. If the hunter was badly injured, they ought to be hurrying. They should be bringing in first-aid supplies, calling the paramedics, preparing Lassiter for evacuation. Then, too, maybe he wasn't hurt badly. Maybe it was just a sprain. She hurried toward the stretcher to see if she could help.

As she broke into the clearing, Wolfson blocked her path.

"I think you'd better stay," he said.

"Why? Is it Lassiter? Did you find him?"

"I don't think you want to see."

"Why? Is he . . .?"

"He's dead," Wolfson answered flatly.

"Oh, God! Oh, no!" Kimberly gasped. A shudder ran through her body. Not Lassiter. Lassiter dead? How could it be? A thousand questions rushed through her mind. How did it happen? How could it happen? They had just been with him a few hours before. How had he been killed? Had he fallen off his horse? Where had he been found? In her shock, the only thing that came to mind were the hounds.

"And the dogs?" she asked in disbelief. "What happened to his dogs?"

"Dead," Wolfson said. "The lion has killed them all."

44

"Special Delivery. Priority First Class" read the label; the address: Station KPXL, San Francisco. Kimberly hand-carried the package to the Elkhorn airport at eleven in the morning. By noon the videotape was on a jet aircraft traveling west.

If the report had been created near San Francisco, Kimberly might have used a satellite or microwave mobile truck for the transmission. Here she had no such luxury. And the Internet in Elkhorn was much too unreliable for her to trust.

At 4:30 that afternoon, Jeremy Wong, the station's lead engineer, received the report. He viewed the narrative on a small monitor adjacent to the main programming console. Wong called two of his associates. The three watched the video together.

Kimberly's report ran less than three minutes, unedited. A little cutting here and there, and they could condense the story to 120 seconds, the two-minute target for special features. Their decision was unanimous. The story should run at the top of the news.

Wong hurried to the office of Patrick Noonan, chief programmer for the station. Noonan did not need the station manager's permission to alter the evening news. At first, he was irritated by the interruption. After watching the tape, he realized the report was something special. He made the instant decision that Kimberly Benson's video would follow the national news, preceding weather and sports. An editing assistant was pulled off an assignment to tighten the sequence. In thirty minutes, the videotape was ready.

The segment aired in San Francisco at 6 p.m. By eight that evening, national networks had picked it up. By midnight, more than 47 million people had seen Kimberly Benson's report. Like it or not, the interest of a nation was becoming focused on the developing story of a mountain lion in Elkhorn, Montana.

The video began with a shot of Kimberly standing in front of a mountain valley. A pair of firs framed the scene. The reporter's face was covered with scratches. Although she had touched her cheeks with makeup, her hair appeared blown and matted. She wore no lipstick. There was a breathless urgency to her voice that seized the viewer and did not let go. The scene appeared harsh. She looked scared.

Viewers realized there was no way a reporter could fake this. The story was real news in the making. Her voice seemed throaty. Her hands, holding a page of notes, were trembling.

"The video tape you are about to see contains the last photographs of Howard Lassiter, remembered by many as one of the great players of the National Football League. Mr. Lassiter is a government trapper who works for the state of Montana. He left on horseback yesterday to the chorus of three hounds chasing a mountain lion."

The scene cut to a sequence showing Lassiter riding down into the valley. He was pushing his horse hard, and in the background you could hear the faint yelping of the dogs. As Kimberly's voice continued, the scene switched to a video of the helicopter bringing in the body, the litter dangling by a long line, swinging like a coffin towed at sea.

"Last evening, Mr. Lassiter's body was found, along with those of his three dogs, all killed by a mountain lion," Kimberly paused, trying to control the grief in her voice. "This brings the death toll to four individuals over the past two weeks, all thought to have been killed by a large male *Felis concolor*.

"State department officials indicate they will be sending more hunters to the area. Early this morning, in an unprecedented move, the governor of Montana called an emergency press conference."

The report zoomed to a close-up of Montana Governor Leonard Erickson. He stood behind a makeshift podium on the Elkhorn town square. Behind him rose the statue of Jeremiah Bates, Indian fighter and cavalryman. Attached to the wooden podium were a dozen microphones. The governor dressed in a coat and tie. His lips were pursed, the jaw muscles set. He looked disconcerted and angry. "I am announcing today that the state of Montana is offering a $100,000 reward to anyone who is responsible for tracking down and killing this lion. In addition, we are considering calling a state of emergency and sending troops from the National Guard."

"Townspeople feel this is too little, too late," Kimberly continued. "Many say they will not sleep well until this big man-killing cat is brought in. And now there is hope that a $100,000 reward will help where other measures have failed."

The sequence switched to stock film of a stalking mountain lion as Kimberly's voice carried over. This was the only segment the station had inserted. The editors had felt the footage would add to the story.

"It is unclear why this mountain lion has begun attacking humans. In several of the deaths, the bodies were not consumed. Perhaps it is the lion's response to being threatened or chased. Perhaps man has encroached too close upon its territory.

"In the evening before he was killed, Howard Lassiter said there is a fine line between a lion's perception of what is prey and what is not. And once it crosses that line, for some individual cats, there is no return . . ."

Stafford's camera zoomed to a close-up of Kimberly's face. Her voice rose, her message terse. "The Blackfoot Indians are calling this animal a 'spirit cat.' They say it is an ancestor of great lions that existed in these mountains centuries ago. They say it has come back for a reason. Some think it has returned to block a mining company from building a road across sacred Blackfoot lands. Others say it has returned to help tribal members elect a new chief. But exactly what the reason is, no one is willing to say . . ."

"Holy Christ! This is hot!" Alvin Kessler exclaimed after he reviewed the tape. "Do you think we need to send another crew?"

Noonan shook his head. "I think Kimberly's doing great. She's been there from the beginning. Let's let her follow it to the end. We need to express Stafford a backup camera, though. I'll send it in the morning."

"One hundred thousand dollars!" Kessler whistled. "That's a hell of a reward for one measly lion."

"I don't think we are talking about 'measly' here," Noonan said.

"The funny thing is . . ." he added with a wry smile. "I kind of find myself rooting for the lion."

Part IV

The Cry of Fang and Claw

"And so close did some of the people
Come to their feathered and furred friends
That in true brotherhood
They spoke a common tongue . . ."

(Luther Standing Bear, Sioux)

45

THE TEEPEE STOOD AT THE EDGE of a small stream, a quarter mile behind the housing settlement at Weasel Creek. There was no road, only a footpath that led from the end of the houses. The trail wandered across a broad meadow and then through a section of aspen and scattered fir. The dwelling was a traditional conical Plains Indian structure, its canvas weathered brown with age. The painted shapes of buffalo ran along the base. Two geometric patterns circled the top.

As Robert Wolfson approached the clearing, a wisp of smoke rose from a small fire. Next to the teepee were several wooden tripods used for drying meat.

"Hello!" he shouted. "Anyone here?"

No answer.

The fire burned brightly, the coals warm and glowing. A stick held by two rocks ran over the blaze, holding an iron pot. The liquid was boiling, the odor like an aromatic broth.

From out of the trees, a crow swooped overhead and lit on one of the poles at the top of the teepee. The bird called twice, arched its head, and peered downward at him.

"Where is Raven Crow?" Wolfson asked, as if expecting an answer. The crow shuffled, changing its position on the perch.

"Go on! Sha! Tell her she has a visitor."

The crow gave a croak and flew off, disappearing toward a section of forest that ran along the edges of the stream. In a few minutes, a figure emerged, walking slowly. A gray blanket covered her head. When she reached the teepee, she eyed Wolfson but said nothing.

Moving toward the fire, she held out a long stick. Here, speared like beans, was a string of objects. She bent over the kettle and took a second stick and scraped the wriggling forms into the boiling broth. Wolfson recoiled at the sight. The objects impaled by the stick were still alive. Steadily, she began to stir the boiling liquid with a wooden spoon.

"Tea?" she asked.

"No thanks." Wolfson tried to swallow. A surge of bile rose in the back of his throat. "What is that?"

"Grasshoppers. Grasshoppers, beetles, and grubs," she answered. "They're easier to catch in the morning. The cool air slows them down."

"You eat that stuff?" he asked with repulsion.

"Our people have been eating these for centuries."

A lark fluttered into camp and landed on a fallen log. Hopping next to her, the bird began chirping for attention. She spooned out one of the floating beetles and tossed it to the bird. The lark darted forward, grabbed the insect, and flew off. Raven Crow continued stirring the broth, crouching by the fire.

"The lion has killed again," she said.

"Yes. How did you know?"

She glanced up at him. "There are ways, old ways of our people, Bobby, that make us aware of such things. Your grandfather knew of such things. But you? You are covered with too many layers of civilization."

As she poked at the fire, he studied her face. Her eyes were black, her features tanned. Her hair, from what he could see beneath the blanket, was speckled with strands of gray. He judged she was in her early fifties. She looked as if she might have been quite beautiful once. He wondered where she had come from. Raven Crow was someone he had never heard of until he came back for his grandfather's funeral.

"The paw prints . . ." He spread his fingers. "They're bigger than a man's hand. The tracks showed the lion circled and came in behind the hunter. Followed him as a lion might have stalked a deer."

"This lion is from the old times, Bobby," she said.

"There is a $100,000 reward," he continued. "With this kind of money, there will be dozens of professional hunters coming into Elkhorn looking for the lion."

"And they can comb the mountains for a hundred years, and they will not find him," she answered.

"I don't think you understand," Wolfson said. "These hunters will have guns, and they're going to bring in a lot of dogs. Many lions will be killed in the process."

"So, you'd better end it, Bobby."

He crouched, poking a stick into the fire, and then stared upward at her.

"Why me?"

Raven Crow continued stirring the broth. For a long moment, she did not speak.

"Long before you were born," she started slowly. "Long before your father and your father's father, the Blackfoot were spread across the plains. There was no leadership, no unity amongst the tribes. There was a young brave who went out into the wilderness on a vision quest. He was caught by the Shoshone and terribly wounded. Somehow he managed to escape. In the forest, he encountered a huge lion. The lion shared his kills with the brave and gradually nourished him back to health. With time, he became a great chief . . ."

Wolfson nodded. The legend of Eyes-in-Shadows was a story passed down through generations of Blackfoot. It was the story etched on the back of the buffalo skin he'd found with his grandfather's belongings.

Raven Crow glanced over at him. "Now that your grandfather is gone, you are the last link with the past. There is no one left but you."

Wolfson stared at the fire, mulling over her words, trying to make sense of what she was saying.

"I am not a hunter," he answered. "And even if I wanted to kill this lion, what chance would I have? Where would I even start?"

"You will need to prepare. You will need strong medicine," she said. "Without this medicine, the lion will kill you, just as it has every other man who has pursued him. You will need to Sundance."

"Sundance?" A shudder worked through Wolfson's body. "It would be crazy."

Raven Crow glared at him. "You have been gone from your people for a long time. Your mind is covered with a thick bark of Anglo civilization. You live in the city. Every night you see, smell, and hear the sounds of man. You have been away too long."

She raised her arm, her fingers sweeping past the clearing and the forest, directing his gaze from the trees to the white-covered peaks beyond. An eagle soared above the forest, drifting along the upper current of air.

"Here you can smell the grass and the trees and the mountains." She paused. "Here the sounds of bird and animals and the wind speak to you. These are ancient rhythms of this world. I do not have to tell you such things."

Turning away, she began to stir the boiling kettle again. "What I have to say, you may not want to hear, Bobby. But these people need you. The tribe needs you to return, to set a course for the future. And to do this, you must face the lion."

Wolfson stared at her. "It makes no sense."

"Do you remember the sweat bath you took?"

He nodded.

"You saw the eyes of the lion in that sweat bath, Bobby. And you felt the spirit of the forest and the strength of the lion. Do you remember?"

234

Wolfson felt a shiver pass through his spine. It was exactly as she described. But how did she know what he'd seen in the sweat bath? He had told no one about his experience. Her revelation was beyond his comprehension.

He stared at her in disbelief. "Who the hell are you?"

"The sweat lodge was the beginning," Raven Crow answered. "The lion will be the end."

She took a spoonful of broth, smacking her lips.

"Here. Take some."

Shaking his head, Wolfson rose from his haunches to a standing position.

"Even if I wanted to," his voice raised, "there's a thousand miles of wilderness out there. I don't know how I could find the lion."

"For that, you don't have to worry," Raven Crow answered. "You go into the forest. *Omahkatayo* will find you . . ."

46

IT WAS NEARLY NOON BY THE TIME Hayden reached Helena for
the funeral of Howard Lassiter. Before he left for the state capitol,
he dressed in a freshly starched uniform and polished his shoes
until they shined. Lassiter was a good man, he thought, and he
wanted to pay his proper respects.

The church ceremony was small and intimate and in keeping
with what Lassiter would have wanted. The hunter had two children and an attractive wife. The Methodist pastor asked the age-
old question of why a fine man like Lassiter would be taken from
the world. Sometimes, the minister reflected, only God had the
answers.

A testimonial ceremony was held an hour later at the Russell
Center for the Performing Arts, a large auditorium with a seating
capacity of a thousand. Hayden sat in the balcony and listened in
amazement to people who had flown in from across the country to
give their fond remembrances of the man. There were ex–football
players, coaches, and college professors, plus coworkers from Fish
and Game.

The testimonies were intimate, often stirring—some humor-
ous, others sad. An ex-quarterback from the Denver Broncos
remembered Lassiter's capacity for eating following big games.
After a win against Dallas, Lassiter had gone to a restaurant where
seven main courses were offered. When the waiter asked what he

wanted, he ordered one of each. Lassiter was a man of extraordinary presence and immense appetites.

A friend from Fish and Game recalled how Lassiter had once stared down a grizzly. They had been working outside Glacier when the two men accidentally stumbled upon a sleeping bear. The grizzly leaped up and roared. It happened so quickly there was no time to bring out a gun. Lassiter faced it, eyeball-to-eyeball, and roared right back. The bear took one look and ran.

"He was the only animal that grizzly ever met that was equally as large and twice as mean," the speaker concluded. Everyone applauded.

The most moving testimony came from a young man who had worked with Lassiter in recent years and had had the privilege of going out with him on several hunts.

"I don't think he would have wanted it any other way . . ." the man said with choked emotion. "Outdoors, with his hounds, chasing an animal which he had the utmost respect for."

The ceremony ended with a church choir singing "Amazing Grace." At the conclusion of the piece, Hayden paid his respects to the family and told them how much he had enjoyed their last night together, having dinner before the campfire. Except for Kimberly Benson and the photographer, Eric Stafford, Hayden was the last person to see Lassiter alive.

Just before he left the auditorium, the administrator of Fish and Game drew Hayden aside. Dr. Will Taylor was a short gray-haired man with a friendly demeanor.

"Sergeant, it was nice of you to come. I know Lassiter enjoyed working with you."

"I thought it was the least I could do," Hayden replied.

Taylor lowered his voice so that others nearby could not hear. "Lassiter called about a television crew shortly before he started out. We encouraged him to take them along. The governor thought it might be a good idea, but I wonder now if Lassiter got into trouble looking out on their behalf."

"I don't think so," Hayden said with a shake of his head. "We went over the incident pretty carefully. Both members of the film crew were not with him at the end. He was following the lion by himself. The tracks seemed to indicate his horse threw him and ran."

Taylor eyed him closely. "What's your fix on this lion?"

"I'm not an animal expert," Hayden replied. "But I can tell you from all I've seen, this is not an ordinary animal in any sense of the word. It systematically took out all of Lassiter's dogs, one by one. It has been right in the middle of town. And it has now killed four people. It doesn't seem to act like mountain lions are supposed to act. And it doesn't have any fear of man."

"The governor wants this thing brought to an end. But I must say," Taylor added, "I wasn't pleased with the $100,000 reward. The governor may have acted too impulsively. I worried it might bring in a lot of yahoos out there trying to shoot up the countryside."

Hayden nodded. "And, I'm not sure how you're going to tell one cougar from the next. If somebody brings in a big cat, how are we going to know if it's the right one?"

"That part shouldn't be a problem," Taylor replied. "We'll send out a special team to do an autopsy. If it's attacked a human recently, usually DNA tracings in the tissue can be found on scrapings beneath the claws. Plus, the stomach and intestinal contents can be very revealing. Sometimes hair, sometimes body parts. You bring in the cat; we'll make sure it's the right one."

"You know my men will be at your disposal," Hayden answered.

"One other thing, Sergeant."

"Yeah, I'm listening."

"In the investigative report, there was information that Howard Lassiter had fired his rifle. Several witnesses confirmed they heard a shot."

"That's right."

"Do you suppose he wounded the lion?"

"Nope," Hayden answered. "I think he shot one of his wounded dogs."

"God Almighty, "Taylor muttered. "Well, if it's any consolation, the autopsy report on Lassiter showed he broke his neck from the fall. I don't think he would have ever walked again."

"Thanks." Hayden nodded grimly. "His death was a great loss."

As HE LEFT THE STATE CAPITOL AND BEGAN the long drive back to Elkhorn, Hayden had time to reflect upon the lion. So, what was different about this big cat they were dealing with? The footprints were huge, and the courage and fierceness of the beast exceeded anything he had ever heard about. Mountain lions were supposed to be timid creatures that were rarely seen and lived largely in isolation. And what was this concept of a "spirit cat," the Blackfoot were murmuring about?

He thought about his strange encounter with the woman named Raven Crow and her mention of Bobby Running Wolf. His housekeeper said she had known the Running Wolf family over the years. Hayden could make no connection there. Bobby Running Wolf, or Robert Wolfson, or whatever he wanted to call himself, was a single person. Even if he was of Blackfoot ancestry, it made no sense for Hayden to call off the search so Wolfson could hunt the lion. If anything, Hayden needed everyone he could get.

Hayden reached Elkhorn by five. When he pulled into the sheriff's station, the parking lot was full. Many cars he did not recognize. Two large trucks were parked next to the street with large antennae on their roofs. Both were painted with the insignias of television news stations. A general uneasiness tightened his stomach.

As he approached the entrance, he could hear a number of voices inside. Stepping through the doorway, he was suddenly blinded by a row of lights. A microphone was shoved in his face. A woman spoke with a Japanese accent. Hayden looked wildly around. The waiting room was packed with visitors. Reporters with television cameras and recorders rushed toward him.

"Sergeant, can you tell us about this lion? What steps are you taking to ensure the safety of the town? Have there been any new sightings?"

Hayden searched frantically for his secretary. "Mabel, what the hell is this?"

"Sam, I'm so sorry." Mabel appeared agitated and out of control. "They barged in here and have been waiting for hours. I couldn't get them to leave. At least the Italian film crew was nice enough to set up an appointment."

"Holy Jesus," Hayden muttered.

When he turned back, three microphones were thrust in his face. Too late, he realized they had already begun filming.

47

B Y EIGHT O'CLOCK THAT NIGHT, the tables at the Cattleman were full. A jukebox played softly in the background. Kimberly had wanted to do an interview in a better place than a western saloon, but given the available meeting sites, she had no other option. Certainly her motel was not an appropriate place. When Wolfson suggested this as a meeting spot, she was pleased he had given her time for an interview. She didn't want to be presumptuous. She could always try a casual meeting first. Once Wolfson was more comfortable, she could suggest a television interview later on.

So far, few of the Native Americans would speak about the lion. When she tried to ask around town about who was the best person to talk with, Wolfson's name kept coming up. It was only after they'd made it back to camp that she had learned Wolfson had been flown up to the mountains by Sergeant Hayden to track Lassiter down. It was he, she was told, who had found Lassiter's body and the dogs.

They sat in a rear booth of the saloon. Kimberly opened a small notepad and began making notes. At first, Wolfson seemed guarded, and his answers brief. As they spoke further, he started to relax. She began the interview trying to learn more about Wolfson, the man. The lion business was in the back of her mind, but it was not something she wanted to bring up at the start. Lassiter's death was still difficult for her to comprehend.

There was a side issue, too, that tugged uneasily at her mind. She liked the deep color of Wolfson's eyes and the sharp contours of his face. There was a gentle yet tremendous strength about the man that seemed to underlie his presence.

"I understand you're a teacher," she began.

"High school, American history, South Side Chicago." He watched her write down his comments on the pad. "I understand you are a television reporter."

She caught a faint twinkle to his eyes and wondered if he was truly as handsome as she imagined. She sensed there was a certain wildness about him. She wasn't sure if it was because she knew he was of Blackfoot ancestry, or if there was something foreboding about his features she couldn't understand. Although Wolfson seemed calm and collected, she sensed there were dark, turbulent aspects of his personality that were beyond her reach.

"People say that you are not part of the reservation anymore. That you rarely come back."

"Depends on who you're speaking with," Wolfson replied.

She smiled, trying to ease the tension. "I've been talking around. It's my job. I ask here and there, and people give me bits of information, and pretty soon I put the whole picture together."

"People say a lot of things," he answered carefully. "In all candor, maybe they're right. It's probably a valid criticism. I left the reservation to go to college when I was sixteen. I was the youngest in my class. As it turns out, I was one of the few to graduate from college. I think it was the influence of my grandfather. He mostly raised my sister and me after our father died. Grandfather was it, and we pretty much listened to his wisdom."

"What happened to your mother?"

"She died when I was eight. They said she had some type of internal hemorrhage. My dad was busy in politics at the time. He'd gone to Washington to speak with the Bureau of Indian Affairs. She died when he was gone. When he came back, he was never the same. He started drinking heavily and died in a car crash six months later. Even before his death, he was often gone. Mostly, day-to-day, we were raised by my grandfather. Thinking back, I don't think I would want it any other way."

She looked away, shyly, as his gaze met hers. "Do you think of yourself as Native American?"

"I'm aware of my heritage, if that's what you mean," he shrugged. "In Chicago, no one gives a damn. It's a great melting pot, and I'm just part of the brew."

"And how do you feel about what the government has done for the Indians?"

Wolfson's jaw tightened. "You should ask about what it hasn't done."

"I'm listening," she said.

He paused, mulling the question in his mind. "Part of me, the realistic part, says that the buffalo are gone, as is the land, and it went the way of the wolves—plundered and annihilated. No matter what the government did to us or against us, we could have never continued as a tribe living off the land. Too many settlers were coming into the country. The end of the Plains Indians was just a matter of time. We couldn't have stopped it any more than trying to stop the crest of a rising flood.

"But there is another part of me that knows what happened to my ancestors. Some Native Americans say the only difference between the way the United States treated the tribes in the nineteenth century and the Nazis treated the Jews was the gas chambers. They tried to exterminate us. They knew once the buffalo were gone, we couldn't survive, so there was an intense effort to put an end to the herds. And once they had the tribes starving, they placed us on reservations so that they could control us. Maybe concentration camps would be a better word."

Wolfson looked down, staring at a glass of water. Kimberly saw a deep sadness work its way across his face.

"Grandfather was forced to go to a school away from home when he was six," Wolfson said. "It was an Indian school, and all tribes were sent to this boarding school in western Montana. Indian kids didn't have a choice to stay home. They were picked up and taken away from their families. They were treated like institutionalized orphans. They lost all day-to-day contact with their parents.

"And when grandfather was seven—in the second grade, he told me—he and some school friends cut out cardboard feathers and pasted them on their heads and began playing with some makeshift bows and arrows. They played after school with a couple other children in the woods. It was a life they had known. They dressed up using wrapping paper and colored their outfits with crayons.

"When the schoolmaster heard of this, he gathered them up and paraded them in front of an assembly. He forced them to take off their clothes. Then he soaked them with buckets of water and made them sing the national anthem. They stood naked and wet in front of all their classmates.

"You ask me how I feel about my heritage? I know the bitterness many Native Americans have toward the government. There was a time when I heard stories like this that I wanted to kill these men."

"I can understand," Kimberly answered softly.

"I think a seed was planted in my grandfather's mind that he never wanted me to be subject to such humiliating treatment. Even though he was a respected elder of the tribe, he realized it would be better for me to get away. I've thanked him for that, many times over. Had I stayed here, I might have joined some of my high school friends . . . drunk, on heroin, ending up in jail. The options left for kids when I was growing up on the reservation were not great."

"And what about this lion?" she asked carefully.

Wolfson's lips tightened. She thought, at first, he was going to make a joke. Then his expression changed. It was as if a switch had flipped.

"I'm very concerned," he answered slowly. "I've had no encounter with this lion. To the best of my memory, I have never heard of an animal like this. Had I not been there myself, I wouldn't have believed it. I saw the tracks. I saw the dogs. What happened is hard to believe."

"They are saying no white person can kill this lion. That it can only be taken by a Native American."

"People say a lot of things." Wolfson frowned. "Mostly, I think it is a very big lion that has followed the deer and elk down because of the drought and got mixed up with some people. I don't see any reason why the hunters won't kill it. With a $100,000 bounty on its head, I don't think it's going to last very long."

"There is a rumor this lion is a 'spirit cat,' that it has come back from the past."

"Some of the medicine people of the tribe have been hinting a lot of things," Wolfson pulled at his chin. A frown crossed his face. "My grandfather thought *Omahkatayo* had returned. He'd seen some images in the clouds. He also envisioned a herd of buffalo trekking through the living room. So, you've got to understand that a lot of 'spirit' talk may be a figment of somebody's imagination."

"Lassiter was supposed to be the best in the state."

"Lassiter was thrown off his horse. Yeah, the lion killed him, but part of his injuries may have been from the fall. From the tracks we followed, it looked like he was pushing the lion about as hard as you can. Sooner or later, a big cat like that's going to turn. Clearly, he underestimated the size and strength of this animal. I'm told he was a good man. I feel badly for his family."

"Are you going after it?" she asked bluntly.

There was a faint hesitation that Kimberly missed at first. It was not until she thought about the interview later that she realized there was perhaps a seed of indecision that had been working steadily on his mind. On the surface, Wolfson sounded firm and unshakable in his response. Later—much later—when she reflected upon it, she wondered if the deeper, turbulent waters of his soul had been considering the decision more seriously than he cared to admit.

"I have no dogs, no gun, no way to go after this lion," he said flatly. "If it was up to me, I would leave the damn thing alone. You harass and pursue it enough, and it's going to strike back. I came to bury my grandfather, and that's my only reason for being here. I have a flight back in a couple of days."

Someone put a quarter in the jukebox. Garth Brooks' began singing; "The Dance." His voice carried across the saloon. The sound was too loud for them to continue. Kimberly listened to the music for a few moments and then shook her head. "I'm afraid we'd better stop."

"Do you dance?" Wolfson asked.

"Depends," she shrugged. "Is this part of the interview?"

"Could be . . ." he answered with a smile.

Wolfson escorted Kimberly out on the floor. They danced conventional ballroom-style for several numbers. Then the music changed, and a western line dance started. A dozen couples came forward.

"I'd better sit down," she said with embarrassment.

"It's not difficult," he urged. "You just need a couple of basic steps. Here, follow my lead."

Patiently, he showed her how to advance forward with her foot and then rock backwards, step sideways, and slap her heel. She tried again, with the opposite leg. With a little practice, she was able to alternate her feet and get through a repetitive eight-beat step.

The jukebox started a new song. Before she knew it, she found she was dancing. She surprised herself. She hadn't danced with anyone like this in years, and here she was, western dancing with an Indian, of all people, line dancing in a bar in Elkhorn. She almost felt like she was a teenager again.

48

CAMERAMAN ERIC STAFFORD DIDN'T HAVE MUCH to do that Saturday evening. He loitered around the motel for a while and then decided he would go into Elkhorn and have a drink. Kimberly had called earlier to say she was meeting with Wolfson for an interview but had decided not to do any videotaping until she felt Wolfson was more comfortable. She wanted to do a story on the Native Americans but was worried that a formal video might scare Wolfson off.

Before he left the motel, Stafford called his wife and learned Janet was doing well. He also had an opportunity to speak with his two-year-old son. He apologized for missing his birthday party and promised he would bring him something special when he returned.

"And when are you coming home?" his wife asked.

Stafford had to tell her he didn't know. A two-day assignment had turned into a week, and now twelve days had passed. He was pretty sure they wouldn't be gone a month. By then, the weather would turn, and the majority of tourists would be gone. He was not as convincing as he would have liked.

He didn't speak much about the lion. He didn't want to. Janet was spooked enough by the news reports they'd sent back. So he played it down and assured her everything was all right. A lot of things were better left unsaid.

When he entered the Cattleman, it was 10:30 in the evening. The saloon was packed to capacity. He saw Kimberly dancing with Wolfson and waved to her as he passed. She was struggling with some type of dance step, and Wolfson was showing her what to do. She appeared immersed in trying to learn the steps.

He approached the bar, took a seat, and ordered a beer and basket of chicken wings. Then he swung around to face the dance floor. He watched the line dancing with interest, humming with the music.

Stafford was vaguely aware of two men who came out of the crowd and took seats at the bar alongside him. They were dressed in jeans. One had a black baseball cap with the logo "G.S.M.C." along the top. The other wore a dark jacket showing the picture of a molecule with atoms spinning around its nucleus. The words "Gold Stone Mining Company" were stenciled across the back.

The photographer continued eating, enjoying his beer, when he heard a comment from one of the men. The voice was low and gruff.

"Aren't you the television man who came with that lady reporter?"

The photographer turned. "Were you speaking to me?"

"You deaf?"

Stafford wiped his mouth with a napkin. "Sorry, the music is pretty loud."

The man's tone was hostile. "I said, fat man, aren't you part of the television team from California?"

"He means Californicating," his partner laughed.

Stafford tried to ignore the menacing tone. "We've been out here for a couple of weeks."

"This is mining country," the first man said. "We don't appreciate outsiders like you coming in and making a lot of news. Your reports have brought some people who aren't welcome. You understand?"

"You're pretty sweet," his partner added. "You got a cute earring there. Maybe Jake and I could come over to your motel and have a go. What do you say, big boy?"

Stafford felt his lips tighten. He couldn't remember when he'd last been in a fight. He didn't like confrontation, and he especially didn't want to get into a fight with two locals at the bar.

The bartender came forward and wiped the counter. "Hey, guys, come on. Jake, Billy, knock it off! I don't want trouble."

"No trouble." Stafford bowed graciously. "I need to be going. I'll take the bill, please."

Gaining his feet, he reached into his back pocket for his wallet and placed a twenty-dollar bill on the counter. "Keep the change," he said.

"You tell that lady reporter we don't appreciate lion huggers around here," Jake interjected. "A good lion is a dead lion. If she's going to bring a lot of bad press to this town, you're in for a bit of trouble. You tell her that, big boy, would you?"

Stafford tried to ignore the comment, but he could feel his anger rise. Abruptly, he was beyond his boiling point. "We're going to report the story how we see it," he answered firmly. "And quite frankly, I don't give a rat's shit what you think."

He turned on his heels and started for the doorway, feeling good he'd told the bastard off. A boot caught his ankle. Tripping, he fell forward, landing with a crash.

A woman gasped. Someone dropped a glass. As the music ended, everyone's focus turned toward the heavy-set man sprawled across the floor.

Jake moved off his bar stool and stood with his friend, hovering over Eric Stafford. "So, you give her this message, would you?" Sneering, he spat a wad of tobacco onto Stafford's chest. "Folks here don't like pussy lovers, you understand?"

Jake had started back to the bar when he felt a steel grip clenching his shoulder. He tried to break free, but the strength of the fingers twisted him around.

249

"I think you owe my friend an apology," Wolfson said.

The miner took one look at Wolfson and snorted. "What the fuck business is this of yours?"

"Try me," Wolfson answered.

The punch started from his waist and shot toward Wolfson's chin. Wolfson twisted sideways. At the same time, his fist came out of nowhere. Jake's head jerked back, splattering blood. His legs buckled. He crumpled to the floor.

Billy edged forward. There was a flash of movement as a knife appeared. He stood in front of Wolfson, waving the blade, the point glinting dangerously close to Wolfson's face.

"You come a little closer, Indian," he hissed. "I got a little present for you."

A dark man with braids stepped forward on Wolfson's right. He was dressed in jeans and a black leather vest. A large tattoo rippled across his biceps. A second man advanced from the audience. A third came from the bar. A fourth, fifth, and sixth stepped forward until a dozen Native Americans had materialized from the crowd. They edged toward the man with the knife.

"I didn't come here for a fight," Wolfson said with a nod. "And if I was you, sir, I would take your friend and leave."

The man glared at Wolfson and then eyed the dozen individuals moving into a circle around him. One of the Native Americans had a huge knife at his belt and started to unsheathe it. Another placed a hand inside his vest. His fingers appeared to be reaching for a gun.

Billy scowled. The knife slipped back into his belt. "I got no beef with you people," he muttered. He resignedly bent down to help his friend. Jake was still out on the floor.

Wolfson nodded to the men gathered around him. "Thanks, gentlemen." He then added an expression in Blackfoot that only his comrades could understand: "*Iniiyi'tapo batale* . . . It's good to have your help."

As the Blackfoot tribal members dispersed back into the crowd, Wolfson helped Stafford to his feet. The western music started again. Voices sprang up. Couples began dancing. No one took further notice. For Elkhorn, Montana, it was just another Saturday night.

49

Wolfson escorted Kimberly and her photographer back to their motel. The cameraman thanked Wolfson for his help, laughing nervously at the incident. Stafford said good night, and Wolfson walked Kimberly back to her room.

A full moon edged above the horizon. The Montana sky twinkled in a brilliance of stars. Kimberly found her hand seeking Wolfson's arm. They stopped in front of her doorway.

"I want to thank you for the evening," she said. "I don't think I've had such an interesting night in years."

"You should have warned me your interviews end with a fight," he replied with a smile. "Next time, I'll be more prepared."

"And thanks for that, too," she said. "I know Eric appreciated your help."

"Tonight we had a lot of friends."

"Will I see you again?"

A frown crossed his face. "I don't know."

"I know I shouldn't ask . . ." She paused. "Was there . . . is there someone?"

"No one that matters."

The moon flooded across his face and caught the glint of his eyes like reflections in polished steel. Kimberly felt a shiver. Later, she was embarrassed yet thrilled with what she did. It was so unlike her, yet something that seemed right.

"Do you mind?" she asked. She did not give him time to answer but brought her lips to his face and kissed him softly on the cheek. She could feel his arms slowly come around her, and with them, she could feel his strength envelop her in a pool of dizziness. His lips found hers, and they stood in the cool evening, surrounded by an embrace of warmth. When she pulled away, she found she was trembling.

"I don't know if I have ever met anyone quite like you," she whispered. "I don't want this evening to end."

He did not answer. Instead, she could feel his lips softly explore the skin along her neck. An uncontrollable shudder rose deep inside her.

The first time they made love, she was consumed with fires of urgency and desire. Somewhere in her adolescent life she had heard—was it something she read or a rumor?—that Native Americans were incredibly well-endowed, and Robert Wolfson lived up to all expectations.

The second time they made love was what she really remembered. It was Wolfson's softness, the tenderness with which the great hidden strength of his hands caressed her body. No one had ever fired her passions like this before.

They had lain upon the bed, the sheets pulled off, their naked bodies touching head to toe. And ever so gently, he massaged her, his fingers caressing her toes, running up her legs and then into her soft parts, and later, along her abdomen and breasts and her inner arms. She felt great comfort in his presence. Slowly, he stroked her body until she wanted to scream.

Afterwards, she felt a warmth of peace and tranquility, as if her strength had ebbed from inside her body and gone to his. She rested here as if she could no longer move.

She awoke once during the night. The moon flooded through the window and fell upon his bare, muscular chest. She glanced at the outline of his body and ran her finger across his breast. He seemed to stir but did not awaken.

In the pale moonlight, she saw a small dark spot on his left breast, just below the nipple. She lifted her hand and ran her finger across the surface of his skin. She thought, at first, it was a bruise or perhaps some type of birthmark.

She would ask about it later, she thought. But she never had the chance. When she woke in the morning, the sun was flooding through the window, and the warm shape next to her was gone.

She thought, at first, he was in the bathroom. She called out, but he did not answer. She got up quickly, wrapped a blanket around herself, and looked through the room. His clothes were gone. On the counter, she found a note.

The words brought tears to her eyes. Mostly, they made her realize how little about Robert Wolfson she could understand.

> *Dear Kimberly,*
>   *You will never know what a special person you are, and if we don't cross paths again, I want you to know how much I care for you. There is something, however, I must to do for my people. If I don't see you for a while, I hope you'll understand.*
>
>   *Bobby*

50

WITHIN SEVENTY-TWO HOURS of Governor Erickson's announcement of the $100,000 reward, Elkhorn had the makings of a boomtown. Old-timers hadn't seen a rush like this since the Bartlett silver discovery in 1935. Unofficial estimates indicated the town of 7,000 had doubled in size. By the weekend, you couldn't get a place to eat without a reservation. Even then, there was a two-hour wait.

First, the television and news reporters came. They were the most mobile, and some arrived within hours of the governor's proclamation. Over the next few days, drifters and squatters from Idaho and Wyoming began to arrive. These first visitors were the transitory work force and the unemployed, individuals who had part-time jobs or spare time on their hands. Many had dreams of killing the lion. A few were just hoping to see the beast.

Along with this rush of people came another thousand tourists who were vacationing in the area—families who had seen the television reports and altered their plans. They wanted to witness what the press was touting as the "Greatest Lion Hunt of the Century." After all, where else could you find a lion walking through the middle of town? Word of the four deaths and the $100,000 reward spread through the West like wildfire.

When Hayden came to the station early the next morning, Mabel greeted him at his office. He could tell by her expression that things were not going well.

"Good morning, Mrs. Lincoln," he said, trying to make a joke. "How was the play?"

"Sam, you're absolutely not going to believe this," she answered. "Look at this!"

She shoved a six-inch pile of telephone messages onto his desk. "By my count, twenty-seven calls came in since midnight. The place has gone absolutely crazy. Dispatch told me last night they could hardly get their job done, there were so many inquiries. God help us if we had a real emergency."

She began to thumb through the messages. "People want your home phone number. They want to know what we're doing about the lion. What kind of precautions have we set up? How big is the lion? When was it last seen? Is it black or tan? Is everyone carrying a gun?"

She threw up her hands in a gesture of futility. "What do you want me to do with these?"

"Just put 'em in a box," Hayden grunted. "We'll save them for later."

On top of his desk was another pile of telephone messages. Glancing through the slips, Hayden counted nineteen. Mixed in with the communications was a late evening call from the sheriff's office in Helena. Hayden was behind on a justification report for "after hour" deputies that was due last week. Administration wondered when the report would be finished. The damn lion business was starting to get him behind on everything, he thought, frowning.

A sudden commotion rose in the hall. The office door burst open.

Mayor Miller rushed into the room. "Sergeant . . . God, am I glad to see you!" His face looked haggard and flushed. His shirt was wrinkled, as if he'd slept in it.

"I'm getting calls from all over the damn world!" he exclaimed. "There was an Italian film crew that came to my home last night. They had to speak through an interpreter, for Christ's sake. How the hell did they find my address? This lion thing is getting out of hand, Sam. We've got to get some law and order here."

The mayor took a seat at the conference table, shaking his head. "What calmness and civility we've had in this town is getting blown to hell. I don't like it, Sam. Quite frankly, I don't think you've got enough resources to handle this."

"I put in a call to the central office yesterday. You know what they told me? I've already used too many overtime hours. They want me to cut back! I'm not sure where else to turn. I've already got my men working eighteen hours as it is."

"Then what are we going to do?"

Hayden thought for a moment. "What if we set up a command center of some type to coordinate communications? It was something we did in Seattle when there were major emergencies in progress."

"I like that!" the mayor said, clapping. "I can free one of my secretaries. Maybe we could add some volunteers."

"Good," Hayden replied. "It will get us out of the communication loop. We can rig up voice mail or an 800-number with a repeating message. Try to put routine announcements on it, with an updated recording every morning. Then, if it gets really crazy, I would suggest we set up a central booth so that we can give daily news briefings."

"How about the town square?"

"Weather permitting, that should work."

Hayden's secretary came over the intercom. "Governor for you, sir."

Hayden rolled his eyes. "Now what?" He picked up the telephone.

"I saw you at the funeral yesterday," Governor Erickson said. "I just wanted to let you know my thoughts are with you. I was a great admirer of Howard Lassiter. When I heard he'd been killed, I was stunned. He was one of the best hunters in the state."

"Yes, sir," Hayden answered. "It was hard for me to believe, as well."

"I wanted to tell you if there is anything my office can do, please let me know. Has there been any news?"

"I have the mayor here now. We've been talking over some of the problems."

"Any way I can help, you let me know. National Guard. State Police. I don't know how good these men are at chasing lions, but I want to get that damn animal killed."

"Well, sir, not only with the lion," Hayden answered. "I was thinking too, we may need some assistance just to keep law and order. This reward has caused a lot of crazy people coming into town. I don't have enough deputies as it is."

"You give me the word. I can have a unit of thirty guardsmen overnight."

"All right, sir. We will certainly appreciate your help."

"And, Sergeant, good luck with the lion."

"Yes, sir. Thank you, sir."

Hayden hung up the phone. "Well, that's a start," he said.

AT NOON, DEPUTY CAMPBELL TOOK HAYDEN and the mayor for a reconnaissance drive through town. On the outskirts of Elkhorn, not far from the baseball field where Ashley's team held practice, they found a growing tent city. By Hayden's count, there were twenty-seven tents of various sizes and descriptions. A couple dozen RVs and mobile homes were parked nearby. Makeshift clotheslines were strung. Rows of shirts and underwear flapped in the breeze. The park had the look of a refugee camp.

"Incredible!" Miller shook his head.

"We've had three calls here to stop fights, just since last night," Campbell said.

"Where in the hell did these people come from?"

"You ain't seen nothing yet."

Campbell took them across town to a second RV park. The place was overflowing. Where the lot had a capacity for forty, it looked as if it was packed with a hundred. Every space was crowded with trucks, cars, and motor homes.

When they drove into the town square, they found a squad car on the sidewalk. A deputy had two men in handcuffs, face down on the pavement.

"Little argument about a parking spot," the deputy said. "A couple of citizens called when they saw somebody pull a gun."

"You need help?" Hayden asked.

"Nothing a paddy wagon and a few dozen deputies won't solve."

Hayden motioned for the mayor to follow. The two walked across the town square. Both were astonished by what they saw. A dozen campers were parked along the street. The sidewalks were crowded with people. At one corner, an argument had sprung up over a minor collision between two cars. Vince Bertolli stood in front of his art store cursing a youth who had blocked his parking spot. A storeowner yelled at a man leading three dogs along the sidewalk. One of the animals had peed on his welcome mat.

A deafening roar stopped Hayden in his tracks. Driving up the middle of the street were a dozen motorcycles. To the mayor, a man of principle and peace, the bikers looked like an armada from hell.

The bikers rode two and three abreast, moving in tight formation, their engines rumbling. Beneath an assortment of World War II helmets, they wore long hair. Some had unkempt beards. Many were in sleeveless vests, with leather chaps and mud-stained boots. And riding along the backs of the motorcycles were a half a dozen young women, buxom girls with leather pants and skintight blouses.

The mayor tried to say something, but his voice was lost in a roar of engines. As Hayden approached the street, the leader of the bikers flagged him down. They came to an abrupt stop next to the sidewalk.

259

"Hey, sheriff," the biker shouted. "We've come to find the lion. You got any suggestions where we can stay?"

"Yeah, try Whitefish."

"And where is that?"

"A hundred miles west." Hayden pointed with his thumb.

"Oh, man, you're a real joker," the man snorted. "Anybody see the lion today?"

"With this noise? Not a chance."

"Well, we're the Panthers. We were heading over to Missoula when we heard about the reward. Thought we'd come to town and park for a while. Got any good places to eat?"

"You'll find some along the square," Hayden nodded. "Just keep it respectful and pay your bills. And if any of you got guns, I need to check them."

"Guns?" the man laughed. "Do we carry guns, boys?" His words were drowned out by an impatient revving of engines. With a hand signal, the procession started up again.

"Be cool, bro'." He nodded to the mayor. They continued along the street with a deafening roar.

Mayor Miller looked pale. For a moment, Hayden thought he was going to collapse.

"If it's all right with you, I think we'd better call the governor and bring in the National Guard." The mayor said with trepidation.

"I'll call him when we get back to the office." Hayden tried to smile. "We get much more of this, I'm thinking we'll need a battalion of marines."

51

KIMBERLY BENSON SPENT THE MORNING talking with several ranchers who expressed worries about the lion. As far as they were concerned, a good lion was a dead lion. They had cattle to protect, and losing any of their livestock meant losing income. They considered all predators the same; wolves, coyotes, lions, and bears had no business on their property. If an animal crossed the line, it would be killed.

A fishing guide took a more cautious position. "Look," he told her. "I can understand why people want to protect these animals; and I understand, too, why the ranchers are so violently opposed to their presence. But I can tell you, my son was playing out in the backyard, a couple of years ago. He was maybe six, and we had a set of swings. I was watching out the window when I saw a mountain lion edging along a row of hedges behind him. It took my breath away. He'd been stalking my son and was perfectly camouflaged in the brush. I grabbed for a gun and ran outside, yelling. By then the lion was gone."

The guide's voice faltered. "God knows what would have happened, if I hadn't intervened."

Kimberly contacted KPXL in San Francisco at noon. Everything was fine, Jeremy Wong told her. Keep up the good work. Her reports had raised keen interest from the public on the lion. And Stephanie Peterson had done a few fill-in segments as an anchor. That too was going great. A poll showed viewer numbers increased by ten percent.

The mention of Stephanie's name raised an uneasiness in Kimberly's mind. What kind of a job would Kimberly be given when she returned? Were they gradually phasing her out?

She gave her cameraman the afternoon off. When she returned to her room, she tried to rest, but the memory of Robert Wolfson kept returning. When she shut her eyes, she saw him. Her skin still trembled at the memory of his touch. Everything about the man she liked, yet she knew so little about him.

Had he been married? Did he have children? Was she just another casual affair among a long list of women? She sensed not. She thought she was a good judge of character. Wolfson didn't seem the type that would run through a number of loose relationships. Why she had slept with him was the real question, she reflected. She had no easy answers.

Kimberly went into the bathroom, washed her face, and changed her clothes. The least she could do was try to say good-bye. She could always tell Wolfson there were a few details in their interview that needed further clarification. It sounded like a reasonable excuse. If he was cold and unemotional toward her, she would write the night off as a simple mistake.

She thought first she would try to reach Wolfson by phone. She had no telephone number and no easy point of contact. Perhaps Sergeant Hayden would know, but she didn't want to bother him with this type of question.

She considered driving out to the reservation. Her first experience there with Eric Stafford had not been not good. But having the cameraman with her had made everyone suspicious of their intent. By herself should be easier. Besides, she wanted to poke around the reservation anyway. There was a lot about the Blackfoot she didn't understand.

The day was warm, the sky an immeasurable blue. On the outskirts of Elkhorn, she stopped at the Dairy Queen. She would grab a sandwich and be on her way. A young man approached and began wiping down the table. He had a dark complexion and wore his hair in braids.

"Excuse me for asking. Are you Native American?"

"Blackfoot," he acknowledged.

"I'm Kimberly." She held out her hand.

"You're the woman doing the television story?"

Kimberly nodded. She hadn't realized she was so widely recognized.

"I've seen you filming here and there," he continued. "You and the big cameraman. My name is Franklyn Yellow Pine. It's nice to meet you?"

"I'm looking for a man named Robert Wolfson," she told him.

Franklyn smiled. "Everybody's looking for Bobby Running Wolf. You a friend of his?"

"You could say that," she replied.

"He's been staying with his sister out on the reservation. Her name is Sarah Running Wolf. If you want to reach him, I think she has a listed number. If nobody answers, they may be at the Sundance."

"Sundance?"

"Indian thing," Franklyn replied. "Can I get you something to eat?"

Franklyn took Kimberly's order and disappeared inside the building. In ten minutes, he returned, carrying a sandwich and drink.

"Is the Sundance something I could see?" Kimberly asked.

"Do you know your way around?"

She shook her head.

"I'm not sure I should be giving you this type of information," Franklyn said with a bit of hesitation. "I guess if you're a friend of Bobby's, it would be all right."

He took a napkin and drew a map, sketching Route 29 and Browning to the south and then a turn at the Beaver River, ten miles east.

"Look for mile marker 121," he said. "Shortly afterwards, you'll find a sign for the river."

Kimberly took her food and thanked him. She started for the reservation, eating along the way. She tried to use her cell phone to find a number for Sarah Running Wolf but could not get a signal to work.

When she reached Browning, she stopped at a gas station and looked in a local phone book. Here she found a number listed for Sarah Running Wolf, 32 Weasel Creek. She called twice. No one responded. There was not even an answering machine.

She wondered about the Sundance. If no one answered the phone at Sarah Running Wolf's, maybe everyone was at the celebration. The ceremony was probably an Indian festival involving a bunch of dancers with someone chanting and beating a drum. Most likely, there would be tourists taking pictures. Maybe there would be a set of bleachers where she could sit and watch. She wasn't sure what to expect.

Following Highway 29 east, Kimberly slowed at mile marker 121. Within a quarter of a mile, she found a sign pointing toward the Beaver River. Here she turned off the highway. The road descended a gentle ravine next to a dried riverbed. Within a mile, it rose toward a wide, flat basin. The sage spread out before her like a sea.

A herd of antelope flashed by. The animals kept even with her car for a bit and then bolted across the road. She slowed to watch them pass, amazed at their leaping bounds.

As she continued driving, a flock of sage hens erupted from the road, clattering wildly away. A hawk perched on a single leafless tree watched her pass. At the base of a steep ridge, she noted a group of large dark animals. At first, she thought they were cattle. Soon she was driving through a herd of buffalo.

Huge, thick-shouldered bulls, dozens of cows, and small calves passed in front of her. She stopped and rolled down the window. Grunting and snorting, they ambled a few feet from her car. Some were close enough to touch. When she started up, she honked to get them out of the way.

She hadn't imagined there would be buffalo here, and the abundance of wildlife caught her by surprise. She felt like she had driven through a time warp. She wondered if this was what the prairie was like a century before.

The road dipped unexpectedly, descending into a steep ravine. Below was a lush, green valley filled with magnificent trees. A river flowed through the valley, twisting and turning in a multitude of strands.

At the base of the valley, she discovered a number of vehicles parked in a field. The cars and trucks were the first signs of humanity she had seen. If she'd taken a wrong turn, at least she could ask someone for directions.

When she reached the parking area, she stopped. At first, she could see no people, and she wondered where they might have gone. As she stepped out of her car, she heard a distant high-pitched whistling sound.

She followed the direction of the noise. At the base of a small stream stood a grove of cottonwood trees. Beyond the trees was a large circular structure made from wooden poles. The walls were lined with boughs of willow. By her estimate, the edifice was a dozen feet tall and thirty yards in diameter.

The structure appeared to have been strategically placed in a niche along the western side of the ravine. At one side of the edifice was a small arched doorway covered with blankets. She could see there was no roof. Poles had been strung across the open ceiling like rafters.

As she moved closer, she became aware of a deep repetitive drumming. A hoarse voice rose and fell, following the primitive drumbeat. Through cracks in the branch-covered walls, she could see shadows dancing back and forth in front of a fire.

As she drew nearer, the noises of chanting became louder. In the background were women's voices, rising in periodic shrieks. Mixed with these sounds came the piercing noise of a whistle.

She had a sudden impulse to turn back. This was not the type of tourist festival she'd expected. She wondered if she had stumbled upon some type of ceremony that she had no business attending.

Moving next to the walls, she carefully spread a tunnel through the branches. She had imagined a group of Indians dancing around a central fire, shuffling feet, moving in a circle. What she saw took her breath away. She stared in disbelief.

At the center of the structure was the trunk of a large tree, rising thirty feet above the edifice, like the central pole of a colossal tent. Cut limbs composed the open ceiling, radiating outwards, fastened to the walls by cords. Lined along the walls stood a large audience of Native Americans. Some wore leather vests and leggings; others were covered in blankets. All were intently focused on the ceremony unfolding at the middle of the enclosure.

A cluster of buffalo skulls hung from the central pole. At its base was a blazing fire. A man with a wolfskin headdress danced in front of the flames. Two yellow circles were painted around his eyes. Leaping back and forth, he shook a pair of rattles, chanting in rhythm with the drums.

A lark swooped down and landed by her head. The bird eyed her suspiciously and began squawking loudly. Kimberley was so focused on the scene that her eyes scarcely moved. Her attention was riveted to the form of a man hanging from the center of the scaffolding poles.

Except for a cloth draped around his loins, he was naked, his body painted a ghastly white. Two cords attached to small stakes impaling his chest, lifting his body off the ground. Blood streaked down his thorax and across his abdomen.

As the form slowly twisted on the suspension strings, she saw he was held by pieces of wood that had been skewered through his breasts. The weight of the man's body pulled heavily at these attachments, stretching the skin in a grotesque fashion. The man's head lolled at his shoulders. At first, she thought he was dead.

Looking closer, she observed a faint rising of his chest. The man's hands were contracted into fists, held stiffly at his side. Gripped between clenched teeth was a small whistle. She realized now the high-pitched whistling came from the figure as he blew repeatedly with each breath.

As the body twisted, she could make out the outline of the head. It was the visage of a man in intense pain, the muscles pulled taut around the jaws, the eyes glazed. The body swung a few degrees until she could see the face.

"My God!" she murmured. She could feel her senses sag as if a wind had blown out a flame. Her knees buckled. She staggered and was beginning to fall when strong hands propped her upward.

She looked into the fierce eyes of two Blackfoot men glaring at her. Standing beside them was a strange woman whose head was covered by a blanket.

"You are not welcome here," the woman said.

"The man . . . he's dying . . ." she gasped.

The hands grabbed her tightly, pushing her toward the parking lot.

"We don't want trouble," one of the men said. The barrel of a shotgun pointed at her face.

"We would kindly ask you to leave," the second Blackfoot added.

The two men escorted her to the car. She looked back once, a hundred feet from the parking lot. The strange woman had turned to go inside the enclosure. The lark perched on her shoulder. With a flick, she dislodged the bird. Then the woman ducked through the blankets and disappeared.

Kimberly stepped into her car and drove steadily up the ridge, following the dirt road back across the sage. For half an hour, she could hardly catch her breath. Once, when the dizziness seemed to fog her mind, she pulled over and vomited.

A hundred times she played the scene over in her mind. She should have refused to leave. She should have run into the enclosure and screamed for the man's life. Yet the Blackfoot had made it incredibly clear she was not welcome. You don't argue with a man pointing a shotgun at your head.

Inside, hanging from a ceiling pole, skewered by two cords through his breasts, was the slowly twisting form of a man. The visage—the nose, the lips, even in their agony—were unmistakably his. It was Robert Wolfson. He was dying, his life slipping away in some horrible Indian ceremony, and there was nothing she could do to help.

52

DURING THE FOLLOWING WEEK, the Native Americans from the Blackfoot reservation were surprisingly quiet. Several newscasters tried to get statements from the "Indians" about the lion, but they preferred to give no response. What they wished to talk about was a controversial mining company that wanted to build a road across their sacred land. Tribal members had few jobs and little pay. Perhaps the road would help. But the Blackfoot were not so sure. It would not take much contamination to ruin their land.

A Japanese film crew thought this was interesting and completed several interviews in Elkhorn with a few locals who were familiar with the situation and who were willing to talk. It made good copy back in Japan, to tell how the United States government had sold out to the mining companies and screwed over the Native Americans again and again.

The American reporters were not so intrigued. Mostly, they wanted news about the lion. Hayden, by now, had pretty much dismissed the talk about the "spirit cat" as so much hokum. Rumors had come to him that there had been some type of special ceremony out at the Blackfoot reservation, but he could find out no further information. He had his hands full in Elkhorn as it was, trying to keep law and order.

For the first several days after visiting the Sundance, Kimberly tried to call the reservation but no one would answer her calls. Was Wolfson alive or dead? None of the Blackfoot would say. She was an outsider, and it was mostly none of her business, she began to understand. Even Hayden had no idea what she was talking about. Finally, she decided to bury herself in her work.

There were a lot of different people coming to town. Some were advocates of animal rights, and she set up as many interviews as she could.

During this time, she put together two contrasting video-tape reports. The first involved a rancher named Doug Butler who owned ten thousand acres of cattle land. He was tolerant of wild animals but rightly pointed out that lions had the potential to kill his livestock, and every winter he lost a dozen head to lions. These losses cost him real money. Even if the government was willing to reimburse him for the loss, someone had to come out to the ranch and examine the kills and certify the death was due to pre-dation. Furthermore, cattle chased or wounded often ate poorly, lost weight, and became secondary casualties. Butler felt he was caught in an unsolvable bind.

Kimberly's second interview was with the president of an ani-mal rights group who had come to town to try to place a morato-rium on any further killing of lions. Peggy Evans was an articu-late, bright woman in her forties from Washington, DC. She had majored in biology, with a graduate degree in animal science. Not surprisingly, she was very knowledgeable about *Felis concolor.*

A "bad" lion should be hunted down, she agreed. What Ms. Evans didn't like was the wanton killing of other innocent lions in the process. The problem was, dogs couldn't differentiate between good lions and bad ones, and the ranchers didn't give a damn what they killed. So, pregnant females, immature males, and sometimes lion clubs were taken in the frenzy.

"Two hundred and fifty lions killed in Montana last year," she reported. "And, the body count of lions massacred from fear or sport over the past century is in the thousands."

After Kimberly sent off these reports, she drove by the Dairy Queen and searched for the young man she had spoken with about the Sundance. She learned Franklyn wasn't on duty. He wouldn't be back for a couple of days.

She tried calling Sarah Running Wolf again. When she finally reached Sarah, Kimberly had the sense that Sarah was trying to protect her brother from any outside calls. Yes, he was fine, she said. Her responses were brief and abrupt. At least Kimberly learned Wolfson was alive. She was embarrassed to ask more about the Sundance, and even if she had, she was sure Sarah wouldn't give out further information. Sarah finally promised she would tell her brother that Kimberly had called, but he never returned her call.

On Friday, seven days after the Sundance, when there was still no tangible news on the lion and the dozens of reporters were going crazy looking for a story, any story, she went to the Dairy Queen. Franklyn Yellow Pine was back at work.

She took a seat at one of the outdoor tables, patiently waiting for Franklyn to come outside. After a few minutes cleaning tables, he drifted over. "Hi," he said.

"Do you remember me?"

"Of course. You're the television lady from San Francisco."

"How are things at the reservation?"

"Good, very good." He nodded. "Did you come to eat?"

"Mostly, I wanted to talk."

"How can I help?"

"You've been hard to find."

"Sorry." He shrugged. "I've been staying with my uncle. He doesn't have a phone."

"I went out to the Sundance." She waited carefully for his response.

"Yeah, I heard."

Kimberly tried to hide her surprise. "What did they say?"

"That you became faint and had to leave."

"That's one way to put it." She coughed. "Did they tell you I was escorted off at gunpoint?"

"I'm sorry." Franklyn frowned. "It was my fault for telling you it would be all right. It's not a good place for Anglos. Especially a reporter like you."

Kimberly forced a laugh. She tried to make light of the situation. "I saw Robert Wolfson."

Franklyn nodded solemnly, biting the corner of his lip. "What Bobby did . . . That was amazing. I wish I had the courage to do something like that."

"I thought he was dead," Kimberly said.

"To do that . . . to put your life on the line like that . . ." Franklyn stared across the parking lot. "I don't think many members of our tribe have done that this century."

"But why?" Kimberly carefully chose her words. There was much about the ceremony she didn't understand.

"In the old days . . ." Franklyn replied. "Back in the eighteenth century, there was a time when the Sundance was used as an initiation ceremony to bring young braves into the tribe. The piercing was reserved for only the most courageous. It was a voluntary thing. Only those with the most stamina could survive."

He shook his head. "I tried piercing once. I asked them to cut a small wound in my chest to see what it would be like. The pain was so horrible, I couldn't stand it."

"Why Robert Wolfson?" she asked.

"Do you know who he is?"

"He's a man from Chicago. A teacher. He told me he rarely came back to the reservation anymore."

"He is also a direct descendant of one of the great chiefs, Eyes-in-Shadows. He has a lion's paw tattooed beneath his left breast. It's like a sign of royalty. After his grandfather died, he's the last member of his line."

So, it wasn't a birthmark, Kimberly thought with surprise. It was a tattoo she'd seen in the moonlight that night.

"Is . . . Is he all right?" she asked hesitatingly.

"Sure, he's doing well. I saw him this morning."

"Could you tell him I asked about him?"

Franklyn shook his head. "For the next couple of days, I'm afraid that would be impossible."

"I don't understand," she replied.

"Because he's gone into the mountains."

A bewildered expression crossed Kimberley's face.

"He left on horseback this morning. He's gone to hunt the lion."

"Alone?" she gasped.

"I know it sounds crazy," Franklyn answered. "But he wouldn't have it any other way."

53

THE SEND-OFF COULDN'T HAVE BEEN less spectacular. A Blackfoot elder pounded a steady rhythm on an elk skin drum. A medicine man raised dust in his hands, blowing the soil in the four cardinal directions like smoke. At most, a dozen individuals came to watch him go. James Black Kettle and David Lame Elk were there along with some of the tribal elders with whom he had shared the sweat bath. So were his sister, Sarah, and Franklyn Yellow Pine.

They stood next to a dirt road beneath the ceremonial bluff where George Two Feathers's funeral had been held. A half dozen cars parked nearby. A truck and trailer brought the horse.

It was a small turnout for such a precarious adventure, yet Wolfson didn't want a pretentious end-off. He had what he would need to hunt the lion. Black Kettle lent him a 30/30 lever-action rifle. Franklyn gave him a sleeping bag, and Sarah had prepared some dried food. Other than the horse, he required little else.

Wolfson placed one foot in the stirrups and hoisted his leg over the saddle, pulling his sleek frame onto the horse's back. Taking the reins, he turned his mount and nodded. He was ready to leave.

Franklyn had placed a whitewashed handprint on the horse's left flank, a mark the Blackfoot used to decorate their war ponies. Three small hoof prints were painted along the rear hip. A red circle adorned one of the horses' eyes.

Wolfson was dressed in a deerskin vest. A grizzly claw necklace looped around his neck. His hair fell freely onto his shoulders. A pair of painted yellow flashes marked his left cheek. These were marks Blackfoot braves used for battle.

"I will bring you fresh supplies in three days," Franklyn said.

"How many shells did you give me?"

"Twelve."

"That's not a lot."

"If you shoot straight, you need one."

"Thanks for the confidence," Wolfson said, smiling.

He had a long ride ahead: fourteen miles as the crow flies, eight hours left until sunset. If he pushed hard, he would make the great cliffs above Buffalo Ridge by nightfall.

As he swung the pony around, Sarah reached up and kissed him. The others came forward and extended their hands. He touched each of them, exchanging farewells, one by one. Black Kettle was the last to speak.

"May the Great Spirit be with you. Your father would be proud."

Wolfson turned and kicked his horse into a trot, following a dirt road that led like an arrow toward the hump of Medicine Mountain. Beyond that rose the snowcapped peaks of the Continental Divide.

As Wolfson rode up into the mountains, he had a lot to think about. So much had happened—so much was happening—he needed a period of solitude to sort things out. Settling in the saddle, his body soon adjusted to the gentle sway of the horse.

The Sundance had been a horrendous experience. For six hours, he had hung from the cords before they pulled through his skin. By the time he collapsed, he was unconscious. He lay on the ground as the elders chanted over him. Periodically, Raven Crow gave him broth, which helped him regain his strength. Then they carried him back to Sarah's house. The next two days were lost in delirium.

Later, his sister told him how many of the reservation had come to pay their respects. The pain had been so intense, his mind had blocked it out. He had trouble remembering much of the ordeal. Even when he began to recover, he refused any medical assistance. After it was over, Sarah scolded him for his insanity. For the next several days, she tended his wounds and nourished him back to health. Although she wouldn't admit it, Wolfson sensed she was very proud.

A month before, he would never have dreamed of such a thing. Maybe it was a combination of events that turned him over. Maybe seeing the boys playing basketball without a coach. Maybe hearing of the mining company's plans to build a road across sacred land. Maybe tracking the lion with the sheriff's deputies and coming upon the body of Howard Lassiter. The lion was real, and its size was huge; and, if he was going to get involved, he needed to do it right.

And then there was the reporter named Kimberly Benson. Once, during his delirium, he had called out her name. He knew he wanted to see her again, but that would have to wait, wait until after the Sundance, and the matter with the lion. There were things about his life she wouldn't understand.

It was dusk by the time he reached the abutment. He dismounted at a clearing beneath the cliffs, hobbled his horse, and went to collect some wood. As he searched for suitable branches, he walked over to a broad vista where the mountain fell away, dropping in a precipitous chasm for more than a thousand feet. He stared across the immense space as darkness overtook the land. A hawk soared past. There was no sound, only the dark form gliding through the night.

He returned to the clearing and made a fire. As he squatted before the surge of flames, he thought about his grandfather. George Two Feathers had come to this sacred place many times in his life. It was a place where the old man had looked for spiritual guidance.

On several occasions, his grandfather had brought him here. As a youth, he recalled staring with wonder at the pictographs painted along the buttress of rock. The drawings were still a marvel to him. Who had created them? Two Feathers said they were from his Blackfoot ancestors. Later, he learned some of the drawings went back a thousand years.

Here were figures of buffalo and wolves, elk, and moose. In at least two areas, his grandfather pointed out images of lions. Lions played a role in the history of the Blackfoot and maybe the people before. And now a lion was playing a significant role with its presence again. Strange, he thought, how sometimes things at the beginning had a way of coming back at the end.

Huddled before the small fire, his horse a short distance away, Bobby Running Wolf ate a piece of jerky Sarah had prepared. He drank some water and pulled in closer to the flames. A chill descended upon the mountains. He unrolled his sleeping bag and placed the rifle next to his saddle. He was tired. His legs were sore from the ride. The two wounds on his chest hurt terribly.

For a time, he stared into the fire, letting his thoughts wander. He would spend one night here. Then he would move into the forest past Elkhorn, looking for tracks. On the third day, he would rendezvous with Franklyn Yellow Pine. If the lion was here, he would find it.

He stood up and placed more wood on the fire, gradually stoking the flames until there was a leaping blaze. The reflections of fire flickered across the cliff walls, illuminating the drawings. Trying to get comfortable, he pulled a blanket around his shoulders. From a cloth bundle, he unwrapped a flute. George Two Feathers had taught him to play it as a child. Wolfson was not an accomplished musician, but the music had always brought him solace.

Leaning back, he began to play, softly at first, then gradually louder, until the melancholy notes of the flute reverberated off the rock, echoing through the forest beyond. Sparks from the fire dazzled and glowed, fluttering toward the cliffs in showers. He felt a growing oneness with the land. He loved this place. He loved the mountains and the plains and the animals and the solitude of it.

This was his mission. His vision quest. Here, he could touch the past, and it was as much a part of him as the blood that surged within his veins.

Raven Crow was right. He'd been gone too many years, lost in a mass of people, buried beneath buildings of glass and steel. He'd forgotten the lifting scents, the noises of the forest, the beckoning whisper of the wind.

As the reflection of flames leaped and pulsed across the cliffs, the noise of his flute played tantalizingly to the moving shadows. For a moment, it was as if the figures were alive. Their horns and hooves danced to the endless rhythms of life. And with them came an echo from the ancient world, a time that existed long before the coming of his tribe.

54

Secretary Mabel Browning stepped into the Elkhorn town square, eyeing the crowd with astonishment. Between the small fountain at one end and the prominent statue of Jeremiah Bates at the other, tables, booths, and various tents of partisan groups were erected, each supporting their position regarding animal rights and the hunting of lions. The Sierra Club and Audubon Society were there. So was a booth from the National Rifle Association. The Montana Ranchers Foundation even had a small kiosk hastily constructed in the hopes of soliciting funds.

The informational booth established by Mayor Miller and Sergeant Hayden appeared wildly successful. Volunteers manned the station twelve hours a day. A large slate board was erected with up-to-the-hour information on sightings, footprints, and kills for everyone to see. At the top of the board, written in large purple letters, was "Lion Watch: Elkhorn Montana."

Registered each day, underneath the title, were the dates and sightings of lions. An 800-number listed at the base of the board gave a telephone recording updated every hour. The number received over fifty calls a day.

A volunteer had written: "6:30 a.m. Female lion with two cubs, killed one mile south of Crazy Horse Reservoir." Below that: "10 a.m. Male lion, 167 pounds, taken, Tompkins Ranch."

A table representing the Boone and Crocket Club stood a few yards away. On a hunch the lion might be a truly colossal animal,

Mayor Miller had asked the club to make final skull measurements once the animal was killed. No one wanted to miss an opportunity to establish a world record.

Nearby was a second table that had been taking bets like a pool for the Super Bowl. You could pick two numbers for a dollar. If the numbers corresponded to the date and hour the lion was brought in, you could win $250.

A woman stood in front of a booth near the statue of Jeremiah Bates. "Stop the killing! Save the lions!" she shouted. "We need only a few more signatures. You don't kill animals indiscriminately just because one animal has made a mistake. If a man has committed a crime, do you shoot his neighbors?"

She waved at Mabel as the secretary passed. "Sign up here, ma'am. It's a worthy cause. Every signature counts."

Mabel politely declined. Continuing across the grass, she weaved through the crowd. Along the side of the square, she observed a small cluster of people circled around a television camera.

Moving closer, she could see it was Kimberly Benson. The reporter was completing an interview with a middle-aged rancher named Steven Jeffries. The man was speaking about a lion that had broken into his pasture and killed three of his sheep and injured seven more. All of the wounded animals had had to be put down. Behind him, laid out across a table, was a dead female lion with two young cubs. The kittens still had their spots. Mabel felt a sudden heaviness in her heart. Sure, the rancher had lost some sheep, but killing the cubs seemed to be going too far.

The secretary worked her way toward a prominent table holding a group of microphones. A dozen television reporters were bunched together, hurriedly arranging their cameras. Off to the side, standing casually, were two men. They had similar facial characteristics and appeared to be related. So, these must be the men everyone was talking about, Mabel thought.

Rumor of the brothers' arrival had passed rapidly through Elkhorn. They had come all the way from Texas. They'd killed over a hundred lions. There were no lion hunters their equal in all of North America, and they were scheduled to give a news conference at noon. Hayden had gone to complete some business in Browning and asked her to attend.

She studied the two men closely. They seemed to be in their mid-thirties, both of medium height, with blondish hair. One had a slightly ruddy complexion. He was dressed in blue jeans and a vest. The other was thinner with the beginnings of a receding hairline and wore light-colored slacks and a tan safari jacket.

Mayor Miller stepped up to the microphones. Raising his hands, he tried to gain everyone's attention. "Ladies and gentlemen. Please!"

Gradually, the crowd began to quiet. More people pushed forward to see what the commotion was about.

"It gives me great pleasure to introduce the Bowden brothers from El Paso," the Mayor said. "They are professional hunters. They have boasted there is no lion they cannot bring in. Hank, Jethro . . ."

An enthusiastic applause rose from the crowd. Reaching over, the mayor twisted a microphone toward the closer of the two. The man in the safari jacket swaggered to the table.

"It's good to be here, folks. Henry and I haven't been in Montana for a couple of years, and we're glad to visit your blessed country and see if we can help you with your problem."

"Were you called in by the governor?" someone asked.

Jethro smiled patiently. "Well, not exactly," he drawled. "We're pretty well known in hunting circles. We've had several calls from a mining company, early on. They were worried about some of their surveyors getting killed. When we heard there was a $100,000 reward, we thought we'd better pack up and head north."

"You and everybody else!" a man in a cowboy hat snorted. A chuckle rose from the bystanders.

"When did you get in?" a reporter questioned.

Jethro spit a slug of tobacco near his foot.

"Near seven last evening. We put in twenty-eight hours coming from El Paso. Took us a day and a half just to get through Texas . . ."

He smiled as the audience laughed. By now, there was a large gathering around the table. Mabel watched quietly from a corner of the crowd. Even at the beginning, she had a sense these brothers knew what they were doing, although the technology they were about to demonstrate was beyond her imagination.

"And what makes you think you will be able to end this when someone like the state hunter couldn't?" a woman asked.

"With all due respect to Mr. Lassiter, ma'am," Henry answered, "you just don't go after a lion like this by yourself. A big Tom can chew up a couple of dogs pretty easily. We got fourteen of the best lion hounds in the country. This, plus we got radio collars on six of 'em. We can follow the direction they're going, and when they get a lion treed, we hear a different signal. And we always bring a half a dozen fresh horses. When one set gets tired, we use the next. I don't think there's going to a problem."

"Like the man said," Jethro chimed in, "we've got a lot of lions under our belt. Killed one over 200 pounds in Arizona last year. Helluva' big Tom. Had paw prints wider than your boot."

"Here, take a look at some of our dogs," Henry added. "You want to bring 'em out, Rufus?"

A short man went over to a large truck parked next to the street. He disappeared in the back section of the cab, then emerged with a half dozen dogs. The hounds began barking wildly, lunging and pulling at their leashes.

Jethro paused. "Sir, keep your dog on its leash over there, please." He pointed toward a man with a German shepherd. "I don't want anyone hurt. These dogs will kill another dog in a second."

The man nodded and pulled his dog protectively away.

Jethro held up a small white squirt bottle filled with fluid.

"Now, watch this, folks."

282

Making several sprays into the air, he started off across the green, jogging in a wide circular path around the square. As he ran, he squirted little tufts of mist at his heels, marking the trail.

At first scent, the hounds went absolutely crazy, howling and lunging wildly. It was all Rufus could do to keep from getting dragged across the grass. These were big-boned animals, with large feet and ferocious-looking fangs. They appeared to Mabel much meaner and stronger than the dogs Lassiter had used.

When Rufus could no longer hold the hounds, he dropped the leashes. The dogs bounded off, roaring hot on Jethro's trail. People fled in every direction. Everyone tried to get out of the way. As the dogs rushed around a corner, they turned over a table. Two chairs went sprawling. Everyone cheered with delight.

The lady in the "Save the Lion" booth began shrieking for them to keep away. An observer slipped on the grass. The hounds trampled right over him. When he got up, there rose an excited cheer. It was as if someone had unleashed a bolt of electricity into the square.

"Nothing like a little lion scent to get 'em stirred up, eh Jethro?" Henry laughed.

"Question there?" Jethro pointed into the audience.

"And what are you going to do if the lion gets away from the hounds?" a skeptic asked.

"Well, we got one final *pièce de résistance*," Jethro chuckled.

"Go ahead. Put the dogs back, Rufus," Henry yelled.

The short man struggled with the hounds, finally getting them collected back into the truck. Once the back gate was closed, Henry called to another assistant. "William, bring out Roxanne, please."

A handler came out from the back of a second truck. A gasp rose from the crowd. An astonished murmur flashed through the reporters.

It was a mountain lion—a real live lion, right in their midst. And it walked casually onto the green, right in the middle of the town square. The handler had the lion on a chain, as he coaxed

283

it gently up to the front table. Here, the lion sat on its haunches and waited.

The handler gave the lion a small piece of meat and stroked its ears. The lion glanced around the audience. Its piercing eyes studied every movement of the crowd. Finally, it yawned, its large canines glinting in the sun. With a bored expression, it settled onto its haunches and began to groom one of its paws.

"Ladies and gentlemen, meet Roxanne," Henry announced. "She is the star of our team."

Mabel Browning watched with astonishment. She couldn't keep her eyes off the lion. The female was one of the most beautiful creatures she'd ever seen. The lion was sleek and well-contoured. Its coat looked as if it was made of velvet. Jethro moved forward and began to scratch the animal's head. The lion stood up and rubbed against his legs like a tabby cat.

"Roxanne has been with us, how long, Henry? Four years?"

"We got the idea when we were having a particularly difficult time chasing a male up in the Grand Canyon. Dogs couldn't keep up with the rough terrain, and the lion we wuz chasing kept doubling back and escaping up one of the ridges. So we figured, why chase the lion? Why not have it come to us?"

"So, we hooked up with Roxanne," Jethro added. "She is a five-year-old female. She's already borne three litters for us. She came from one of the lions we killed a while back, and we raised her outside, but close enough to be friendly."

"Are you saying that you let her loose to chase the male?" a reporter asked with surprise.

"Even better." Henry reached into a satchel and pulled out a small Velcro collar. Holding the device above his head, he waved it so everyone could see.

"Radio collar. The latest in electronics. Made by the same company that placed an electronic transmitter on the back of a bee. The device weighs less than a pound. Attaches with a Velcro collar and transmits a signal we can pick up by satellite a hundred miles away."

He reached over and gently applied the collar to the lion's neck. The animal rolled its head, eyed him for a second, and then dropped down on all fours, resting like a sphinx.

Jethro chimed in. "Once we find that a male is in the area, we give her an injection of hormones. Within six hours, she'll come into heat. Then we take her out to the forest where we found the male and turn her loose. She's pretty good at taking care of herself. Even likes to chase a deer every now and then, don't you, Rox?" Jethro rubbed the cat's head.

My God, Mabel thought. She could hear the lion begin to purr.

"So, she goes out and begins screaming at night and scents up the place, and the male will find her. We let them pair up for a couple of days and then go after them. She knows the routine well. The dogs come. She jumps up a tree. Most times, the male climbs right up with her.

"In the past several years, we've taken more than twenty lions this way. We especially like to use her with the difficult ones. Like this cat you got here in Elkhorn. Once a male mates with her, he'll stay in the area. You know they mate maybe thirty, forty times over twenty-four hours, and when they are mating, the male is thinking only about one thing. Kind of like falling off a log—eh, Henry?"

Henry began to laugh. "So, if the governor wants to make that check for a hundred thousand, we'll be glad to pick it up . . . say, tomorrow or the next day."

"One thing for those of you interested in conservation and preserving the lions," Jethro commented. "I see Sierra Club and Audubon represented here. Because we use a female that attracts a mature male lion, we avoid hunting down the female cats or mothers with cubs. This type of hunting also avoids young, immature males. That's why we've got a good system."

Mabel shook her head. It was an intriguing operation. It sounded as if they had covered every angle.

"There's supposed to be a Blackfoot Indian out there hunting the lion," a young man said. Mabel craned her neck to see who the speaker was. She recognized one of the local wranglers. Amongst all the rumors that were circulating around town was a crazy, unsubstantiated story that a teacher from Chicago had gone through some type of mutilation ceremony and was in the mountains hunting the lion.

"An Indian?" Jethro coughed incredulously. "What about an Indian?"

"What if he kills the lion?"

"An Indian by hisself? Do you hear that, Henry? He ain't got no dogs, no horses, and no satellite-tracking devices. What if a bull has tits, eh?"

Loud guffaws rose from the audience. The television cameras swung back and forth, trying to keep up with the responses.

"I would just say if there is any man in the area we're hunting, he'd better clear out. These are lion dogs, son. These dogs don't take lightly to anyone in their way. They're used to chasing bear and lions, and they're ferocious fighters. Safest place for an Indian is up a tree."

"Maybe get all three on the same limb," Jethro quipped.

A chuckle came from the observers.

"Dogs near killed a man when we was hunting back in El Paso last year," Henry said. "Mexican fellow. When they got through with him, he lost an ear and nearly part of a leg."

"Almost lost his balls," Jethro grunted.

A murmur of amusement rose from the audience. The crowd pushed toward the Bowden brothers, trying to see the female lion better. Abruptly, everyone began asking questions at the same time.

Mabel chuckled to herself and started back toward the station. She passed Kimberly Benson and her cameraman. They nodded briefly. Then Mabel saw Franklyn Yellow Pine. The youth had been standing behind the table, watching the presentation. He remained for a moment, smiled at her, and drifted off into the crowd.

Of the hundred or so people packed into the town square, there were few others she recognized. Elkhorn was a small town, and she had thought she knew everyone. In this crowd, there were dozens of people she'd never seen before.

This lion stuff was getting pretty crazy, she thought. In truth, she wanted it to be over. The beauty of the female lion brought a new appreciation for the cats she'd not previously considered. Still, there was a man-eating member of the species out there that needed to be stopped. As long as the killer remained free, it was turning Elkhorn into a three-ring circus. And in the middle, now holding center stage, were the two brothers from El Paso.

What they proposed was shockingly simple. Yet there was something about it that tugged at her sensibilities. Something that seemed unjust. Somehow, they seemed to be using techniques on these magnificent beasts that were not quite fair. When she thought about it, the sheriff's department used female decoys in crime work all the time, didn't they?

And what was fair about Tracy Reynolds jogging down a logging trail, or Lute Olsson trying to chase the lion? Or Howard Lassiter, one of the great hunters in Montana, getting killed? What was fair about that to their families?

In a way, it was like holding a torch at night to catch a moth. No matter what the moth thought, it would be pulled irresistibly to the light, trapped by a million years of instinctual orientation toward the moon. And now the Bowden brothers were using the sexual drive—a drive so powerful in most species, the male would be rendered totally helpless—to lure a male lion to a decoy female.

There was no way that the Bowdens could fail, Mabel thought. How incredibly clever. How horribly precise.

55

IT WAS A MAGNIFICENT OLD-GROWTH CEDAR, two hundred twenty feet tall and eleven feet in diameter. Despite logging efforts around Elkhorn in the early 1900s, the tree had somehow escaped. Its wood was the kind that built great ships or sturdy cabinets or varnished chests worth $1,000 when sanded smooth and carved with the genteel touch of an artisan. The bark had been marked once with an ugly, yellow splash. There was even the scar of a saw along its base. Maybe the winter storms had come early that year, or perhaps a flash flood during the spring. Whatever had happened, the loggers had abandoned it.

At the cutting, had it occurred, a detailed cross section would have identified over seven hundred rings. In 1297, when Edward I ratified the *Magna Carta*, the cedar was thirty-seven feet tall. In 1492, when Columbus discovered the New World, the tree had occupied this spot for over two hundred years. Little had changed geographically during the past five centuries. Certainly, the streambed had altered its course, but the entrance to the canyon was much the same, and the venerable old tree still occupied a strategic position at the trailhead.

From an osprey's nest, you could see Eagle Lake two miles away. If you followed the stream out from the canyon to the south, you would find a junction with the Arcata River. Looking back toward the mountains were the great, ridged walls of Porcupine Canyon. A thousand feet they rose, in ledges of sedimentary rock, the top incredibly steep and devoid of vegetation. At the end of the canyon was a waterfall. Here, a stream cascaded downward, leaping and bounding until the filamentous strands disappeared along the sides of a talus slope.

The base of the tree formed the hub of a number of radiating trails. Some came from the canyon and followed the stream, working their way toward Eagle Lake. Others penetrated the forest and crossed the water, moving gradually toward the mountains. Deer, elk, and moose traveled these paths. So did rabbits, squirrels, and foxes. And on this particular day, in the soft earth next to the tree were the paw prints of a lion.

By now, practically everyone in Montana was aware of the "Blackfoot Lion," as the press called it. Hardly a day passed without a lead article covering the largest lion hunt in the history of the western United States.

To those who would listen, the Native Americans called this creature *Omahkatayo* or "spirit cat." A few said it was not an animal of these times. Others merely referred to the beast as the "Great Lion" to distinguish it from all other cats of lesser size.

To be sure, there were other large lions in Montana that season. And on this particular afternoon, lounging seventy-five feet up, with his legs draped over a limb as big as a man's thigh, rested a lion of formidable size. He was a mature male, ten years old, weighing well over two hundred pounds.

Years ago, he had chipped his right front canine on the takedown of an elk, and now his fangs were worn to a third of what they used to be. In the accelerated aging of *Felis concolor*, by the age of twelve, these great teeth would further erode, a product of wear and dietary factors. Eventually, the teeth would become so worn they would no longer be the rapier-sharp killing devices that served the animal so well.

A mature lion at the age of seven is at the height of his prime. At ten, like a great athlete past his peak, he has lost a step. A second of lost speed means there are deer and elk that can beat it at the run. Another year, another step lost, and the number of animals that it can successfully kill lessens. At that point, when age and speed and tooth decay take their inevitable toll, he will die.

Yet to look at this particular lion, you could hardly imagine a more superb specimen. He was sleek and muscular, and where he had lost a step, he made up with increased cunning. Now his stalks were performed upwind. Now he carefully positioned himself closer to the herd before he charged. Whereas before he could often outrun the game, he no longer had that luxury. Now his charges were close ambushes, rushes made with a single leap, cleverly positioned, using all his strength.

In this way, he was able to remain solid, heavy, and strong. But his genetic time clock was running out. If not this year, the next. There was no exact predictability when it would come. A particularly hard winter, a drought season with little game, a misstep chasing a mountain goat, and he was gone.

Still, his life could be considered enviable by some. He hunted and ate when he wanted, and mated with an assortment of captivating females when nature dictated they were ready. The rest of the time he traveled, sometimes defending his territory from other males, and sometimes, like today, sleeping fitfully as cats will do, dreaming in the luxurious warmth of a patch of sun.

Toward evening he decided to come down. His movements were leisurely and unhurried. It was as if he had all the time in the world.

Stretching, he began to descend from his perch, moving headfirst down the trunk. The cedar gave a slight tremor as he stepped from crook to limb. When he reached the bottom forking of branches, he dropped to the ground in a graceful leap. He landed in the soft earth with barely a sound.

It was six in the afternoon. Having no particular direction in mind, he followed a game trail that led alongside the stream. He was not hungry. He had fed heavily the night before on a young moose he had stumbled upon. Now his mind was more on sex. It had been two months since he had mated, and he was curious to see if he could find a female he knew lived in the area of Porcupine Canyon.

As he padded up the trail, he came to a narrow clearing. He remained at full alert, ears forward, whiskers fanning. His nose twitched with each newfound scent. Abruptly, he paused. A sudden odor stopped him in his tracks.

He made a circle, carefully sniffing around the clearing. At a corner next to a hidden path, he found an area of loose grass pushed together in a mound. Raking with his paw, he uncovered the droppings. Three elongated pieces of lion scat were buried here. The smell was unmistakably that of another male, and the odor made his hair bristle.

A dead tree stood next to the clearing. Chest puffed, tail thrashing, he walked stiff-legged to the tree to make his mark. Standing on his hind legs, he scratched at the decaying bark with his claws. He would mark the bark so that other lions would note his size. If there was another male nearby, perhaps it would push on, not wanting to tangle with a lion as formidable as he. Yet, as he shredded the tree, he saw to his astonishment that there were higher scratchings.

A foot above his reach were the marks of another lion. As high as he could stretch, he could not match them. He was a large lion. By Montana standards, there were few cats in the state his size. Before him were the markings of a giant.

Had he been smart, he would have left. There was plenty of land for him to patrol. But his actions were controlled more by instinct than by reason. And on this particular evening, the discovery of another male made his blood boil.

He backed down from the dead tree and sniffed around the base of the clearing, spraying his scent. Then he defecated, marking the spot with his hind legs, creating a mound by scratching loose twigs and branches. Every place the other male had left scat, he obliterated the signs, scattering the debris until there was nothing left.

He tried to smell which way the other lion had gone. The scent seemed to lead in the direction of Porcupine Canyon. Were he to follow the stranger, he realized, he would have to be extraordinarily careful. But the challenge was too great for him to resist. If the other were still in the area, he would find the male and chase it off. His instinctual drive for dominance gave him no choice.

With nightfall, he worked his way two miles into the interior. Peaked ridges of the canyon began to crowd on either side. He paused at a curve in the stream and crouched to drink. It was then he heard the cry. It came once and did not repeat. In centuries past, out on the prairie, it was the type of sound that made a settler's blood run cold. Some likened it to a woman's scream.

The cry was from a female lion in heat, looking for a mate. His pulse rose, his breath came in rapid pants. A surge of excitement drummed inside his loins.

The call seemed to come from a cluster of trees at the base of the cliffs, and he started at a lope, attempting to home in on the female. As he drew closer, he slowed to a stalk.

A twig snapped. His muscles tightened. His ears probed for the slightest sound. Cautiously, he began to creep forward, placing one foot in front of the next. He scanned the trees ahead. He was so focused on finding the female that he didn't notice the immense form that materialized out of the shadows behind him.

The odor of the Great Lion reached his nostrils like a blast. The impact was so great he sprang in the air, twisting sideways, landing in the opposite direction. By all standards, he was a big male. But there, standing before him, was the largest lion he'd ever seen.

For the old male, his actions honed by thousands of years of evolution, there was only one response. There was no turning back. He would fight to the death. Until this moment, he had been king. To the victor would come the rights of mating and territorial dominance.

A deep rumble erupted from his chest. His lips curled in a snarl. Steadily, he advanced toward his enormous adversary, ears back, claws unsheathed, looking for some weakness, some vulnerability toward which he could attack. Finally, when he could control his rage no longer, he charged, his voice rising in a scream.

56

A MILE FROM THE ENTRANCE TO PORCUPINE CANYON, a small campfire blazed. Crouched next to the fire was the figure of a man, dwarfed by the immensity of surrounding trees. By nine that night, Wolfson had eaten the last of his rations and made a pot of coffee. He sat for a time listening to the sounds. Hell of a fight out there, he thought. He rose once and stared into the darkness but could see nothing. He grabbed his rifle and pulled the weapon closer to his side. A chill permeated the air. He shivered once and pushed in closer to the fire.

He'd spent most of the day following tracks. There were lion prints everywhere. Along the riverbed, in scattered trails along the ravines, in soft mud at the edge of clearings, he found them. Some of the tracks were huge. There were at least two very large males in the area, and he wondered if they had gotten into a fight.

So far, finding the Great Lion had proven extremely diffi-cult. He was sure the lion had crisscrossed the area several times. Where the animal was now, he could only guess. In the morning, he would search out the location of the fight and then go deep into the canyon, following the stream to its origin. It was the one place he hadn't searched. Perhaps the lion had a cave up there.

As Wolfson sat by the fire, an owl hooted off in the trees. He stopped and listened. The hooting came a second time. Cupping his hands, Wolfson gave an answering call.

His horse shifted on its feet. A moment later a branch snapped. Then came the sound of a heavy foot. A figure on horseback emerged in the firelight. It was Franklyn Yellow Pine.

"Hi. How goes it?"

Franklyn slipped off his horse and walked up to Wolfson. The two shook hands. There came a sudden whinny as a second horse emerged from the shadows. Wolfson spun backwards, reaching for his rifle.

"No, it's OK," Franklyn said. "I brought a friend."

Wolfson eyed the approaching rider. He was disturbed Franklyn had invited a second person. Their rendezvous was supposed to be a secret.

"We agreed you would come alone."

"Sorry," Franklyn answered. "This seemed to be an exception."

"There were to be no exceptions," Wolfson replied angrily.

Franklyn helped the other rider down. The two came into the firelight. Wolfson caught a glimpse of the face, the eyes, the faint smile. His heart twisted.

"Kimberly!"

"Franklyn told me that you were here," she said, breathlessly. "I thought I should come."

Wolfson stared at her. "This is no place for you."

She paused for a moment, not quite sure what to say. Then the words tumbled out. "I was so worried. I went to the Sundance. I saw you there. I thought you were dead. I tried to call several times to let your sister know I wished you well, but she wouldn't let me through. When I learned you were hunting by yourself, I convinced Franklyn it would be all right. I wasn't sure when you were leaving. I was afraid you might get hurt . . . afraid I wouldn't see you again . . ."

"I see you two have met," Franklyn said dryly.

"This is not what I wanted." Wolfson frowned.

He glanced at Kimberly, his eyes scanning her face. "I didn't want to get you caught up in this."

"Bobby, they have a second lion, a female decoy. They've given her an injection of hormones, and they've put her out to attract the male. They have a radio collar on her. They will track her every movement. They tried to keep secret where they're searching, but the word's out: they've placed her here in Porcupine Canyon. When Franklyn told me he was going to meet you, I had to come."

"What she says is true," Franklyn added. "I wouldn't have believed it if I hadn't seen it. They paraded the female out in the middle of the town square. She's like a tame cat. She's helped them kill over twenty lions. Once she goes into heat, she will attract a dominant male for miles."

Wolfson turned away, wiping a hand across his forehead "That certainly adds a complication to this hunt I hadn't dreamed of," he fretted. "It means we've got to move much faster than I thought."

He stepped back toward the fire. A grim expression lined his face. Taking a fresh log, he tossed it onto the coals. "Well, we can't do anything tonight," he finally said. "Let's sit down and talk. Maybe there is some way you two can help."

THAT NIGHT, FAR PAST MIDNIGHT, when the fire burned steadily down, Kimberly rolled up in a blanket with her head on a saddle. Franklyn was sleeping on the other side of the coals, snoring quietly. He had said he would go back and leave them together, but Kimberly knew now was not the time. Wolfson must have realized this too, for he asked Franklyn to stay. "I will be needing you tomorrow," he told him. "Kimberly will have to leave. It's too dangerous for her here."

She lay with her head on the saddle and tried to sleep, but every time she opened her eyes, she could see his form curled in the blanket. She wondered if he was awake and what he was thinking.

The wounds in his chest had apparently healed, for he made little mention of them now. As far as she could tell, he was back to normal. Maybe a little gaunter than she remembered, but there was little other difference.

Sometime in the early hours, a troop of coyotes howled far down the canyon, and then came the soft hoot of an owl. Kimberly fell asleep for a time. When she opened her eyes, she saw Wolfson sitting before the fire. A blanket was wrapped around his shoulders.

"Bobby?" she said softly.

He stirred, glancing across the fire. "I thought you were asleep."

"Hard to sleep."

"Yeah, I know," he answered.

"What are you going to do if you find the lion?"

"I've got to kill it," Wolfson answered simply. "I don't think I have any other choice. It's crossed the line. There is no telling how many more could get hurt. My personal feelings are out of it now. No one will let it live under these circumstances."

"But why you? Why do you have to be the one to hunt it down?"

"I'm not sure I have a good answer," he replied.

"Why don't you just let the Texans come in here and take it, and the whole thing will be over?"

"I wish it was that easy," he said. "Part of it is my lineage. Part of it is the feelings of the Blackfoot and their relationship to the lion. And part of me just doesn't like the thought of a lion sitting in a tree with dogs jumping around it, waiting to be shot. Not this lion. This lion is something special. He's too big, too strong, too magnificent to end like that."

"But if you're going to kill it, what difference does it make?"

"I guess it's an Indian thing."

"And you're willing to risk your life?"

He shrugged and did not answer.

She watched in the glow of the fire, as the flickering light played across his features. His eyes glinted with the reflection of coals. It was all she could do to keep from reaching over and touching him. She wanted to tell him that she was afraid for him, that she did not think he had a chance in the forest by himself. She'd been with Lassiter when he was killed. Wolfson was not a hunter. She wanted to say he was a fool, that this lion was a powerful, colossal beast that could kill him in a second.

Instead, Kimberly rolled back in her blanket and rested her head on the saddle. She would go back to Elkhorn in the morning and keep up with the Bowden brothers and the various events in town.

Such different worlds, such different backgrounds, she thought. Wolfson was the first person in years who had made her body tremble. And this second meeting, here in the forest, confirmed what her heart had told her the first night they had talked.

Just as at the Sundance, she had a growing feeling that she was powerless to help. Maybe if she prayed, one of her prayers would wrap him in a protective shield. There was not a lot else she could do.

57

THEY STARTED AT FIRST LIGHT. Franklyn took Kimberly back to town. Kimberly would keep abreast of the Texans' plans. Franklyn would ride with Wolfson for the day and then return to Elkhorn later that evening. Now there was a certain desperation to Wolfson's hunt. Time was running out, and Wolfson realized Franklyn's help was a considerable asset. Like many Native Americans, Franklyn was a solid tracker and had a good knowledge of game. By spreading out, the two could canvass an area much better than he could do alone.

By seven, Wolfson had come upon the tracks of a large lion in the soft ground. He whistled for Franklyn to join him. For an hour, they tracked the male until they found the clearing where the lions had fought. The place looked as if it had been hit by a cyclone. Saplings were broken. The grass was matted and swirled. Smudges of blood were scattered across the ground.

They spent several minutes carefully searching the area. It was Franklyn who heard the sound. He held up his hand, listening. From a deep thicket came a faint, rasping sigh. Wolfson moved through the brush, searching carefully. In a shallow depression, they discovered the old male on his side, panting heavily. The lion had crawled into the brush to die. It was too weak to lift its head. A pool of blood trickled from its mouth.

Wolfson wondered for a moment what they should do. If he fired his gun, it might scare other lions out of the area. But he couldn't leave the wounded animal. Death for it was too long, too cruel, to tolerate.

"We've got to end it," he said.

Placing his rifle to the lion's head, Wolfson pointed the barrel at a deep puncture wound on the right side of the skull and mercifully pulled the trigger. The old cat shuddered once and was gone.

Franklyn cut down several branches from a fir and placed them over the body. It was a fitting burial for an old lion. It would not keep the coyotes or the ravens away for long, but perhaps this day, the lion would rest in peace.

They spent the remainder of the morning searching further into the canyon. Next to a stream, a quarter mile away, Franklyn found fresh tracks of a lion that could only be the one they were pursuing. The paw prints were huge. And then it all made sense.

During the night, there had been a fight of mammoth proportions, and the Great Lion had won. The spirit cat, *Omahkatayo*, was here. And the tracks before them were less than an hour old. Even as he studied the colossal four-lobed prints, Wolfson had the uncomfortable feeling the lion was aware of their presence. Some sixth sense told him silent eyes watched them from the forest.

They rode for eight hours that day, penetrating deep within the canyon, following the small river upward until they reached the base of the waterfall. Wolfson searched on one side of the stream, Franklyn the other. Whistling or using game calls, they communicated back and forth, alerting each other of their finds. Their conversations were brief and often at a whisper.

At the edge of a meadow, Franklyn found a place used as a lion scraping. There was a tall dead tree that had claw marks high along its trunk. Further into the canyon, Wolfson discovered the carcass of a young moose, half-eaten and freshly killed. The work was tedious and time-consuming, and their yield frustratingly small.

It wasn't until they emerged from the canyon in the late afternoon that they began to see tracks again. Just outside the cliffs, Franklyn whistled softly. Here were two prints, half-buried in earth. A dozen yards away was a second set along the edge of the stream. The pugmarks were fresh.

"I don't remember seeing these prints when we rode upstream this morning," Franklyn said.

"It must have come here after we went into the canyon."

"Do you think it's aware we're here?"

"I think it's known all along."

As he reached down to measure the width of the prints, Wolfson knew it was the animal they were after. The freshness of the tracks sent a renewed sense of uneasiness up his spine. The lion knew they were in the canyon. It must have waited until they came upstream and then crossed in behind them. Was it hunting them? Had it been following them all along?

They had just crossed a stream and entered a thick cluster of pines, when Wolfson noticed his mount had become progressively nervous. The horse seemed fidgety, shying at every bush. Soon both animals began to jerk.

"Whoa! Whoa!" Franklyn yelled. His horse pawed nervously at the ground. He tried to rein the horse, but the animal wouldn't stop. "What's the matter with you?"

"Franklyn, we have company," Wolfson said quietly. He nodded toward the forest.

When they reached an open meadow between two broad swaths of forest, Wolfson reined his horse to a halt. He pulled the rifle out of its scabbard and dismounted. He handed Franklyn his reins.

"I'm going back on foot."

Franklyn stared at him in disbelief. "You crazy?"

"I think I can entice him out in the open."

"How?"

"Ride ahead. Go fast enough to clear the area. If you hear a shot, come back."

"If not?"

"Then you better bring a body bag," Wolfson grunted.

"Bobby, this is absolutely insane," Franklyn protested.

Wolfson shook his head. "Leave me here with him . . . alone."

"Come on, Bobby. This makes no sense."

"He'll never come out in the open if we're together with the horses."

"It's stupid and foolhardy, and you're going to get killed," Franklyn answered.

"Leave me," Wolfson said.

Scowling, Franklyn shrugged and did what he was told. Wolfson watched the youth disappear with the horses and turned back toward the forest.

He stood for a long time without moving, carefully surveying his surroundings. Where was the lion? Nothing around him moved. If the lion was there, it was totally invisible.

He remained here, trying to catch his breath, trying to calm the surging of his heart. How was he going to lure the lion out into the open? What chance did he have on foot?

Movement. A small bush shimmered near the base of a tree. Wolfson stared at the forest, trying to penetrate the gloom. He could feel the skin prickle at the back of his neck. So, the lion was here, he thought. And it was close. He could sense it was moving toward him, stalking, coming in for the kill.

He felt his rifle, checked the loading mechanism to be sure a cartridge was in place, and then slipped off the safety. He took a deep breath and tightened his jaw. This was it, he told himself. This was what he had come for. There would be no turning back.

Suddenly, he darted across an open spot, keeping low, bent over, his profile like that of a moving deer. He paused, hesitated, and started again, running in short, erratic bursts through the trees. As he ran, he made a soft calling sound, the noise a frightened elk might make, looking for its herd.

Out of the corner of his vision, he caught a glimpse of something moving. Then came a shift of shadows and a flash of tawny brown.

He started up again, this time in an irregular, sprinting fashion, just as a desperate elk might do in a panic-stricken run. It was a clever ploy, a trick his grandfather had taught him as a boy. Act like prey—look, sound, and move like prey—and a predator will follow.

With an animal cry, Wolfson took off again. He ran for another hundred feet, darting and springing through the forest, sensing the beast was right behind him. At the last instant, he jumped sideways.

He would have a point-blank shot at the brain of the charging animal, the rifle thrust practically in its mouth. But as he turned, his foot caught a root. He tripped and fell forward, landing on his side. The fall dislodged the rifle from his fingers.

He was trying to get his hands up to protect his head when the impact of the lion flattened him to the ground. The breath was knocked out of him. Gasping wildly, he curled into a ball and lay there stunned.

For a second, he could sense the lion's head so close he could smell its breath. If he could get a hand around its throat, maybe he could jam a fist into its jaws. Then maybe he could twist away and reach his rifle. It was a desperate move. It was the only chance he had.

"Now!" his senses screamed. Flipping sideways, he rammed his left hand toward the lion's mouth while his right hand groped wildly for its neck. It was then he grasped the Velcro collar.

58

THE EXPLOSION RATTLED OFF THE STOREFRONTS. A tongue of flame pierced the morning darkness. A gasp came from the crowd. Jethro Bowden stood in front of his truck as a plume of smoke rose from his gun.

"Load up," he yelled. "We got a lion to kill!"

A large group had gathered in the town square before dawn. Nearly a dozen cars and trucks pulled up alongside the statue of Jeremiah Bates. Their lights were on, engines running. Some of the observers were members of the press; others were from state agencies such as Fish and Game. Many were townspeople or tourists who wanted to come along. Kimberly Benson and her cameraman, Eric Stafford, arrived at 4:45. By 5:30, everyone was ready.

"Hell, you'd think we were giving free tickets to the Dallas Cowboys," Henry drawled.

He turned and swung into the lead truck. The brothers had two large trailers. Six horses were carried in the first; six additional mounts would follow in the second. Behind them came two pickups loaded with their hounds.

The convoy pulled out of Elkhorn and headed toward the mountains. They traveled for forty minutes in darkness. As the faint blush of dawn began to spread along the horizon, the line of vehicles came to a halt. In the distance, glowing in the rising dawn, rose the steep rim of Porcupine Canyon.

A lump worked its way into Kimberly's throat. Where was Wolfson? she wondered. Was he safe? Was Franklyn with him? Were they still in the forest?

She worried now about a confrontation with the Bowden brothers. They had a lot of hounds, and they would be on horseback; and, if somebody got in their way, she was afraid they might turn the dogs on him, or worse, he might be shot.

Leaving Wolfson was one of the hardest things she had ever done. He seemed too determined, too fixed in his intentions, to alter his plans. If she was to be his friend, she knew she must honor his wishes. She hoped he had left the area, perhaps gone above the canyon rim. There he would be safe. At least Franklyn was with him. But where the two were now, she could only guess.

As the Bowdens began saddling their horses, two huntsmen brought out the hounds. There was a sudden flurry of barking and yelling. The dogs lunged wildly on their leashes.

Most of the occupants of the caravan got out. Several of the photographers began filming. To Henry Bowden's annoyance, someone fired a flash. Jethro placed a portable laptop on the hood of one of the trucks. With a couple of keystrokes, he began searching for the radio collar of their tame lion. On the computer screen, a target of concentric circles lit up. In the middle was a blinking dot.

"Right on the money!" Henry exclaimed. "Roxanne should be right there." He pointed to the canyon ahead. "And the big male should be right with her."

Rufus moved out from the first horse trailer and handed Jethro a vest. The hunter raised his hand to get everyone's attention.

"A couple of things I should tell you," he began. "During the hunt, please try to stay here along the road. We'll leave the laptop with one of our assistants so you can follow the chase. We have two-way communications, so you can hear from base what's going on. You're welcome to stay here by the cab and listen."

Pausing, he buttoned a heavy safari jacket over his vest. "You can see I'm putting on some protective gear. The vest is Kevlar, a bulletproof vest for police work, but it serves for lion claws as well. If we get charged or wound the animal, it's better to have a margin of safety."

His assistant handed him a double-barrel shotgun. Jethro opened the breech and thrust two shells into the chamber. He closed the gun with a metallic snap.

"We always use shotguns for this work," he said. "You need the safety of a spread of twelve to fourteen inches using double-O shot. Up close, no lion can survive. The problem with a rifle: if you're shooting at a charging animal, a single bullet makes it harder to drop. We want no room for error."

Kimberly listened with interest. They ran an extraordinary operation, she thought. As much as she'd been impressed with Howard Lassiter, these men covered every angle.

Jethro put his foot into the stirrup and swung effortlessly across the saddle. Kimberly glanced around and saw Eric Stafford filming in the background.

"One of the reasons we use a female is to show the male what to do," Henry added. "He'll see her go up into a tree and follow. So we'll take him first and then coax Roxanne down with some food."

"Jethro, you ready? Bill? Rufus?"

The three men mounted. One of the assistants brought Rufus an H-shaped tracking device. Holding the receiver in one hand, the small man attached a pair of earphones to his head.

The dogs began milling about, nervously pulling at their leashes. A ferocious clamor rose as a dogfight started. An assistant waded into the pack, cursing and kicking the animals apart.

"We'd better be off before the dogs kill each other," Jethro grunted.

Rufus raised the H-shaped radio receiver, listening intently. Slowly swinging the device back and forth, he pointed directly toward the mouth of the canyon.

"Signal's there."

"Let's get us a lion!" Jethro cried.

A wash of light flowed through the trees. Birds flitted in the upper boughs. Kimberly walked over to the Bowdens' truck and waited by the two-way transmitter. She stood next to a dozen others. Give them an hour, she thought. By 7:30, she hoped it would be over.

JETHRO BOWDEN SLOWED HIS HORSE to an easy canter as he followed the game trail ahead. He kept at the lead, while the others followed closely behind. Rufus continued to listen on his earphones, periodically checking the frequencies to be sure they were on the course.

For a time, Jethro could hear the hounds working the scent. It was always amazing to him how the forest could hide all sounds. In the dense trees, even the scattered barks and chips of the dogs were hard to locate, especially on the run. Without a radio transmitter, he wasn't sure how a hunter could manage.

The dogs broke into a series of deep-throated howls. Jethro kicked his horse to a gallop.

"Come on, boys!" he shouted. "Sounds like the dogs are on!"

A herd of elk crashed across their path. Several of the dogs broke off the trail and went after the elk. Jethro whistled shrilly after them. The hounds were fresh and excited, and it was hard to keep them focused on the lion. Give them another ten minutes, he figured, and they should begin to settle down.

Jethro hoped the big cat would stay and fight. He hadn't witnessed a good battle between a lion and his hounds in over a year. He enjoyed the thought of dismounting and wading into the midst of the melee, then blasting the lion with his gun. That's when the hunting became exciting—up close and personal. Maybe he could open the microphones and let the audience hear the fight.

There were a lot of reporters in the convoy banking on their success. If it ended in fifteen minutes without a struggle, it would look too easy. Henry could make a hell of a lion imitation. Maybe if the lion was treed early, they could fake a fight, get the dogs to howl, and have Henry screech as if he was dying. Jethro could envision the reporters gathered around the truck, eyes wide, listening breathlessly to the struggle. He smirked at the thought.

When he reached a clearing, he reined his horse to a halt. Rufus stopped to listen on the earphones. The short man rotated the antennae slowly. "Signal's there," he said, pointing. "Directly ahead."

The hunt carried to the base of the canyon. Then came a subtle shift in the direction of the chase. For the first time, Jethro began to have a hint something was wrong. He pulled his horse to stop. Rufus reined behind him. Then came Henry and William.

"You sure we got them in this direction?" he puzzled.

Rufus checked the receiver. "The lion is beeping there." Pausing, he flipped through the frequencies of the collared dogs. "And the dogs are moving southeast as well. I think maybe the lions have begun to run."

Makes sense, Jethro thought. Maybe the dogs flushed the lions and scared them. Despite his optimism, he knew that every lion hunt was different. Always, there was the unexpected. That's why he enjoyed the chase. If they just rode up and blew a lion out of a tree, how monotonous it would be. Listening, he could hear the dogs at full voice, but the direction seemed to be changing. The animals were moving east.

As THE SUN CONTINUED TO RISE, Jethro began peeling off his clothes. First came the zippered safari coat, then a turtleneck sweater. Finally, he was wearing only the Kevlar vest.

"I don't think I've ever seen a lion run like this, Henry," he gasped. "I'm dying out here."

"Let's give the horses a break and follow them in the truck," Henry replied. "God, that lion's giving us a run."

When they reached the trucks, they trailered the exhausted horses, checked the laptop, and began driving slowly along the road, following the blinking light on the computer. The road gradually climbed up the side of a mountain.

Ahead, the valley narrowed. Below was a thick-forested depression. The hollow ran for nearly a mile before it ended in a ridge. Here was a natural saddle between two mountains.

"Treed!" Rufus cried.

He rapidly switched the frequency of the radio receiver. The tracking pings of the dogs changed to a high-pitched clang. "Treed from number two . . . and there's number three."

"We got 'em!" Jethro shouted.

Across the valley, the sounds of the hounds rose in a wild cacophony. The barks and howls grew in intensity, carried by gusts of wind.

"You want the horses?" Hank asked.

"No time," Jethro answered.

The brothers piled out of the truck. Rufus leaped from the back seat. "Still treed," he added, tapping on his earphones.

Grabbing their guns, the Bowdens started at a run into the valley. The sound of the dogs was close, and the hunters covered the last hundred yards at a sprint. They arrived at a ridge out of breath. A number of hounds were milling around the base of a large tree. Several were leaping up the trunk, scratching at the bark, trying to climb into the branches

Jethro pulled them back. Henry moved around the base of the tree, gun raised, searching for the lions.

"Can't see them." He shook his head. "If they're up there, I can't find them."

He spent a moment tramping around the base of the tree, looking upwards.

"Nothing," he grunted. "Where's the rest of the dogs?"

Rufus adjusted his earphones, swinging the H-shaped antenna first to the right, then left, trying to amplify the signal.

"Shit," he grunted. "They're moving again."

"Crazy," Jethro said. The chase had lasted much longer than he expected. He was clearly in no shape for such a vigorous sprint. His heart struggled inside his chest. His legs shook. Both brothers were soaked in sweat.

The hunters struggled to the top of the ridge, passing through a field of boulders, picking their way laboriously up a twisting trail. Jethro found a gap in the trees and sat on a rock. He took out his binoculars and began to glass the area beyond. The ridge gave way to a forested area that opened onto a broad plain.

Jethro sucked in his breath. There, visible through a space in the trees, was the town of Elkhorn. He could see telephone lines and scattered houses and then a highway with passing cars. As he swept his binoculars along the road, his gaze came to the Dairy Queen. Beyond that were several filling stations, a motel, and a large building that looked like a high school. Next to the school was the beginning of a residential section with a row of houses. He couldn't believe his eyes. Were the damn lions going right into the middle of town?

"Get the horses," he cried. Then he took the two-way radio and raised the transmitter to his lips. "Base, we got a problem . . ."

MABEL WAS SITTING AT HER DESK behind the switchboard when the call came in. She was stunned. She was so sure that the lion would be killed that she had been expecting an announcement the Bowdens were returning to collect their reward. The emergency alert caught her by surprise. The lions were moving in toward the perimeter of town. Both animals should be considered extremely dangerous.

Hayden sat in his office, presiding over a meeting about teenage violence. Mabel interrupted over the intercom.

"Sam! You'd better get on this right away!"

He was up in a second, grabbing a gun, barking out commands.

"Where are they coming from? The north? That's out by the Dairy Queen. I'll go there immediately. Have Campbell join me as quick as he can."

Inside the patrol car, Hayden slammed down the accelerator, squealing out from the station, siren shrieking. He ran through the drill in his mind. Call the schools. Keep the children inside. Alert the local radio station. Get everyone off the streets. There were lions coming into town. And wherever the animals were, shoot them on sight!

THE HUNTERS CAME THROUGH THE LAST SECTION of trees at a gallop. The visibility was poor, there were no good trails, and the horses were crashing heavily through the brush. At one point, Jethro tried to avoid a low branch and nearly lost his balance. Ducking forward, he managed to stay on.

Jethro didn't want to waste time. Once they got back to the trucks, they rolled fresh horses off the trailer and took off. They could cross the ridge and follow the chase far quicker on horseback than with the vehicles.

The dogs had been running nonstop. For most of the chase, they were hidden in the forest, located only by their telemetry units. As the hounds moved out into the open, Jethro had an unobstructed view of the animals for the first time. Clearly, they were hot on the trail. He'd seen them chase too many lions to think otherwise. The dogs had their heads down, their voices in full chorus.

Ahead, Jethro saw a pair of trucks rolling up the interstate. He tightened his jaw. Even from a distance, he could hear the hum of passing traffic. If the dogs got onto the freeway, they would be slaughtered. He held his breath and then exhaled with a groan. The dogs veered to the right, moving en masse toward the Dairy Queen.

Jethro spurred his horse, trying to go faster. Out on the highway, a squad car approached, siren warbling. On the patio of the Dairy Queen, people began running for cover. Drinks spilled; sandwiches and fries went flying. Moving in a tide of leaping bodies, the hounds lunged through the outer section of the building and disappeared around the back.

Jethro reached the restaurant first. He dismounted rapidly, flying off the saddle. Hank and Rufus were right behind. A group of customers cowered in one corner of the building. Hayden pulled the sheriff's Bronco into the parking lot, skidding across the gravel. A second patrol vehicle braked next to him.

Rufus rushed up, adjusting his radio receiver. The crowd of bystanders pushed in beside him. "Hold it!" he cried. He held up his hand for silence. Raising the H-shaped antennae, he fanned the receiver back and forth, searching for a signal. Suddenly, the ping-ping of the transmitter grew louder. "There!" he pointed. The bystanders pushed back to clear a gap in front of him.

Pulling out from the Dairy Queen, a large eighteen-wheeler shifted gears and accelerated onto the highway. A minute later, it was a blinking dot on the Bowdens' computer screen. The collar was moving west, hooked to the back of a truck, traveling 45 miles an hour up Highway 29.

59

THE EAGLE WAS A MILE HIGH, coming fast, following a stream of air that spilled down the snowcapped mountains. From a distance, it was little more than a speck. Raven Crow heard its piercing cry and smiled. They were old friends, this bird and she, friends from a distant past, a friendship that had developed over many years.

She answered by pulling her lips taut, aiming her high-pitched whistle toward the sky. The call she produced did not sound exactly like an eagle. The noise was not intended to. They were different beings on these broad plains, communicating with each other in their own special language, and each recognized the other's call.

The eagle soared above her in a high-altitude glide, its pinions scarcely moving. She pulled the blanket off the top of her head and shielded her eyes, following the great bird as it passed. She could make out its head and hooked beak. She noted it was looking down, scanning the bluff on which she stood. It was a cautious bird, always on the watch for enemies or animals by which it might be harmed. Over the years, she had found it never came close when anyone else was there. She was not quite sure why, but she had learned to accept this as one of the rules of their friendship.

The dead rabbit she had snared lay on the top of a rock a hundred feet away. She watched quietly. With a graceful dip of a wing, the eagle came around in a half-circle, losing altitude as it turned. This time, it passed so close she could hear the swish of wings.

It was reassuring to see this bird. Its presence was a good sign. She had not seen it for a month. Although she had come up to the bluff on three occasions, the eagle had not returned.

"Where have you been, my friend?" Her words were in Blackfoot and uttered in a hoarse whisper.

For a moment, the eagle disappeared below the edge of the cliff, then caught an updraft that brought it past the gnarled tree. The great bird moved both wings only once, and that was just before it landed. Spreading its talons, the eagle came down on the rock, hovering with such precision nothing stirred.

Raven Crow made no movement. She could not approach the eagle without scaring it off. Theirs was a precarious relationship of respect and understanding. She lowered herself to a crouched position and waited. The eagle took several bites of the rabbit and then clenched the dead animal in its talons and hopped to the edge of the rock. With a scream, it was off, catching the rising currents like a rocket.

She watched the bird until it was a speck, drifting across the prairie. She whistled to it once, just as it turned back toward the mountains, as if to say goodbye. There came a distant high-pitched answering call.

Raven Crow stood on the bluff where George Two Feathers's funeral had been. Next to her was the twisted tree with its leafless limbs. Below, as far as she could see, the prairie spread before her in a sweep of sage and grass like a sea of undulating waves.

A small bird came out of a crevice and fluttered toward her. The thrush had hidden while its huge enemy was near. Landing on her arm, it scolded noisily, as if to reprimand her for having such horrible friends. The thrush flitted to a rock and pecked at a seed.

If Raven Crow squinted hard, she could see the distant crest of Buffalo Ridge, just beyond Medicine Mountain. She knew Bobby Running Wolf had spent the first night there, by the great cliffs with the ancient drawings. Half-hidden to the left was the outline of Porcupine Canyon. It was there he would find the lion.

He would need great medicine for this confrontation, she thought. For that, he had done his part. How long had it been since a member of the tribe had performed a Sundance? Fifty years? A hundred? She knew the pain he had endured was not easy. Yet, before him, other great chiefs had performed such feats. To do extraordinary things, sometimes extraordinary men had to make extraordinary sacrifices.

She hobbled to the boulder where the eagle had stopped to feed. She spent a few seconds looking carefully around the rock until she found it: wedged between two small stones rested a single eagle feather. She grabbed it deftly and rolled it in her fingers.

She moved back to a sheltered area beneath the tree and crouched, laying the feather on the ground. Reaching into a leather pouch, she pulled out a small, mummified lizard. To the feather and the lizard, she added a clump of sage. She made a circle in the soil with her finger. Placing all three items inside the circle, she began to chant.

Across the plains rose a huge thunderhead. The summit of the cloud spilled over in curls and twists, glowing in the afternoon sun. There came a flicker of lightning. A faint rumble reached her ears.

She waited here, watching the ominous cloud approach, until the first raindrops stung her face with biting velocity. There in the clouds was a shape. With every flash of lightning, she could see its eyes, the claws, the enormous fangs. *Omahkatayo* was coming. And the last male progeny of Eyes-in-Shadows stood directly in its path.

60

FROM HIS PERCH ON A SMALL KNOLL near the entrance to Porcupine Canyon, Robert Wolfson searched the meadow with a pair of binoculars. Franklyn was an hour late, and he worried something had gone wrong. He breathed a sigh of relief as two riders approached, emerging from the forest.

Franklyn was in the lead. He rode easily, coaxing his horse along a trail that followed the tree line. The second rider appeared less comfortable but followed gamely behind. For a woman who had not ridden much, Kimberly looked nice on a horse, Wolfson thought. She had good posture and an attractive figure. When Franklyn kicked his horse into a gallop, she kept up, moving in a graceful, rolling motion behind him.

Kimberly's presence raised a great conflict in Wolfson's mind. Seeing her brought a feeling of tenderness that he could not deny. At the same time, he didn't want her to come into harm's way. There was a significant risk hunting this lion. He would have preferred she remain in town.

The pair galloped across the meadow and approached through a grove of trees.

"Greetings." Franklyn held up his hand.

"You had me worried," Wolfson said. "We were supposed to meet at noon."

"I know," Franklyn said, nodding. "It's just that leaving became a little dicey. I was afraid we might be followed."

"And you?" Wolfson turned to Kimberly. "I thought you were supposed to stay in town."

Kimberly gave him a sly smile. "I'm afraid you're stuck. I thought maybe I could help."

The two dismounted and joined Wolfson on the grassy overlook.

"Well, how was the run?" Wolfson asked.

Franklyn gave a thumbs-up sign. "Better than expected."

"God, you should have seen them at the Dairy Queen!" Kimberly exclaimed. "No one knew what to expect. Everyone had their guns drawn. It didn't make sense the lion would be there, but with this lion, you never knew. When the truck pulled out of the parking lot, I thought the Bowdens were going to explode."

Franklyn grinned from ear to ear. "Leaving the radio collar on the back of the eighteen wheeler was a good touch."

Wolfson slapped his friend affectionately on the shoulder. "I think I owe you one."

"And you were right about the lion scent," Franklyn added. "One of the elders on the reservation had a couple extra bottles. When I thought the dogs were close, I stopped and squirted the scent up a tree as high as I could. I think it bought some time. I didn't beat them by much. Ten minutes, maybe. I was going to try to run into town, but when we reached the Dairy Queen, I kind of ran out of steam. I saw the truck getting ready to leave and looped the collar onto a rear bumper. Then I went into the employee locker room and changed."

"Maybe if you get to the Boston Marathon, we can pace you with a set of hounds," Wolfson joked.

Franklyn reached into his belt and pulled out George Two Feathers' mummified paw. "The lion foot was a good thought, too. I used it in a couple of spots near the river. Places where I thought they would find the tracks."

Kimberly shook her head in amazement. "Quite a plan, gentlemen."

"Well, at least we've bought some time," Wolfson reflected. His expression became serious. "After the dogs came through, I spent the morning searching the canyon. I followed some fresh tracks near the entrance. If I had to guess, the big male is using a spot along the north face for his resting place. He probably holes up there in the daytime and then comes down at night."

"What about the female?"

"They must have paired up. Both of their tracks are all over the place. I say we start there . . ." Wolfson pointed to a trail leading deep into the canyon. He glanced cautiously at Kimberly.

"You game for this?"

"I wouldn't want it any other way," she said.

THE THREE MOUNTED AND RODE INTO THE CANYON. Wolfson took the lead, followed by Franklyn, then Kimberly. The trail ran next to a small stream. Thickets of willow grew along the water. Large cliffs rose on either side. At the entrance, the granite walls were spread widely and separated by almost a mile. Inside the canyon, however, the ridges quickly narrowed into steep, tightly placed stone.

Wolfson paused every hundred yards to glass the cliff walls. He was meticulous in his search. Sometimes he studied an area three and four times before he handed the binoculars to Franklyn. But there was no sign of the lions.

A mile into the canyon, Wolfson found an elevated ridge and stopped. Here he dismounted and asked Kimberly and Franklyn to sit with him while he searched the northern rim. He had just started glassing a high bench along the canyon wall when he sucked in his breath. "There!" he whispered. "There!"

He handed the binoculars to Franklyn. The youth took the glasses and squinted in the direction he was pointing. "I don't see anything," he murmured.

"Find the dark outcropping of rock. A hundred feet to the right is a small cave. Look right below."

318

Franklyn stared for a moment, then let out a low whistle. "You're right!" he exclaimed.

Franklyn handed Kimberly the glasses. She studied the cliff face, trying to spot what they were seeing. Abruptly, she gave a low gasp.

"It's the lion!"

"Lions," Wolfson corrected.

She searched through the binoculars again. There, high on the wall of the canyon, resting next to a small ledge, was a magnificent male mountain lion. She had not seen it at first. The coloring of the lion so perfectly blended with the rocky background that the animal had been invisible. It was only when the lion stood up that she noticed movement.

A few feet away rested the lioness, lying on her side, apparently asleep. As Kimberly watched, she saw the huge male readjust his position. Even from the great distance up the cliffs, Kimberly sensed the keen eyes of the male had been watching. With every movement they had made, the lion had observed their approach.

"So, what do we do?" Kimberly asked.

"We hike up there and see how close we can get."

"Aren't they going to run?"

"Maybe," Wolfson replied. "But remember, we have a tame female up there. She might not want to leave. If she's in heat, I doubt he will abandon her. If we're lucky, we'll get close enough for a shot."

Observing these two magnificent animals in their natural setting, Kimberly began to contemplate actually seeing the lion killed, and for the first time, she began to feel a sense of discomfort. She had to remind herself this was a dangerous lion, that this lion had already taken four people and almost killed Ashley Hayden. If they could take it now and prevent this from happening again, it would make everything worthwhile.

"Some pretty black clouds to the north," Franklyn observed. "It looks like a storm's coming."

Wolfson took the binoculars and studied the sky. The crest of a thunderhead pushed steadily above the cliffs. He glanced at his watch. They had six hours of daylight left. The hike to the base of the north wall would consume an hour. It would take another hour to climb along the steep face rock.

They could ride the horses a mile ahead, and maybe, if they pretended they were proceeding into the canyon, he could fool the lions. Then Wolfson could retrace their steps and try to climb the cliffs where the lions could not easily spot them. It would be a difficult stalk, but he had no other options. Finally, the lion seemed within his reach.

Wolfson led them into the valley for nearly a mile. At a hidden spot behind a cluster of trees, he dismounted and hobbled the horses. He tried to keep out of sight in the forest as long as he could, finally slipping upward through a field of broken rock and gradually ascending the cliffs.

Along a sheltered plateau, Wolfson halted. It was an arduous climb, and Kimberly was breathing heavily.

"Want to stop?"

She shook her head.

He nodded to Franklyn. "See anything?"

The youth raised the field glasses and scanned the cliffs. He shook his head. "I think we lost them."

Wolfson took the glasses and searched along the lateral ridges. The small pine tree and deep-colored rock where the two lions had been resting was clearly visible. But there was no sign of the lions.

"I smell rain," Franklyn said. A dark section of clouds hung ominously above the northern rim. The storm crept steadily toward them. A faint wind began to blow.

"Let's go up to the cave," Wolfson said. "I don't want to get caught in the open. If we get heavy rain, we're going to need shelter."

Steadily, they ascended a series of step-like buttresses, leading upward along the cliff face. From across the canyon wall came the occasional bleating of mountain goats. Periodically, Wolfson scanned the area of the cave and outcropping of rock, but the lions did not reappear.

As the three worked their way upward, the canyon floor spread out far below. The view was spectacular. A waterfall cascaded over a precipice, tumbling hundreds of feet toward the valley floor. Here their footing became progressively more difficult. In places, the path disappeared. Small rocks dislodged beneath their feet, ricocheting into the depths below. Kimberly slipped once. Wolfson caught her arm.

"Keep moving," he said firmly. "Don't look down."

The clouds continued to gather along the canyon rim. The day, which had started so clear, was now marked by the darkened pall of coming rain. A twinkling of lightning flashed. A storm was brewing, and it was coming far faster than Wolfson had anticipated.

Got to keep going, he thought. If they were caught in the open, with hail or lightning, their return could end in a disaster. One slip would end in a five-hundred-foot fall.

Ahead stood a narrow ledge that jutted out from the cliffs like a platform. Wolfson was the first to reach the ledge. Kimberly followed, then Franklyn. The two men spread out and searched across the plateau. Kimberly watched them with amazement. Wolfson had eyes like a hawk, she thought. She saw his expression change, the tightening at the corner of his eyes, as he tried to put together small signs that were totally invisible to her. He paused to point out a footprint in the dust. The irregularity seemed no more than a smudge.

"Lion print," he said.

"The male?"

"Hard to tell," he replied. "It looks like the beginning of a pad mark. There are some goat prints here, too, but I don't see a lot more. Franklyn?"

The youth shook his head. "It's a tough surface to read."

A gust of wind rushed at them. Dust and debris rattled off the granite walls. Wisps of moisture drifted past. Then came the stinging drops of rain.

"We need shelter," Wolfson said. "Let's get up to the cave."

He was starting to move along the longitudinal plateau when something on the wall caught his eye. He paused and then stepped forward and brushed the rock with his hands. Hidden behind layers of dust were faint pictographs. The drawings were made with faded pigment. As he scraped away the layers of dirt, images of buffalo and elk emerged. He took a bandana from his pocket and gently wiped at the surface. Drawings of running antelope appeared. The artwork was good, the figures strikingly realistic in their rendition.

A shaft of lightning flickered along the horizon. An ominous rumble echoed through the canyon. Kimberly reached for Wolfson and grabbed his arm. When she released it , she was trembling.

"Sorry." Her lips were taut, her face pale. "I never got used to lightning and thunder even as a kid."

"Go down to the end of the overhang and wait for us at the cave," Wolfson ordered. "We'll join you shortly."

Lingering at the wall, Wolfson scraped off more of the dust covering the drawings. Abruptly, he came across the unmistakable shape of a lion. The tail and paws were sketched in silhouette, the face turned sideways. Were these made by his Blackfoot ancestors, he wondered? Or were they much older?

A sudden scream. Kimberly stood at the cave entrance, frozen. Wolfson bolted across the ledge. Franklyn rushed after him. Kimberly had climbed up a series of stair-like rocks to the cave. She stood now, facing the grinning sockets of a skull.

"Mountain goat," Wolfson said. "You're okay."

He grabbed a horn, tossed the skull to the side, and turned his attention to the cave. The opening was nearly twenty feet wide, surprisingly larger than he had expected. The smell from inside the space was one of pungent heaviness.

As they stood at the entrance to the cavern, a bolt of lightning dazzled the sky. The flash was closer now, and with this brief illumination, Wolfson could see into the depths of the opening. Searching along the floor, he found a handful of sticks and grasses. He bunched these together and lit them with a match. The straw flickered as the flame took hold. Holding this makeshift torch above his head, he illuminated the interior.

The cavern opened into a large room rising thirty feet above. The space led into separate corridors that disappeared into the blackened interior. A fine layer of sand and debris covered the floor. In several areas, small boulders stood where they had fallen from the ceiling.

Along the entrance, Wolfson noted a place with burnt wood surrounded by a half-circle of rocks. It was the spot of a previous fire. How long ago man had been here, however, he could only guess.

"Bobby, here!" Kimberly exclaimed.

Wolfson raised the flare and moved toward her. She was standing next to one of the cave walls. Here, too, were pictograph-like figures. Etched along the surface were swirls and circles drawn in faded white.

By now, Wolfson's flare had burned almost completely down. Feeling the flames begin to scorch his fingers, he laid the torch on top of one of the boulders. The last ends of the straw blazed, then dimmed.

A flash of lightning stabbed the sky, followed by a crash of thunder.

"That was a little close," Franklyn remarked.

"We'd better get away from the entrance," Wolfson said. He had started to edge deeper into the cave when Kimberly grabbed his arm.

"Bobby . . . something moving . . . something there . . ."

Abruptly, Wolfson could smell the heavy, damp scent of an animal. It was the odor of fur. Raising his rifle, he took off the safety. A shadow was moving into the cave.

Outside the opening came another flash of lightning. There, in the flickering light, standing at the cave entrance, was the form of a lion. In the split second of illumination, Wolfson could make out the tail, the rounded ears, the shape of its back.

He pulled Kimberly protectively behind him. "Franklyn, stay close!" he ordered.

A second bolt of lightning danced across the cave entrance.

"It's the female," Franklyn murmured.

"How the hell do you know?"

"Too small for the male."

The lightning flashed again, and with the fresh illumination, Wolfson could see the lion advance into the interior of the cave. Franklyn was right. This was not a huge lion. He followed the form with his rifle. It took the greatest restraint to keep from firing. What if they were wrong? What if this was another lion that was using the cave as its lair?

Then from out of the darkness came an unmistakable purring sound. Kimberly stifled a gasp. She could feel the lion rub against her legs.

"Oh, my God," she whispered.

"Don't panic. Be calm," Wolfson said in a low voice. He moved in next to Kimberly and reached out, expecting to feel the lion's fur, but the animal drifted away.

Another stroke of lightning flashed. The bolt was followed by a concussion, which reverberated through the cave. At the same time, Wolfson saw a second form fill the entrance. The shape of this lion was huge, almost twice as large as the female. The lion entered the cave with an ominous growl.

"It's here!" Wolfson said quietly. "Don't move."

The display of electrical discharges now occurred with increasing frequency. A constant flickering of light danced outside the cliff walls, casting the cave in an ever-changing illumination of light and shadows.

The massive beast took a step forward. The hair raised along its back, its ears flattened, its body coiled.

Wolfson readied his rifle. It would take a single shot at close range placed neatly between the eyes of the cat, and it would be over. He pushed his finger around the trigger, feeling the cold touch of steel. With a small millimeter pull, he could end it.

He had started to squeeze when the cave was thrown into darkness. Between flashes, the inky blackness was absolute. With another flicker of lightning, he saw the lion had changed position.

There was time for a single shot. He had to be sure. It would be a rapid pull, and if he somehow missed or wounded the lion, they would be in trouble. In close quarters, there was no way to defend themselves. He'd get no second chance.

Behind him, from somewhere back in the cave, came a soft, bird-like chirping sound. He thought at first it was Franklyn imitating a bird and then realized it was the female lion. The call repeated. The lioness was calling for her mate.

There came an enormous flash followed by a tremendous concussion, an explosion so great it jolted Wolfson backward. A streak of electricity shot into the cave like an incandescent tongue, darting through the darkness, surging into the deepest recesses of the cave. The interior glowed like a thousand candles.

With the lightning came a shudder of some great force deep inside the mountain. A rain of rubble tumbled from the ceiling. Everything went black. And then from the darkened cave rose an enormous cry. It was an unearthly sound Wolfson had never heard before. The sound was clearly from the Great Lion, and the cry erupted through the darkness in a rising scream that ended in a wail.

"Shoot!" Franklyn shouted. "Shoot it, now!"

There came a flicker, a warning rumble from outside the cave, followed by an ear-splitting crash. A finger of lightning rushed into the cave, shooting a bolt of electricity that ran like fire down the walls, encircling the lion, lighting the animal in a dazzling halo. The beast's eyes shined as if they were spheres of cobalt.

"Now!" Franklyn screamed.

Wolfson charged at the beast and began to pull the trigger. Fire erupted from his gun in tongues of flame. Between each concussive explosion, he screamed at the lion in Blackfoot. The rifle clicked on empty. He was still pulling the trigger when Franklyn grabbed his shoulder.

"It's over, Bobby . . ."

Now there was only blackness and the pungent smell of electricity and burning fur. A faint dripping sound came from water falling from the cave entrance. Inside, along the floor of the cave, erupted tiny flames where scattered grass and debris had been ignited by the lightning.

Wolfson stumbled to the cave entrance and sat down, crossing his legs beneath him. Staring across the valley floor, he watched the storm move steadily away. There were tears in his eyes. Kimberly stepped behind him and placed her hands on his shoulders. Franklyn edged next to him.

Far below, along the southern edge of the cliffs, sputtered a faint glow. It looked to be the size of a match, a dot of flame, flickering precariously at the base of the cliffs. A growing plume of smoke drifted upward from the blaze.

Wolfson turned toward Franklyn with an imploring glance. His voice was unsteady, the words choked.

"Lord, what have I done?" he said.

Part V

Raven Crow

"It does not matter where the body lies,
For that is grass.
But where the spirit goes,
That would be a good place to be."

(Black Elk, on the death of Crazy Horse)

61

BY NINE O'CLOCK THAT MORNING, Mabel was sitting at her desk, trying to look busy. Secretly, she had turned on the intercom and was listening to the conversation in Hayden's office. The Bowden brothers had been inside for almost an hour. At times, their voices were so loud she could have followed the conversation through the closed door. At other times, when the four-letter words erupted like gunfire, she winced. Once, she was tempted to call one of the deputies for help. She didn't want Hayden to get into a fight with these cursing, unsavory hunters from Texas. For the most part, though, Hayden seemed to be holding his own.

Inside the office, both brothers stood in front of Hayden's desk. Occasionally, one pounded the surface with his fist. With one of the crashes, Mabel jumped. She wondered if something had broken.

"Hold your temper!" Hayden roared. "You're in a law enforcement office, and by God, if you can't act in a respectful fashion, I'll have you thrown in jail!"

"Well, you tell us what we're supposed to do, Sergeant!" Jethro Bowden shot back. "Our female lion is worth at least twenty thousand dollars. And now she's gone, Lord knows where. I say she's been captured or killed, and I bet I could point to a dozen Indians who know damn well where she is."

"These are pretty big accusations, sir."

"Who the hell else could catch a lion and take a collar off like that?" Henry exclaimed. "Then we go into Porcupine Canyon

329

this morning, and there's a forest fire so big, we can't get near the entrance. If I had to guess, the damned Indians started that as well. What kind of a charade you got going on here, Sergeant?"

"There was a big electrical storm up there last evening, gentlemen. This morning, there are a dozen blazes covering half the county. You telling me Indians started fires in Butte and Birch Creek and Cedarville? Come on, guys, that's pretty hard to believe."

"Why the hell can't you understand?" Jethro stormed. "I'm not sure Roxanne can feed herself. She's got a stiff hind leg. She'll die out there in the brush without our help."

"Then maybe she'll come in on her own."

"Yeah, and maybe the tooth fairy will bring her back. With a $100,000 reward out there, somebody sees a lion coming, what you think they're going to do, give her a kiss? This is bullshit, man! What the hell we need to do to get some help from your office? Am I speaking to a wall?"

Hayden's voice rose. "You got no proof, gentlemen, and Goddammit, you got no evidence of stolen property. Hell, maybe the collar got caught on a branch and slipped off and somebody found it. I'll be damned if I'm going to harass a bunch of Native Americans in an inquisition-style interrogation. You want an investigation, we'll do it in a methodical, fair way, in the spirit of justice of this office."

"All right! Give 'em hell, Sam!" Mabel smacked her fist. But the next words that erupted from Henry Bowden's mouth made her blush. The oaths were followed by a sudden silence.

"I tell you what we're going to do, Sergeant." Jethro's words rose in a hoarse, deliberate voice. "I'm going to call our lawyers this morning, and we're going to have this town so tightly wrapped in lawsuits, you're not going to be able to shit."

"Well, you just do that, Mr. Bowden," Hayden replied. "And while you're at it, I'll send one of my deputies over to search your trucks. Seems one of your men was trying to sell cocaine at the

Cattleman Saloon last night. You boys peddling a little drugs, are you?"

"Ah, screw you, Sergeant!" Henry growled. "Your town makes me puke. Let's go, Jethro."

Glowering fiercely, the Bowdens stormed out of Hayden's office into the parking lot.

Hayden leaned back in his chair and tried to ease his anger. The two brothers were so obnoxious, he was glad their female lion had escaped. Yet try as he might, he had trouble concentrating on the morning's schedule. Whether he liked it or not, Elkhorn was becoming increasingly famous. It was as if the town had a blinking neon sign advertising "Lion Country. $100,000 Reward!"

People were driving into the area by the dozen. The station fielded seventy to a hundred calls a day, and ninety percent of his work was related to the lion. And then there was the mail. Letters were pouring in by the bagful.

The correspondence came from all over the United States—some typed, some handwritten, some from children, others from adults. To Hayden's surprise, a great number of letters were sympathetic to the lion.

A typical envelope came from an elementary school in Orlando, Florida. The first page contained a note in pencil on three-lined paper. The introduction was followed by several dozen pages in which each student had drawn their version of the lion in crayon. The letter was signed by twenty-two members of the class.

Dear Townspeople of Elkhorn:
We pray every night that you will catch the lion. We are afraid the lion might come down here some day and we hope you find him. If possible, please don't kill him. There is a good zoo here and we could keep him for you. We love all living creatures and killing is a bad thing. We have watched you on television and we are wishing you the best

2nd grade class
Green Lake Elementary School
Orlando, Florida

The office had sifted through hundreds of letters like this. Behind Hayden, resting on the floor, were several bags of mail stuffed with correspondence. At first, Hayden tried to keep up with the letters, but he quickly gave up. In the end, he asked Mabel to sort through anything that looked like official business and pile everything else in the corner.

He found it increasingly difficult for the department to keep focused on day-to-day business. With the influx of tourists, gawkers, and self-proclaimed lion hunters, the robberies, assaults, and criminal activity in general had risen threefold.

The Elkhorn jail was built to contain six. Now it was holding nine. Because of crowding, some of the more serious offenders were being shipped to Bozeman. His telephone rang constantly. It seemed the governor, the sheriff, and anyone else with an interest in the lion wanted updated information twenty-four hours a day.

As he turned to an "all-points bulletin" covering a missing child from Twin Falls, a faint honking rose from outside the building. Half listening, he tried to concentrate on the report. The noise of the beeping became louder. Soon, the horns were joined by a chorus of yells. The cacophony grew steadily until it seemed to be right outside the station. Hayden rose from his desk as Mabel came bustling through the door.

"You'd better come see this, Sarge."

A motorcade drove up the street, led by a dozen bikers. They were followed by a rusty gray pickup truck. Behind the truck came a procession of cars. Everyone was shouting and whistling. The windows to the vehicles were open. People stuck their heads out, yelling in a massive celebration.

"Town square!" someone yelled. "We got the lion! The lion's killed!"

My God, Hayden thought. Was it true? Could this be possible? "Sam, look!" Mabel exclaimed.

Hayden followed her gaze. There, on the front of the truck, was the tawny shape of a huge lion. The body was strapped by ropes across the hood. He couldn't tell the size of the lion, but by the way it was tied, it looked very large. The head and forepaws dangled from one side of the truck, its tail touching the ground on the other.

The procession passed with much tooting and shouting and then progressed to the corner of Elm. More cars came out of side streets. In the midst of the commotion, Hayden could see residents emerge from their houses, cheering.

Hayden glanced at Mabel. A grin spread across his face. Had they really killed the lion? Was it over? He could hardly suppress his joy.

"Did you see who was driving the pickup?" he asked excitedly. "I wonder who killed it?"

"I'm not sure," she answered. "It looked like a couple of Native Americans."

"Well, hallelujah!" Hayden exclaimed. "Maybe the ordeal is over. Let's go down to the square and see what's going on."

"No, you go, Sarge," Mabel replied. "I'll man the phones. Tell me what you find."

It would have been quicker if he'd walked. The closest parking spot Hayden could find was two blocks away. When he arrived, the square was jammed with people. A group of helpers untied the legs and front paws of the beast. Then they hoisted the limp form off the truck. The lion was so big, it took six men to lift it. The body was carried over to the statue of Jeremiah Bates and placed on a patch of grass beneath the statue.

The press materialized out of nowhere. Television cameras were hastily assembled, tripods expanded. Half a dozen reporters scrambled to hook up their gear. Everywhere, cameras flashed.

Someone raised a horn and blew it wildly. Dozens of people poured out of the shops and cafés. The atmosphere had the markings of a carnival. Mayor Eliju Miller worked his way through the crowd, spotted Hayden, and rushed over.

"What fantastic news!" he exclaimed. "I'm so pleased. I'll make a proclamation to shut all businesses this afternoon. We're going to have a band and refreshments. Good work, Sergeant! This is a great day indeed!"

"Well, I hope it's over," Hayden answered. "I'm not sure how much I had to do with it, but thank you."

"No, we all did. We kept our cool. We didn't let things get out of hand. People are safe again."

"*If* this is the right lion," Hayden cautioned.

"Damn straight it is the right lion!" the mayor replied with a flash of anger. "Did you see the size of it? And it's got a tooth chipped off, just like the one that stalked your daughter. There's no question. This is the cat we're after."

"Who killed it?"

"Two Indians. Franklyn Yellow Pine and Bobby Running Wolf. It's just like they were saying on the reservation. Don't you see, Sam? It all makes sense. No one can sniff out a lion like a redskin. Not even with the dogs and all this fancy electronic tracking gear. I knew it would be Indians who killed this lion. I knew it all along."

The mayor's attention suddenly diverted to a crowd of waving people. Miller slapped Hayden on the back and strode triumphantly toward the gathering. Everyone gave each other high fives. It was a great day in the history of Elkhorn, the mayor thought, and there were going to be no doubting Thomases or conversation naysayers like Sergeant Hayden to get in his way. It was time for celebration.

Someone set up a makeshift podium next to the statue of Jeremiah Bates. A dozen microphones were hastily taped to the platform. Hayden noticed Kimberly and her cameraman across the square, but they were too far away to say hello. As the crowd funneled in toward the podium, Hayden watched Robert Wolfson push toward the front.

Wolfson appeared sweaty and exhausted. His hair was unkempt. He wore a pair of mud-streaked jeans. Large smudges of dirt stained his shirt. He stepped up slowly, almost reluctantly, to face the cameras.

Suddenly, the press erupted with a dozen questions. Everyone began yelling at the same time. "Where were you? What happened? How did you kill it?"

Wolfson raised his hands for silence.

"Franklyn, come join me," he said.

The youth stepped out of the crowd and stood next to the podium. Like Wolfson, he seemed exhausted. There were bramble cuts across his forehead. His right arm was scratched. He, too, was covered with mud.

"Some of it was luck," Wolfson began. "Being in the right place at the right time. Some of it was persistence and continued tracking, trying to put together all the signs with the location."

"How did you know to look in Porcupine Canyon?" a reporter asked.

"Indian thing," Franklyn answered.

Everyone laughed.

"Mostly a hunch," Wolfson said. "I figured the lion was operating somewhere close to Elkhorn. If you trace the known encounters, first at the Arcata River, then Lute Olsson's ranch, and finally next to Diamond Creek where Howard Lassiter was killed, all of these spots are within a lion's travels during the night. I tried to think where I would hole up if I were a lion. Porcupine Canyon seemed a logical choice."

"What about the Texas lion? The lion that was collared? Did you see the female up there?"

"She was with him at the end," Wolfson replied.

"Did you kill her, too?"

Wolfson shook his head. "There's been no problem with the female."

"Then maybe we should send the Texans up there to find her," a newscaster suggested. "They're saying she might not survive on her own."

"Don't think you're going to be able to do that," a rancher countered. "Half the canyon's in flames."

"Then how did you get out?" a second reporter asked.

"Franklyn and I went in at first light this morning. If we look a bit ragged, it's because there's still a lot of water and mud in there from the storm. The smoke was everywhere. Sometimes we couldn't see. The riding was difficult. At times, we had to break our own trail."

"And just how we going to know if this is the right lion?" a woman shouted.

One of the townspeople spotted Hayden standing near the back of the crowd.

"Yeah, Sergeant," he yelled. "How you going to be sure it's the right lion?"

Hayden moved quickly to the podium. Nodding to Franklyn and Wolfson, he turned to address the crowd.

"I'll be in touch with the state," he said. "We'll request a team of experts in the morning. I want a formal autopsy. We'll let the body remain here for another couple of hours, then transport it to the hangar for safekeeping. Until the postmortem comes back, we won't know for sure. For everyone's sake, let's hope it's the right lion."

A chorus of cheers rose from the crowd. Mayor Eliju Miller pushed his way through the audience. His face radiated delight.

"Folks, I don't know about you, but I think this is a great day for Elkhorn, and I'm proclaiming the afternoon off as an official holiday. No further business and no more school. Take it easy and enjoy yourselves. And let's keep our fingers crossed what we've been praying for is true. If it is, we owe these Indians— er, Native Americans—great thanks."

Television cameras blinked. People cheered. After the mayor stepped down, the reporters pushed in toward Wolfson and Franklyn Yellow Pine. There were dozens of questions. What kind of gun did he use? Where did they shoot the lion? Had it charged? How close were they? Had he been afraid?

Finally, when the questions were exhausted, some of the reporters turned their attention to the lion. Soon they were hovering over the body like a swarm of flies. Everyone agreed the animal was huge. Even draped across the grass, the body measured over ten feet. And its paws were the size of waffle irons.

Hayden watched for another ten minutes and then started back to the station. A feeling of satisfaction rushed across his mind. He could hardly believe it was over. As he walked across the town square, a tug came on his arm. Kimberly moved next to him.

"How come you're not in with that frenzy of reporters?" he asked.

"Too much competition," she answered. "We'll shoot a few long shots. I think I'll wait until the crowd settles, then try to put something together this afternoon. I'm really more interested in the autopsy. What are you going to do if it's not the right animal?"

Hayden pulled at the corner of his moustache. "I guess we go back to the drawing board. You know this business as well as I, Kimberly. There are always false alarms, false hopes." He hesitated. "What are you going to do if it is the right lion?"

"I still have a condominium in San Francisco." She paused, smiling faintly. "If they haven't fired me yet, I suppose we'll head home."

"Well, you know you always have a place to stay with Ashley and me. We owe you a lot for negotiating the sale of the photographs."

"You're sweet to think of me, Sam." She pressed him affectionately on the shoulder. "There is one favor I would like to ask."

"Of course," he said, nodding.

"I want to take a look at some of the station's archives. There are a few things about the Blackfoot I'm interested in."

"I don't think that'll be a problem," Hayden answered. "They're stored at the hangar. Most of it is public record."

"Thanks." She turned and waved to Stafford motioning for the cameraman to change position. The photographer picked up his gear and edged toward the corner of the square.

"I'd better go," she said. "We need to get some cut shots of the crowd before they disperse. You'd think somebody's won the lottery."

"I think maybe we have," Hayden smiled. A broad expression of relief crossed his brow.

Before noon, Hayden picked up Ashley at school and brought her into town. The high school band had assembled next to the town square. A table was set up for ice cream and cake. Hayden arrived in time to see Kimberly finish her videotaping. To the right of the statue formed a line of children and adults waiting to have their pictures taken with the lion. An enterprising photographer had set up a booth and was charging five dollars a print.

"Ashley, you don't have to look if you don't want," Hayden told her.

"No, I want to see it, Dad," she said.

Ashley walked up to the back of the crowd. Slipping through a gap in the line, she moved next to the dead beast. She crouched, gently stroking its fur and then pulled softly at its ears. Carefully prying open the lion's lips, she stared into its mouth. Hayden was surprised at the close exam she gave. After she had almost been killed by the lion, he was amazed she was able to touch the animal with no apparent fear.

To Ashley, the lion looked like some great stuffed animal lying on the grass. Its lips were pale. Its gums felt as if they were made of rubber. The tip of its tongue protruded through its teeth just slightly, so that she could see a glob of pink erupting from its mouth. Ashley reached over and touched the tongue and then ran her fingers along the fangs, trying to feel the sharpness of the teeth.

"Hold it, young lady." A camera flashed. "You're the girl the lion chased, aren't you?"

Ashley nodded.

"Charlie Adams. *Denver Chronicle.*" He held out his hand. "We'll run this tomorrow. Front page. You're a famous lady, you know. Do you have anything to say about the lion?"

"I'm just kind of sad for the animal," she answered.

"Sad for a lion that almost killed you?" Adams asked incredulously. "I can hardly believe it."

"No, it wasn't that close." Ashley shrugged.

"Come on, sweetheart, let's go," Hayden said, glowering at the reporter.

"No, I'm cool, Dad," she said.

Hayden watched protectively as the reporter asked several questions, jotting notes on a pad. Adams snapped two photographs of Ashley with the lion, and then Hayden grabbed his daughter and pulled her away. "I don't want you to stay around here if you don't want to," he said.

Hayden waved to Deputy Campbell standing at the back of the crowd. The deputy held a large black canvas folded under his arm. It was the type of bag the department carried bodies in.

"Give them another hour to finish up the photographs, then load the animal and take it out to the hangar," Hayden told him.

"Sure thing, Sarge," Campbell replied.

"I think I want to go home," Ashley said.

"You don't want any ice cream and cake?"

"Not this afternoon," she replied. "Let's take the horses for a ride."

It was to be one of her last television reports from Montana, filmed this warm September afternoon behind the booths and tables and crowds of milling people who'd come to see the lion. The scene was the town square where Kimberly had taped several video reports before. Behind her, stretched beneath the statue of

Jeremiah Bates, was the huge, tawny body of a mountain lion, *Felis concolor.* The head was propped up so the camera showed its face. The animal looked peaceful and asleep, its large amber eyes closed.

It was hard to believe this animal, resting in such quiet repose, could have terrorized an entire town. Yet, the sinewy strength of its large forearms was clearly evident when Kimberly compressed a paw and unsheathed its enormous claws.

Crouching next to the head of the cat, Kimberly faced the camera. She spoke into a handheld microphone. Her voice was clear, her words precise.

"The chapter of the Elkhorn lion may have come to an end this morning when two Native Americans, Robert Wolfson and Franklyn Yellow Pine, brought in a large male lion which they killed in the area of Porcupine Canyon. The paw prints of this lion are similar to tracks of a lion that has now attacked six people, and there is growing evidence this lion may be the animal for which the governor of Montana has placed a $100,000 reward.

"The beast weighs over two hundred pounds and is unusually large for lions of this area. There is also a small chip on the right front tooth, similar to photographs taken by Ashley Hayden, the ten-year-old girl who barely escaped an attack several days ago. What remains is irrefutable evidence that links this lion with the human deaths.

"Tomorrow morning, state officials will be coming to Elkhorn to perform an autopsy. If investigators can find evidence of human elements in the lion, items like human hair in the digestive track or microscopic DNA samplings of human skin beneath its claws, the final chapter to one of the largest lion hunts in the history of the United States will come to an end."

"Until then, this is Kimberly Benson from Elkhorn, Montana," she concluded. "Stay tuned and I will keep you posted . . ."

62

EVENING CAME. THE SUN SLIPPED below the horizon in a subtle downshifting of light. It was nearly nine by the time Kimberly reached the sheriff's hangar. Except for a single flood, the surrounding runways were dark. Private planes were tethered along the pavement in a row. Kimberly parked at the side of a large two-story building and walked toward the entrance. Peter Campbell waited in a sheriff's Bronco. The deputy blinked his lights, stepped out of the vehicle, and escorted her to the hangar door.

"I'm sorry to bother you with this," she said.

"No problem," Campbell answered. "Sergeant Hayden apologized he could not be here himself. He told me to accommodate you any way we can."

Campbell unlocked a padlock securing the hangar. The two moved inside the building. The space was the size of a gymnasium. Here the helicopter was stored along with various equipment used for search and rescue. The deputy led her around the aircraft and then proceeded toward the back of the building.

"We got some quarters for the flight crew upstairs. A couple of beds. A small kitchen. Sometimes they need to stay over. Everything's pretty quiet tonight."

Kimberly nodded. It was the way she liked it. This way there would be no interruptions. The lighting was harsh, cast by two overhead bulbs that created darkened shadows. A mouse scurried across the floor and disappeared beneath a row of boxes.

341

As they came around a darkened corner, Kimberly accidentally bumped into the side of a table. She sucked in her breath.

Stretched out on the table was the body of the lion. Kimberly had not seen it at first, and the closeness of the animal caught her by surprise. She was astonished the dead beast would be laid out like this, left uncovered.

"I should have warned you," Campbell said. "I brought the body out this afternoon. We're trying to get everything ready for the autopsy tomorrow."

"Let's hope we've got the right lion," she replied.

"I think we have," the deputy answered with confidence. "It's a damn big lion. Some of the hunters are saying it's the largest animal they've seen in years."

At the back of the hangar, Campbell led Kimberly to a row of rooms. Each door was marked with a stenciled sign. "Sheriff's Department—Official business only."

"Here are the archives," Campbell said. "Thirty years of history of the Sheriff's Department in Elkhorn, Montana. Where would you like to start?"

Kimberly pointed to a doorway at one end. Campbell opened the door, and they stepped inside. Lined along the walls were stacks of cartons, each identified by year. Kimberly searched the stacks, moving from the highest row to those along the floor.

"Anything you're specifically looking for?" Campbell asked.

"I'm guessing the late 1980s."

"Sorry, I can't help you there," Campbell said with a frown. "That was a little before my time."

"Some of the Native Americans have spoken about a sergeant that was particularly difficult for the Blackfoot. Anyone come to mind?"

"There was one," Campbell said, nodding. "I don't remember when he was here, but maybe twenty years ago. Every now and then his name comes up. A guy named Ronald Iverson. Very controversial character. Had quite an eye for Indian women. They still use his name when they try to impress us what not to do. I think he was finally run out of town. Retired in Florida, I'm told. Nothing like Hayden. Hayden's the best sergeant we've ever had."

"I've heard that." Kimberly continued looking through the files.

"Yeah, there's no one that doesn't like working for him. Always willing to help. Last year, when I broke my leg, he came over and visited me every day. Had Ashley bake a cake."

Kimberly smiled at the mention of Ashley's name. She had promised Ashley she would do a short interview with some of her Little League friends before she returned to San Francisco. Eric Stafford would run the camera. Ashley would act like a sports commentator reporting on the team. It sounded like great fun. In return, Ashley had promised she would take Kimberly for a ride with her horses.

Kimberly found a section marked "1988." Campbell helped her pull down the box. Kimberly placed the container on the floor and began searching through the contents. The reports were filed alphabetically. She spent a few moments looking through the "R" section but could not find the name she was looking for.

The ring of a cell phone startled the silence.

"Sorry," Campbell said. He stepped outside the room to take the call then came back inside. "There's a fight at one of the tent camps. Somebody's got a weapon. They're calling for help."

"I'll be all right," Kimberly said. "If you want to go, I can find my way."

"I suppose there's nothing much to get in trouble," Campbell replied. "Just pull the door and close the padlock. I'll check back later to be sure everything is secure."

Kimberly listened to the deputy's footsteps echo through the darkened hangar and then turned back to the files. Along an upper shelf, she found three boxes marked with the year 1989. The boxes were heavy, and she pulled each down with difficulty. A film of dust covered the folders. It didn't look as if anyone had touched the files in years.

A small table stood in a corner of the room. Next to the table was a folded chair. Kimberly pulled the table over so she could examine the boxes better.

The name she was looking for was not there. With a frown she searched through the next section. Methodically reviewing the list of names for each year, she scraped at the labels, trying to identify the contents. She looked through "1990" and then started on "1991." Maybe it was a wild goose chase, she thought. She had almost given up when her gaze fell upon the name she was looking for. Buried in a stack of folders was a file titled "Running Wolf."

Her breath quickened. She took off the top of the box and carefully searched through the contents. Toward the rear was a folder labeled "Martin Running Wolf." That could be Bobby's father, she reflected. A second folder was titled "Mary Running Wolf." If she was lucky, this would be his mother. A double asterisk marked the name. Had someone tagged the file for a reason?

She lugged the box over to the table and sat down. Withdrawing the folders, she placed them on the desk, blowing off a layer of dust.

She studied Martin Running Wolf first. The file contained a dozen reports plus several newspaper articles. At a brief glance, the news clipping talked about Martin Running Wolf heading a delegation of Blackfoot Indians that traveled to Washington in order to convince the government to spend more money on school programs on the reservation. A photograph showed four of the Native Americans in suits and ties, standing awkwardly in front of the Lincoln Memorial.

She thumbed through several reports covering various fights and misunderstandings involving Martin Running Wolf. Apparently, Robert Wolfson's father had been a strong-willed individual who was not easily intimidated by authority. In one report, he accused the sheriff's department of dropping an investigation of stolen goods. Toward the end was a folded newspaper article:

"December 9, 1991. Martin Running Wolf was found dead this morning on Highway 29, where his car flipped off the road

at a curve. *The Highway Patrol theorized the death was an alcohol-related accident.*

Mr. Running Wolf was 45 years old. He had led the tribal council on several trips to Washington to help the cause for Indians on the Blackfoot Reservation. Interviews with tribal members report that Mr. Running Wolf had become depressed since the death of his wife and had been drinking heavily. He is survived by his two children: Sarah, age two, and Bobby, age eight. The children will be placed in the custody of their grandfather, George Two Feathers."

Kimberly placed the folder back into the box and opened the second file. Under the name Mary Running Wolf were a dozen pages. She glanced quickly through the folder. Here she found an investigative report followed by several pieces of paper with notes written in long hand.

She turned to the investigative report. It was authored by a senior officer named John Seaton. The date: March 19, 1991. As she read the report, her eyes widened. Little by little, fragments of the incident began to unfold.

Internal Investigative Report

—For Department Use Only—

March 19, 1991. A complaint filed today by Mrs. Mary Running Wolf, a 26-year-old Blackfoot Indian, alleged she had been sexually assaulted by Mr. Ronald Iverson, sergeant for the Tri-County Sheriff's Department. According to the report, Mrs. Running Wolf was returning from a tribal affair in Elkhorn when her car was pulled over by a sheriff's vehicle just outside of town. Mrs. Running Wolf admits she had had some "beers," although she is emphatic no more than two. She denies that she was either impaired or driving in an erratic fashion.

The claimant states the sergeant told her he was going to throw her in jail if she did not cooperate. By her report, he tried to make advances, touching her breasts and legs, telling her he would let her go if she cooperated.

When she did not accept his advances, he became hostile and threatening. She states Mr. Iverson forced her to the ground at gunpoint and raped her. Then he left her alongside the road. She was able to get into her car and drive home.

A doctor's exam showed bruising on her arms and legs and around her vaginal area, although the doctor was not specific as to how these injuries could have occurred. In a later interview, the physician reported that such bruising could have happened with a fall.

Sergeant Iverson has called the accusation "ridiculous and absurd" and the ranting of an intoxicated woman who was trying to get out of having her car impounded. Further investigations are pending.

Addendum: On May 15, 1991, Mrs. Running Wolf stated she is withdrawing her accusations for fear of the publicity and possible damage to the reputation of her children. Charges are currently placed on hold until more information is forthcoming.

So this was Sergeant Iverson, the man Deputy Campbell had spoken about. Such men had a way of preying on the weak and disadvantaged. Often they liked to take positions of authority, Kimberly thought. The sheriff's department in a small town like Elkhorn would be perfect for him. Still, there was no hard evidence. It was the sergeant's word against that of an Indian woman who was allegedly drunk.

She turned a page and found an old faded photograph of Mary Running Wolf. My God, what a beautiful woman, she thought. Mary Running Wolf had a thin, curvaceous figure. Her face was punctuated with deep black eyes. Long black hair fell to her waist.

On the last page was the autopsy report. The report was dated June 5, 1991, approximately three months after the alleged rape. The last page recorded three calls to the sheriff's department from the reservation. Apparently, someone had called multiple times asking for help.

Kimberly scanned through the report, stopping at the cause of death. She read it once, then twice. As she tried to piece together what had happened, how this vibrant woman could have died so young, Kimberly's eyes dilated. Her lips pursed. Steadily, her anger rose.

The facts made her sick. She felt as if she wanted to vomit. How could they have done something like this? Not to this woman. Not to the mother of Bobby Running Wolf. But there it was in black and white, clearly documented in the autopsy report, buried for twenty years in a cardboard box on a dusty shelf in the Sheriff's hangar.

Kimberly closed the folder and placed the file inside the box. She lifted the container and replaced it on the shelf. She switched off the light and walked out into the darkened hangar.

A horrible injustice had been done to an innocent family on the Indian reservation. But who else knew? Not Robert Wolfson. He'd been only eight then and would have never known. Maybe his grandfather, George Two Feathers, knew, but she was doubtful he would ever tell the children. Maybe this was why he had encouraged Bobby to leave the reservation. And Iverson, the sergeant? Retired somewhere in Florida, Deputy Campbell said. Maybe he was dead.

Kimberly passed the lion's body, resting stiffly on the table, and navigated around the sheriff's helicopter. As she stepped out into the night, the cool air was welcome. The hangar and its records were like a rotting bog back there, she thought. She had taken a step into the quicksand of it and she had been sucked under by the stench. But what could she do? How could she make things right?

She took a deep breath, trying to steel her courage, and then plunged back into the hangar. Deputy Campbell would be returning soon. She would have to hurry. She set her jaw. A grim determination crossed her face. She couldn't change what had happened to Robert Wolfson's family. Those things that happened were history. But maybe, just maybe, she could change the future.

63

ON FRIDAY MORNING, the State Department officials arrived in Elkhorn shortly before ten. Following a brief press conference, Hayden escorted the examiners to the sheriff's hangar. Here he helped set up a makeshift table for the postmortem exam. Illumination came from a large lamp attached to a stand. A hose with running water was supplied. Beneath the table were several buckets to catch the runoff. By eleven, they were ready to proceed.

Five individuals composed the autopsy team. The lead examiner was a forensic pathologist named William Perkins, the man Hayden had communicated with early in the investigation. Two others were state veterinarians. One of these was a woman. A technician would assist with measuring and bottling the organs for further study. A fifth person came along as a recorder. He would be responsible for making notes and writing details of the findings. Perkins would further document the proceedings in a formal dictation.

The examiners put on surgical gowns and wore masks and disposable caps. Each donned a pair of hospital gloves. Special autopsy instruments were supplied in two black bags. The recorder remained outside the light, scribbling with his pen. The rest of the audience, mostly Hayden and his staff, looked on, peering over their shoulders.

The exam had the appearance of a medical autopsy performed at a university medical center with one exception: Dr. Perkins had refused access to the press. The incident had enough of a circus atmosphere as it was. The last thing state officials wanted was frequent interruptions from a lay audience.

Hayden politely asked Kimberly and the others to wait outside. As a gesture of cooperation, he set up chairs in the shade next to the hangar. As soon as the autopsy was finished, Hayden promised he would give them a full report.

"This is Dr. William Perkins recording postmortem exam on specimen *Felis concolor* taken in Porcupine Canyon," the pathologist spoke into a Dictaphone. "The autopsy is performed at the sheriff's hangar in Elkhorn, Montana, on the sixteenth of September, commencing at eleven a.m. The specimen is a male. The weight of the lion is 211 pounds. These measurements were taken yesterday after the lion was brought in and verified again this morning. The measured weight here at the hangar is 209 pounds, three ounces. This difference may be due to insensible evaporation from skin and mucous membranes postmortem."

Perkins ran his hands over the lion, carefully exploring each of the limbs. The two veterinarians searched through the fur. The exam was meticulous and thorough.

"Several recent lacerations here," one said. "Looks like this big boy was in a fight."

"And here on the left hind leg is a deep puncture wound. Possibly associated with a fracture."

"Without X-rays, hard to tell," Perkins said.

"You think maybe he was crippled and that was why he was killing humans?"

"No way to know," the woman veterinarian replied.

"There are several deep puncture wounds in the skull, possibly from another lion," Perkins continued. "The most striking finding is a large bullet wound, right upper forehead, with an exit behind the left ear. There are powder burns on the fur," he added. "I would say this was a relatively close shot."

"Indians like to shoot 'em close," the technician snorted.

A quiet chuckle rose from the observers.

Perkins held up his hand. "We're recording, ladies and gentlemen. Please keep irrelevant comments to yourselves."

"Good healthy claws," one of the vets observed. He scraped beneath the talons with a pair of forceps, taking tissue samples. Minuscule fragments of meat and flesh were placed in specimen bottles. Each container was carefully labeled. Later, these would be studied for DNA evidence of human tissue.

The team now directed their attention to the teeth. Taped measurements were taken of the length of the teeth as well as the distance between canines. When possible, these would be used to compare with puncture wounds found on the victims.

"Tooth age gives you what?" Perkins asked one of the examiners. "Seven? Eight?"

"I would say ten years," the female vet replied.

"That old?"

"The broken canine looks pretty worn."

"Let's compromise. Make it nine."

The examiners now turned their attention to the body of the lion. Using a scalpel, the pathologist opened the chest wall and abdominal cavity with a typical Y-shaped autopsy incision. Perkins continued announcing his findings. Methodically, the team inspected the heart, lungs, and upper abdomen of the lion. The internal organs seemed healthy and robust. The liver, spleen, and pancreas were normal. The heart appeared firm and strong.

An examination of the lion's gastrointestinal tract came last. Carefully, Perkins grabbed the stomach and brought the organ into view. Using a pair of sharp scissors, he opened the outer lining. Along with some bilious green-looking juice, several dark, hairy objects popped out.

"Stomach contents," Perkins announced. "Small, half-digested shape of a rodent. Looks like a wood rat. And here, a half a dozen feathers. What do you make of these?"

The vet took one of the feathers and washed away the digestive coating. "Maybe a mountain grouse."

The autopsy moved to the intestines. Perkins followed the small intestine with his fingers, inspecting the long, hose-like organ from top to bottom, gently squeezing the lining, feeling for masses and imperfections.

"Whoa! Something here," he paused.

A small, irregular bulge, dark in color, lodged inside the intestine.

Perkins cut into the bowel and shelled the object out. A large piece of black-and-white hair came into view. Abruptly, a horrific stench permeated the room.

Perkins backed away from the autopsy table, gasping for breath. Noxious tears flooded his eyes. The female veterinarian turned away and retched. The recording technician bent over as if he had been punched in the stomach. Hayden stumbled backwards, clawing for air. The group bolted for the doorway.

"The lion ate a skunk!" someone cried.

For twenty minutes, there was coughing and retching from all the observers and most of the crowd. One of the deputies produced a fan. The hangar door was raised, the interior sprayed with deodorant. Once the skunk tissue was placed in a jar, the smell began to dissipate. The specimen was tightly capped and hustled outside the building.

Gradually, the foul odor disappeared. The examiners returned to the autopsy table. A few gave scattered coughs as they began.

"We're returning to the postmortem exam on *Felis concolor*," Perkins dictated. "It appears that the lion recently devoured a portion of *Mephitus mephitus*, which necessitated a brief intermission. It is now eleven forty-five . . ."

He continued to examine the small bowel, working his way along the intestines until he reached the large balloon-like sac of the colon.

"Appendix normal," he said. "Surgeons didn't get him yet."

"Must be managed care," a vet chuckled. Perkins shot him a frown.

Each organ was weighed on a set of portable scales.

"What do you think the gall bladder of a lion would bring in the Asian market these days?" Perkins commented. He cut into the organ, releasing a crystal-golden fluid.

"Five hundred for a grizzly. I would suspect higher for a lion, especially one of this size."

"Maybe a thousand?"

"Supposed to guarantee an erection for a month."

"With or without the skunk?" one of the vets chided.

Several snickers rose from the examiners. Gradually, their humor was returning.

The pathologist continued working further, dissecting the remaining caecum and transverse colon, and then the descending colon. It was here along the terminal portion of the large bowel he uncovered their most significant find.

Dissecting carefully, Perkins followed the large intestine, working his way toward the lion's rectum. The fecal material of the cat appeared well-formed. Approximately ten inches from the anus, Perkins felt a thick, bulky section of scat. Opening the tissue with a scalpel, he produced an oblong piece of dung.

"Something unusual here," he said.

Everyone at the table leaned forward to see his findings better. The pathologist took the mass and began pouring water over it, washing away some of the well-formed debris. Out from beneath the fecal material came a clump of matted hair, reddish blonde in color. Perkins washed the specimen further, spreading the strands of hair onto his fingers. Some were six inches in length.

"We'll need to do a species identification on this," Perkins said cautiously. "But I would say this is very suspicious for human hair."

"By the texture and length, I would say more than suspicious, Bill," the female vet commented. "There's no wild animal that has long strands of blondish hair like this."

Hayden tried to stifle a cry. "Tracy Reynolds!" he exclaimed.

"We'll need to do more studies to be sure," Perkins nodded. "If this hair turns out to be human, I think you've got your lion."

64

Tobey jumped onto the foot of Ashley's bed. Pushing his way upward, the little dog found a space near the crook of her arm and scratched at the blankets until he created a suitable nest. Turning several times, he trampled the covers to his satisfaction and settled next to her shoulder. The terrier looked up as Hayden reached over and kissed his daughter goodnight. "Ready for sleep?"

"Yeah, I'm just kind of sorry the summer is ending."

"Me, too," Hayden answered. "I was thinking now this lion thing is over, I need a break. Maybe we could go into Great Falls for a couple of days. Do some shopping and have a good time. We haven't been on vacation for a while."

"I'm okay with you taking off," she said, "but I really like it here, Dad. Much better than the city. If you're going to take some time, why don't we ride the horses up into the mountains and take Tobey with us and do some camping?"

"I thought with all this lion business, you might be afraid to go up there," Hayden replied.

"No, I'm all right, Dad. I don't think the lion was a bad thing. I just think it was doing what it's supposed to do, and some people got in its way."

"Well, you have a good philosophy about it, Ashley. Some ranchers think all lions need to be killed."

"You don't believe that, do you?"

"No, I lean more to your side, but I understand the ranchers' concerns. They have sheep and cattle to protect, and we can't just let an animal go around killing their livestock. Especially if it begins to threaten humans. What if Tobey had been killed? Think how terrible that would be."

"Yeah, but he wasn't," Ashley said. "And we got some money for me to go to college."

"I guess we should thank the lion for that." Hayden smiled.

"I kind of mostly feel sad for the lion, Dad. It seemed so out of place. And lying dead there on the square. It was really a beautiful animal. Why did they have to kill it?"

"Because it harmed people."

"But wasn't it just doing its thing?"

"Maybe," Hayden answered. "What if it begins to start hunting people? Then you would have to kill it, wouldn't you? Or what if it took some child? That would be pretty awful, wouldn't it?"

"I guess," Ashley said. "But that was different with this lion. I don't think this lion would have killed children."

"Why not?"

"Because I think it had plenty of time to, if it wanted. It could have gotten me, and it could have killed kids here in town. I think mostly we were just in its way. And the rancher and the hunter, they were trying to kill the lion, weren't they? What else could the lion do?"

Hayden nodded. He didn't want to argue the point, especially with his daughter. If she was not scared about the lion, that was great. So far, she seemed to have adjusted to the incident pretty well. She wasn't waking up screaming with nightmares or wetting her bed, as he had feared. Her life had returned to normal. In reality, he reflected, she had come through the ordeal much better than he.

"Time for sleep, young lady," he said. "Tomorrow, I'll take the afternoon off. We can ride or do whatever you want."

"Kimberly told me she wanted to take a ride. I said we could take the horses and go into the meadow. Is that okay?"

"Of course. You like Kimberly, don't you?"

"I think she's wonderful."

"Maybe you can be a reporter like her someday."

"That would be pretty neat."

"You ready for sleep?"

"I think so."

Hayden stood up from the bed. He gave Tobey a good-night pat and started for the door.

"Dad?"

"Yes."

"I don't think they killed the right lion."

"What?"

"I don't think the lion we saw in the square is the same one that chased me in the barn."

"What brings you to that brilliant conclusion?" Hayden asked.

"It didn't look as big. I mean, that is a big lion, but the lion that was here was a giant."

Hayden chuckled. "On the square, it's really hard to tell how big the lion was. And its paws were huge," he added patiently. "And it's got a tooth chipped on the right front just like the one that chased you. The state pathologists' exam found convincing evidence it was the lion that had attacked the other people. I think it's the same one, Ashley. Don't worry. They wouldn't make a mistake like that."

"Remember the photographs of the team on the roll of film I took?"

"Yeah."

"Remember the team numbers were backwards on some of the photographs in the news, and you said that sometimes the papers, when they print photos, they accidentally reverse them? The photographs that were reversed show the broken tooth on the right, just like the animal down there at the square."

"I'm not sure I follow," Hayden said, frowning.

"The reversed photograph had the broken tooth on the right, remember?"

"All right."

"But the lion that chased me had the broken tooth on the left."

"How did you figure this out?"

"Because after we looked at the dead lion in the town square, I went back and looked at the newspaper photographs. The lion that chased me had a chip on the left tooth, not the right."

"Are you sure?"

"Dad, go look at the photographs. See for yourself."

"Maybe the lion that chased you was a different lion, Ashley. I mean, there are a lot of lions out there. Maybe it was two different lions."

"I don't think so, Dad," she said firmly. "There is only one."

"The exam at the hangar was pretty convincing," Hayden answered softly. "I think they got the right one. Now, it's time for bed."

"I hope it's a different lion, Dad."

"How so?"

"Because I feel sorry for the big lion. I think it's out of place. I want it to keep on living."

"I understand, sweetheart." Hayden reached forward and kissed her on the forehead. "Lights out, please. And you, too, mister." He pointed at the dog.

"Good night, Dad."

"Good night, Ashley."

HAYDEN WALKED INTO HIS BEDROOM, stripped to his underwear, and washed his face. Then he lay down. He tried to read a magazine for a while, but had difficulty concentrating. What the hell was Ashley talking about?

It couldn't be the wrong cat. If it were the wrong lion, they would have to start all over. It would bring a nightmare of bad publicity to the department. It would mean the continued killing of more lions. It would mean more people trekking into Elkhorn seeking the reward. The town seemed about to burst as it was.

Hayden swallowed hard, trying to calm his rising concern. Suddenly, he leaped out of bed and raced downstairs, taking two steps at a time. Yanking open a desk drawer, he pulled out a manila folder. Inside were the original prints Ashley had taken of the lion.

Could this be possible? his mind screamed. What if Ashley was right? What if they had the wrong lion?

65

THE SHERIFF'S BRONCO ROARED into the parking lot, stopping with a squeal of brakes. A door slammed. Moments later, Sam Hayden came charging through the station entrance. A frown was etched across his face.

"Good morning," he said briskly.

"Good morning, Sarge," Mabel answered. "Can I fix you coffee?"

"Not today."

There was no friendliness in his voice. Hayden stomped past the secretary into his office.

"What the hell's eating him? she wondered. She heard Hayden's desk squeak, followed by the sound of a drawer opening. Then silence. Mabel waited five minutes before she walked to his door, knocking softly.

"There are some telephone messages for you, sir."

"Just put them on the table," he grunted.

As she moved into the room, she noticed Hayden had placed half a dozen photographs across his desk. One was a large black-and-white blow-up of a lion's mouth. An examiner's fingers pulled back the lips. A tape measure had been thrust between the teeth.

"How can this be?" he muttered. "How could this happen?"

She laid the telephone messages in an in-box at the corner of his desk.

"Is something wrong?"

"Mabel, Goddammit, I think we've been duped," he said angrily. "We've been completely fooled! I think this is the wrong Goddamn lion!"

With a look of surprise, she stepped closer to his desk.

"Look at this!" Hayden exclaimed. "Ashley told me last night, and I didn't believe her. But she's right. Look at the photographs."

"I don't understand."

"Here is the photograph Ashley took the night the lion chased her. This came from a roll of film in one of those small disposable cameras. And here is a copy of the article that appeared in the Rocky Mountain Times. See the background? See the numbers of the baseball players? The photographs are reversed.

"The lion that chased Ashley had a tooth chipped on the left. But the photographs were reversed in the article, and the chipped tooth appeared on the right instead. And here is a postmortem photograph of the lion taken yesterday at the autopsy. This lion's tooth is chipped on the right. We've got a different lion."

"How can you be sure?"

"Photographs don't lie," he growled.

"It's got to be a mistake," Mabel argued.

Hayden raised a cautious finger. "We were so eager to bring this thing to a close, we jumped at the most obvious conclusion. Maybe Wolfson and Yellow Pine shot a big male and brought it in."

"It still doesn't explain the human hair."

"Yeah, that bothers me too," he answered. "I called Perkins this morning. He said sometimes foreign material like this can stay in a lion's digestive track for days. But I think I know where I can get some answers."

He stood up. "Hold my calls," he said gruffly.

Marching out of the room, Hayden hurried through the station and slammed the door. Mabel watched the Bronco speed out of the parking lot and turned back to her desk. The wrong lion? she wondered. How could this be?

66

ASHLEY STOOD WITH KIMBERLY BENSON outside Hayden's corral. The reporter was dressed in blue jeans with a pair of cowboy boots and colored scarf. She was about to mount when Hayden's Bronco roared up the driveway. Hayden stepped out of the car and moved briskly toward them.

"Hi, Dad," Ashley said. "We're going for a ride. You want to come?"

"I need to speak with Kimberly."

He motioned for the reporter to follow him over to the side of the fence. The two moved beneath a grove of Aspen next to the corral. Ashley tied the horses to a post and began brushing them down.

"I'm kind of stuck on a couple of issues with this lion," Hayden said. "I thought maybe you could help."

"Go ahead, I'm listening."

"Let's just say that maybe Wolfson and Yellow Pine shot a big lion. There were pictures in the paper when Ashley was chased by the lion that showed a lion with a chipped tooth. Anyone could have seen that. And let's just say when the $100,000 reward came out, it might lead some people to do some strange things."

Kimberly's eyes narrowed. "I'm not sure what's your question, Sam?"

"You seem to know Wolfson pretty well," Hayden said. "Word is you were with him during the dust-up at the Cattleman Saloon a while back."

"That's right," she answered. "I was doing an interview."

"So let's just say Wolfson and Yellow Pine brought in this big lion and they had seen the photos and they worked on the tooth a little bit. Filed it down to look as if it was chipped. Only they got it wrong because they were working off the photos that appeared in the news with the chipped tooth on the right."

"That's a little far-fetched, isn't it?"

"You got a $100,000 reward out there, anything fits."

"What about the human hair in the lion? "

"Yeah, well maybe they stuffed that in there as well."

"Where you going to get hair like that on the reservation? How many Native Americans with light-colored hair have you seen out here?"

"Well, maybe they got friends," Hayden grunted. "Something doesn't smell right. And if I've been duped, or this is some type of cover-up, I don't want any part of it."

"You want to talk about cover-ups?" Kimberly glared at him. "Go look in your files."

"What are you talking about?"

"Robert Wolfson was a kid—an eight-year-old Indian boy named Bobby Running Wolf—and his mother was one of the most beautiful women on the reservation. His father had gone to Washington to fight some kind of political battle with the government. And the sergeant heading your department, a man named Iverson, had an eye for young women, especially Indian women."

"What does this have to do with anything?" Hayden scowled.

"You'll find her records under Mary Running Wolf, 1991," Kimberly shot back. "They're in a storage box in the hangar, in case you're interested."

"Hey, Dad!" Ashley yelled. "I'm ready for our ride."

"Hold on!" Hayden held up his hand. He turned back to Kimberly. "So, what's your point?"

"I'm telling you Mary Running Wolf died of a hemorrhage from a tubal pregnancy. She died because she'd been raped by a sergeant in your office. The sheriff's department denied it, of course. They said she was a crazy Indian woman who'd been drinking, and under the circumstances, who was going to believe her?

"You want to talk about cover-ups, Sam? The night she died, the records indicate they called three times, pleading with the sheriff's office for help. The bastards ignored her. Iverson knew she was in trouble. Maybe if he ignored her calls, she would die. And if she died, his problems would disappear. They didn't show up for two hours, Sam. They let her bleed to death."

"Where did you get all this?"

"From your archives. It doesn't take rocket science to put two and two together."

"Does Wolfson know of this?"

Kimberly shook her head. Moisture clouded her eyes. "I would never have the heart to tell him."

"Well, I need to know what happened with this lion, Kimberly. And if the Indians pulled one over on us, we're going to look pretty stupid."

"It wasn't the Indians," she answered flatly. "Wolfson wouldn't have a clue."

"What are you talking about?"

"Your deputies left a dead lion on a table in the hangar the other night. If the pathologist found some convincing evidence, the case would close. All they needed was a bit of confirmation to connect this lion to one of the human deaths."

"I don't understand."

Kimberly shrugged. "Just suppose you've got a big lion on a table and you need some convincing evidence it's the lion that's been killing people. And just suppose someone's got hair the color of Tracy Reynolds's and they take a lock and stuff it up the lion's rear."

"You did this?" he asked incredulously.

"I'm not saying I did anything, Sam. I'm just telling you this thing has got to end. And now it's over. The evidence is there."

"Who else knows of this?"

Kimberly shook her head. "I don't know what you're talking about."

"Goddammit! "Hayden fumed. "If you're part of some kind of a hoax, I could have you thrown in jail."

"Yeah?" she answered. "Then cuff me."

Her voice rose. "But if you want to open this up again, I urge you to think long and hard. Everybody's ready to go home. The Reynolds family will be satisfied with the knowledge that the lion that killed their daughter has been brought in. So will Lute Olsson's family and Lassiter's wife. There is closure for the pain and suffering these families have gone through.

"You like this circus in Elkhorn, Sam? By next week, all the lowlifes lurking around town will crawl back into their holes. And you can get about your business of running a good law enforcement agency, as you have. Everyone loves you here, Sam. You've got an opportunity to end it. Let it go."

Hayden glanced toward the corral. Ashley mounted and began riding slowly around the ring. When he turned back, his voice was almost a whisper.

"If we have the wrong lion . . . Just say it is. It means we have a murderous lion still on the loose. How the hell can I live with myself knowing that tomorrow or the next day somebody else is going to be killed?"

"Where you going to look? You've got a fire roaring through Porcupine Canyon, and these animals are going to be running from here to the Canadian border. In another month, the snows will start. At what point is this thing going to end? How many more lions you want to kill? How many weeks you going to tolerate your town torn apart by all the gawkers and idiots crushing in here, looking for the reward?"

"Dad, I'm ready," Ashley yelled.

Hayden shook his head. "If they don't find human DNA in the claws, somebody's going to raise some questions."

"If they're doing their job, they're going to find human DNA." Kimberly rolled up her sleeve. A circular gauze bandage marked the inner surface of her arm.

"Jesus, God . . ." Hayden muttered.

"You got a bronze statue in the middle of the town square," she said fiercely. "A man named Jeremiah Bates. Cavalryman and Indian fighter. A local hero. Someone the town can be proud of.

"You want to know what he did, Sam? In 1882, he took a troop of soldiers and raided an Indian camp. The braves had left on a hunt. Jeremiah Bates killed twenty-seven Indians. Most were women and children. So go fuck yourself and your department. If that's what you call law and order in this country, then put me in jail."

She turned and started back toward the corral. Halfway there, she stopped.

"You want a cover-up?" she yelled at him. "I figure you owe Robert Wolfson a cover-up or two. Otherwise, take your damned department and go to hell!"

Hayden stood in the shade of the aspen and watched her go. Down in the corral, Ashley helped Kimberly climb onto her horse. The two rode out of the gate into the pasture.

"Thanks, Dad," Ashley called, waving. He raised his hand with a slight nod.

Ashley kicked her horse into a gallop. Kimberly followed closely behind. Tobey raced out from the barn, barking and yipping, trying to catch up.

A lark sang from a post. The leaves of aspen shimmered in the sun. In a couple of hours, the governor of Montana was flying into

Elkhorn to give Robert Wolfson a $100,000 reward. What the hell was he going to do?

He turned back toward the sheriff's Bronco, walking slowly. There were some hard decisions to make in life, he thought. Sometimes you couldn't go by the book. Sometimes you had to make choices by the heart.

67

A T THE DRUM MAJOR'S WHISTLE, the Elkhorn High School marching band started up Main Street. They were led by six cheerleaders, a team of drill cadets, and a dozen girls in tight shorts and white cowboy boots, carrying pom-poms. The dancers were followed by a color guard of four uniformed soldiers holding the United States and State of Montana flags. Next came twenty-three members of the high school band.

Behind them drove a well-polished 1957 Chevrolet convertible with the mayor and two members of the city council, who blew kisses to the crowd. A second convertible of similar vintage brought Robert Wolfson and Franklyn Yellow Pine. After them came a loose assemblage of Native Americans, some playing flutes, other shaking rattles or tapping drums. Half a dozen dogs wandered along with the participants. Someone had even brought a goat.

At the rear of the parade came a group of horseback riders. They were dressed in Stetson hats and cowboy shirts, with silver buttons flashing in the sun. The clap of hooves echoed off the surrounding buildings as the parade turned the corner and steadily advanced. A crowd of observers lined the main concourse, cheering as they passed.

Along the western edge of the square was a small stand. Here a speakers' podium had been erected with a number of folding chairs. Crepe banners of red, white, and blue decorated the scaffolding. Nearby was a refreshment stand.

Across the street at the Bank of Montana building, beneath the national flag, someone had run up a yellow pennant showing the black silhouette of a stalking cougar. The cloth was snapping in the breeze. It reminded Hayden of the flags deep sea fishing vessels fly when they have caught a marlin.

Hayden took a seat at the speakers' table and watched the procession work its way around the square. Various dignitaries began to file into seats behind him. The mayor stepped out of his convertible. Robert Wolfson and Franklyn Yellow Pine followed closely behind.

Wolfson's hair was pulled back in a ponytail. He wore a white shirt, sports coat, and flowered tie. A pair of thin wire-rimmed glasses made him appear quite studious. He looked to Hayden like a college professor. Perhaps more handsome than most, he reflected.

Franklyn was dressed in polished boots, designer jeans, and a resplendent cowboy shirt. A bright red bandanna hung around his neck. He came to the speakers' stand and took a seat alongside Wolfson. In a few moments, all the seats were filled.

Over the past twenty-four hours, some of the story had come out. Many of the audience were still whispering about it as they gathered along the Elkhorn square. It was a tale related by Native Americans in the bars, the stores, and the various cafés they frequented. They said Bobby Running Wolf had participated in a Sundance. He had undergone the piercing ceremony alone. For six hours, he had hung until his skin had broken through and he had fallen to the ground. Blackfoot braves had not undergone such painful initiation for as long as anyone could remember.

Wolfson had shown his people that he was as courageous as any member of the tribe. The piercing ceremony was a way of uniting him with the past, the elders claimed. And now that he was back, he was eligible to take over his inherited leadership, passed from chief to son to grandson for generations.

Bobby Running Wolf had gone into the wilderness. For five days, he had hunted the "spirit cat," and Raven Crow had used her magic to protect him. On the fifth day, Wolfson had come face to face with the Great Lion. In a cave, high upon the cliff walls of Porcupine Canyon, Bobby Running Wolf had counted coup. This, Franklyn Yellow Pine attested, was fact.

The Indians were more evasive as to how the tracking collar of a tame female lion could end up on the back of an eighteen-wheeler leaving the Dairy Queen. They said the captivity of a wild animal such as a cougar was never meant to be. It was the Great Spirit who had ordained the removal of the collar. Likewise, the Great Spirit must have brought it to the Dairy Queen. How else could it happen? No person could outrun three men on horseback with a dozen lion hounds.

As people settled into their seats on this bright Montana day, the town square hummed with excitement. A helicopter buzzed overhead, landing in a nearby park. Governor Leonard Erickson stepped out. Soon he was moving through the crowd, shaking hands, working his way to the speakers' podium. Only when the National Anthem started did everyone rise.

What had happened was a great victory for this town, the governor said. Women, children, and citizens of every description could be proud. And it was all due to Robert Wolfson and Franklyn Yellow Pine. He likened the feat, the courage, the heroism of these two men to that of the great pioneers who had come across the prairies in covered wagons and blazed a trail for others to follow. Men like Jeremiah Bates, whose statue adorned the square. The governor concluded by holding up a check for $100,000.

"It gives me great pleasure to present this reward to Robert Wolfson," he exclaimed with a broad smile. "Bobby Running Wolf, we thank you."

A loud cheer rose from the audience. Four rows of Native Americans sitting along the right-hand side of the podium began to stomp their feet.

"Running Wolf! Running Wolf! Running Wolf!" they chanted.

Soon the entire ensemble took up the call. Everyone began whistling and yelling. Then the band started playing "America the Beautiful."

Wolfson stood before the podium, patiently waiting for the crowd to quiet. Bowing graciously, he held up his hands for silence. The wind gently ruffled the crepe paper behind him. Down in the front row, his sister was watching closely. She stopped for a moment to hush her two children. Lindsey had already stained her dress with ice cream.

"If you had told me a month ago I would be standing in front of this crowd in Elkhorn, Montana, accepting a check for $100,000 from the governor, I would have fainted . . ." he began.

A murmur of laughter passed through the audience.

His voice rose. "A lot of things have happened over these past three weeks. I have had the opportunity to come back and share things with people whom I dearly love. It has been an opportunity for me to realize my heritage again. You are special people here in Elkhorn, and you have been very special people to me at the reservation."

Taking a sip of water, he paused to carefully choose his words.

"I have thought a lot over the past twenty-four hours about how I should handle this reward. Since it was my grandfather who brought me back, I have wondered what he might want me to do. In the old days, the wealth of a single member of the tribe was always shared by its members. No one kept riches for himself.

"Accordingly, I will be donating a check for $90,000. This money will be given to the reservation with the stipulation that 20 percent be used with matching government funds to help repair the gymnasium. The floor is bent and the roof leaks, and I would like to see the community build up its basketball program again.

"I am also concerned about the elementary education program for our people. The remainder of the reward should be used to assist with the teaching program at the first three grade levels. I will help direct these funds. I learned this summer that not all of our children attend school regularly. If we are to be competitive and participate in our share of the common good, we must do this through the education of our children.

"And finally, to my brethren, to whom I owe so much. The Blackfoot have asked me to assist with the tribal council, which I will be willing to do. For this next year, I have a commitment to teach in Chicago. More and more, however, I need to look at how I might return and help my people."

He was interrupted by loud applause.

"So, I will be back," he promised with a smile. "Perhaps this was my past; now it is my future."

People stood up and cheered. The band interrupted with the beginning stanza of a Souza march.

"One final thing," Wolfson added. "If I can add . . ." He paused with a smile to count his fingers. "There still remains ten thousand dollars. I have spoken with our tribal council. I would like to create a scholarship fund for that young Native American with the most outstanding potential for continued education. This award I present with great pleasure to Franklyn Yellow Pine."

Franklyn came forward and shook Wolfson's hand. The youth was beaming. The audience rose to their feet, clapping and cheering.

"Lastly, I would like to honor the Great Lion that brought me here," Wolfson said. "Mountain lions are part of the heritage of my people. When an animal kills or injures a human being, it is a bad thing. But for those of you who cannot understand, I would ask you to forgive an instinct of survival that is far stronger than our own. There will be other problems of this nature, I'm sure. But I would pray for that day when man and beast can co-exist in harmony again."

The band started up. There was clapping and cheering and the chatter of uplifted voices.

"Don't forget the refreshments and cake!" Mayor Miller shouted. "Hallelujah! The streets of Elkhorn are safe again."

It was inevitable they should come together and speak. For an hour after the ceremony, Kimberly Benson continued finishing her interviews, but always her eyes sought out Robert Wolfson. Within her heart there was a terrible ache of urgency.

What had happened the last two days was not something she had wanted. If it had been up to her, they would have been together more. In reality, she had scarcely seen him. When they had come out of the canyon that night, Wolfson was strangely silent. She, too, was shocked at what had happened.

There, in the blackness of the cave, between the flashes of lightning and the strange glow of electricity, she had heard the explosive concussions of Wolfson's shots, seen the deadly tongue of flame from his rifle, and watched in horror as he advanced toward the lion, screaming. With the next bolt of lightning, the lions were gone. The female had been undoubtedly scared off. And the male? Had he killed it? There were still many things about the night she did not understand.

Once they had reached the horses, they had hurried out of the canyon, trying to make the road by dark. As they drove home in silence, she felt like something within her had died. Franklyn dropped her off at the motel. Before they parted, Wolfson took her hand. "I will call," he said, yet there was a distance to his voice she had not heard before. Two days had passed. She had scarcely seen him since. In twenty-four hours, she would be gone. And now, it seemed she would have to share him with everyone in town.

Kimberly watched as small children asked for his autograph. Wolfson was constantly being pulled by the mayor or one of the city council members to speak to this official or that. She glanced at him out of the corner of her eye as he was being interviewed by another television station and watched jealously as he gave a story to an attractive newspaper reporter.

She knew more about his encounter with the Great Lion than perhaps anyone else except Franklyn Yellow Pine. But there were still things about it that did not quite fit. Yes, she would report it as it seemed. Her cameraman had taken a video of Wolfson accepting the reward. The rest she could fill in with other interviews. This would be the last piece she would put together on the Blackfoot Lion. Surprisingly, she found herself dreading its coming to an end.

She was due back in San Francisco tomorrow. She had a flight out at nine in the morning. She wondered how she could go back and work on stories like the mayor's new plan for the homeless in San Francisco or a toxic spill that tied up commuters for hours. It seemed to her the real stories in life happened out here in the "wilderness." Here she had been her own boss and done pretty much what she wanted. Here she didn't have anyone looking over her shoulder or someone like Stephanie Peterson to compete with.

And what about Robert Wolfson? She looked for him again and saw he had moved toward the refreshment stand. He was talking with three people, a woman and two men, smiling graciously, involved in an animated discussion. Her heart skipped a beat when he glanced in her direction.

As she moved toward him, she felt like a swimmer about to take a dive into a darkened pool. She didn't know what the outcome would be. She only knew there were things she wanted to say.

She met Wolfson coming out of the refreshment line.

"We should speak," she began.

Wolfson nodded, excusing himself from the people surrounding him. He held a cup of punch in one hand, a piece of cake in the other. They walked together toward a corner of the town square where they could talk privately.

"Want to share?" he asked.

She shook her head.

He led her to a split log, where they took a seat.

"When are you leaving?"

"I should finish up this last segment tonight. There's not a lot else to stay for. I have a plane out in the morning. You?"

"I fly to Chicago Wednesday."

"They wouldn't give you more time?"

"They would, but I need to get back in time to start the fall semester. I feel badly enough missing the end of summer school. There are some tough kids there I didn't want to leave."

"That was a good speech. I was taken with what you said."

"Thanks."

"I was impressed you gave all the reward money away. That was a courageous thing to do."

He shrugged. "I owe it to my grandfather to do something for the reservation."

A man stepped forward and interrupted. "Mr. Wolfson, I wanted you to meet my family," he said. "We live on the outskirts of town. I can't tell you how thankful I am for what you have done for this community."

Wolfson smiled politely and stood up. "Stay here," he told Kimberly. "I'll be back."

He walked with the man a short distance across the square and greeted a family with three young children. Kimberly watched him crouch down and speak with the kids. He had a way with people, she thought. She wondered what he would be like as a high school teacher. Probably interesting, probably demanding, probably tough, yet compassionate. And then for a brief moment, she wondered how he would be as a husband. She stopped herself from dwelling on the thought. It would be ridiculous to consider. How could it ever be?

Wolfson excused himself from the family and walked back toward her. He took a seat beside her on the log.

"There are a few things I need to tell you," she began, "before I lose you to the crowd."

"If it's about our night together, you don't need to apologize," he answered. "It was my fault. I understand."

"No, I don't think you do," she replied. She studied his strong features: the sharp outlines of his chin, his dark eyes, the ponytail carrying his hair across one shoulder. "That night was very special to me."

"It was to me, too," he answered.

"It would be absurd to think anything would come of it," she found herself saying. Yet as soon as the words were spoken, she regretted them. She knew she was trying to harden herself for the loss. There was a point where realism and pride and self-respect took over. They had had one intimate night together, that was all.

"You are a very special person to me, Kimberly," he said softly. "You will always be."

Wolfson looked down and brought a piece of cake to his lips. Then his eyes rose and met her stare. A hint of moisture welled within her eyes.

"We lead different lives."

"I know," he agreed.

"We have very different backgrounds."

"I hope you'll write." He searched her expression like a hawk.

"You will have to give me your address."

Out of nowhere, Sergeant Hayden appeared and loomed over them. "Sorry to interrupt you two," he said. "Bobby, the governor wants to speak with you."

Wolfson stood up. He turned back to Kimberly. "I guess I'd better go."

He held out his hand.

She took his fingers gently, feeling the controlled strength in his grasp. She remembered the first time they had touched during her interview at the Cattleman Saloon. She gazed up at him, her eyes searching for an answer she was afraid to hear.

"Will I see you again?"

His expression suddenly became serious. The faintest frown worked its way across his face. "I promised I would participate in a tribal council this evening. Sometimes they go on for hours. We might not be finished until after midnight."

"My flight doesn't leave until nine in the morning," she said.

"Where could we meet?"

"I'll keep a light on."

His eyes darkened. "Our worlds are so different, Kimberly . . ."

Her hand reached out and touched his fingers.

"I'm not sure I care," she said.

68

FOR TWO HOURS, KIMBERLY BENSON PACED the motel room. First she rearranged the bed. Then she ruffled the pillows and smoothed the blankets. She watched television for a time and then restlessly stepped outside to feel the night air. She tried to keep her mind occupied, yet as each minute passed, her confidence began to ebb.

It was impossible that they could see each other with any seriousness, she reflected. They lived half a continent apart, and they had totally different lives.

They had known each other for little more than a couple of weeks.

A quarter moon rose to the east. In the pale light, she could see the tips of fir trees swaying in the wind. She turned on the porch light, hoping it would act like a beacon.

A car approached. Headlights flashed across her window. She held her breath. The vehicle continued down the road. Most of the motel guests were asleep. Except for her small porch light and a "No Vacancy" sign, the grounds were dark, the building quiet.

Perhaps he would call, she told herself. She didn't like the thought. If he called, he would likely say he got tied up at the last minute. Of course, he would suggest they write. But writing never quite said the things you wanted—and she wanted Robert Wolfson this night. She wanted to feel his strength and his caress. She wanted to recapture that night so many days before, to see if it was real, to see if what had happened was an accident or there was still a passion so strong it made her mind spin.

Midnight came and passed. She gave a last look outside. A cool breeze drifted into the room. Going to the front door, she turned off the porch light. She took a seat by the window. As she switched off the light, the room was cast into darkness.

A glint of silver fell across her face. She closed her eyes and let her head lean back on the chair. A tear worked down the corner of her cheek. She tried to put up a mental wall, to steel herself from dwelling on it further. He's not coming, she told herself. She shouldn't have expected more.

She was not sure how long she'd been asleep. When she awoke, she was aware of faint music playing. She thought at first it was a tape or someone turning on their radio. The drifting melody of a flute came to her ears. The music was haunting, the tune melodious and wild. She raised her head and looked out the window. There, silhouetted by the faint light of a dying moon, was the figure of a man. He held a flute in his hands.

Standing up, she wrapped a blanket around her shoulders and stepped outside. She closed the door so quietly it did not make a sound. Following the music, she slid across the pathway to the grove of trees where the figure stood.

Even in the darkness she knew it was him.

69

ROBERT WOLFSON SAT IN THE MIDSECTION of the plane gazing out the window. The twin-engine jet accelerated down the runway and climbed steeply into an azure sky. To the north, cumulus clouds lined the horizon like tufts of cotton.

The plane rose steadily, swinging over the southern edge of Glacier Park. As it gained altitude, it banked to the south, toward Denver. Wolfson had a connecting flight at noon. With luck, he would be in Chicago by dinner.

As he stared absently out the window, his mind was already on the task ahead. The last three weeks of the summer session had ended. They would have finished up finals by now, and the fall semester would be beginning soon. Taking time off had not been as problematic as he had thought. Over the years, he had accumulated a month's sick leave, and the school had found an acceptable sub.

The moral breech of leaving the kids, however, bothered him, especially the difficult ones. But sometimes, some things had to give, he thought. If he had to do it over again, he wouldn't change a thing. It was important that he'd returned to the reservation. For his grandfather. For the tribe. For the lion.

Loren Rodgers, the school superintendent, had told him to get his affairs in order; his job would be waiting when he returned. Besides, freshman basketball didn't start for another month.

"And good work on the lion business," the superintendent said.

"How'd you know about that?" Wolfson replied with surprise.

"Where've you been?" Rodgers answered. "It's all over the national news."

Wolfson did not respond. The two exchanged pleasantries, and hung up. By month's end, he would be up to his neck in lesson plans, teaching history, and the beginning of basketball practice. Thinking back on the past three weeks, he wondered if he would every fully comprehend what had happened. His life had changed irreversibly—and so had his future.

Before he had left Elkhorn, at the tribal meeting that last night, the council had asked him to return, to help bring the various factions of the Blackfoot tribe together. They wanted him to be their leader. They had some tough decisions to make. A vote on the mining company's proposed road was coming up. No one could represent the widespread differences between the conservative elders and the left-wing youth like he could.

The words were flattering. They meant well. He told Black Kettle he would give it careful thought. First, he had a contractual obligation to return to Chicago to teach. Maybe next year, he reflected. There were a lot of time and a lot of unknowns to consider.

As the plane banked, Wolfson could see the huge, snow-peaked mountains marking the Continental Divide. To the east spread a wide plateau of rolling plains. He followed the serpentine line of the Arcata River until he could see Elkhorn. The town looked like a cluster of dots at the end of a valley. To the north rose a dark, billowing cloud forming over Porcupine Canyon. The newspapers had said the forest fire was contained. Looking out the window, Wolfson wasn't so sure. The large smoke cloud indicated there was a lot of acreage burning.

And then he thought about the lion. He'd not been able to kill the beast. The cry rising in the darkened cave had certainly come from the Great Lion. Wolfson had been only a few feet away.

Erupting from the darkness had come a sound that sounded like a primordial shriek of enormous sadness, a scream from across the depths of time, which spoke of the death of a hundred thousand animals: animals chased, persecuted, and hounded by man. And with the scream, he recognized the voice of his own people, herded onto reservations, left to starve, driven from their hunting lands.

In desperation, he'd charged at the beast, firing his rifle, screaming in Blackfoot. He'd come close enough in the darkness, for a brief instant, to feel the fur of the lion touch his hand. The noise and the unexpected insanity of his charge must have scared it. When a flash of lightning illuminated the cave seconds later, both animals were gone.

In days past, it was often considered a greater feat of courage for the Blackfoot to touch an enemy, or "count coup," rather than to kill him. And he had, as Franklyn attested, "counted coup" with the Great Lion.

It wasn't until later in the evening, after they had left Kimberly at her motel and were returning the horses to the reservation, that Franklyn Yellow Pine had spoken up.

"What are we going to do?" he asked.

Wolfson shrugged. He didn't know what else they could do.

Franklyn pressed him. "The fire will chase these lions for miles. There's no way the hunters will find them."

"Not now, Franklyn. But, there's still a $100,000 reward. No lion will be safe. In the end, it will just cause the deaths of a lot of innocent animals."

"So, we bring it in."

"And how could we possibly do that?"

"We bring in the old lion you shot."

"And pass it off as the man-killer? No one will believe it."

"Fish and Game wanted all lions that are killed brought in."

"I don't get your point."

"Can you still find it?"

"Of course."

"Then let's go back in the morning and get it."

"You crazy?"

"We need to bring it back," Franklyn persisted.

"And what the hell are we going to do with it?"

"Have it weighed, catalogued, autopsied. They can do with it what they are doing with all the other lions that are killed."

"It's just another lion."

"Yeah, but what if . . . just what if you're wrong, Bobby? What if the old lion was involved in some of this? You saw yourself; it was a damn big animal. The prints are not a lot smaller than the Great Lion's. And sometimes, old lions get ornery and crippled and take to killing people. What if it killed just one of these people? Just what if it killed one? It's not going to hurt to turn it in, is it?"

"The tracks were different."

"But not that different. That old lion has an awfully big paw. You and I can recognize the difference. I'm not sure how many others can."

Wolfson smiled. "Still trying to figure out how to get that reward, aren't you?"

"Hell, I'm going to need some tuition to go to school next year. What the heck is it going to hurt? The worst thing that can happen is they find nothing and declare it the wrong lion."

"So, you want to go back in the morning and trek through the forest and dig out an old dead lion? I would do a lot for you, Franklyn. But this is a lot to ask."

"Hey, I just spent four hours risking my butt with a pack of hounds running up my ass. It's the least you could do in return."

"All right." Wolfson finally gave in.

At dawn, they'd ridden back. By then, the entrance to Porcupine Canyon was engulfed with smoke. They found the old lion, rolled it in a blanket, and hauled it out on the back of Franklyn's horse. When they hit Elkhorn, everyone went crazy.

"Two Indians killed the lion!" someone cried. Within minutes, rumors flew through town. "The Blackfoot have killed a big lion. It may be the one we're after." Then: "The redskins have killed the man-eater! Bobby Running Wolf and Franklyn Yellow Pine. It's the big lion! No question about it!"

Mayor Elihu Miller was so excited he ordered a motorcade to follow Franklyn's truck with the lion tied across its hood. Everyone piled behind, honking horns, shouting the news.

"Sir, wait a minute," Wolfson had tried to protest. "Please don't jump to conclusions until the autopsy reports come in."

"No way this is not the lion," the mayor exclaimed. "Look at the size of it! Look at its paws! They're huge! It must weigh over two hundred pounds. Congratulations, gentlemen! This is the one!"

And then when they performed the autopsy on the lion, Wolfson was flabbergasted. He knew the prints didn't fit, only it took someone with his tracking ability to tell the difference. The paw prints of the old lion were huge. Pushed out and splayed widely, they almost looked the same. Wolfson had seen the size of the great beast up close, and he knew there were no other lions like it in Montana, and for that matter, probably not in North America.

"Traveling far?" A woman's voice.

Wolfson turned from the plane window. "Denver, then Chicago," he answered.

The woman looked grandmotherly, gray-haired, with a pleasant smile. "Have you been following that horrible lion thing in Elkhorn?" she chatted. "I was visiting my daughter's family. Scared me to death. I'm so glad they finally brought it in. I was just petrified it was going to kill one of the children. Two Indians got it, you know. They said it was some kind of a 'spirit cat.'"

Wolfson nodded politely. "That's what I heard."

As he leaned back toward the window, his thoughts turned to Kimberly Benson. He had her address and her telephone number, and he had promised he would call. A tiny part of him wondered about quitting his job and moving to San Francisco, but he knew that wouldn't work. He had a commitment to his profession, and the last thing he wanted was to be hanging around Kimberly in a new city, with a part-time teacher's job and no clear direction. That would sink their relationship from the start.

And then his thoughts returned to the lion. The lion had done a lot for him. It had brought him back to the reservation, and it had given him his rightful place with the tribe. Perhaps this was the destiny that Raven Crow had spoken about. Perhaps this was why he had returned. And maybe therein was the trade.

Franklyn Yellow Pine had received his scholarship. Wolfson had donated $90,000 to the reservation. With matching funds, there would be enough money to begin repairs on the gymnasium and help with education for the kids. Yet, there was still a tiny, nagging doubt in his mind. He couldn't explain the human hair in the dead lion's stomach. In the end, there were things about the autopsy he didn't comprehend.

Not everything had worked out exactly as he expected. But when does it ever? he thought. The truth, he ultimately decided, was somewhere beyond his reach.

70

A LIGHT DRIZZLE OBSCURED THE HIGHWAY. Brake lights flashed. Kimberly slowed her car to pull around a stalled vehicle and then accelerated into an open space. A minute later, she was stopped again. By the time she reached KPXL, it would be nine. She was already a half hour late. Not a good way to start the day.

Although she'd checked in over the weekend, Monday would be her first full day back. She wondered how her reception would be. After she had gotten settled, Kessler had told her to come up to his office. He wanted to schedule a conference with one of the station's owners. Was she getting two weeks' notice? She wondered if they were going to tell her to look for another job.

She watched the line of vehicles creep around a curve into San Francisco and switched on the car radio to the morning news. A prominent Arizona senator admitted to an affair with a young woman. The worst season for forest fires in history was still in progress. And the governor was threatening to roll back payments for state workers to the minimum wage.

She remembered how excited she used to be when she was an integral part of the breaking news. Now things didn't seem to matter. More and more her thoughts returned to Montana. She wondered where Robert Wolfson was. Probably teaching, she thought. Probably working with the kids. Probably getting ready to coach the freshman basketball team. Already she missed him. But what was she going to do? Their lives were impossibly different. She could feel the separation, the distance, the stress of different professions pulling her away.

It was 9:30 by the time she arrived at the station. She moved up the stairs and headed for the main editing room. Along the way, she passed an open set with assorted props and television cameras. Here KPXL filmed its daily reports. Donald Casper, the station's chief weatherman, sat behind a desk pulling off his mike. He looked up as Kimberly passed.

"Hey, Lion Lady!" he shouted. "Good work out there. Welcome back."

She nodded with surprise. Casper had never been particularly friendly before. She wondered at the change. Continuing, she entered the main editing room. Stephanie Peterson was watching one of the monitors, reviewing a morning report. Two assistants crowded next to her, editing footage for the afternoon news. Stephanie stopped what she was doing and waved.

"Kimberly. Good to see you," she exclaimed. "I wanted to tell you what an inspiration your stories were." Stephanie held out her hand. "What you went through. I couldn't believe it. You did the station proud."

Kimberly grasped her fingers. She was tempted to give Stephanie a Robert Wolfson handshake but held back. No sense breaking her rival's hand.

"I was wondering if we could have lunch," Stephanie said. "I want to hear all about your trip."

"Of course," Kimberly replied graciously. "Call me when you're free."

She continued through to the back of the editing space. Jeremy Wong waved from behind one of the consoles. Hustling over, he gave her a hug. "Welcome back," he said with affection. "I'm glad you're still alive."

"Ah, it wasn't that close," Kimberly said, smiling.

"Yeah, ask Stafford. He said you two were almost killed."

"Only twice," she laughed.

"Well, Kessler's in, and he told me he wanted to see you immediately when you arrived."

"I want to look over tomorrow's assignments," she said, hesitating.

Jeremy shook his head. "I think he wants to see you now."

"That man never lets up, does he?"

"Hey, rumor is, he's putting you up for an Emmy."

"Kessler? Not in a million years."

"If I was you, I wouldn't keep him waiting."

"Thanks." She held up her hands with a shrug.

Turning, she walked down the corridor to the station manager's office. She knocked lightly on the door.

"Come in," a voice shouted.

She pushed into the room. Alvin Kessler sat at a conference table. Next to him was a silver-haired man in a blue blazer and red tie. Both men stood up as she entered.

"Kimberly!" Kessler said effusively. "We were just talking about you. You know our boss, Peter Magnum, don't you?"

"We've met." Kimberly reached forward and shook Magnum's hand. Taking a seat, she settled across the table.

"We've got a lot to talk about," Kessler said.

Magnum nodded. "I wanted to thank you for putting KPXL on the map. Your reports brought in some of the highest ratings we've ever had. I was astounded at your work. I wanted to personally congratulate you."

"Just doing my job," Kimberly replied. "Most of it, I probably owe to a very big lion."

"You had us all on the edge of our seats, Kimberly. Thank goodness, the Indians got it."

She nodded. "I don't think it will be bothering anyone again."

"Peter and I have been talking about the best place for you at the station," Kessler continued. "We were thinking you would probably be well suited for your own program. Something like 20/20 with a 'Jane Pauley' slant. Something you could bring to us once a week. You pick the topics. We'll have two assistants available for research."

"We're talking about a slot, Thursday evenings, eight p.m.," Magnum added.

"We would like you to begin early October," Kessler said. "We need a little time for advance advertising. Let's try it for six months. See how it plays."

"I'm honored, "Kimberly answered. "But I'd like to think it over for a couple of days."

"Money?" Magnum leaned forward. "If that's your concern, I'll triple your salary with an incentive clause. Potentially, you're looking at more than a hundred grand."

"Don't turn this down, Kimberly," Kessler urged. "We'll make it work. Tell me what you want, and I'll get it for you."

"Cameraman?"

"You can have anyone at the station."

"There is only one. Eric Stafford."

"Done," Kessler replied emphatically. He seemed pleased. He nodded to Magnum then turned back to Kimberly. "Anything else?"

"A couple days off."

"Take a week. We'll need some time before you start, anyway. We need to put the marketing in place. This thing takes off and you got the world at your feet."

"And while you're off, be thinking about topics. We want something provocative. Something that will bring controversy. Something that will knock the public off their respective butts."

"You willing to take some risks?"

"Absolutely," Kessler answered. "That's exactly what we want."

THE TELEPHONE CALL TUMBLED THROUGH THE LINES, across 2100 miles of circuitry, from San Francisco to Chicago. Kimberly could hear the distant ring at the other end. She stood at the back of the station, phone to her ear, heart pounding in her chest.

"Hello." The voice was deep, firm, strong. Exactly how she remembered.

"Bobby?" The words spilled out before she could even think. "They've given me a couple days off. I was wondering . . . ?"

The reply crossed the lines like a bolt of lightning. There was no pause, no hesitation to the voice. "I can hardly wait," he said.

71

BY MID-OCTOBER, THE TREES WERE ablaze with crimson and saffron. Winds began to pour across the prairie, pushing heavy clouds from the north. Days were crisp. The wind chill factor dropped the temperature to minus five. A few last elk bugled in the canyons. An occasional bear foraged for berries, now bitter in taste. Sheet ice formed on the ponds, as migratory waterfowl pushed south, the ducks joining cackling strings of geese that threaded across the evening skies.

Inside the front entrance of the sheriff's station, Mabel sat at her desk. She fielded a call from the mayor. Miller wanted some information on a conference scheduled for the spring. She forwarded the call to Hayden's office and turned back to a stack of files.

A faded folder sat on the top of her desk. The report was labeled "1991." She thumbed through the pages, stopping at a black-and-white photograph of a woman named Mary Running Wolf. Hayden had brought the file from the sheriff's hangar a couple of weeks ago. For a time, he had been thinking of opening a long closed investigation. The sheriff's legal team advised him too much time had passed. A state official checked on retired Ronald Iverson and discovered he died a decade ago. It made no sense to open the investigation again.

Mabel stared at the photograph. Mary Running Wolf was an incredibly beautiful woman, she thought. She placed the image back in the folder and turned to a second report on Martin Running Wolf. She closed the files to take an incoming call. Hayden wanted the documents returned to the sheriff's archives. One of the deputies would carry them out to the hangar later in the day.

FOR MOST OF THE MORNING, Hayden had been at his desk, working on administrative matters. Ashley was in school. Things in Elkhorn were quiet. There had been no robberies for a week. No stolen cars, no busts for illicit drugs, no complaints of assaults or insulting behavior. Even the drunks appeared to be behaving. The biggest call for the search-and-rescue helicopter had been a pair of climbers stuck on a ridge at Deadman's Peak.

Gone were the hundreds of tourists from the summer season. Some Hayden missed; a lot he didn't. Gone, too, were the newspaper writers and television cameras. When he thought about it, Kimberly Benson was an attractive reporter; the rest he could do without. At last count, Hayden had completed twenty filmed interviews and been quoted more times than he could recall. He'd even received some letters from Japan. He had no idea what they said. Someday, when he had time, he would have a translator interpret their contents. For now, they were piled in a corner, along with a dozen sacks of other mail.

All the hunters and self-proclaimed lion killers who flooded Elkhorn with their RVs, their trucks, and their makeshift buses had left. Their tents and guns and dogs were gone. These, for all he cared, could fall in a hole and disappear. Mostly, he hoped they were out of his life forever. The body count: five lions, two cows, a horse, and a kid that shot a hole in his foot. He didn't think he could go through another season like this. He wasn't sure anyone could.

As he worked at his desk, Hayden became aware of a fluttering outside the office window. He tried to ignore the disturbance. When the noise became unusually persistent, he looked up. At first, he thought it was some kind of moth. He could see the wings flapping as the object repeatedly surged at the glass. Looking closer, he saw it was a thrush. The bird pecked at the window, charging the pane as if it was trying to get in.

He returned to his work and continued reading. Before him was a report from the state asking for a review of the department's official vehicles. The government was cutting back. Elkhorn had five official cars, and he was twenty percent over budget. What the hell do they want? he thought with exasperation. Did they expect him to patrol five hundred square miles on foot?

The bird continued pecking. There seemed be a frenzied urgency about it. Out of annoyance, Hayden left his desk and walked to the window. The thrush crouched at the glass, peering upward at him.

Hayden rapped on the pane. The bird flew off. Following its course with his glance, he recognized the form of Raven Crow. She stood across the courtyard, patiently waiting. He wondered how long she had been there.

Hayden waved to her in acknowledgment. She replied by bringing two fingers to her lips. She wanted to speak. She motioned for him to step outside.

A week, ten days ago, Hayden had driven to the reservation on other business. He had stopped by Weasel Creek looking for Raven Crow. Out of curiosity, he wanted to learn more about her. But the reported teepee and small encampment where she lived was gone. Except for remnants of a campfire, there was nothing there. No one knew who she was or where she was from. The tribal members he spoke with said she just appeared one day, a while back, and they weren't sure where she'd gone.

Hayden nodded to Mabel as he passed.

"I think we got company."

The secretary glanced up with puzzlement. "I haven't seen anybody, Sam, and there's no calls for you."

"Outside," he said, motioning.

Mabel walked to a side window and watched as Hayden moved into the courtyard.

Raven Crow held up her hand in a greeting.

"Good morning," he said.

"I'm told you were looking for me?"

"Where are you staying?" Hayden replied. "I came out to the reservation. I couldn't find your place."

She glanced toward the thrush and gave a little cluck. The bird was back on the windowsill. As if on command, the thrush flew toward Hayden, hovering about his head.

"You'd better put out your hand," she said.

Hayden extended his arm. The thrush landed on his sleeve.

"The last time I did this, he left a little present."

"I think he sensed you didn't like him."

"He's got a hell of a way of showing friendship," Hayden said. "Were you passing by?"

"I thought we should talk."

"Go ahead."

"I wanted to thank you."

"For what?" Hayden asked with surprise.

"For ending the hunt."

"There was no reason to continue."

"The lion, the 'spirit cat,' is gone," Raven Crow said. "You don't have to worry about it anymore."

"It's dead, if that's what you mean," Hayden replied. "Robert Wolfson killed it."

She gave him a funny look as if she didn't believe what he was saying. As if she knew more about the incident than she should. It was as if she knew what had happened and she understood what he told her was not quite the truth.

"My daughter would like you to come by her class sometime," Hayden told her. "Kids love birds. She would like to see how you touch them."

She stared at him with an odd expression. "I'm sorry about your daughter. There are things about the lion that are difficult for an Anglo to understand. It did not come back to harm children."

"I wish I could believe that," Hayden said, frowning.

"It killed people who were hunting it," she responded. "People who were trying to track it down."

"Tell me about this lion," Hayden said. "Tell me so that someone like me can understand."

Her words came slowly. "Your people have caused great injustices to the animals and the people here."

"So the lion came back?"

"*Omahkatayo* returned to make things right."

"And Robert Wolfson?"

"As it was, it shall be."

Hayden eyed her, trying to piece together what she was saying. He held up his arm and watched the bird pecking on his sleeve.

"Where do you go from here?" he asked.

"I'll be leaving soon."

"Will we be seeing you again?"

"I don't think so," she replied.

"Well, thank you for stopping by."

"There were things I wanted to say."

Inside the station, Mabel moved across the room. She stood at the doorway, watching intently. The bird that had been hopping on Hayden's arm fluttered off. Raven Crow shuffled out of the courtyard. Just before she left, she made a subtle motion with her arm. A corner of the blanket whipped across her shoulder. At the same moment, a black form came out of nowhere. Mabel thought the crow might have been sitting on the roof. Hayden had a second's warning before a swoosh of feathers hurtled toward his head.

"Sam, watch out!"

Hayden ducked as the crow shot past. Cawing once, it swung above the hedge and vanished beyond the shrubbery toward the disappearing figure of Raven Crow.

Raven Crow looked back once with a faint smile before she walked away, and it was this expression that clicked in Mabel's mind. It was a connection that she'd been reaching for, a remembrance that came to her with a sudden shock. The face, the familiar look to the eyes, the angle of the chin. It was similar to the expression in a faded photograph, crammed in the pages of a twenty-year-old investigation.

"Sam! My God . . ." Mabel cried. But as quickly as the thought came, the connection submerged within her rational mind. No way, she caught herself. The thought was too ridiculous to consider.

Maybe if Mabel saw her again. Maybe if she could observe her up close, there were questions Raven Crow could answer, things about the Blackfoot and the lion maybe she could put to rest. But the woman was on the other side of the hedge, moving rapidly away. Her form glided off into the shadows.

"Sam! Stop her!" Mabel yelled. She bolted out the door.

As the secretary raced toward the hedge, her first thought was the woman was gone. There was no one there. Then came an explosion of feathers, as a covey of quail rocketed skyward, scattering in every direction. High above flew a string of geese. A faint cackling reached her ears.

"That was one strange woman," Hayden said quietly. "I wonder if we'll ever know who she is?"

Turning back, Mabel's legs began to wobble. For an instant, her world spun. Hayden caught her by the shoulder and steadied her balance.

"You all right?"

"Sorry. I got a little dizzy."

Gradually, the secretary could feel her senses return. Leaning heavily on Hayden, she walked back toward the building, holding onto his arm. As she entered the doorway, Mabel glanced back, searching for Raven Crow. But the quail were gone and the geese no more than a spider's thread, drifting along the horizon.

Inside the station, a FAX machine rattled. Then a voice came over the radio. A deputy was calling dispatch. There had been a car accident at Benson's Creek. It was time to get back to work. The station's commitment to law enforcement never ended. Time to get back to business again.

72

A STREAM CASCADED THROUGH AN ALPINE MEADOW, sparkling and surging until it disappeared into the shadows of a forest. Here the water flowed in slow-moving, turquoise pools. From the depths glittered pebbles of garnet, beryl, and quartz, their surfaces smoothed by untold centuries of liquid froth.

Massive trees grew along its banks, a thousand years old and eleven feet in diameter. The trunks lined the stream like ancient colonnades. Beneath their limbs grew a carpet of ferns, interrupted by tiny orchids called fairy slippers. Beams of sunlight penetrated the shadows. Through these shafts flew flocks of warblers, their chirps like the tinkling of chimes.

A magnificent stag moved cautiously along an ancient trail. In places, the pathway was overgrown by a maze of creepers and vines. When he reached these impasses, he lowered his antlers, clearing a swath of vegetation. He was an immense animal, nearly a ton in weight and six feet high at the shoulders. On his head grew a rack of velvet antlers. He was followed by a herd of eleven elk: six mature females, three juveniles, and a pair of yearling twins.

When he reached the stream, he paused to let his family drink. One by one, they stepped down to the water, taking in the sweet, clear liquid as if it was ambrosia. Only the leader of this handsome clan refrained. Crossing the stream, he paused to test the wind, searching for the slightest hint of danger.

He waited for a minute and then snorted impatiently. In tight quarters, with poor visibility, he was anxious to proceed. He gave a low-pitched grunt as the last of the fawns sipped from the crystal pool. With a graceful leap, he bounded up the embankment, urging the others to follow.

For a mile, he led them along the serpentine path. At one turn, a huge hemlock had toppled, downed by a winter storm. The stag detoured around the fallen tree, breaking ground for a new trail. With time, as they traveled back and forth from the deep forest, this bypass would become part of their regular route. For now, he chose his footing carefully.

The month was June, and for the first time, he led his harem to a broad meadow at the base of cliffs. Here he knew the sun would melt the snow. Tender green shoots rose through the ice. It was a large, open space where the herd could feed safely.

At the eastern edge of this meadow was a talus slope bounded by a steep walled cliff. The rock rose for a hundred feet and then stair-stepped upward to the crest of a giant mountain. A glacier curled around one shoulder of the peak. Across the other, fell a waterfall, plunging in a wisp of spray.

When the herd arrived at the meadow, the sun was unusually warm. Melting snow lined its edges. Tiny shooting stars had begun to bloom. Along one side, a clump of bear grass grew, its cream-colored stalks like a row of candles. In two weeks, the field would be ablaze with flowers.

The elk grazed here for the afternoon. There was little motivation for them to leave. The yearlings fed heavily and then began to play, romping across the field. Mothers and aunts browsed peacefully, lingering in the warmth. If the insects got too bad, they strolled over to a snow bank where the cooler temperature acted as a repellant. One of the mature females, an aunt, became so comfortable she lowered to her knees, resting in the shade of a fir. For the herd, it was an idyllic afternoon.

As the sun began to drop, some inherent instinct alerted the stag it was time to go. The yearlings quit frolicking and moved closer to their mothers. The herd, once spread across the meadow, began to merge into a group. The stag became unusually watchful, scanning the clearing with vigilance. Suddenly, he trotted to the center of the meadow, head raised, nostrils flaring. He snorted once and pawed his hoof. An unseen scent had touched his nostrils.

By now, the Great Lion had reached the edge of the forest. He was directly across from the female elk resting beneath the fir. Slinking forward, ears flattened, he crawled the last ten yards on his belly, moving through the grass with imperceptible stealth. He rose ever so lightly, head tilted, eyes just above the grass. His pupils dilated, his breath quickened.

When the resting female stared in his direction, he froze. His tawny shape blended perfectly with the terrain. Then the elk lowered her head, distracted by a fly. It was the moment he'd been waiting for.

He came out of the grass like a rocket, claws gripping, his great hind legs propelling his body in powerful, leaping thrusts. He covered the first ten yards in a blur. The elk jumped up, trying to get her legs beneath her. In three strides, she would be at full speed; in another ten, she would reach the safety of the trees. She never made it. In an instant, the lion was upon her.

Leaping onto her flanks, he grabbed her chest with his claws. At the same time, he twisted her head. Then he was at her throat, cutting off her wind.

Only when she quit shuddering did the Great Lion stand. His mouth was covered with blood. He was panting heavily. He watched the rolling motion of the herd as they fled across the meadow in panic. Then he bent down and tugged at her neck. Using all his strength, he began to drag the carcass across the meadow.

He worked at this labor for nearly an hour, pulling the body along the edge of the cliffs. Every few minutes, he had to rest. For half a mile, he hauled the elk until he reached the stair-stepped layers of rocks. At the edge of the forest, he stopped.

Here he fed for a few moments and then rose from the carcass and began to bury the body beneath a pile of sticks. Finished, he ambled into the brush and lay down. He fell into a light slumber. His eyes closed, his huge claws relaxed inside their sheaths.

As evening came, the last rays of light illuminated the ridges in an alpine glow. Across the summits came the bleating of goats. The air chilled. A pair of marmots whistled and then scurried to their beds. Growing shadows flooded across the trees.

From deep within the timber came a strange bird-like chirping call. The sound repeated twice, and then all was quiet. Suddenly, two amber eyes appeared. The face pushed through the brush, carefully surveying the clearing.

Only when everything seemed safe did the female lion approach. With her right paw, she gently pulled off the branches, uncovering the body. Resting on her haunches, she called again and then proceeded to feed.

From out of the darkness came a small, furry figure with spots along its sides. The cub had blue eyes and ears like tiny saucers. As it approached its mother, it made a soft mewing sound. Moments later came a second and then a third.

The cubs were two months old and still heavily dependent on their mother. The sight of the elk provided great excitement. Immediately, they tumbled and wrestled across the body, tasting its blood, grabbing its fur, snarling and growling as if they were giants.

The mother gorged herself and then lay back on her side, patiently letting the three cubs nurse. One of the kittens was decidedly larger and more aggressive than the others. It was he who finished first. He stood at the head of the elk, facing the forest, testing the wind with his nose. There came a scent that made him rise up and hiss. He watched, wide-eyed, hair standing on end, as the immense lion drifted out of the shadows.

The male stopped a short distance from the female. An unheard communication passed between the two. It was behavior atypical for an American mountain lion. Scientists think male *Felis concolor* lead solitary existences except to mate. Some are known to kill their cubs. But the extraordinary circumstances for this lion family were different from most.

The female, raised in captivity, was not a good hunter. Her right hind leg did not move well, and she depended upon the male for food. Perhaps with time she would learn to hunt. During this first season, out in the wild, Roxanne needed help.

As she stood protectively next to the cubs, they gradually began to relax. Soon they were tumbling about, spitting and hissing, in mock combat. When one approached too close, Roxanne cuffed it back with a growl.

The Great Lion watched this mayhem for a few minutes. Then, with an impatient leap, he navigated a ten-foot ledge. Loping along this path, he climbed another hundred yards until he reached a cave in the side of the cliffs. Here he plunked down, facing the forest. The evening breezes caressed his face.

Spread before him was a vast tract of untouched wilderness. Far below glinted the waters of Kintla Lake. Forests of spruce and pine lined the base of the mountains. Behind rose the massive peaks of the Continental Divide.

This was his home. This was where he belonged. He had learned from his wanderings there were places to the south that he did not like, lands populated by strange beings that stood on two legs. These were animals that used sticks that fired and occupied wooden structures by the thousands.

He could kill these beings, this he knew. Yet the price of living in their territory was great. Theirs were lands where loud things clattered through the air and zooming objects traveled across blackened paths. And everywhere spread the odor of man. He felt a constant uneasiness there.

Certainly, there were dangers here. Wolves came from the north and harassed the animals in this land, and there were grizzlies who were always unpredictable and cantankerous. Yet these were creatures he knew and felt assured he could overcome. He seemed to have a purpose here, a sense of satisfaction, missing in his travels south.

As he lay along the ridge, contemplating the forest below, he heard a distant crashing sound. A tremble rushed through his bones. He wondered with a thrill what chase was occurring. Perhaps a grizzly pursued a moose. Perhaps a herd of deer were spooked and running for their lives.

An echoing cry drifted through the mountains. The howl split the silence and hung along the ridges in a lingering wail. Wolves!

The Great Lion leaped to his feet. In a series of rapid bounds, he descended the cliffs into the clearing. In seconds, he was in the depths of the forest, following a game trail north. The excitement of the night rang like drumbeats in his ears. His senses focused; his great body became a fluid motion of muscle and bone. No noise, no movement, no minuscule scent escaped him.

He was like a ranger on patrol, moving along the perimeter of his territory, checking who was there and who had passed. He would be gone on this foray for four or five days. Not so long that Roxanne and her cubs would get into trouble, but long enough to roam the outer boundaries of his land. Then he would return and bring her food.

At midnight, he stopped at a fork in the trail, five miles from the den. Here he rose to his full height and scratched the bark of a dead tree. The trunk served as a signpost for many animals. The highest lion scrapings were at a height of ten feet. A grizzly had shredded a portion of the bark along its side. At its base, a porcupine had chewed. He could even smell where one of the gray shapes had peed.

When "*Omahkatayo*" rose to his full extension, his talons clawed the trunk at twelve feet. No mark by any other beast rose to this height. He remained for a moment, scratching and gouging the bark. Then he was off, plunging through the night. Except for the markings on the tree, nothing betrayed his presence.

To all that passed, the warning of these immense claws was unmistakable.

"Here goes a Blackfoot Lion.
All you that enter here, beware."

Author's Note

Although this is a work of fiction, the description of animals and their behavior in this story should be consistent with current scientific data. Readers should note, however, that I have taken some artistic liberty with fictional names depicting locations of geographical interest in the Browning and Glacier Park area.

In referenced to the names; "Blackfoot" vs. "Blackfeet," I have tried to be consistent using the term "Blackfoot" to describe the Native American tribe and its reservation in the Browning area. The term originally comes from the singular use of the word "*siksika*" from which the English translation originated.

During the early formulations of this story, I had opportunity to visit with several individuals from the Blackfoot tribe, and always found them extremely courteous and friendly. Of these, "Curly Bear" was especially helpful in showing me the reservation plus helped fill in background details of their tribal history.

The writing of this novel took several drafts and a number of years to complete. During this time frame, I was heavily involved in clinical medicine, and often diverted to hospital projects which required immediate attention. On occasion, the story was shelved for weeks, sometimes months. Because of the time involved, the characters became like old friends. Often during a quiet time in the day or middle of the night, they would come to me and ask how we were doing. When I finally told them I was in the final stages of editing, they gathered together and cheered.

Several individuals deserve special credit in the concept and execution of this story. Early in its formulation, I had the privilege of working with Tom Schlesinger (tfilm23@gmail.com), story consultant "*extraordinaire*," who introduced me to the concept of the Hero's Journey and the works of Joseph Campbell and "*The Hero of a Thousand Faces.*" Michael Palmieri was also instrumental in guiding me through the nuances of character development and back story.

Bob Scheibel, Jacquie Scheibel, Bob and Helen Landman, and Al and Jane Baron were extremely helpful in their encouragement and support through a number of drafts; as well as my wife, Ellie, who was never too tired, or too busy, to listen to a fresh idea. Thanks, too, to Jane Baron (janebaron.com) for her wonderful creation of the cover for this book; as well as Waights Taylor Jr. with McCaa Books (waights@sonic.net) who made this publication possible.

And finally, thanks to a young mountain lion who attacked several dogs while I was vacationing with our family in Montana some years ago. At night, coming back to our cabin in the dark, I was able to understand the fear we humans have in dealing with predators and dangers we cannot see. It was here **The Hunt for Blackfoot Lion** was born.

TWH

About the Author

T.W. Hard is a physician and author who lives with his family in northern California. Previous works include three short stories: "*Molokini*", "*The Island,*" and "*The Leopard*" published in the *Saturday Evening Post*; plus two novels; ***Oasis*** and ***SUM VII***. Foreign editions of ***SUM VII*** were printed in Italy and the United Kingdom with film rights purchased by Twentieth Century Fox. Over the past several years the author has written a number of articles for the Sonoma County Medical Society. Two of these; "*Into the Valley of Wolves,*" and "*Touched by the Dragon's Tongue*" were selected for "Article of the Year" awards.

CPSIA information can be obtained
at www.ICGtesting.com
Printed in the USA
LVHW080448200221
679376LV00014B/350/J

9 781735 807492